STUART MACBRIDE

ALL THAT'S DEAD

HarperCollins*Publishers*

The quotation 'Clap in his walie nieve a blade...' is from Robert Burns's 'Address to a Haggis', published in 1786.

HarperCollins*Publishers*
1 London Bridge Street,
London SE1 9GF

www.harpercollins.co.uk

This paperback edition 2020
1

First published in Great Britain by HarperCollins*Publishers* 2019

Copyright © Stuart MacBride 2019

Stuart MacBride asserts the moral right to
be identified as the author of this work

A catalogue record for this book
is available from the British Library

ISBN: 978-0-00-820829-5 (PB B-format)
ISBN: 978-0-00-833646-2 (PB A-format)

Set in Meridien by Palimpsest Book Production Limited,
Falkirk, Stirlingshire

Printed and bound in Great Britain by
CPI Group (UK) Ltd, Croydon, CR0 4YY

MIX
Paper from
responsible sources
FSC™ C007454

This book is produced from independently certified FSC™ paper to ensure responsible forest management.

For more information visit: www.harpercollins.co.uk/green

For Grendel (again)

Without Whom

As always I've received a lot of help from a lot of people while I was writing this book, so I'd like to take this opportunity to thank: Sergeant Bruce Crawford, star of Skye and screen, who answers *far* more daft questions than anyone should ever have to, as do Professor Dave Barclay and Professor James Grieve; Sarah Hodgson, Jane Johnson, Julia Wisdom, Jaime Frost (who enables my sushi addiction), Anna Derkacz, Isabel Coburn, Alice Gomer, Charlie Redmayne, Roger Cazalet, Kate Elton, Hannah O'Brien, Sarah Shea, Abbie Salter, Damon Greeney, Finn Cotton, Anne O'Brien, Marie Goldie, the DC Bishopbriggs Naughty Monkey Patrol, and everyone at HarperCollins, for all things publishy; Phil Patterson and the team at Marjacq Scripts, for keeping my numerous cats in cat food; and Allan Guthrie for being an excellent pre-reader.

Like all writers I also owe a huge debt of thanks to all the librarians and booksellers out there who put books in people's hands and enthuse at them till they go away and read them. Then there's you, the person reading this book! In a world that seems hell-bent on dumbing down, you're a magnificent sexy beast of a thing and none of us would be here without you.

I've saved the best for last – as always – Fiona and Grendel (with honourable mentions to Onion and Beetroot who didn't really help, but haven't interfered too much).

— I want you to pretend —
that nothing bad is going to happen to you...

1

The study cupped itself around him like a hand around a match, guarding the flame until it can ignite the fuse. A dark room, filled with the sounds of Led Zeppelin, lit by a single Anglepoise lamp and the three huge monitors that hung above his ancient wooden desk. Awaiting his next words. Hungry.

Nicholas reached out with two liver-spotted forefingers and fed them: 'this is what any *sensible* person can easily diagnose as "Referendum Dementia".' He sat back and smiled through the fug of cigarette smoke. *Referendum Dementia.* Yes, he could work with that. Expand the metaphor to something a bit more—

A curl of ash tumbled down the front of his old Rolling Stones T-shirt and blood-red hoodie.

'God damn it...' Brushing at it just smeared the powdery grey deeper into the fabric.

Abigail really wouldn't approve of that. Bad enough going around dressed like a stroppy teenager, never mind a tramp.

An electronic *ding* broke through 'Communication Breakdown' as a new tweet appeared on the right-hand screen.

Nicholas adjusted his glasses and peered at it. Cleared his throat and read it out loud. '"Shut your mouth you upper-class English tit." Three Exclamation marks. "You can spout your plumby voiced treason all you like, but you know bugger all about it. Sod off and die." Hashtag, "IndeRef F.T.W."'

How lovely.

A smile pulled at his cheeks as his two fingers rattled across the keyboard.

'While I would love to debate constitutional legislation with you, I fear you lack the requisite number of brain cells to appreciate the nuance. And it's *"plummy*-voiced" not "plumby". Hashtag, not enough brain cells. Hashtag, learn to spell. Hashtag, independence from reality... Send.' A click of the mouse and it was winging its way back to whichever Alt-Nat troglodyte was hiding behind the username '@WeAll8TheEnglish'.

Well, it was important to enjoy the little pleasures life presented from time to time.

Now then, where were we? Ah yes: Referendum Dementia.

His fingers hovered over the keyboard.

Now, what we need, is something—

A small bark crackled out in the hallway, and Stalin hobbled through the study door. Wheezing and whining. Fading brown spots. Legs stiff with arthritis. A clockwork Jack Russell that was slowly winding down.

'I know, I know. Just let me finish this bit, Stalin.'

Stalin hobbled closer and scratched a paw at Nicholas's leg, staring up at him with those rheumy eyes. Manipulative little sod that he was.

'All right, all right.' Nicholas levered himself out of his chair, stuck one hand in the small of his back as his spine straightened – vertebrae making sounds like crunching gravel. 'Urgh...'

Stalin wagged his ridiculous little tail, turned, and lumbered off.

'Nag, nag, nag...' Nicholas limped after him.

Should probably do something about cleaning the hall. All those bookshelves, crammed with dusty volumes. Thick lines of dark-grey fur on top of the picture frames.

He reached out a hand and ran his fingers along the one of Abigail, feeling the dip where the wood had worn away over the years. Past the stairs. Following Stalin's white bum in the gloom.

'Honestly, between your rotten old bladder and mine, it's amazing I get any work done at all...'

Dark in the kitchen, but at least it hid the dirty dishes, pots, and pans, leaving nothing but vague shapes in their place. More piles of books and newspapers. The lonely remains of a microwave meal-for-one on the kitchen table.

Abigail wouldn't be pleased at all.

Stalin scrabbled at the kitchen door.

'I'm doing it! Stop nagging.' Nicholas turned the key and opened the door, letting Stalin hurple out into the gloom. 'And don't be long!'

He clicked on the outside light and a pale orange glow oozed from the plastic fitting. Bloody energy-efficient light bulbs. What was the point of saving the planet if you broke your neck waiting for the damn things to come on?

Wind battered through the trees, making them judder against a vermilion sky, their tips tinged with red and gold as the sun said its final farewell to the land of men. Leaving nothing but the pathetic outside light to illuminate the long weedy grass, thick with dock, nettles, and thistles. The hen run, sagging and rotten in its wire cage.

Pffff... Cheery.

Maybe a glass of wine or three would lighten the mood?

Stalin clockworked his way across the rectangle of pale orange light, growling – hackles up as he disappeared into the undergrowth, heading for the woods.

'Oh for God's sake.' Stupid animal.

Nicholas stepped outside, slippers scuffing through the windwhipped grass. 'Joseph Vissarionovich Stalin, you get your smelly old rear end back here this instant!'

Which, of course, he didn't. Because when did a Jack Russell *ever* do what it's told?

'STALIN! COME ON, YOU LITTLE SOD, DADDY'S GOT WORK TO DO!'

Still no sign of him.

'Should've got a cat.' Nicholas sagged, sighed, then zipped his hoodie up. Reached in through the open kitchen door to grab the torch hanging there and his walking stick.

Dog was a bloody menace.

The torch beam played across the windy grass, across the waving spears of thistle, across the boiling mass of nettles, towards the woods.

Deep breath. 'STAAAAAAAAAAAA-LIN!'

Wind tugged at his hood, pattering it against his bald spot.

'Bloody dog.' He cleared a path into the woods with his walking stick, swinging it like a machete, following the torch beam towards the trees. Their trunks and branches shone like ancient bones in the darkness.

'STAAAAAAAAAAAAAAAAAAAAAAAA-LIN!' He dropped his voice to a disgruntled mutter. 'Should've buried you when we buried Abigail, you horrible stinky little monster.'

Another breath: 'STAAAAAAAAAAAAAAAAAAAAAAAAA AAA-LIN!'

A *crack* sounded somewhere deeper in the woods and Nicholas froze...

'If you don't get your rear over here *right now*, young man, I'm going inside and you can spend the rest of the night shivering in the dark. Is that what you want? Is it?'

He brought the torch round, sweeping across the skeleton branches and bone trunks.

A pair of eyes glittered back at him – too far away to make out anything but their reflected glow.

He stayed where he was. 'Stalin? Stalin, that you?'

No answering bark. No response at all. Whatever it was just stayed there, staring at him from the darkness.

'Hmph.' Nicholas pulled his chin up. 'Well, what are you then: a fox or a badger?'

And that's when he feels it. A ... *presence*. There's someone behind him!

The smoky tang of whisky catches in his nostrils as they step in close, their breath warm against his cheek.

Oh God...

His mouth dries, pulse stabbing its way through his throat.

There's a papery rustling sound. Then a cold metallic one as a ghost-white arm appears from behind Nicholas, painfully

4

bright in the torch's glow. The arm holds an axe, the blade chipped and brown with rust.

'A fox or a badger?' A small laugh. 'Oh, I'm something much, *much* worse...'

— and then there was screaming —

2

'Urgh… Look at this place: so bucolic it's *sickening.*'

Una pulled her Fiat onto the gravel driveway and grimaced out through the windscreen.

A crumbling farmhouse with a small wood behind it, a bunch of hedges and bushes and flowers and trees and things. Nothing for miles and miles but hills and fields and sheep and trees and whatever the hell that was swooping about through the blue sky. Like bats, only in the daytime. Daybats.

Off to the side, a bunch of outbuildings and barns and the like were in various stages of being done up – one of them caught in a web of scaffolding, the slates stripped off the roof and replaced by blue papery stuff.

Urgh.

Joe's voice boomed out of her car's speakers, '*So is he there?*'

She killed the engine, grabbed her phone from its cradle, and climbed out into the… Oh dear Lord, it was like climbing into an *oven*. One filled with the contented sound of stupid bumble-bees staggering their way through the baking air en route to extinction. Barely out of the car thirty seconds and already her nice floaty paisley shirt was clinging to her back.

'*Hello, Una? Helllllo?*'

'Hold on.' She dipped back into the car for her Frappuccino and sunglasses, pinning the phone between her ear and shoulder so she could plip the locks. Stuck her shades on.

'*So, is the old bugger there or not?*'

'Well I don't know, do I?' The gravel scrunched beneath her feet as she marched for the front door. 'With any luck he'll be dead in a cupboard with a scarf around his neck, an orange in his mouth, and his cock in his hand.'

'*Oh thank you* very *much for that image. I'm eating a banana!*'

Una mashed her thumb against the bell and deep inside the house something went off like a distant Big Ben. 'Oh come on, he's a stranglewank waiting to happen.'

No answer.

'*Going to have nightmares, now.*'

Another go.

Una checked her watch. Nearly ten already. 'For goodness' sake.' Because it wasn't like she had a dozen faculty meetings to get through today, was it?

She tried the handle: locked.

Then Una turned and looked across the drive to a manky old Volvo estate painted a shade of used-nappy brown. 'Professor Stranglewank's car's still here.'

So he couldn't have gone far.

She thumped the palm of her hand against the front door, making it rattle. 'NICHOLAS, ARE YOU IN THERE?' Pause. 'COME ON: IT'S TOO HOT OUT HERE FOR DICKING ABOUT!' A bead of sweat tickled its way down her ribs.

'*If it* is *a stranglewank, fiver says he's wearing women's underwear.*'

'Hold on I'll try round the back.'

She picked her way past the bins and through a patch of grass landmined with small grey jobbies. Around the corner the garden opened up. Well, if you could call it that. The whole thing was a sea of weeds. Oceans of them. Some high as your hip. A strange tiny shed looking about ready to collapse inside a chicken-wire prison. Place was a disgrace.

She took a sip of creamy cold coffee, then pinned the phone with her shoulder again and hammered her fist against the back door.

Boom! Boom! Boom!

Joe sighed in her ear. '*Do you think they'll let me have his parking space?*'

'In your dreams.' Another three booming knocks.

Still no answer.

Well, can't say she didn't try.

'God, can you imagine the press release?'

A grin. 'Aberdeen University is delighted to announce the passing of its least favourite professor, due to sexual misadventure.'

'He died as he lived, being a wanker.'

OK, one last try: Una turned the handle ... and the door swung open.

She stepped over the threshold into a manky kitchen. Dirty dishes in the sink and stacked up on the work surfaces. Piles and piles of dusty books. A half-empty bottle of white wine sitting out on the filthy kitchen table, bathed in sunlight. The stale smell of hot pennies and mouldy food.

No doubt about it, the man lived like a pig.

'Nicholas?'

She stood there, head cocked, listening.

A faint whining came from the other side of the door through to the rest of the house, accompanied by the scrabble of paws. Urgh... That revolting little dog of his, Satan, or whatever it was. The one responsible for all those landmines.

'NICHOLAS? IT'S DOCTOR LONGMIRE! NICHOLAS?'

'Speaking of eulogies, it's Margaret's retirement bash on Thursday. You want to give a speech?'

'Do I jobbies, like.'

She walked towards the scrabbling door... Then stopped. Stared down at the kitchen table with its lonely bottle of Chardonnay, paired with a single, untouched glass. From the doorway, the table had looked filthy, maybe spattered with mud, but from here, closer, it definitely *wasn't* mud. It was blood. Lots, and lots of blood.

On the other side of the door, Satan whined.

'Well they better not ask me *to give the old cow's going away speech. You've heard her "opinions" on gay rights. Honestly, that woman can—'*

'Joe...' Una swallowed and tried again, but her voice still sounded like she was sitting on a washing machine approaching the spin cycle. 'Call the police, Joe. Call the police now!'

11

3

Bloody stairs.

Logan lumbered his way up them, peaked cap tucked under one arm, his cardboard-box-full-of-stuff in the other – a spider plant sticking its green fronds out of the open flaps.

They hadn't updated the official Police Scotland motivational posters on the landing while he was away. Oh, they'd mixed things up a bit with a handful of new memos; regulations; guidelines; and 'HAVE YOU SEEN THIS MAN?' posters; but there was no getting away from 'OUR VALUES'; 'RESPECT'; and that beardy bloke in his high-viz and his hat, standing in front of the Forth Bridge, looking about as comfortable as a cucumber in a pervert's sandwich shop: 'INTEGRITY'.

Two doors led off the landing, one on either side.

Logan stopped in front of the one marked 'PROFESSIONAL STANDARDS', straightened his epaulettes, took a deep breath and—

The door banged open and a chunky bloke with sergeant's stripes burst out, lurching to a halt about six inches from a collision. He flashed a wide grin, showing off a golden tooth, then stuck out a signet-ringed hand for shaking, the other signet-ringed hand holding the door open behind him. 'The prodigal inspector returns! How's the...' He mimed stabbing someone. 'You know?'

Logan shook the hand and did his best to smile. 'Leonard. Your kids well?'

'Rabid weasels would make less mess.' A sniff. 'Need a hand with that?' He reached out and took Logan's box off him, gesturing with it towards the open door. 'Looking forward to your first day back at the Fun Factory?'

Not even vaguely.

'Yeah... Something like that.'

Another grin. 'Deep breath.'

Logan did just that, then stepped through into the main office. Sunlight flooded the open-plan room. Meeting rooms and cupboards took up one side, with cubicled workstations filling the remaining space. A squealing laser printer, more of those motivational posters, only this lot were 'personalised' with sarcastic speech balloons cut from Post-it notes.

Every desk was populated, more officers bustling about, the muted sound of telephone conversations.

Wow. 'OK...'

Ballantine's mouth pulled wide and down, keeping his voice low. 'I know, right? We're helping our beloved Police Investigations and Review Commissioner look into a couple of Strathclyde's more recent high-profile cock-ups. And on top of that we've got a home-grown botched raid in Ellon that ended up with a geography teacher having a heart attack; and a fatal RTC in Tillydrone last night.' A grimace. 'High-speed pursuit between an unmarked car and a drug dealer on a moped. Wasn't wearing a helmet, so you can guess what's left of his head.' Then Ballantine boomed it out to the whole room: 'Guys, look who it is!'

They all turned and stared. Smiling broke out in the ranks, accompanied by shouted greetings, 'Guv!', 'Logan!', 'Heeeero! Heeeero!', 'McRae!', 'Welcome back!', and 'You owe me a fiver!'

Logan gave them a small wave. 'Morning.'

A matronly woman marched out of a side office, her super-intendent's crowns shining on her epaulettes in the sunlight. Her chin-length grey bob wasn't quite long enough to hide the handcuff earrings dangling from her lobes. A warm smile. Twinkly eyes, lurking behind a pair of thick-rimmed glasses. She popped her fists onto her hips. 'All right!' Her full-strength

Kiwi accent cut through the chatter like a chainsaw. 'That's enough rowdiness for one day. Back to work, you lot.'

Her smile widened as she raised a hand. 'Inspector McRae, can I see you in my office please?'

Great. Didn't even get to unpack his box.

Logan followed her inside, past the little brass sign on the door with 'Supt. JULIE BEVAN' on it.

The room was surprisingly homey, with framed pictures of an orange stripy cat; photos of Bevan and what were probably her children, going by the resemblance, in front of London and Sydney landmarks. But pride of place was given to a big frame containing a faded photo of an ancient green-and-white car and what looked like a speeding ticket. The usual assortment of beige filing cabinets played home to a variety of pot plants and a grubby crocheted elephant with its button eyes hanging off.

Bevan settled behind her desk. She was probably aiming for encouraging, but there was no disguising the note of disappointment in her voice: 'Inspector McRae, I appreciate that it must be a shock to the system, having to get up in the morning after a year recuperating at home, but I really need *all* my officers to be here at the *start* of the working day.

Yeah...

Logan eased himself into one of the two visitors' chairs. 'You emailed me yesterday and told me not to come in till twelve. It's eleven fifteen, so I'm actually forty-five minutes early.'

Bevan raised her eyebrows. 'Did I? Oh...' Another smile, then she set her grey bob wobbling with a shake of her head. 'Right, well, let's say no more about it, then.' She sat back, watching him. 'I know we've not worked together before, Logan, but I'm sure we'll get along famously. Superintendent Doig spoke very highly of you in his handover notes.'

'That was nice of him.'

'*Lovely* man.' She pursed her lips and did a bit more Logan watching. 'As you can see, this is a very busy time for us. I've had to draft in support from N Division, so I'm afraid your desk is currently unavailable. Sorry.'

14

It wasn't easy not to sigh at that.

Her smile reappeared. 'But not to worry! I have something nice and straightforward to ease you back into the swing of things.' Bevan reached for her Pending tray and pulled out a file. 'I believe Sergeant Rennie used to be your assistant before you were … injured?'

'Only if I didn't move fast enough to—'

'A fine officer. Credit to the team. I can't spare Rennie from his ongoing cases at the moment, so you'll be flying solo on this one.' She slid the file across the table towards him. 'I'm sure you'll be fine. After all, you didn't win a Queen's Medal for being the station cat, did you?'

Nope, he got it for being an idiot.

Logan accepted the folder with a nod. 'Thank you, … Boss?'

'Julie. Please.'

Oh, great: she was one of those.

'Right.'

'One more thing.' Bevan dipped into her Pending tray again, only this time it produced a biro and a birthday card with a teddy bear on it. 'It's Shona's birthday tomorrow, so if you can write something nice in there and don't forget to bring a plate.'

Logan opened the card. The inside was liberally scrawled with various ball-point wishes and indecipherable signatures. 'A plate?'

'I'm making my famous lemon drizzle cake; Karl's doing his Thai fishcakes, which are *super* yummy; Rennie's bringing doughnuts; I think Marlon's doing devilled eggs. What's your speciality?'

'Erm…' Phoning for takeaway probably didn't count. 'I burn a lot of sausages on the barbecue?'

'Excellent. Then you can bring a plate of those.'

'OK…' The pen had 'BOFFA MISKELL' printed on it, which sounded like some obscene sexual practice. He clicked out the end, wrote 'ONE DAY, YOU'LL BEAT THAT PRINTER INTO SUBMISSION!' and signed it.

'Thanks.' Bevan took the card and pen back and consigned them to 'Pending' again. 'Well, if you'll excuse me, I've got

15

review boards to organise.' She pulled her keyboard over and poked at it, frowning at the screen.

'Right.' Logan stood. Picked up the file. 'I'll go and...' He pointed over his shoulder, but she didn't look up. 'OK.'

You are dismissed.

Bloody stairs. Again.

Logan limped down them, phone pressed to his ear, trying not to be too overwhelmed with the view out the stairwell windows. It would take a hardy soul not to be moved by the arse-end of Bucksburn station and the car park hiding behind it. A faint heat haze lifting off the vehicles as they slowly roasted in the sun.

Ringing, and ringing, and finally someone picked up: *'Operation Overcharge?'*

Overcharge? Whoever was running the random word generator for naming investigations needed a kick up the bumhole.

'Hi, I need to speak to DI King.'

There was a pause, then, *'Can I ask who's calling?'* The voice was sort of familiar: a Yorkshire burr, starting to warp under the strain of talking to Aberdonians all day.

'Logan McRae.'

'Oh.' Another pause. Then a touch of panic joined the accent blender. *'Erm... Inspector, didn't know y' were back. Feeling better?'*

'Detective Constable Way?' Logan kept lumbering downwards.

'We was all worried about you, you know, after the stabbing.'

'Where is he, Milky?' Logan pushed through the doors at the bottom of the stairs, into a bland corridor lined with offices and yet more sodding motivational posters.

'Where's who?'

'DI King!'

'Oh, right. Yes. Erm... You know, it's a funny thing, but he's just this minute run out door on an urgent job.'

What a shock. 'And when will he be back?'

Logan stepped outside. The car park smothered in the heat of a far too sunny day – its surface sticky beneath his boots, the air thick with the scent of hot tarmac and frying dust. He screwed his eyes half shut as the sun drove red-hot nails into them. God, it was more like Death Valley out here than Bucksburn. 'Milky?

'*Erm...*'

Typical: soon as Professional Standards started asking questions, everyone developed amnesia.

'OK, where's DI King *going*, then?'

'*Erm...*'

'And bear in mind I can just call Control and check. Then come pay *you* a visit.'

'*Oh* that *DI King!* *Yes, course, I've yon address right here. You got a pen?*'

Gorse and broom lined the road, their yellow flowers boiling like flames above the reaching branches. Beyond the conflagration lay swathes of green, carved into an irregular patchwork by drystane dykes. The hills on either side thick with Scots pine, beech, and fir.

All of it slipping past the windows of Logan's Audi.

A cheery voice brayed out of the radio, trampling all over the tail-end of a song. '*How does that set you up for a sunny Tuesday? Great. We've got Saucy Suzy coming up at twelve, but before that here's a quick traffic update for you: the B999 Pitmedden to Tarves road is closed following a fire at the Kipperie Burn Garden Centre. So look out for diversions.*'

A burst of drums and the howl of guitars started up in the background.

'*Now, here's Savage Season with their new one, "The Wrecker". Take it away, boys!*'

The road twisted around to the right, revealing a cluster of manky outbuildings in the process of being converted, and a manky farmhouse in the process of being managed as a crime scene.

A throaty voice growled over the music:

'*Darkness deep and thoughts so wild, it's—*'

17

Logan switched the radio off and pulled onto the wide gravel driveway.

The Scene Examiners' grubby white Transit sat right outside the farmhouse, next to an unmarked grey Vauxhall pool car, a Volvo in shades of rust and gastroenteritis brown; and a perky little red Fiat.

He parked next to it, grabbed his hat, and climbed out into… Holy mother of *fish*.

The burning air caught in his throat, wrapped itself around his Police Scotland uniform, and tried to grind him into the ground.

Bees bumbled their way between the flowering weeds that lined the drive, hoverflies buzzing amongst the thunderheads, house martins reenacting the Battle of Britain – jinking and swooping and diving, while a clatter of jackdaws looked on from the farmhouse roof.

Logan pulled on his hat and limped for the front door.

It wasn't locked. Or even guarded, come to that.

Which was a bit lax.

He stepped into a dusty hallway, the walls punctuated by dusty photos in dusty frames, between dusty bookshelves stuffed with dusty books. A half-dozen doors led off the hall, most of them open. A staircase leading up, with dusty piles of yet more books at the outside edge of every tread.

The clicker-flash of cameras burst out from one of the door-ways, into the hall. Logan paused at the threshold and peered inside.

It was a kitchen, full of yet more books. Stacks and stacks of them. Newspapers too. And a manky bin-bag-left-in-the-sun kind of smell. Two figures, one short and pregnant, one tall and broad, both in full SOC get-up, busied themselves around the kitchen table, taking photos and swabs. Fingerprint powder greyed nearly every other surface.

They'd rigged up a half-hearted barricade by stretching a line of yellow-and-black 'CRIME SCENE – DO NOT CROSS' tape across the doorway.

Logan waved at them. 'Hello?'

The pregnant one looked up from her DNA sampling, features obscured by a facemask and safety goggles. 'You're back at work then?'

'Apparently. DI King about?'

The smile vanished from her voice. '*His Majesty* is swanning about somewhere. If you find him, tell him we're out of here in twenty. Got *other*, more *important* crime scenes to deal with.'

'Thanks, Shirley.' Logan carried on down the corridor, past the stairs, past the bookshelves and their dust-furred books – ninety percent of which seemed to be Scottish history with the occasional Mills & Boon thrown in.

A clipped voice came from a room off to one side, as if every word was being throttled to stop it screaming, emphasising the Highland burr. '*No, Gwen, I didn't. And you repeating it over and over doesn't make it true.*'

Logan stepped into the doorway of a cluttered study, lined with yet more overflowing bookshelves. One wall was devoted to a cluster of framed photos – proper full-size head-and-shoulder jobs – each one depicting a different grey-muzzled Jack Russell terrier. And crammed in, between everything else, were newspaper clippings, stuck to the wallpaper with thumb-tacks. A desk sat in front of the room's only window, piled high with papers, three monitors hovering above it on hydraulic arms. An ashtray as packed with dog-ends as the bookcases were with books.

And in the middle of all this stood a man in his shirtsleeves. A bit overweight, his swept-back blond hair a bit higher on his forehead, the dimple in his chin a bit more squished up by the fat that gathered along his jawline. Big arms, though, as if he used to be a prizefighter who'd let himself go after one too many blows to the head. His silk tie hung at half-mast and his bright-blue shirt came with dark patches under the arms.

His features creased, as if whoever he was on the phone with had just stabbed him in the ear. 'No. ... Because I'm *working*, Gwen. You remember what that's like? ... Yes.' Then a longer pause. 'Yes.' A from-the-bottom-of-your-socks sigh. 'I don't know: later. OK. Bye.'

He hung up and ran a hand over his face.

'DI King?' Logan knocked on the door frame. 'Not interrupting anything, am I?'

King smoothed himself down, slipped his phone into his pocket, and forced a smile. 'Inspector McRae. Thought you were still off on the sick?'

'I get that a lot. So... Missing constitutional scholar?'

'Can we skip the foreplay, please? You're not here about Professor Wilson – the call only came in an hour ago, not enough time for anyone to have screwed something up.' King popped an extra-strong mint in his mouth, crunching as he talked. 'So come on, Mr Professional Standards, what am I supposed to have done wrong?'

Logan wandered in, hands behind his back as he frowned his way along the articles pinned to the wall. The headlines all followed the same theme: 'Scotland Is Setting Itself Up To Fail.', 'Rise Up And Be The Failure Again.', 'Why The Scots Need The UK More Than It Needs Them.'...

He nodded at them. 'Looks like the Professor was a man of strong opinions.'

'The man's a Brit-Nat tosser. If he thinks Scotland's so crap, why doesn't he move back to Shropshire?'

'Interesting you should say that...'

King stood there, being aftershavey.

Logan skimmed the nearest bookshelf. The whole thing was dedicated to volumes on economic theory and political science. 'It's a bit overkill, isn't it? This is a simple missing person case, wouldn't have thought it warranted a full-blown Detective Inspector. Especially not one as *esteemed* as yourself.'

King folded his arms. Chest out. 'OK, what's this all about?'

'Just wondering why they sent you.'

'When Professor Wilson's colleague reported him missing at eleven-oh-two this morning, she told Control the kitchen was covered in blood. We thought it might be serious.'

'Ah. That clears it up.'

A sigh. 'And it's politics. He's been having a go in the media about our handling of these White-Settler arson attacks. Says we're complacent. Says we don't care about Alt-Nats burning out English businesses. The brass don't want anyone saying we didn't take his disappearance seriously.' Another extra-strong mint disappeared between King's crunching teeth. 'And you still haven't answered the question.'

'Alt-Nats?'

'You know how the Alt-Right is full of white supremacists, gun nuts, racists, and neo-Nazis? Well, Alt-Nats are our own home-grown version. Only without the guns and Nazis. And it's the English they hate.'

Strange the things you missed being off on the sick for a year.

Logan shook his head. 'Makes you proud to be Scottish, doesn't it?'

'You see "Alt" in front of anything these days, you know what you're getting: Arrogant Lowbrow Tossers.' All said without the slightest hint of a smile.

'Teaching my granny to suck eggs, I know, but have you tried the hospitals? Maybe Professor Wilson cut himself and rushed off to accident and emergency?'

'Don't be daft, of course we checked. Besides, that's his manky Volvo outside, how was he going to get there, fly?'

Good point.

'Hmmm…' Logan moved on to the wall of dogs. Nine photos, each with its own little plaque. '"Vladimir Ilyich Ulyanov – 1966 to 1984." And this one's "Lev Davidovich Bronstein – 1985 to 1999". Bit of a mouthful when you're calling them in for their dinner. Whatever happened to "Spot" and "Stinky"?'

The muscles tensed along King's jaw for a moment, his face closed and unhappy. 'Do they teach you this at Professional Standards School? How to avoid answering questions and be *phenomenally* annoying.'

If only he knew how close to the truth that was.

Logan gave him a nice bright smile. 'The *Scottish Daily Post* emailed us tomorrow's front page, wanting a comment.' A couple of swipes and the front page popped up on Logan's phone screen: a photo of DI King scowled out beneath the headline, 'TOP MURDER COP WAS IN SCOTNAT TERROR GROUP'.

He turned the phone, so King could see.

It was like watching chunks of ice falling off a glacier as King's face sagged, eyes wide, mouth open in an expression of complete and utter horror. 'Oh God...'

Logan nodded and put his phone away. 'Maybe we should have a wee chat?'

4

The living room wasn't much better. Books, books, dust, and more books – heaped up on the floor around a tatty leather sofa. A massive stereo system complete with racks and racks of vinyl took up the space where a TV should have been, the speakers big enough to pass for sarcophaguses. Or was it sarcophagi?

King looked as if he was ready to be buried in one of them, anyway. He half-sat, half-collapsed into the sofa, sending a puff of dust billowing out from the underside. Motes of it glowed in the sunlight as he put his head in his hands. 'They're going to fire me, aren't they?'

Logan shrugged. 'Well, you can see how it looks: here you are, working the disappearance of a prominent Brit-Nat academic, and all the time you were a member of...' Nope, drawing a blank. Logan pulled out his notebook and checked. '"The People's Army for Scottish Liberation". Soon as the media get hold of that it'll be like throwing an injured piglet into a bathtub full of piranhas.'

'I was *sixteen*! Sixteen and stupid. And she was pretty and Welsh.' King sagged even further. 'I just wanted to impress her.'

'Welsh?'

'And I only went to a couple of meetings! Till I found out Cerys was shagging Connor O'Brien behind my back.' He rubbed at his face. 'She said it was all about "uniting the Celtic nations to cast out the English oppressors and break the final bonds of imperialist subjugation".'

Which was probably code for a threesome. 'Well, she does sound fun.'

'After all, India managed to win its independence, why couldn't we?'

'Only, from what I remember, the PASL weren't so keen on the peaceful protest approach, were they? More into blowing up statues and abducting politicians. Not very Gandhiesque.'

King waved a dismissive hand. 'That wasn't the People's Army for Scottish Liberation, that was the Scottish Freedom Fighters' Resistance Front.'

Don't smile! 'Splitters.'

'I didn't *do* anything!'

'*The Post* says it's got proof.'

'I don't hate the English – my *wife's* English, my *kids* are half English. Hell, Josie was born in Newcastle!' He curled forwards, knees against his chest, arms wrapped around his head for a muffled scream.

Which, given the circumstances, was understandable.

There was a photo in the hall of a handsome woman in what had to be her late forties. Fiery red hair swept back from a high forehead, green eyes, and a twist to her mouth that made it look as if she was about to burst out laughing at any moment. The wooden frame was worn through, nearly to the glass along the bottom.

Logan ran his fingers along it. Smooth.

King's voice growled out through the living room door. '*For God's sake, Gwen, can you just support me for* once *in your life? ... No. And to be honest, I think it's the least you could do!*'

Probably best to give him a bit of privacy. So Logan eased that door shut and opened the only one he'd not seen inside yet.

Bathroom: and not a huge one, made to feel even smaller by all the towels on the floor, and the overflowing bin, and the skeletal remains of long-dead loo rolls, and the discarded empty boxes and pill packets, and the impressive collection of bleachy / toilet-cleanery bottles around the pan. All smothered by the ever-present geological layers of dust. An archaeologist would have a field day in here...

Was that a scraping noise?

Logan stopped, head on one side, ears straining to pick up the—

Yup, there it was again. Not in here, though.

He backed into the hall, just in time to see the taller, broader, less pregnant of the two Scene Examiners lumber out of the kitchen in his rustly SOC suit, carrying a blue crate with a couple of brown-paper evidence bags in it. He'd pulled down his facemask, revealing a swathe of glowing shiny red skin, coral pink lipstick and a bit too much blusher for the natural look. Grimacing as a drip worked its way down his cheek. 'Gah... Never join the SE, Inspector. You think it's bad wearing black in this heat? Try a sodding Tyvek suit. It's like a waterfall of sweat from my balls all the way down to my socks.'

'You make it sound so romantic, Charlie.'

'I *squelch* when I walk.' And to prove the point, he squelched away down the hall and out the front door.

That scratching noise sounded again.

And was that a whimper?

Logan peered up the stairs.

Yup, definitely coming from up there.

He climbed up to a tiny landing, where yet more books lay in wait, narrowing a space that was already claustrophobic because of the coombe ceilings. Two doors led off it, one of them rattling slightly as whatever it was scraped and whined.

The noise stopped as Logan turned the door handle.

He pushed it open, revealing a bedroom littered with yet more books. Discarded clothes lay heaped up on a wicker chair in one corner, a laundry basket overflowing in the other. A mound of cigarette stubs, ground out in a saucer. The whole room reeked of stale washing, fags, and a sort of dirty sweaty funk normally reserved for spotty teenagers.

No doubt about it, King's missing professor was a bit of a slob.

But other than the mess, there was no sign of Captain Scrapey McWhinesalot.

'Hello? Anyone there?'

Another whimper.

Logan hunkered down onto his haunches. Pitched his voice soft and low. 'Who's that?'

A manky old Jack Russell terrier tottered out from underneath the bed – cobwebs in his ears and dust bunnies on his flanks. He wobbled on his stiff little legs, tail going like a manic windscreen wiper as he stared up at Logan with cloudy eyes and whined.

Logan held a hand out for sniffing. 'Hello, little man, did you get shut in here by mistake?'

The terrier did a shaky lap of him, yipping and yowling.

'You need a wee, don't you? I know that dance – Sergeant Rennie does the same one.' He stood and clapped a hand against his leg. 'Come on then.'

Then back down the stairs, the dog thump-lumping along behind him, scampering around Logan's feet as they made their way along the hall to the front door.

Charlie squelched in through it before they got there, evidence crate swinging from one hand, and the ancient terrier went berserk – hackles up, barking and growling, making little feinted charges.

'AAAARRRRRGH!' Charlie flinched back against the wall, crate held out like a lion-tamer's chair, eyes wide. 'What the hell did you let it out of the room for?'

More barking, tiny brown teeth flashing.

'He's only—'

'GET AWAY FROM ME, YOU LITTLE HORROR!'

Logan picked the poor wee thing up, holding him against his chest. The dog trembled in his arms, still growling at Charlie. 'He needs a piddle.'

'He needs a bloody *muzzle*! Get him out of here!'

'All right, all right. Keep your squelchy pants on.'

Logan carried Professor Wilson's dog out through the front door and into the sunshine. Popped him down on the gravel, where he immediately turned around and directed a bark towards the house. Charlie let loose a high-pitched shriek and slammed the door shut, sealing them outside. The terrier stared at it for a moment, then scuffed its back paws on the driveway, announcing that he'd won that argument, then tottered away around the side of the house.

Logan followed him, past the bins, through a patch of grass that had clearly seen a lot of pooping, but no scooping, through a clump of docken that was nearly shoulder-height, and into what might have been a back garden at one point. Now it was just a vast collection of weeds and unmown grass, with the corpse of a hen coop decomposing in its chicken-wire mortsafe. Butterflies danced whirling polkas through the hot air, flitting from one tangled clump of nettles to another. The rat-a-tat-tat of a belligerent woodpecker.

Shirley and Charlie had already done this bit, going by the back door's liberal coating of fingerprint powder and the spiky white remnants of plaster in the grass where they'd taken casts of footprints.

Just a shame they hadn't bagged and tagged the disaster area in the rumpled linen suit; grey hair, styled by lightning conductor and earwax; eggy stains on her lime-green shirt – unbuttoned so far it showed off *way* too much leathery cleavage; wrinkly face turned towards the sun. Basking, like an iguana crossed with a gonk. Phone clamped to her ear with one hand, massive e-cigarette in the other, puffing out plumes of strawberry-scented vape. Voice a gravelly growl, 'Tell you, my arse is on *fire* today. It's like the Battle of the Somme down there, only with fewer soldiers and more explosions. I'm...' She froze for a moment, then opened one eye and looked at him. 'Have to call you back.'

Logan sniffed. 'Well, well, well, if it isn't Detective Sergeant Roberta Steel.'

She pocketed her phone as the wee dog snuffled around her feet. 'Oh it's you, is it? Those sodding sausages have had my guts like—'

'"The Somme". Yeah, I heard. And there was nothing wrong

with my sausages yesterday. Perfectly good barbecued sausages.'

'Then why are my innards trying to become outards?'

The terrier wobbled over to the hen run and cocked an arthritic leg.

'I think it *might* have something to do with the Long Island Iced Teas you were knocking back all afternoon. No wonder your eyeballs look like two oysters drowned in Tabasco.'

'Mmmph...' She pulled out a pair of sunglasses and popped them on. Then nodded at the house. 'So, you here for me, or for His Royal Highness? Can't be me – I'm a paragon of sodding virtue, me.'

Aye, right.

Logan stuck his hands in his pockets. All innocent and casual. 'So what's he like to work for, King?'

'Pff... You asking me to clype on my beloved DI? Cos you can ram that right up your liquorice allsort.'

King's voice boomed out across the back garden / weed patch. 'Should think so too.' He scraped his left foot in the long grass a couple of times, nose crinkled in disgust. Matching suit jacket on over his blue shirt, face all pink and shiny in the heat. He frowned at Steel. 'Is there any...' A blink. Then he watched the ancient terrier snuffle his way past. 'Is that Professor Wilson's dog?'

'Yup.' Logan smiled. 'He's having a wee.'

'OK...' Back to Steel. 'Any progress?'

She took another long draw on her fake cigarette – a huge metal tube of a thing with rings and protuberances all along its length, making it impossible to tell if the person who'd designed it had been going for 'Sonic Screwdriver' or 'Steampunk Sex Toy'. Steel puffed out her strawberry fog. 'Forensics aren't finding much. Whoever did it, they didn't break anything on the way in and wiped everything down before they left.'

Steel dug out her phone again and poked at the screen. 'The Alt-Nat trolls are out in force, mind. And I quote: "Ha, ha, ha, ha, ha. Hope you burn in hell you traitor bastard", says Tartan Numpty One Three Six. "Couldn't have happened to a nicer guy. Where's your English superiority now?" asks Willy Wallace Was Here.'

King sagged a bit, eyes screwed shut. 'Great. So it's *already* all over antisocial media.'

'Oh I'm no' finished yet. "For sale, both of Prof. Wanky Wilson's balls. He won't be needing them any more." Hashtag, "One less English scumbag. LOL." With three exclamation marks. Cybernat Ninja Thirteen Twenty.'

'All right, we get the point.'

'"What do you call one dead constitutional scholar? A bloody good start. ROFL", according to We All Eight the English. That's the number eight, not—'

King's voice grew a sharper edge. 'Enough! OK? Enough.' Then he stifled a burp and winced. Crunched down another mint, rubbing at his chest. 'When does this stuff start showing up in his timeline?'

Steel checked. 'First one's yesterday morning, nearly twenty-four hours before he was reported missing.' She looked left, then right, then dropped her voice to a whisper. 'Which kinda implies someone out there was involved, doesn't it?'

She had a point. Logan leaned against the chicken wire enclosure. 'So what's the plan?'

King pointed at Steel. 'Right. Once ... whatever the dog's called has had his wee, I want you out there doing something useful. Interview the neighbours.'

Steel stared at him as if he'd just pulled a live squid from his trouser, then she turned on the spot, pantomiming a good hard look at the weeds and the trees and the whole middle-of-nowhereiness of the place. 'What, the *squirrels*?'

'Doesn't matter how far out in the sticks someone lives, there's always neighbours. *Find them*, Sergeant.'

That got him a scowl and a sarcastic, 'Yes, *Boss*.' Then she rolled her eyes at Logan, tucked the old-age terrier under her arm and ruffled the fur on top of its head, till it kind of resembled her own. 'Come on, little man, let's take you away from these nasty police officers that stink like a wino's Y-fronts.' Marching off around the side of the house.

King shook his head. 'I swear to God, I'm going to end up killing someone. Probably her...'

'Ahem.' Logan waved. 'Hello? Professional Standards, remember?'

There was a small flinch. 'Don't remind me.' Then King straightened up, all in charge again. 'Now, if you'll excuse me, I've got an investigation to run.'

'*Actually*, if you don't mind, I'm going to hang about for a bit and observe.'

A pained look crawled its way across King's face. 'I—'

'You'll barely notice I'm here. Promise.'

'Oh for... I didn't *do* anything! I told you, I only joined—'

'To impress a girl. I know. But...' Logan shrugged. 'I wouldn't be doing my job if I just turned up for a quick five-minute chat, then sodded off again, would I?'

A deep and bitter sigh left King looking hollowed out and grey. 'Right. Well, I suppose I'd better find out what happened to Professor Wilson, then.'

House martins massed over the outbuildings, chasing bugs, as Logan followed King along a dusty path. Past scaffolding and stacks of slates. Timber and bags of sharp sand. A cement mixer with teeth painted around the mouth, as if it were a World War Two fighter plane.

Most of the steading was an empty shell, stripped back to the bare granite, but the unit nearest the farmhouse was much nearer being completed. A crisp new roof and a coat of off-pink harling. The double glazing still had the blue sticky plastic on, but the hollow studwork was clearly visible through it. Watertight, but nowhere near finished.

King led the way between an overflowing skip and the remains of a cattle byre, to a stack of breeze-blocks where a middle-aged woman in a floaty paisley shirt sheltered out of the sun. She looked up from her phone when King cleared his throat.

'Dr Longmire?'

She put her phone away. 'Can I go now? Only I've got a faculty meeting at two and it's my turn to bring the milk...'

'It's OK.' King forced a smile. 'My *colleague* and I just want to ask a couple of questions. Professor Wilson: did he have any enemies?'

'Nicholas?' A laugh sent her hair jiggling. 'Did the man have anything but?'

Yeah, that wasn't normal. Normally people shovelled on praise for the missing and the dead. Lifelong dicks were suddenly transformed into beloved role models and all it took was getting stabbed, strangled, bludgeoned, or abducted.

Dr Longmire sniffed. 'Oh, don't look at me like that. Nicholas Wilson will argue water isn't wet for the sheer joy of winding someone up. Never met anyone who relishes a fight more, and I've been married twice.'

Logan leaned back against the byre. 'He seems to have a lot of trolls on Twitter.'

'Nicholas isn't the kind of man who keeps his opinions to himself. All that hate hammering in his direction every day – any *sensible* person would've shut down their account and burned their computer, but not Nicholas. Not when he could call people "knuckle-dragging nationalist morons" in two hundred and eighty characters or less.'

King shot Logan a look that wasn't exactly subtle: shut up, this is *my* investigation. 'Are you saying Professor Wilson isn't popular at work?'

'He isn't popular *anywhere*. I'm only here because I drew the short straw. And I mean that literally: we drew straws and I lost.' She sighed and stood, picked up an empty plastic container that looked as if it'd housed an iced coffee in happier times. 'Look, I'm not saying I wanted him *dead* or anything – and before you ask, yes I do have an alibi – but if someone were to rough him up a bit I wouldn't exactly complain, OK?'

5

The kitchen still smelled like a butcher's shop, the air in here thick and heavy and stifling. Uncomfortably warm.

Logan stood at the kitchen window, giving Dr Longmire a wee wave as her Fiat pulled out of the drive and disappeared down the lane.

King watched her go. 'You'd better *believe* we'll be checking her alibi.'

Bless his little sweaty socks.

Shirley and Charlie packed their equipment away in more blue plastic crates, the top halves of their SOC suits stripped down to the waist, sleeves tied around their middles. Showing off sweaty red faces and sodden Scottish Police Authority polo shirts.

Charlie's blusher was all smudged by the heat, and his lipstick didn't look much better. His eyeshadow and mascara might have started out as a perfectly crafted smoky eye, but they'd ended up more Heath-Ledger's-Joker-meets-drunken-panda.

Shirley pulled off her Alice band and had a hearty scratch at her long blonde hair. 'Gah... When I get back to the shop I'm going to climb into a cold shower and stay there till I evolve gills.'

Logan gave her a smile. 'So ... crime scene?'

She pointed at the table. 'Just between you and me? That's a *lot* of blood. Not a fatal amount, but you'd notice you were missing it. Want to know what else is missing?' Shirley left a dramatic pause... 'Fingerprints. And I don't mean whoever-it-was-wore-gloves, I mean *every* surface that's not covered in books or crap has been wiped. Don't quote me, but from the lemony-fresh smell I'd put money on those disposable antibac wipes.'

King folded his arms. 'You check the bin?'

'No, because I've *never* done this before.' She turned back to Logan. 'Whoever it was, they weren't your usual thickie. The two footprints we pulled from the garden are flat rumply things. No tread.'

'So...?'

'Take a bit of cardboard, cut it to the same shape as your shoe's sole, then put it in a wee blue plastic bootie like this.' She lifted one leg, showing off the blue plastic bootie on the end of it. 'All you leave are the rough outline and some crinkles from the plastic.'

Great.

She nodded. 'We managed to lift some good fingerprints from the study, just in case, you know: for elimination purposes. But there's nothing in here to eliminate them against.' A sigh. '*Maybe* we'll get some DNA, but I doubt it. Your boy's forensically aware.'

Scottish crime fiction had a lot to answer for.

King tried exerting his authority again. 'What about fibres?'

Didn't work though, because Shirley kept her eyes on Logan. 'There's something really ... careful about this. We'll do everything we can, but my gut says your guy's a ghost.'

Charlie wiped a hand across his shiny forehead, smearing what little foundation he had left up there. 'Aye, and as long as he wants to *stay* a ghost, we're not going to find sod all.'

King's nose came up. 'That's a double negative.'

'So's your mum.' Then Charlie barged out the kitchen door, taking his crate with him.

Always nice to have a happy workplace.

Logan tried not to sigh, he really did. 'What about photos?'

'*Technically* I'm not allowed to give you anything unless you go through official channels, in triplicate, but here…' she pulled a cheap iPad-knockoff from her crate, poked at the screen and handed it over. 'You've got till we're tidied up. After that you'll have to wait till the report's done and the Gods of Pointless Paperwork and Half-Arsed Procedures have been appeased.' She stood there, giving King a look that could've curdled holy water, then turned and marched off with her crate. Leaving the two of them alone in the kitchen.

Logan watched him seethe for a bit. 'You made a lovely impression there. They really like you, I can tell.'

'They've still not forgiven me for that Martin Shanks disaster.' He stuck a hand out, for the fauxPad. 'My crime scene, remember?'

Yes, it *was* his crime scene, but he was being a dick, so no.

Logan put the fauxPad on the work surface between them and flicked through the photos to the ones of the kitchen, stopping at a shot of the bloody tabletop with its half-full bottle of wine and accompanying glass…

Now that was interesting.

He turned and stared at the table. A thick oak job, with scarred legs – probably where generations of Russian Revolutionary Jack Russells had scratched the wood raw. Logan hunkered down and had a damn good frown at the blood-spattered surface. Three dried circles marred the red-brown stains, two were perfectly smooth, but the third was dotted around its circumference. That would be the bottle's dimpled bottom.

Logan took out his phone and snapped half a dozen shots of the tabletop and the blood spatters. 'Did you see this?'

King snorted. 'If you're planning on amazing everyone with your Sherlock Holmes impression, don't. *Obviously* Professor Wilson knew his attacker. You don't open a bottle of Jacob's Creek and swig it with a complete stranger.'

'Hmmm…' Three circles, pressed into the blood.

'We need to work our way through his colleagues at the university – you heard Dr Longmire: they all hated him. But this must've been someone he felt comfortable with. Someone who hid it. Pretended to be his friend. Someone he'd invite into his house and crack a bottle of wine for.'

Logan stayed where he was. 'Check out the table: tell me what you see.'

'It's a table.' He took one look at Logan's face and sighed. 'OK, OK. It's oak. It's old. It's a bit manky. Lots of blood spatters.'

'What about the wine glass?'

Sounding bored now. 'They took it away for testing.'

'I know *that*. I'm asking what happens if you put a glass down on the table, then someone does whatever it was they did to get blood everywhere.'

Another sigh. 'Do we really have to play—'

'Humour me.'

King tramped over and examined the tabletop. 'Well, there'd be...' And finally the penny dropped. 'Oh sod and buggeration.'

'That's what I was thinking.'

'The glass would act as a mask, or a windbreak: there'd be a clear patch on the table where the blood wouldn't spatter. The bottle too.' King swivelled around, facing the door. 'So our attacker gets in, attacks Professor Wilson, gets blood all over the table, then pours him a glass of wine? Well that's just perfect: we're dealing with a nutjob.'

'Looks like there was enough wine out the bottle for two, maybe three glasses.'

King narrowed his eyes, then marched over to a scuffed off-white dishwasher, snapped on a single blue nitrile glove, and pulled the door open.

It was empty, except for a single wine glass.

He took the glass out and held it up to the light, where it sparkled and gleamed, sending chips of rainbow swirling around the kitchen. Not a single smudge or smear on it. 'Our attacker does ... whatever it was, then pours them both a glass of wine and has a drink. Puts his glass in the dishwasher, cleans up, and walks right out of here taking Professor Wilson with him, leaving not a single forensic clue behind.' King returned the glass to the dishwasher. 'This is going to be an utter bastard of a case, isn't it?'

It certainly looked like it. But, on the bright side, it was *King's* utter bastard of a case and not Logan's.

Which made a nice change.

They hadn't given King one of Divisional Headquarters' swankier incident rooms. No fancy-pants digital whiteboards and projector systems here, this was old-school. Which in police parlance meant 'scruffy, bland, and a bit tattered around the edges'. The ceiling tiles sagged in one corner, and the handful of cubicles lining the walls looked as if they'd been installed sometime around the end of the last ice age. The whiteboards – analogue, not digital – had been used and cleaned so often they'd taken on a manky shade of grey that looked like a dead person's dentures.

Two plainclothes officers and a uniformed PC were gathered in the middle of the room, sitting on creaky office chairs, watching King finish his briefing.

Logan perched his bum on one of the desks at the back of the room. Doing his best to stay out of the way. To be inconspicuous. Didn't work, though. That was the trouble with being Professional Standards – the uniform might be the same as everyone else's, but it exerted a strange gravitational pull that grabbed people's attention. Like a black hole, lurking at the edge of the room. Sinister, dark, and all devouring.

King risked a glance in Logan's direction, before dragging himself back to his tiny team. 'So, right now, that's all we know.' He folded his arms. 'Any questions?'

A wee nyaff with a pale-ginger crewcut stuck his hand in the air. 'Are we sure he's been abducted? Maybe he cut himself and—'

'Wheesht, Tufty.' One of the plainclothes officers chucked a crumpled-up Post-it at his furry head. She was an older woman with a soft Weegie accent, greying brown bob, lilac jacket, jeans and a shirt. Stylish and relaxed. As if she was off to audition for a TENA Lady advert. 'Don't be such a neep. Why would he pour himself a glass of wine afterwards?'

'Heather's right.' The other PC punched Tufty on the arm.

'Shut yer cakehole, you twonk.' Milky: mid-twenties, in black jeans and a Klangers T-shirt, her shoulder-length hair dyed an unnatural shade of mahogany. 'He'd have got bloody fingerprints on the bottle too.' She hit him again, for luck.

Heather nodded. 'Exactly. And...' She swivelled her ancient office chair around till she was frowning at Logan. Then back to King. 'No offence, Boss, but are we really doing this in front of Professional Standards?'

Logan smiled at them all. 'Don't mind me.'

'I mean it's a bit ... you know. If we have to take a care every time we open our mouths, it's going to stifle the free flow of information and ideas. Plus he'll write it all down and use it against us later.'

'Try to pretend I'm not here.'

King grimaced. 'If only.' He pointed at Tufty's tormentor. 'What about you?'

Milky sucked her teeth for a moment, then let her Yorkshire drawl loose on the world once more. 'I'm worried 'bout all these death and rape threats.'

Tufty shifted in his seat. 'But we can't risk it, can we? Say I'm right—'

'Which you're not.' Heather lobbed another crumpled Post-it at him.

'Yeah, but *say* I'm right and Professor Wilson's slit his wrists then wandered off to die somewhere. We're going to look a right bunch of spuds if his body turns up in the woods, two hundred yards from the house, aren't we?'

Milky groaned. 'Media will love that.'

'Agreed. It's not worth the risk.' King crunched his way through another mint. 'Heather: get a dog team organised. I want those woods search-and-sniffed ASAP.'

A lopsided smile. 'We could take Gibbs instead? He could do with the exercise.'

'A proper dog team, H, not you and your mental cocker spaniel again.'

She sighed. 'Guv.' Then pulled out her phone and went to stand in the corner, one finger in her ear as she made the call.

'Good.' King pointed at Milky and Tufty. 'And you two: Professor Wilson's colleagues need interviewing. We're looking for enemies, fights, threats. Was he depressed? Do they think he might have harmed himself? Make sure you check *every single* alibi – you know what academics are like.'

Tufty's hand shot up again. 'Ooh, ooh! What about the social-media side of things, Guv? There's all these Alt-Nat accounts gloating about the Professor being dead, and all these Unionistas wading in to do battle against them. It's Keyboard Armageddon out there.'

'What about it?'

A slightly puzzled look. 'We need to investigate, don't we? Who are they? How did they know something happened to Professor Wilson before we did? A sticky digital trail of clues could lead us straight to the murderer!'

Milky rolled her eyes. 'It's like he's been half drowned in Idiot Juice…' She checked her watch. 'We could ask the forensic computer-geek team?'

'Have you seen their backlog?' King shook his head. 'We'll have died of old age by the time they get anywhere *near* it.'

Tufty still had his hand up, but now he was bouncing in his seat too. '*I* can do it! I can! I has resources and mad skillz and stuff!'

King scowled at him. 'You're interviewing academics for the rest of the day and liking it.'

'But—'

'Interviews!'

The wee loon sagged in his seat, all the bounce taken out of him. 'Guv…' To be honest, he only had himself to blame.

Logan waved at King. 'We've got someone at PSD who might be able to take a look. Does all our computer forensics.'

A little bounce made its way back into Tufty. 'Honestly, I could do it. It's no trouble.'

'Go.' King pointed at the door. 'Away with you.'

And the last bounce died. 'Guv.' Tufty scuffed his way from the room.

Milky stood. 'Don't worry, I'll keep an eye ont lad.' Then she followed him out.

King turned to Logan. 'This IT guy of yours, is he...'

A kerfuffle in the doorway made them both look as DS Steel appeared, arms out, stopping Detective Constable Way from escaping. 'Hope you're off on a tea run, Milky. Two and a coo for me.' A suggestive wink, then she stepped aside, letting Milky squeeze past.

There was a pause as King pulled himself up to his full height, chest out. Frowning down at Steel. 'Well?'

She stuck both hands in her pockets and sauntered in. 'What-ho, sharny bumholes?'

King stiffened. 'Is *that* how you speak to superior officers?'

Apparently.

'I've finished your stupid door-to-doors and you know what I got? Go on: guess.'

Heather emerged from the corner, stuffing her phone back in her pocket. 'Guv? I've managed to sort us a dog unit, but we'll need to wait till they've finished in Banff. They're dunting a druggie's door in at half one.'

'What I've got,' Steel stuck a hand down the front of her shirt and had a rummage – rearranging things, 'is sore feet, midge bites, and a sweat-sticky cleavage. It's like a teenager's wet dream down here.'

Logan shuddered. 'Urgh...'

King turned his back on her. 'They give you an ETA, Heather?'

'Minimum two hours, plus travelling time.'

Steel extracted her hand and wiped it on her suit trousers, leaving a damp smear. 'Did a three-mile radius and you know how many houses I found? Six. Six houses full of weird wee teuchtery people with webbed feet and no chins cos Mummy married Uncle Daddy.'

'Two hours?' King sighed. 'Not ideal, but it'll have to do.'

Heather tried her lopsided smile again. 'Sure you don't want to give Gibbs another go?'

'Inbred old gits didn't have a pair of teeth between them. Whole place reeked of banjos and "squeal piggy!"'

'We'll need to get on to the Superintendent: try and drum

up some more bodies.' King took out his phone 'Have a word with—'

'HOY!' Steel banged a hand down on the nearest desk. 'Are you tossers even listening to me?'

They might not have been before, but they were now.

King's eyes bugged. 'I *beg* your pardon?'

'Should think so too.' She stuck her nose in the air. 'And you'll be delighted to know that the media have got hold of your professor's disappearance. Bloody Aberdeen University issued a press release.'

With that, all the indignation hissed out of King like a deflating turnip. He sank into one of the recently vacated office chairs and sagged back, staring up at the baggy ceiling tiles. 'Great.'

Then his phone launched into 'Fairytale of New York' again. He groaned and curled into himself, arms wrapped around his head.

Steel grinned at Logan. 'What *you* doing here?' Then pointed at the groaning King. 'Going to fire the wee man?'

'Just popped in on my way to the canteen.'

'Hmph. Nice for some, swanning about like something off Darth Vader's glee club.'

'So you didn't find out anything useful at all?'

'From the Teuchter Patrol? Nah.' She plonked herself down in a chair. '"Professor Wilson is a loner", "Professor Wilson is a pain in the hoop", "Professor Wilson never puts his bins out on the right day". Only thing we know for sure is he went missing sometime between eighteen past eleven on Sunday night and twenty to ten, Monday morning.'

Heather raised an eyebrow. 'How can you possibly—'

'Last tweet he sent was eleven eighteen; first Alt-Nat tweet crowing about his death was twenty to ten. It's no' exactly *Celebrity Eggheads*, is it, H?'

A blush spread itself up Heather's neck and across her cheeks.

Steel pulled out her phone. 'Honestly, you buggers forget I used to be a Chief Inspector, don't you?' She poked at the screen, eyes all narrow and squinty. 'Here you go: "Corrupt Brit-Nat mouthpiece, Professor Wilson, has stained our proud country with his lies and filth for the last time. Death was too good for him. Enemy of the people!" Exclamation mark. Hashtag: "Rise up and be the nation again", hashtag: "Scotland first".'

Logan peered over her shoulder at the screen. 'They leave a name?'

'Aye: "Wally Knieve 1314".'

'OK.' He straightened up. 'So we do a PNC check for—'

'It's from Burns.' Heather pulled her chin up, stressing the words as if trying to redeem herself after Steel made her look like a numpty. "'Address to a Haggis". And I quote:

"But mark the Rustic, *haggis-fed*,
  The trembling earth resounds his tread,
  Clap in his walie nieve a blade,
  He'll mak it whissle ..."'

She held up a hand and curled it into a fist. 'This is *my* "walie nieve".'

King let his arms fall by his sides and stared at the ceiling again. Voice little more than a funeral dirge:

'"An' legs, an' arms, an' heads will sned,
  Like taps o' thrissle."'

Heather nodded. 'And 1314 was the battle of Bannockburn.'

'Oh...' Steel put her phone away. 'In that case, no. He didn't leave a name.'

'Course he didn't.' King sagged a bit further. 'H?'

'I can get in touch with Twitter, but don't hold your breath.'

King didn't move. 'Thanks. And now, unless anyone else has a—'

The door burst open, banging against the wall, and in marched a short man. A bit tubby about the middle, small round glasses and a hairline that looked as if it was planning on parting company with its host any day now. A scowl etched into his pasty face. DCI Hardie stopped in the middle of the room as King scrambled to his feet.

'Boss.'

'You've heard about the university?'

'Press release.'

'Which means we're going to have to do a media briefing. And by "we" I mean "you". Two o'clock sharp. Try to make it sound like we know what we're doing.'

King nodded. 'Boss.'

Then Hardie stared at Logan. 'Inspector McRae, good to have you back after...' Suspicion replaced the scowl as he looked from Logan to King. 'Is there something here I should know about?'

Logan put a hand on Steel's shoulder. 'Just popped by to see how Detective Sergeant Steel's getting on. Make sure she's keeping her nose clean.'

She gave him a full dose of the evil eye. 'Hoy!'

'Good luck with that.' Hardie turned on his heel, snapping his fingers above his head as he marched from the room. 'Two o'clock sharp!'

As soon as the door banged shut, King collapsed into his seat, hands over his face again. 'Aaaargh...'

Yeah, that pretty much summed it up.

6

Logan plipped the locks on his Audi and hurried across the furnace masquerading as Bucksburn station's rear car park. Trying to avoid the stickier patches of tarmac.

Inside, it was a bit cooler, but not a lot. He limped his way up the stairs to Professional Standards, sweat prickling between his shoulder blades. Who decided it was OK for the weather to be so bloody hot? The temperature was *never* meant to hit twenty-six in Aberdeen – what was the point of living nearly a degree and a half north of Moscow if it was going to be twenty-six in the shade? Might as well live in a microwave oven.

At least the air conditioning was on in the main office.

Someone he didn't recognise was lowering the blinds, cutting out the glaring sun and the lunchtime 'rush'. The traffic was barely moving – crawling along Inverurie Road and bringing most of Bucksburn to a grinding halt. Then the blinds clunked down and it was gone.

Whoever-it-was waved at Logan and he waved back.

Yup, no idea at all who you are, mate.

Logan lumbered his way along the line of offices to the one marked, 'FORENSIC I.T.' A laminated sheet of A4 sat underneath it, covered in clipart cartoon characters depicting some sort of bloody Aztec ritual with the legend, 'THE MIGHTY KARL CARES NOT FOR YOUR VIRGIN SACRIFICES: BRING CAKE!'

OK, so a packet of Rice Krispie squares wasn't *quite* the same thing, but it was near enough. Right?

He shifted the pack to his other hand and knocked.

A slightly high-pitched voice sounded on the other side of the door. *'Abandon all hope and enter.'*

Logan let himself in.

The Mighty Karl's domain was an eclectic collection of IT equipment, all of it labelled and most of it stored on the floor-to-ceiling shelves that lined the room. Laptops, desktops, evidence crates full of mobile phones and tablet computers.

More clipart cartoons were pinned up all over the walls and shelves. A halo of them made a wee shrine around a framed photo of Karl shaking hands with the First Minister. Only someone had given her a Post-it note speech balloon with, 'OH KARL, YOU SEXY BEAST OF A MAN, YOU!' on it.

The 'Sexy Beast of a man' sat at the workbench that bisected the room.

Perched on a high stool, with a thin grey cardigan on over his Police Scotland uniform T-shirt, thick-rimmed round glasses, and salt-and-pepper hair in desperate need of a cut, he was just a hookah pipe and a fez away from being the caterpillar from *Alice in Wonderland.*

He clambered down from his mushroom and beamed. 'Logan of the Clan McRae! I heard rumours of your...' His nostrils twitched and he curled forwards, peering at the packet in Logan's hand. 'Ooh, do these ancient eyes deceive me, or are you bearing votive offerings for my humble self? Hmmmmm?'

Logan popped the Rice Krispie squares on the desk and Karl snaffled them up, sniffing the wrapper.

'Ah, the *delights* of puffed rice and assorted sweetly sticky things...' A sigh, long and wistful. 'I miss Norman, don't you? He used to prepare decadent baked treats that would tempt even the most parsimonious of souls.' Karl ripped the pack open. 'I remember once he baked a batch of scones with Mars Bar bits, Gummy Bears, and jelly beans, that—'

'Can I beg a favour?'

Karl tore off a sticky corner and popped it in his mouth,

chewing through a big smile. 'Mmmm... You have made sacrifice to the all-mighty, all-seeing, all-knowing Oracle, so ask away, Brave Traveller.'

'I need you to track down some Twitter accounts for me.'

'Names, addresses, inside-leg measurements – that kind of thing?'

'As much as you can get.'

A nod. 'Luckily, my dear Logan, the only things I have on this afternoon are a pair of tattered pants and a second-hand bobble hat.' He sooked his fingers clean. 'Consider your tweetists found!'

And with any luck they'd have whoever abducted Professor Wilson in a cell by the close of business.

Superintendent Bevan sat behind her desk, hands busy with a ball of multicoloured wool and a crochet needle. Making something that looked disturbingly like a huge willy warmer.

Logan tore his eyes away from it and settled in his seat. 'I'm going to have to go over some of his cases, speak to a few of his colleagues to be sure, but I get the feeling DI King is telling the truth. It was a long time ago and he's genuinely changed.'

She frowned for a moment, crocheting away, then nodded. 'Better safe than sorry, Logan. Better safe than sorry.'

Yup, that was looking more like a willy warmer with every passing second. She'd got as far as the testicley bits... OK, no way that was appropriate for an office environment.

Logan cleared his throat. 'Course, it would help if we knew what the *Scottish Daily Post* had on him. Be easier to manage.'

Bevan didn't look up. '"Manage" is perhaps the wrong word. We're not here to put a positive spin on things, we're here to find the truth and resolve the situation. For good or ill.'

'I don't think he's going to be a risk to the Professor Wilson investigation, anyway.'

'I hope not, Logan. I really do. Politically, there's a lot riding on this one and if DI King slips up...' A pained expression pulled her mouth down. 'Keep an eye on him for me, will you? Be his shadow for a day or two. Actually, better make it three, just in case. Because the fallout would be *horrific*.'

Not quite as horrific as what she was making. Those testicular bits were getting bigger...

Look at something elsc!

Anything else!

How about ... that big frame on the wall, the one with the ancient green-and-white car and the speeding ticket?

'Err... so you're into classic cars?' Pointing at it.

'Hmm?' She glanced up from her crocheted codpiece. 'Oh, no. I keep that as a reminder. Oh, I used to *love* that Hillman Minx. Got done for speeding, when I was nineteen. Five K over the speed limit, so that's about...' Working it out. 'Three miles an hour too fast? But the cops in Auckland were *very* strict about that kind of thing.' More testicalling. 'So I keep it as a reminder.'

Crochet, crochet, crochet.

OK...

'Of what?'

'I was nineteen, I was in teachers' college, and I was in a hurry to get home after yet another day's placement at Blockhouse Bay Primary School – "going on section" we called it, part of the training.' A sigh. 'So I broke the speed limit. And now look at me!' She tugged at the ball bags, flattening them out. 'It reminds me that we all make mistakes, Logan. We all deserve a second chance.'

Fair enough.

'Like DI King?'

'Exactly.' She looked up from her willy warmer. 'I don't like our officers being savaged by the press, Logan. I don't like it one little bit.'

'Have you tried calling the journalist: see if they'll tell you what they've got on King?'

'Tricky. You give credence to the allegations just by questioning them. Next thing you know, the press is full of stories about how Professional Standards are investigating him. That, or accusing us of being involved in a cover-up.' Creases appeared between her eyebrows as she added another layer to the crocheted horror. 'I *suppose*, if you think you can pull it off?

46

But try not to stir up more trouble than we're already in, OK?'

Lovely: a poisoned chalice, all of his very own.

Logan pointed at the door. 'So, should I...?'

There was a *ding*, then a buzz, and Bevan's huge iPhone skittered on the desktop. She peered over the top of her glasses at the screen. Sighed and shook her head. 'Honestly! Some husbands send their wives dick picks, what do *I* get?' She let go of the wool and turned the phone around, so Logan could see.

It was a photo of a man's mid-section, bit of trousers, belt, and waist. A big yellow banana poked out of his flies.

'I swear that man is sixty-one going on twelve.'

So that's who the willy warmer was for.

Logan stood. 'Well, I'd better be—'

'Sergeant Rennie says you taught him all he knows.'

Typical Rennie: rotten little clype was probably trying to spread the blame.

'That depends on what he's done.'

'Inspiring people is *always* a good thing.' She smiled. 'Have you considered what you're going to do when your tour of Professional Standards is over? Which branch of NE Division you'd like to move into?'

'Erm...'

'And you're not restricted to NE Division – now that we're all one big happy Police Scotland family, you could take your pick: Tayside, Highlands and Islands, Fife? I'm sure your Queen's Medal will open all manner of doors.'

'Hadn't really thought about it.'

'You should, Logan. You should. The next ten months will fly by and then ... poof! Professional Standards' loss will be someone else's gain.' She held up the multicoloured willy warmer, letting the dangly bit ... dangle. 'I think it's coming along nicely, don't you?'

Urgh!

'I really don't think I—'

'Now I've got the trunk and the ears done I can move on to Mr Haathee's body and legs.'

Logan looked from the dangly bit to the dirty crocheted elephant perched on top of the filing cabinet with one of its button eyes hanging off.

Oh thank God for that.

'Anyway, I won't keep you.' She went back to her non-willy-warming elephant. 'Let me know how you get on with your journalist.'

No idea whose desk this was, but they had a serious *Twilight* problem. The cubicle walls were covered in posters of various greasy-looking sparkly vampires and shirtless young men smouldering for the camera. Not exactly wholesome.

Logan drew smiley faces on half a dozen Post-its and stuck them over the actors' pouts, giving the desk a much more festive air. Then he logged on to his email and pulled up the front page of the *Scottish Daily Post* they'd been sent. The one with DI King's face and 'TOP MURDER COP WAS IN SCOTNAT TERROR GROUP'.

According to the byline, it'd been written by 'SENIOR REPORTER, EDWARD BARWELL' along with a mobile number and 'HAVE YOU GOT A BREAKING STORY?'

Logan pulled over the desk phone and dialled.

While it rang, he called up a web browser and googled Barwell. The *Post*'s website showed an earnest-looking man in his early twenties, hair slicked back on top and very, *very* short at the sides. The kind of person who thought a checked waistcoat and a tweed jacket made him look both trendy and respectable, but came off more middle-aged Rupert the Bear. The list of articles that accompanied the photo suggested—

A voice in his ear: *'Edward Barwell.'*

'Mr Barwell? It's Inspector McRae from North East Division. Have you got a minute to talk about DI Frank King?'

'On or off the record?'

'Off.'

'Why? What don't you want people to know about?'

Nope, not playing that game.

'OK. I'm sorry for bothering you. Bye.' Logan had the handset halfway to the cradle when Barwell's voice belted out of the earpiece:

'Wait, wait! OK, off the record it is.'

Better.

'You emailed through tomorrow's front page and I'm looking into your allegations.'

'Allegations?' A laugh. *'You're kidding, right? They're not alle-gations, Inspector…?'*

'McRae.'

'Right, and is that M.A.C. or M.C.?'

'It's spelled: "off-the-record", remember?'

'Force of habit.' There was a pause. Then, *'Your DI King was in a Scottish Nationalist terrorist cell. I've enough dirt to run this for three or four days.'*

Well *that* complicated things.

Logan opened his notebook and dug out a pen. 'You've got proof he was involved in terrorist activities?'

'You're investigating him, you tell me.' Then, when Logan didn't, *'The People's Army for Scottish Liberation were big on blowing up statues and guest houses, weren't they? And now there's all these Alt-Nat arson attacks going on. Makes you wonder if someone like King should be out there investigating crimes, doesn't it?'*

'Who told you he was involved?'

'So you're admitting he was in the SPLA?'

'No, I'm asking who *told* you he was. If I told you Donald Trump was a Mensa member, it wouldn't make it true, would it?'

'You want me to hand over my sources to the police? *Yeah, that's going to happen. Let me saddle up my unicorn and I'll ride over with the information.'*

Rupert the Bear does sarcasm.

Logan sighed. 'Look, I'm trying to get to the bottom of this, OK? Maybe it's not a great idea to trash a guy's career without a proper investigation?'

'That a threat?'

'No, it's me wondering why you're so interested in DI King.'

You could hear the big evil smile in his voice, it practically dripped from the handset. *'Read the paper, you'll find out.'* There was some rustling, a clunk, then a swell of voices in the background, as if Barwell had just stepped into a busy room. *'Gotta dash – your media briefing's about to kick off and I don't want to miss a single minute.'* Then he hung up.

Logan put the phone down. Swivelled in his borrowed chair. Frowned at the now smiley-Post-it-faced vampires. 'That could've gone better.'

He opened a new tab on the browser and called up Silver City FM's website, 'THE VOICE OF THE NORTHEAST SINCE 2008!', following a link on their 'NEWS UPDATE!' page to a livestream of DCI Hardie's press conference.

The picture was completely frozen and pixelated – the media briefing room at Divisional Headquarters. The bottom of the screen was taken up with the back of journalists' heads, with a small podium in front of them. It played host to a projection screen, a backdrop covered in Police Scotland logos, and a desk covered with blue cloth. A row of uncomfortable-looking officers behind it – DCI Hardie in the middle, DI King to the left, and the Media Liaison Officer on the right. All three of them sharing a single microphone. Then the circular icon that meant the media player was buffering appeared, whirled for a bit, and *finally* the video started playing.

King was on his feet, mouth open. *'...ask anyone with any information to come forward. Thank you.'*

He sat back down and the Media Liaison Officer nodded at the assembled press pack as the words 'JANE MCGRATH' materialised at the bottom of the screen. Immaculate in her suit, with hair and makeup so perfect she could've been presenting the news. Polished to the point of being slightly creepy in an uncanny valley kind of way. Her voice was much the same. *'Any questions?'*

A flurry of hands went up.

It was difficult to tell who was who, going by the back of their heads, but a few of those journalistic haircuts were familiar, especially the trendy short sides and slicked top of Edward Barwell. Sitting there, between someone from the BBC and the *Aberdeen Examiner*.

Jane pointed at one of them. *'Yes: Bob?'*

'Aye, Bob Finnegan, Aberdeen Examiner. *Is Professor Wilson's disappearance connected to Matt Lansdale going missing?'*

She pulled on a smile that *probably* wasn't meant to look as patronising as it did. *'Not that we know of, Bob. But again, we urge anyone with information to get in touch. Who's next?'*

'Only, see, Lansdale's a high-profile anti-independence campaigner, just like the Professor. Bit of a coincidence, isn't it?'

The smile got even worse. *'Again: we're not currently aware of any connection. Yes: Olivia.'*

The woman sitting next to Barwell lowered her hand. *'Olivia Ward, BBC News. What about all these arson attacks? Isn't it likely that Professor Wilson's murder is part of a coordinated campaign of domestic terrorism?'*

King leaned forward into the microphone. *'For the record: there's no evidence that Professor Wilson's been murdered. This is a missing persons inquiry.'*

Edward Barwell didn't even bother putting his hand up. Cocky little sod. *'Are you sure, Detective Inspector?'*

Logan sat back in his seat. 'Oh God, here we go...'

'You see, the Alt-Nat trolls are all over social media saying he is.' Because cocky wasn't bad enough, he had to be smug with it. *'You have seen the tweets and posts, haven't you?'*

'As I said, the inquiry is ongoing and we ask anyone with—'

'Information to come forward. Yes.' A nod. Difficult to be a hundred percent certain, only seeing the back of his head, but going by the voice? Logan would've put money on Barwell's smile being even more patronising than Jane McGrath's. *'I'll bet you do...'*

7

The keyboard creaked and rattled as Logan picked out a conclusion for his report on Professor Wilson's disappearance. Blah, blah, blah, forensically aware, blah, blah, blah, unknown perpetrator, blah, blah, blah, ongoing investigation focusing on—

His mobile launched into its generic ringtone.

Great.

'Can't even get *five minutes* peace.' He pulled the thing out and answered it. 'McRae.'

King's voice growled in his ear. *'I take it you saw that.'*

So he'd called up to moan. Oh joy.

'Watched it online.'

'What's he waiting for then? Barwell. Smarmy little git.' King's voice sounded ... odd. As if he was being strangled, making the words slightly sharp and mushy at the same time.

'Are you OK?'

Maybe he was having a stroke?

'Oh, fine. Fine. I mean, I'm being investigated by Professional Standards, a national newspaper is threatening to tell the world I was a member of a terrorist organisation, my main case is a booby-trapped nightmare full of burning crap, and my wife's...' He cleared his throat. *'You lied to Hardie. When he came into the office, you told him you were there to see Steel.'*

'I'm not your enemy, Frank. Hardie doesn't need to know we're—'

'Investigating me.'

'Do you *want* him to know?'

'He's going to find out sooner or later.' A bitter sigh. *'Soon as Barwell prints his front page, everyone will.'*

The rattling kettle spewed steam in the tiny kitchen area. They'd managed to squeeze a microwave, toaster, teeny fridge, and a couple of cupboards in here, but there wasn't any room left over for a sink – instead, a couple of two-litre bottles of supermarket water loitered on the windowsill.

Add to that one Logan and a Superintendent Bevan, and the place was packed.

She dropped a teabag into each of the mugs on the work surface. 'And Barwell didn't say *anything* about King's PASL past?'

'Not a word. Just sat there being smug the whole time.'

The kettle finished its juddering song and fell silent.

Logan filled the mugs. 'Best guess? He'll publish tomorrow. Don't see him holding off now he knows King's investigating an abducted unionist.'

'I think it might be wise to get the media department to draft a statement. Better to be prepared than caught with our pants round our ankles. And we'll want to present a united front.' She pulled out a spoon and mashed away at the teabags, as if they'd been naughty. Not looking at Logan. 'And you're sure he's not still involved?'

'"Sure" sure, or "kind-of-certain-but-don't-quote-me-on-that" sure?'

'Then go digging, Logan. Go digging. Because if we're going to stand up there and say he's clean, he damn well better be.'

Ah, the delights of Interview Room Three, with its stained ceiling tiles, scraped walls, and a chipped Formica table covered in badly spelled biro graffiti. It was enough to make you nostalgic for the good old days.

The blinds were open, letting sunlight flood the room, glinting off the recording equipment and the camera mounted in the corner above the door.

For a change, Logan sat on the suspect side of the table – the one where the chairs were bolted to the floor, the one facing the camera, the one where the window was behind him. Meaning that Detective Constable Collins, had to sit opposite, squinting against the sunlight, sweat prickling out across his forehead, the stains under his arms darkening as he wriggled and fidgeted. Wee Bernie Collins: a shaved chimp in a brown shirt, his tie hanging loose like a Labrador's tongue.

Logan gave him a reassuring smile. 'It's OK, Bernie; nothing to worry about. I'm trying to get a feel for DI King's management style, that's all; talking to people who've worked with him. You were on a team of his eight months ago, right? That attempted murder in Kemnay?'

'Erm...' Bernie's eyes drifted up to the camera in the corner. He licked his lips. Blinked a couple of times. 'Sorry, what was the question again?'

Ladies and gentlemen: Aberdeen's finest.

'How do you think DI King gets on with his English colleagues?'

Wrinkles appeared across that sweaty head. 'What, other forces down south?' Sometimes, with Wee Bernie, it was difficult to tell if he was being obtuse, or genuinely thick.

'No, his colleagues *here*. Ones who're *English*. Does he treat them differently?'

'Oh.' The wrinkles deepened. 'He doesn't like Soapy Halstead much. But then Soapy's a bit of a wanker, so no one does. He likes Milky, though, and she's all "Eee-bah-goom", flat caps, and whippets.' A shrug of simian shoulders. 'Other than that? Nah, King was a good boss.'

Heather squinted against the sunlight and scooted her chair over a bit, till Logan's shadow fell across her face. Then leaned back in her chair. 'Ooh, now you're asking.' She brushed the grey fringe from her eyes. 'Not so I've noticed. I mean, you wouldn't, would you? Because he isn't.' A pause stretched for a couple of breaths. 'That I *know* of, anyway.'

Nothing like covering your own arse.

Logan tilted his head to one side, exposing Heather to the

light again. 'OK: what about these arson attacks, has he said anything about them?'

She shoogled her chair over a bit more. 'Only that he *really* hopes it isn't domestic terrorism, or Spevoo are going to be all over us like a wet cocker spaniel.'

OK, no idea. 'Spevoo?'

'Scottish Preventing Extremism Violence Unit. Spevoo. You know what these specialist task forces are like – they've seen one too many episodes of NCIS and think they're all Special Agent Leroy Jethro Gibbs.' Heather scrunched her face up. 'When most of them barely qualify as Timothy McGee. And I mean Season *One*, Timothy McGee, not Season Fourteen.'

He had to ask, didn't he?

Detective Constable Sharon 'Milky' Way chewed on the inside of her cheek for a bit. 'What, you mean like, "is he a racist?"'

'Has he ever done, or said, something that's made you feel uncomfortable?'

'This *is* DI King we're talking 'bout, in't it?' She frowned at Logan. 'Why are you asking?'

Logan shrugged, the sunlight warm against his back. 'You know what things are like these days. We just want to make sure everyone's supported at work and no one's feeling—'

'"Uncomfortable". Yes, you said.' She sat back in her seat. 'King's OK, but I'll tell you who *does* make us feel uncomfortable: Detective Sergeant Brogan. Him with Kevin Keegan perm and permanent sniff. Always ogles me boobs when he thinks I'm not looking, every – single – time.'

'Does he now?' Logan got out his notebook and wrote, 'TALK TO DS BROGAN ABOUT SEXUAL HARASSMENT IN THE WORKPLACE!' then underlined it three times. 'I'll have to have a word with him about that.'

'And make sure you tell him twas me tipped you off. Disgusting sniffy little pervert that he is.'

DS Robertson made a big show of thinking about it. Serious frown. Fingertips stroking his bony chin. A whippet in a charity-shop suit, with horrible sideburns, and droopy eyes.

Logan sighed. 'Come on, Henry: you worked with him on the Martin Shanks investigation, didn't you?'

Robertson shuddered. 'Don't remind me. And before you say anything, the internal inquiry cleared us both, OK?'

'Does DI King treat his English team members differently or not? It's a simple enough question.'

'Oh yes, it's a simple enough *question*, it's the answer that's complicated. See, there's no way I want to land someone in it with the Rubber Heelers.' He raised a stick-insect hand. 'No offence. And there's no way I'm lying to the Rubber Heelers either.' The hand went up again. 'No offence. But you people make me nervous, you know?'

'Just be honest and you've got nothing to worry about.' It was an effort keeping the reassuring smile in place, but Logan did his best.

'Hmmm… Well, he doesn't like Soapy very much, but neither does anyone else. He's even more of a tosser than your lot.' Up went the hand.

'Yeah, I know: no offence.'

PC Oliver 'Soapy' Halstead lounged in his seat, looking at Logan with one eyebrow raised, as if that was the stupidest question he'd ever been asked. Oh the arrogance of youth. Only twenty-four and he was *clearly* under the impression that he already knew everything about everything, with his neat little beard, architect's glasses, and Young Conservative haircut. Even his loosened *tie* looked arrogant. Probably didn't help that his Home Counties accent made him sound as if he was sneering at everything: 'Oh no, I haven't seen anything like *that*, Inspector. When we're out arresting the great unwashed, we are a unit. A team. A tightly knit band of brothers, if you will.'

Logan tried not to sigh, he really did. 'Because I wouldn't want you to think you couldn't talk to me, or one of my colleagues, if someone was making you feel uncomfortable.'

'Oh, dear me, no.' He had a little preen. 'I think you'll find that I'm quite capable of fighting my own battles, thank you very much.'

Logan stared back at him.

Silence.

Halstead shifted in his seat. Picked at the tabletop. Cleared his throat.

More silence.

'All right, I admit that it can be a bit … *challenging* from time to time.' He straightened the cuffs on his pinstriped shirt. 'I see how members of the public look at me sometimes. There I am, arresting some drug-addled junkie who's been sick all over himself, and they're looking down their nose at me, because I'm English and I've had a decent education? That hardly seems fair, does it?'

The arrogant expression had slipped, replaced by one that looked a bit … sad. And disappointed. And a little hurt. Maybe 'Soapy' wasn't quite the dick that everyone thought?

'You do know that you can report hate crimes against you, Oliver? We won't put up with that stuff.'

He waved it away. 'Racism is a by-product of ignorance, Inspector. Are we to punish people for being stupid, now? If we did that, three quarters of the country would be behind bars.'

'And has DI King ever treated you differently to your non-English colleagues?'

A long sigh. Then: 'He's all right, I suppose.' Halstead stared down at the tabletop. 'I'm aware that he doesn't *like* me very much, but at least he doesn't give me all the terrible menial jobs.' A small bitter laugh broke free. 'I only ever wanted to be a police officer. Father wanted me to read Classics at Cambridge, like he did. Rather broke his heart when I told him I was running off to Scotland to "join the Rozzers" instead.'

Logan reached across the table, put a hand on Halstead's shoulder and gave it a squeeze. 'Listen to me, Oliver: if anyone gives you crap for being English, you let me know. I'll make their next prostate exam feel like a teddy bear's tea party.'

Why could Police Scotland never get any decent computers in? Why did they all have to be steam-powered monstrosities the colour of skin grafts? Well maybe not *all* of them, but the one in the tiny office he'd commandeered certainly was.

Tiny *grubby* office.

God knew who'd had it last, but they'd left the bin overflowing with sandwich wrappers, crisp packets, and scrunched-up copies of the *Daily Mail*.

A pile of printouts sat beside the ancient computer. Logan wrote 'FOLLOW UP ON DRUG MONEY? CHECK WITH ARCHIVIST?' on the top sheet, then turned back to the screen. Squinted at the reflected glare. Swivelled his chair around and lowered the blind, shutting out the sun. Then clicked the next link on his search results.

A gaudy web page popped up, festooned with cheesy animated gifs and saltire flags. Whoever maintained PASL-MANIFESTO-FOR-A-FREE-SCOTLAND.COM wasn't exactly blessed with graphic design skills.

> For fifty years, the People's Army for Scottish Liberation
> has been proudly dedicated to ending English impe-
> rialist rule! For too long we Scots have been ground
> beneath the heel of our English oppressors, diminished
> in the eyes of the world and ourselves, as

The office door creaked open and Steel poked her head in. 'Hoy, Limpy: you still here?'

He went back to the screen. 'No. Went home hours ago.'

> in the eyes of the world and ourselves, as they grow
> fat and rich on our oil revenue and whisky duty and
> our land!

She sauntered over, pausing only to kick the door shut behind her, pulled out an envelope and tossed it onto his desk. It landed with a clattery thump. 'Whip-round.'

'What, for me?'

'No' for you, you spungbadger, Ailsa Marshall. You know them woods in Rubislaw Den? Poor cow's been sleeping rough there for months. Someone found her this morning, face-down in the burn. You're chipping in for a headstone.'

'Here.' He added a fiver to the collection and handed the envelope back.

'Ta.' Steel stuck it in her jacket. 'Don't fancy babysitting tonight, do you? I could go an evening in the pub, kebab, and a bit of the old wriggly fun.'

'No chance.'

'Spoilsport.' She hauled the blind open again, turning Logan's computer screen into an eye-watering blare of light.

'Argh...' He backed away from it, squinting.

'Sitting here in the dark like a wee troll.' She cracked the window open, letting in the diesel growl of buses and the seagulls' mournful cries. 'It's no' good for you.' The tip of her e-cigarette / sonic screwdriver glowed as she sooked. A huge cloud of watermelon vape drifted its way around Logan's head, glowing in the sunlight. 'Come on then, what you doing?'

'Investigating.' Logan held up a hand, blocking the glare from his screen. 'Or at least I'm *trying* to.'

'I know that, you idiot; investigating what?'

'People's Army for Scottish Liberation. Apparently they had ties to the Scottish People's Liberation Army, the Scottish Freedom Fighters' Resistance Front, End of Empire, and Arbroath Thirteen Twenty. AKA nutters so extreme that even Settler Watch didn't want anything to do with them.'

Another cloud of fruity smelling fog. 'It's Womble-funting dick-muppets like that who give good old-fashioned Scottish Nationalists a bad name.'

'The whole lot were supposed to get together in the eighties and launch a coordinated attack – you know, tear down that big Duke of Sutherland statue, burn out English-run guest houses, blow up HM Customs and Excise offices so as to "cripple the revenue gathering apparatus of the imperialist oppressor" – but it led to so much infighting they couldn't organise a pervert in a scout hut.'

'You sure you don't want to babysit?'

Logan tapped the top printout on his pile. 'So the People's

Army for Scottish Liberation decided to go their own way: did a big bullion job and walked off with two point six *million* pounds. Word is they were raising money for an armed insurgency. Their leader nips over to Belfast, looking to buy a whole shedload of machineguns from dissident republicans, only he gets picked up by the local plod. Kerb crawling for rent boys.'

She rested her bum against the windowsill. 'I could drop Naomi and Jasmine off at yours. You wouldn't even have to feed them.'

'Turned out he had thirty-two thousand quid's worth of heroin in the boot to pay for the guns.'

'Make sure they do their teeth, then pop them off to bed. You'll barely even know they're there.'

'If he hadn't fancied a knee-trembler in the back of a Vauxhall Astra we could've had our very own version of the Troubles.'

Steel sent another cloud of watermelon in Logan's direction. 'Or are you worried it'll interfere with whatever heterosexual filth you and Ginger McHotpants get up to on a Tuesday evening?'

'Kind of makes you ashamed to be Scottish...' He frowned at her. 'And *stop* calling Tara "Ginger McHotpants"!'

A grin. 'How about Kinky McSpankypants instead?'

He turned his frown into a scowl.

Steel shrugged, pocketed her e-cigarette, shut the window, then bumped his chair with her hip. Voice soft and kind, 'Come on, time for home. No point wearing yourself out on the first day back, is there?'

Pfff... She was probably right.

Logan powered down the computer. 'Suppose not.' He gathered up his printouts as the machine whirred and beeped itself to sleep.

'There you go.' She wrapped an arm around his shoulders as he stepped out from behind the desk. Gave him a squeeze. 'Now, about that babysitting...'

Ah, so that explained the 'nice' act.

'Not a chance in hell. I'm going home to a handful of painkillers, a soak in the tub, and barbecue some sausages for tomorrow.' He poked a finger at her. 'I am *not* babysitting!'

8

'DIE! DIE AND BE DEAD!' Jasmine thundered across the patio, shooting her little sister with a sci-fi blaster. She'd spiked her brown hair up with far too much gel for an eleven-year-old. Ribena stains splotched down the front of her horsey T-shirt, grass stains on her jodhpurs. *Definitely* took after Steel, that one.

'PEW! PEW! PEW!' Naomi tore after her, lumbering a bit from side to side on her tiny little legs, big grin on her face, scuffs on her bare knees, pink and green stripes in her dirty blonde hair. She had Captain Bogies clasped to her chest with one hand, the octopus's legs flopping about as she shot at her sister with the other. 'PEW! PEW! BOOOOM!'

Not exactly restful.

Logan took a swig of IPA from the bottle and turned over a couple of sausages, the warm comforting scent of charcoal and charring fat wafting out into the garden. It'd taken most of the year, but it was looking pretty damn good, thank you very much – a riot of colour and textures, flowers, bushes, trees, and a lawn. An *actual* lawn, not a collection of dandelions, moss, and other assorted weeds. OK, so the rickety old shed probably wouldn't survive another winter, and the greenhouse needed cleaning, but other than that? Domestic bliss.

He popped his beer back on the wrought-iron table, wiped his fingers on his apron, and poked the chicken thighs.

Turned some more sausages.

Naomi and Jasmine screeched their way past again.

'PEW! PEW! PEW!'

'You two monsters: go wash your hands for dinner.'

'DIE, SPACE FIEND!'

And they were gone again.

Typical.

A voice behind him: 'Sure you've got enough sausages? Think the supermarket might still have a couple left.' Tara stepped out through the patio doors, carrying a bowl of salad and four plates. The cowboy boots made her even taller – a clean white T-shirt and spotless blue jeans rounding off the cowboy-who's-never-been-near-a-horse-in-his-life look. Her wolf-blue eyes narrowed in the sunlight, making tiny wrinkles on her heart-shaped face. Her long mahogany hair glowing like— 'Is there something wrong?'

Logan blinked. 'Wrong?'

'Only you're staring at me like I've got a bogey hanging out of my nose.'

'Oh. Right. No.' A smile. 'The only bogies here are the octo-pussy kind.'

She popped the salad and plates on the table as the kids battered past again.

'PEW! PEW!'

'You heard your dad: wash up, horrors!'

They didn't listen to her, either.

Tara helped herself to a swig of his beer. 'I swear to God, those kids take more after Steel than they do Susan. They're like drunken wolverines with ADHD and no volume control.'

Yup.

He grabbed a pork-and-apple sausage with his tongs, and held it up. 'You want yours fruity, spicy, or Cumberlandy?'

She stepped up behind him and slipped her hands into the pockets of his apron. Gave him a *very* suggestive smile. 'I do like a spicy sausage!' And then her hands went a-wandering.

'Arrgh!' Logan danced away a couple of steps, clacking his tongs at her in self-defence. 'Hands off the cook's sausage, you pervert. This is a food preparation area!'

She polished off his beer. 'You hear about this missing constitutional scholar? Professor Watson?'

'Wilson.'

'Met him at an Aberdeen University do last year. I know we're not supposed to talk ill of the dead, but by God that man was a dick.'

Logan shifted some of the more cooked sausages off onto a plate and opened another packet of Cumberlands. 'Was?'

'Well, you know, what with him being dead and all.'

The thick pink tubes sizzled as they hit the hot grill. 'Don't believe everything you read on social media. There's no proof he's dead, just a bunch of Alt-Nat trolls out flapping their gums.'

'Alt-Nat, Brit-Nat, Unionistas, Independunces, Remoaners, Brexshiteers…' She toasted him with the empty bottle. 'Got to love civilised discourse in the modern age.'

'Well, there's always—'

'PEW! PEW! PEW!'

Naomi and Jasmine battered across the garden, once around the patio furniture, and disappeared into the house again. Squealing and screaming and laughing.

Logan sighed. 'Think it's too late to call animal control and have them taken away?'

'Probably.'

Cthulhu burst out through the patio doors, only slowing when she realised she was being watched and it might not look cool for a big stripy cat to be running away from an eleven-year-old girl and her three-and-a-bit-year-old sister. Cthulhu popped up onto the table and settled down for a wash, licking her big furry white paws, massive plumey tail held out at a jaunty angle.

Tara ruffled the fur between Cthulhu's ears, setting her purring. 'You ever think about having a kid of your own?'

'Are Tweedlehorror and Tweedlemonster not enough?'

'Wanking into a cup, so your Lesbian Lothario boss could impregnate her wife with a turkey baster doesn't count.' Tara lowered her head, looking up at him through her eyelashes. 'So … what would you think?'

He opened his mouth. Closed it again. *Stared* at her. 'You're not … I mean, we… Are you…?'

She put a hand on her lower stomach and smiled at him – wide eyed, sappy, and screne. 'The seed of our love has taken root, Logan, and soon it will blossom for all the world to see!'

Oh God.

'I… We… But…' Wait a minute. 'Are you taking the piss?'

She grinned.

'I nearly had a *heart attack* then! Are you trying to kill me a third time?'

'You should've seen your face, it was an absolute—'

'PEW! PEW! PEW!' Naomi stampeded out of the patio doors again, shooting everyone with her laser gun. 'PEW! PEW-PEW-PEW!'

Tara grabbed her, sweeping her up, turning her upside down and dangling her head-first over a wooden planter full of herbs. 'Have you washed your hands yet?'

Naomi shrieked, giggled, and wriggled. 'You'll never take me alive, copper!'

'Go wash your hands or there's no sausages for you.'

The little monster went limp. 'It's a fair cop.'

'Darn tootin' it is.' Tara set her down, the right way up.

Naomi smiled at her, all sweetness and light. Then scampered off. 'Sayonara, suckers!'

Tara shook her head. 'Yeah… On second thoughts, let's not have kids. There's enough horror in the world already.'

Oh God, oh God, oh God.

Nicholas threw back his head and howled his pain into the gloom.

Fire burned up and down his arms, pulsing in waves that matched the beat of his heart. Up and down and up and down. Searing. Scorching. Urgent.

Tears spilled down his cheeks; his chest ached with sobbing, every breath tasting of bitter sweat and hot metal.

He kicked out against the lid again, slamming his foot into

it. The thing barely moved, held fast by the padlocked chain around the outside.

A white plastic box, smeared with blood. His blood. It saturated the bandages that covered his arms from the elbow down, the damp surface busy with the fat greasy bodies of bluebottles.

They glittered in the thin sliver of light that crept through the one-inch gap where the lid had been propped open. One inch: just enough so he wouldn't suffocate. Because that would be quick, wouldn't it? Too easy. Much better to make him endure a slow lingering *hard* death. Trapped in this hideous box. His small plastic coffin – too short to lie down flat in, not deep enough to sit up properly, the sides pressing in against his burning shoulders.

A lifetime spent studying constitutional law and legislation. Lecturing. Educating. Trying to make people understand the truth about how democracy and civilisation *really* work. And this is how it will end.

In a gloomy plastic box.

Eaten alive by bluebottles and pain.

Nicholas dragged in another foul breath and *screamed*.

— this is why we can't have nice things —

9

Something horrible and tinny blared out of the clock radio, followed by, *'Goooooood Morning Aberdeeeeeeen! It's six o'clock – I know, I know – and you're listening to* OMG it's Early!, *with me, Rachel Gray.'*

Urgh...

Logan peeled his eyes open and blinked at the ceiling. The curtains were shut, but bright-white light glowed around the edges, as if the aliens had come to abduct everyone.

'We've got a great *show for you this sunny June morning. So wakey, wakey, hands off snakey, it's time to rock!'*

'Noooo!' Tara's hand appeared from beneath the duvet and bashed him on the head. Voice a pained mumble, 'Make it stop! Make it stop!'

He fumbled with the controls. 'Gnnn....'

'Here's the Foo Fighters with "Learning to Fly", fight that Foo, guys, we can't—'

Silence.

Tara grumbled, turned over – taking a good quantity of the duvet with her – and said something *very* unladylike.

Logan lay there grimacing. Six in the morning. Who got up at six in the morning? Then he sighed, rolled out of bed, and slouched his way through to the shower.

Sod this for a game of soldiers...

* * *

Light spilled in through the kitchen windows, making the tabletop glow as Cthulhu sat in the middle of it washing her bum.

Logan stuck the slice of toast in his mouth, holding it there with his teeth as he ripped open a sachet of chicken-and-liver and *schloched* it into the bumwasher's favourite bowl. It lay there, in a jellied slab, like some foul internal organ. He put it next to her biscuits and dipped into the fridge for the big Tupperware box of barbecued sausages and the smaller one of leftover fried onions. Chewed on his toast as he carried both out into the hall and dumped them by the front door.

No chance of forgetting them there.

Brushed toast crumbs off his black Police Scotland T-shirt.

Yawned.

Slumped.

Mornings used to be a *lot* easier.

He fastened his inspector's epaulettes and stared up the stairs, listening for signs of life.

Nothing. Because *they* were all still asleep. Because none of *them* needed to be at work by seven. Jammy buggers.

'God, I miss being off on the sick...'

He tucked his box o'sausages under one arm, balanced the onions on top and bumbled his way out the front door, into the searing bright morning. The day had barely started and it was *already* far too hot. Like living in a deep-fat fryer. God knew what it'd be like by lunchtime.

He plipped the locks on his Audi and hurried down the steps.

Froze.

Sod.

Hurried inside again and grabbed his peaked cap off its hook at the bottom of the stairs.

Checked his watch: six thirty-seven.

'Gah!'

No doubt about it: whoever invented mornings was a sadist.

It wasn't easy, limping his way up the Bucksburn station stairs, a waxed-paper cup of scalding coffee in one hand, the big box of sausages – topped with the container of onions and his flat cap – in the other. But he hadn't dropped anything *yet*.

He was halfway up when Shona burst out of the PSD office, stomping her way down towards him, face flushed and creased, teeth bared. Deep wrinkles slashed their way across her forehead, barely concealed by a sweaty brown fringe. Mid-forties, going on homicidal.

He tried his best cheery voice, 'Happy birthday, Shona!'

She didn't stop. 'Bloody printer hates me!'

'Oh fine, fine. Thanks for asking. You?'

Shona stomped past him, the muscles bulging in her clenched jaw as she forced the words out, 'You lot better have chipped together and bought me a sledgehammer! Cos when I get back, that printer's dead! DEAD!'

He stayed where he was as she growled her way down to the bottom and away through the double doors.

'Yup. Great to be back.' Logan limped up to the top and pushed through into the main office.

It wasn't as busy as yesterday – most of the desks were unpersoned – but Shona's was *really* easy to spot. Mylar balloons bobbed in the air above it, streamers hung in rainbow-coloured drapes all over the cubicle walls, a big banner with "HAPPY BIRTHDAY!!!" pinned to the wall.

Subtle.

Logan nodded to a couple of officers in the process of logging on to their computers as he made his way across to his desk. Or at least, it *used* to be his desk. Someone had colonised it with Lord of the Rings stuff – posters and film stills on every available vertical surface, an 'Eye of Sauron' mug, and a tableau of action figures Blu-Tacked in place on top of the monitor: Gandalf and Frodo facing off against Saruman, an Orc, and, for some unknowable reason, Postman Pat.

He stared at the Tolkien shrine. 'What happened to all my Gary Larsons?'

Probably went in the bin the day after they signed him off on the sick. Insensitive bunch of bastards.

Logan dumped his sausage collection on the desk, adjusted

his seat, and powered up his crummy old police computer. Might as well do a bit of digging on—

'Is Tufty!'

He swivelled his office chair around and there was Tufty, hurrying across the office towards him: eyes wide and twitchy, bags underneath them, a laptop clasped to his chest and a tin of Red Bull in his other hand. Talking much faster than any normal person ought to.

'Boss, Guv, Sarge! Sarge, Sarge, Sarge, Sarge...'

OK.

'I've been an inspector for *two years*, you half-baked spud. And shouldn't you be off interviewing academics?'

'Too early. Too early. They don't start till nine and it's only five to seven and I've been up all night and is that coffee?' He squirrelled his way over to Logan's desk and stood there, vibrating. A weird grin on his face as he stared at Logan's latte.

'How much Red Bull have you had?'

'Been up all night working on the social media side of things, because I can do that in my spare time, right? Just cos I can't do it in work time doesn't mean I can't do it when it's home time, so I did it at home. Yes indeedy. Home, home, home, home, home.' He put his laptop on top of Logan's sausages and cracked open the Red Bull.

'No, seriously, you need to stop drinking that stuff.'

'But I has a *success*!' The grin got even more manic. 'There's a dark web, lurking below the surface if you know where to look. I did run an algorithm on the first tweet about Professor Wilson and tracked the language usage across a selection of Alt-Nat accounts: Twitter, Facebook, Messageboards. FourChan, ThreeChan, TwoChan, OneChan, we have liftoff!'

'Right.' Logan took the tin of Red Bull from Tufty's hand. 'This is for your own good.'

'But see, I did find the same person running multiple accounts!'

'So you know who they *are*?'

'Ah... Not yet. It's always anonymous usernames and fakeity pseudonyms, and I don't have enough resources to run through *all* the social media accounts that aren't Alt-Naty so I can't find linguistic markers in the outside real world cos that'll take a lot of very big computers and all I've got's a laptop and can I have my Red Bull back?' Reaching for it.

'Definitely not. You're wired enough as it—'

'Course if they've geotagged their posts I could use that to cross-reference their location with the nearest cell-towers and did you know you only need four tagged posts to identify an anonymous account with ninety-five percent accuracy?'

'Great! So, get online and—'

'You'd have to access the customer dataset of every mobile-phone company in the UK to do it, but you could maybe get a warrant...' Tufty stuck his bottom lip out, showing off his teeth in some sort of weird bulldog impersonation. 'Ooh! Or I could try *hacking* in and—'

'No! No hacking things!'

He sagged, going from bulldog to dewy-eyed puppy. 'But Saaa-arge!'

Logan stood and hooked a finger at him. 'Follow me, Caffeine Boy.' Marching across the open-plan office with Tufty scampering alongside – laptop clasped to his chest again.

'Not Caffeine Boy. Caffeine Boy's a sidekick's name, I'm ... SUPERTUFTY!'

Everyone turned to watch as he did the pose in the middle of the room.

'Fighting crime, one bad guy at a time!' Shadowboxing, one-handed. 'Biff! Pow! Kerrrunk!'

Yeah, there was no way Tufty was ever making sergeant. The top brass had a strict no-weirdos policy. Mind you, Karl had made it all the way to Inspector, so maybe it was more of a guideline?

Logan knocked on Karl's door, not waiting for an answer before opening it and ushering Supertufty inside.

Karl was perched on his mushroom again, wearing a pair of big magnifying spectacles that made him look like a character in a sci-fi film. 'Well, well, who's this invading my sanctuary at this early hour? Hmmmmm?'

'Oooh...' Tufty stared at the collected computer kit in its racks and boxes. 'Cool!'

Logan thumped a hand down on his shoulder. 'Tufty, this is Inspector Montgomery. Karl, this is Constable Quirrel. He's weird, but harmless, so you've got a lot in common.'

A wave from Tufty. 'Hello, Boss. Or do you like "Guv" better? We can stick with "Inspector", if that works? Ooh, Ooh, or how about, "Maz Kanata"?'

Karl peered at him over the top of his big glasses. 'I have no idea who that is.'

'It's this really, really wise old character from *Star Wars: The Force*—'

Logan hit him.

'Ow!'

Idiot.

'Tufty's been looking into the Professor Wilson social-media thing, and he's found something, haven't you, Tufty?'

'I *have*, Tufty.'

'Intriguing.' Karl patted the worktop beside him. 'Pull up a stool, kind Sir Tufty, and let us break bread. Well, we can share a Tunnock's teacake, but symbolically it's the same thing.'

'Aye, aye, Inspector!'

Logan shook his head. 'Don't let him have any more caffeine. And if you need to put him down for a nap, do it somewhere no one's going to fall over him.'

Tufty hopped up onto a spare stool and beamed at Karl. 'Have you heard about using geotagged posts to identify anonymous accounts from mobile-phone-cell-tower records?'

Light the geek touchpaper and stand well back.

Logan reversed from the room. 'I'll leave you to it.' Closed the door. 'God, imagine what would happen if they *bred*...'

A shudder.

Some things were too horrible to contemplate.

Ah well, back to work.

He'd nearly made it as far as his desk, when the main doors opened and someone backed in, arms full: Rennie, getting a bit on the chunky side, with a deep tan and bleached blond hair waxed into spiky curls.

Rennie turned, slow and careful. A big box of doughnuts acted as a tray, heaped up with tinfoil parcels and greasy paper bags and two of those cardboard things designed for carrying six take-out coffees at one time.

Logan nodded at the vast collection. 'On a diet again?'

'And I got you a Poseidon's Surprise too, you ungrateful spudge.'

What the hell was a Poseidon's Surprise?

Rennie winked at him. 'How did you enjoy getting up at a proper time this morning? Bit of a strain after twelve months off?'

'Like riding a bike. Barely even noticed the difference.'

Liar.

'Aye, right.' Rennie raised his burden an inch, then lowered it again. 'Little help?'

Logan unloaded the tinfoil packages, bags, and hot drinks onto the nearest vacant desk. 'Do me a favour and call DI King. Tell him I've commandeered Tufty for the morning. I don't know if the silly wee sod's even checked in for work yet.'

'Tsk...' Rennie sighed. '*That's* what you get for recruiting an inferior sidekick. Look what happened last time you were lumbered with that eejit!' He thumbed himself in the chest. 'Sergeant Simon Rennie: shaves as close as a blade or your money back.'

'Maybe, but Bevan won't let you out to play till you've finished all your homework.'

'Then, the dream team shall ride again!' He put the box of doughnuts down, picked up a tinfoil package and tossed it to Logan. 'Exit left, pursued by a bear.' Rennie grabbed a tinfoil parcel of his own and headed for his desk.

'Rennie! Where's the—'

'On Shona's desk.' He threw himself into his seat, unwrapped his breakfast with one hand and grabbed his desk phone with the other, ripping out a bite and dialling as he chewed. 'Yellow? Yeah, I need to speak to Detective Inspector King.'

Logan paid Shona's Happy Birthday Grotto a visit. Nodded at the streamers, banners, and balloons. A DIY poster with 'YOU'RE 46 TODAY!!!' on it in cheerful chunky letters. 'Nice to see they kept it classy and low-key.'

All he got in response was a grunt. She didn't even look up from her copy of that morning's *Scottish Daily Post*. An army of squeezy bottles stood to attention beside her monitor: tomato sauce, brown sauce, fluorescent-yellow American mustard, sweet chilli, mayonnaise, barbecue – both smoky and sweet – and a thing of salad cream for the more sophisticated palate.

Rennie's voice floated across the room. 'Hello, DI King? ... Hi, it's Sergeant Rennie from Professional Standards. ... No, no. Nothing's wrong.'

Another grunt from Shona.

Logan rolled his eyes. 'Why yes, it *is* lovely to be back at work, thank you for asking.'

She sighed, then glanced up from her article. 'You're feeling better then?'

'Not at this time of the sodding morning, I'm not.' He unwrapped his parcel. 'Ooh, fish finger butty!' That called for a celebration, so he slathered it in a mixture of salad cream and tomato sauce, then took a bite. Crunchy and fishy and sweet and savoury all at the same time. Munching around the words, 'Well? How bad is it?'

'Being forty-six? Awful. I used to be a svelte young thing, Logan, pursued by the sexiest of gentlemen, I went on fabulous holidays and ate in the finest restaurants. And now look at me: it's a red-letter day if I can get that sodding LaserJet to print double-sided.'

'No, not being forty-six: DI *King*. In the paper. How bad is it?'

She frowned at him. 'Nope, still not getting you.'

'Front-page splash. You need glasses, Shona, your advanced age is clearly...'

She turned the paper around, so Logan could see the front page. Half of it was devoted to another anti-English arson attack

– this time a bike shop in Aviemore – the other half to 'STRICTLY STARLET'S "BOOZE-AND-DRUGS BINGE HORROR"'. Apparently Professor Wilson's abduction only merited a tiny sidebar and 'CONTINUED ON PAGE 7 →'.

'Oh.'

Shona gave the paper a bash with the back of her hand. 'What there *is*, however, is yet another column by everyone's favourite D-list celebrity nobody, Scotty Meyrick, telling us how Scotland's a bunch of ungrateful scumbags for not appreciating the benevolence of our Westminster overlords. What a great birthday present *that* was.'

Logan gave his butty another seeing to. 'You going to send him a thank-you card?'

'God save us from bloody "celebs" telling us what to think. Someone eats a kangaroo's ring-piece on TV and suddenly they're a political pundit?'

'Can I have that when you're finished with it?'

'Urgh...' She held the paper out. 'Here, take the thing. My blood pressure's bad enough what with birthdays and that buggering printer to deal with.'

'Thanks.' Logan tucked it under his arm and headed back to his desk, finishing his butty as he flicked through what passed for news at the *Scottish Daily Post*. Apparently, unless something happened within an hour of Edinburgh or Glasgow, it really wasn't worth reporting.

The only exception lurked on page seven. For some reason, Edward Barwell hadn't named-and-shamed DI King as an ex-Alt-Nat terrorist, instead he'd spent half a page banging on about Professor Wilson's abduction and how it was *undoubtedly* connected to someone called Matt Lansdale going missing.

Matt Lansdale...

That journalist at yesterday's press conference had called Lansdale a high-profile anti-independence campaigner, but other than that? Never heard of him. And clearly everyone was expected to know who he was, because there was sod all detail about that in the article.

Should probably try to find out, just in case it *was* related.

Logan frowned at the article again, with its accompanying photo of Professor Wilson and 'Alt-Nat Thugs Target Better-Together Heroes' headline. Why hadn't Barwell outed DI King? It was a juicy story – bound to shift a few papers and stir up a whole heap of controversy – so why bury it?

Rennie slouched across the room and perched on the edge of Logan's desk. 'You'll be happy to hear that I've got young Tufters off the hook. And you were right: the silly wee sod hadn't signed in this morning.'

'Thought not.' Logan sooked the tomato sauce and salad cream from his fingers. 'You ever heard of a "Matt Lansdale"?'

'Oh, and King says to tell you the SE have been on the phone. No viable DNA at the scene. Said to say, "They were right, the guy's a ghost."'

A ghost.

Logan frowned out the window. The rush hour was gearing up, but still a good half hour away from clotting like a fat-filled artery. A bus rumbled past.

'Guv?'

Their guy was a ghost...

Two cars. A taxi.

'Guv, you're not having a stroke or something, are you?'

A Transit van with 'The Teeny Beetroot Bakery Co. Ltd.' down the side in cheery letters.

'Hello?'

A ghost.

Soodding hell.

Logan turned back to Rennie. 'He was wearing a Tyvek suit! That's why Professor Wilson's dog went for the Scene Examiners: they were wearing the same SOC kit.'

Rennie puckered his face. 'Oooh... You know, after the BBC did that big documentary about the scumbags who abducted Alison and Jenny McGregor, it's a miracle *more* criminals don't do it. See if it was me?'

'No wonder he didn't leave any forensic traces.' Logan poked at his keyboard, calling up the Police National Computer to run a search on Matt Lansdale.

'He's all dressed in white, he's a ghost... Maybe we should call our abductor "Casper"?'

'Only not so friendly. You didn't see the blood spattered across the kitchen table.' Logan's search results popped up on the screen. Well, result singular, because only one entry came back: 'Reported Missing' and last Wednesday's date. Nothing else. 'OK, back to the topic at hand: Matt Lansdale?'

'Was he a finalist on *X Factor*?'

Logan tossed the paper over. 'Journos are implying his disappearance is connected to Prof Wilson's. All I'm getting on the PNC is that he's missing.'

'Pfffff...' Rennie frowned at Edward Barwell's article. 'Can find out, if you like?'

'Ta.'

'And while we're on the subject: you'll never guess what I've managed to organise for Saturday. Go on, guess. You can't, but try.' Wiggling both eyebrows. 'OK, OK, get this: Princess Unicorn's Magic Bouncy Castle! How cool is that?'

Logan wheeled his chair back a bit, putting a little more distance between them. 'Erm...'

'And Mistress Fizzymiggins is doing a make-your-own-magic-wand-and-fairy-wings thing. And there's going to be a *pony*!'

A pony? Why would there be a...

'Ah, right: Lola's birthday party!'

'Donna's even written a special song for her little sister that doesn't include the words "Bumface Brain". Can you help out with the Fairyland pony rides?'

'Actually—'

'Great. Right, I'll go see what I can dig up about Matt Lansdale.' He sauntered off towards the main doors, taking the *Scottish Daily Post* with him. 'And don't forget, it's BYOT!'

BYOT?

Logan curled his lip. 'What the hell is BYOT?'

But the doors thunked shut and Rennie was gone.

The man was a menace.

Logan stood to follow him ... and stopped as Superintendent Bevan emerged from her office, holding a blue folder.

She gave him a smile. 'Ah, Logan. Good.' Then peered past him, at the desk. 'Oh, are those your sausages? Lovely.' Bevan marched over and picked up the Tupperware box. 'We'll pop these in the fridge, then you can come join me in the conference room.'

Why did that sound as if something horrible was about to happen?

10

Logan shifted in his squeaky leather seat. 'I don't know what else you want me to say.'

Detective Superintendent Young frowned back at him from the oversized TV screen mounted on the far wall. To be honest, Young was a bit intimidating in person – being a rugby-player-sized lump with big meaty fists covered in scars. Throw in the small dark squinty eyes and he looked like the kind of person who'd tear your head off for spilling his pint or looking at him funny, and being on screen didn't really diminish that.

Jane McGrath was sitting next to him, in the boardroom at DHQ, as immaculate as ever, as if she'd been moulded from plastic. The only thing out of place was the expression on her face: as if she really wanted to scrape whatever she'd just stood in off her shoe.

Young picked up his printout of the *Scottish Daily Post*'s front page, or at least the one that was meant to appear today, but hadn't. *'Was he in a terrorist organisation, or not?'*

Logan shrugged. 'He went to a few PASL meetings.'

Jane stared at the ceiling for a beat. *'God damn it.'* Then sat back in her seat. *'Well, that's that, then, isn't it? We're screwed: he's got to go.'*

'Now,' Superintendent Bevan pulled on a serious school-teacher voice, the authority undermined a *teeny* bit by her Kiwi accent, 'before we do anything rash, perhaps we should take a step back and think about this dispassionately.'

'"Dispassionately"?' Jane shook her head. 'It's a PR disaster. Forget "Fingerprintgate" or "Sex-In-The-Woods-gate", every major news outlet will be lining up to jam spiky things up our backsides! Great big spiky—'

Young hit her with his printout. 'All right, Jane, we get the picture.'

'I'm talking pineapples here!'

Bevan tried the voice again. 'That's no reason to indulge in knee-jerk reactions.'

'Jane's right, Julie.' Young held up a hand. 'I know, I know. But DI King has become a liability. He's a diseased limb: we have to amputate before the infection spreads and takes the whole body with it.'

'Who's to say a judicious dose of antibiotics couldn't work every bit as well?'

She had a point.

Logan joined in, going for calm and reasonable: 'DI King says he only joined the PASL to impress a girl.'

'Hmph.' Jane curled her lip. 'We've all done strange things for love, but you should really draw the line at joining a terrorist cell. How am I supposed to spin that?'

'He was sixteen.'

'He was an idiot!'

'Most sixteen-year-old boys are.'

Bevan nodded. 'All I'm saying is that if we throw DI King to the crocodiles because he was a horny teenager, that's it for him. The press will tear him apart. No more career. Even if he changes divisions – they'll find him and drag it all up again.'

'They're going to tear him apart anyway. We got lucky today: the Scottish Daily Post bumped their exclusive, but they're going to print it sooner or later, and when they do…' She banged a hand down on the table. 'This is our chance to get ahead of the story and act like we're on the front foot for a change.'

'But—'

Jane turned to Young. 'Suspend him now, and it'll look like the Post are reacting to our diligent man management. We won't put up with this kind of thing, etc.'

'That's not—'

Young held up his hand again. *'What's the point of having a Professional Standards if we can't use them to hack a festering limb off and cauterise the wound?'* He waved the printout at them. *'My department's not coming down with gangrene!'*

Logan sucked a breath in through his teeth. 'Seems a little harsh.'

'Or, alternatively,' Bevan pursed her lips, frowning, 'and hear me out here: we could take a different route. What if we do full disclosure? Lay it all out for them in a frank and open interview with DI King. "How I stopped being a bigoted tosspot and learned to love the English."'

On the screen, Jane narrowed her eyes. *'I'm listening.'*

'We're always telling people how *racism* and *homophobia* and *sectarianism* and *anti-Semitism* and *Islamophobia* are wrong, yes? Surely, if people are prepared to change we should celebrate that, not keep kicking them because they used to be racist. *Celebrate* that change.'

There was silence and frowning.

Then Young turned to Jane. *'Well?'*

'Hmmm... I might be able to sell that, but we'll need some insulation in case it all goes tits up. Something to stop our fingers getting burned.'

'Agreed. If DI King can catch whoever abducted Professor Wilson, it'll vindicate NE Division for keeping him on the case. Even better if he can get the Professor back alive.' A nod, then a scowl. *'But if he can't, we look negligent for not suspending him. And I, for one, am not bending over for a pineappleing.'*

Jane bit her top lip for a moment, staring off into the middle distance. *'How about this: we put someone in to "support" him? That way, if he fails, we've at least got plausible deniability.'*

Ah the joys of Police Scotland politics. Setting some poor sod up to take the blame if it all went wrong – but the top brass would grab the glory if it all went right. Nothing ever changed.

Logan shook his head. 'And who's going to be the lucky scapegoat?'

The smile Jane gave him was half crocodile, half serial killer.

'Well, who better than someone from Professional Standards? That would show we're serious about it.'

Bevan stiffened in her seat. 'Ah... Perhaps that's not—'

'And who better than a bona-fide police hero? Someone with a Queen's Medal?'

What?

Logan stared at her. 'Whoa, whoa, whoa! Wait a minute: I only got back to work yesterday!'

'I like it.' Young nodded. 'Yes. McRae brings a lot of press goodwill with him.'

'But—'

'This way, if DI King turns out to still be a ... what was it, "bigoted tosspot"? You can yank him off the case, Logan. And if he's not, but he fails anyway, you can vouch that he's really tried his best.'

Not a chance in hell.

Logan turned to Bevan, eyes wide.

Come on, say something. *Tell* them!

She took a deep breath. 'Agreed.'

Agreed?

'No, not agreed. I'm not—'

'Good. Now, if you'll excuse me, I've got a Tulliallan Goon Squad descending in twenty minutes to moan about these arson attacks.' Young stood, his top half disappearing off the TV. 'Keep me informed.'

'Bye.' Jane's evil smile widened a couple of inches as she pointed a remote at the camera. Then the screen went blank, leaving Logan and Bevan alone in the room.

He got to his feet. 'Well thank you *very* much.'

'Oh come on, Logan, don't be like that. You were happy enough keeping an eye on DI King yesterday.'

'"A watching brief", you said!' Throwing his hands out. 'This isn't even vaguely the same thing.'

'Logan, you're—'

'You hung me out like a pair of damp socks!'

A sigh. 'I'm sure it won't be as bad as—'

'I only got back to work yesterday and you've got me set up as the scapegoat's scapegoat!'

Bevan went very still. 'Logan, I know we've not worked

together before, so I'm going to pretend you didn't just talk to your superintendent like that. I appreciate things haven't exactly been easy for you over the last year, but there's only so far I'm willing to bend. Are we clear?'

Oh great, so now it was *his* fault?

Bloody, buggering...

He gritted his teeth. 'Yes, Boss.'

'There we go. All forgiven and forgotten.' She stood and clapped her hands. 'Now, why don't we go sing "Happy Birthday" to Shona, cut the cake, then you can go support DI King. I'm sure he'll be glad of the help.'

There was something slightly surreal about a group of twenty officers, all standing about in their Police Scotland black uniforms, singing 'Happy Birthday' while wearing gaily-coloured party hats. Pointy ones. As if this was some sort of celebration for ninja gnomes.

As the last note warbled away in questionable three-part harmony, a pink-faced Shona hauled in a breath and blew out the candles on her cake. Everyone cheered. Then a handful of them produced party poppers and set them off, draping her with streamers.

Bevan smiled at them all. 'All right, all right. You can have a lot of fun without being stupid.'

Speaking of which...

Logan sidled over to Tufty and Karl – both of whom were wearing their party hats at *very* rakish angles – while Shona cut the cake.

'Have you pair managed to find anything?'

A pout from Tufty. 'Karl won't let me have any more Red Bulls.'

Karl bared his teeth in a big broad smile. 'I have to say, Logan, your young friend here is quite the kid who whizzes, oh my, yes.' He gave Tufty a wee playful punch on the shoulder. 'But I'm afraid we've hit an impasse. Brave Sir Tufty's algorithmic methodology is inspired, but without more computing power, it's like trying to push a ten-tonne blancmange uphill wearing 'nothing but flip-flops and an amusing hat.' He raised his to the height of its elastic, then let go so it pinged back down again.

'Cake?' Superintendent Bevan appeared, bearing three paper plates with slabs of yellowy sponge on them. She handed one to Karl. 'Here we go.'

'Ooh, my! Is this the sainted cake of lemon drizzle I see before me?' He helped himself to a mouthful, chewing with his eyes closed. 'Divine!'

She gave one to Logan and the other to Tufty. 'Birthday lunch at one o'clock. Logan's brought enough sausages to feed a battalion.'

Karl slapped him on the back. 'Good man.'

Bevan wandered off to distribute more slices and Tufty filled his gob, getting crumbs all down himself, mumbling through his mouthful. 'If we had access to a bunch of high-powered servers we might be able to do something about it.'

'But, alas, we are deficient in that kind of kit. So I'm afraid we're done.'

Ah well, it'd been worth a try.

Logan took a bite of cake – sharp and sweet and bursting with lemon. 'So if I could find you someone with a bunch of dirty big computers, you'd be able to track down whoever sent that first tweet?'

A shrug from Karl. 'Possibly.'

A cakey grin from Tufty. 'Definitely!'

'Well,' another shrug, 'we'd stand a much better chance, anyway.'

Logan polished off the last of his cake. 'Then I know just the person.'

Tufty cracked a yawn that made his head look like an open pedal bin, then shuddered and burped in the passenger seat of Logan's Audi. Smacking his lips as he settled back again. Another yawn.

Logan took one hand off the steering wheel to give Rip Van Tufty a thump on the arm. 'If you start snoring and farting, I'm throwing you out of the car.'

Aberdeen slid past the Audi's windows, the traffic thickening along the bypass like clumps of fat in a swollen artery.

Another yawn from the passenger seat. 'Tufty needs caffeine.'

'Well, what did you expect, staying up on a school night? You knew you had work today.'

'But I was beavering for the greater good!'

'Lucky Rennie covered for you, otherwise you'd be up for a spanking, you silly wee—' Logan's phone vibrated in his pocket, then the car's hands-free system got hold of the call, flashing 'SUPT. BEVAN' on the central display and blasting his generic ringtone out of the speakers. On, and on, and on, and on.

Tufty reached for the display. 'Aren't you going to—'

Logan slapped his hand away. 'No.'

'Oh.' He pulled on a sappy look. 'She does make a *lovely* lemony drizzle cake, though.'

Traffic was backed up around the next exit, giving everyone plenty of time to stare down into other people's gardens. Logan changed lanes, bypassing the bypass's vehicular clot.

Tufty puffed out his cheeks. 'Saaa-aaarge? You know there's all this controversy surrounding—'

'If this is about loop quantum gravity again, I swear to God I'm going to pull this car over and stuff you in the boot.'

'Ooh, I do like a bit of loop quantum gravity, but no, it's like, you know all this stuff going on with Alt-Nats hating Unionists? Well, this guy on the BBC website was blatant racism, yeah? But the English aren't a different race, are they?'

'I should've taken Karl with me. At least he's *fractionally* less annoying.'

'No, but listen,' Tufty turned in his seat, bleary little eyes all shiny and dark, 'you can't tell someone's English by looking at them, can you? And what does being English even mean? Rennie says Berwick-upon-Tweed used to be part of Scotland, right? So if you were born there on the twenty-third of August 1482 you were Scottish, but if you were born on the twenty-fourth you were English, but you'd still be the same person, wouldn't you?'

Logan groaned. 'I've changed my mind: *go* to sleep. I don't care if there's snoring and—'

His phone *burrrrrrred* again, but this time it was 'IDIOT RENNIE' that appeared on the dashboard display as 'If I Only Had a Brain' from *The Wizard of Oz* burst out of the speakers. Well, tough: he wasn't getting answered either.

'So it can't be *racist* to hate the English, it's nothing more than good old-fashioned Scottish bigotry. Like when Rangers and Celtic supporters hate each other, because one lot don't like the other lot's flavour of Christianity.'

The tune faded away into nothing. Either Rennie had hung up, or it'd gone through to voicemail. 'Tufty, am I not having a bad enough day as it is?'

'I was supposed to be born in Glasgow, but my mum and dad didn't want me growing up with all that, so they moved up to Banff instead and raised us secular, because—'

'Please shut up, before I kill you.'

'No, but you see—'

It was Tufty's phone's turn, warbling out something cheery in a brass-band kind of way. 'Hey, hold on.' He dug it out and took the call. 'Hello? ... Ooh, Sergeant Rennie, cool. I was telling the Sarge what you told me about Berwick-upon-Tweed and how it— Ah. ... No. Yes. ... Sorry.'

Logan raised an eyebrow. 'Wish *I* knew how to get you to shut up that quickly.'

'Yes, he's here. ... OK. ... OK, I'll ask him.' Tufty put his hand over the phone. 'It's Sergeant Rennie. He says Superintendent Bevan wants to know why you're not at DHQ helping DI King. Apparently, she's not angry, just disappointed.'

Of course she was. Once a schoolteacher, *always* a schoolteacher.

'Tell him to tell her we're on our way now.'

A puzzled look stumbled across Tufty's face. 'But we're not, we're—'

'Well Rennie doesn't need to know that, does he? And if we get access to a load of high-end computers it *is* helping King out, isn't it?'

His eyes widened. 'Oh yeah...' Back to the phone. 'Hi, uh-huh, we're on our way there now, so tell her not to worry. ... No, there wasn't anything suspicious about the length of that pause. ... Nope. ... OK, bye.' Tufty hung up. Grinned. 'Didn't suspect a thing.'

If that was true, there was no hope for Police Scotland.

11

Logan pulled into the visitors' parking area, stopping in front of an Avril Lavigne clone in skinny jeans, Converse trainers, ripped Nickelback T-shirt; pierced nose, ears, and eyebrow; and the kind of hair that would've got you locked up in less enlightened times. She had a clipboard and a little knot of lanyards with her. Big Colgate smile.

Oh God... She was going to be perky, wasn't she?

Quarter past eight on a Wednesday morning was *far* too early for perky.

Logan killed the engine and climbed out into the sauna formerly known as Aberdeen.

Four huge grey warehouses were gathered around the car park, all snug and secure behind an extra-high chain-link fence, guardhouse, and heavy-duty traffic barrier. Each of the warehouses had a number painted on it – 1 to 4 – but the biggest of the lot was home to the company logo too. A huge woodlouse silhouette – at least twenty foot tall – rendered in shiny gold-coloured plastic. Never mind the rest of Altens, you could probably see the thing from Lerwick. If not orbit.

Tufty clambered out of the car, tucked his laptop under one arm and stared up at the buildings. 'Ooooh... Cool.'

Avril bounded up to them. Oh, she was *definitely* perky. 'Inspector McRae, and Constable Quirrel?' She thrust the lanyards at them. 'Great to have you here?' The sentence went up at the end, as if it was a question. 'Now, I need you to wear your passes at all times?' Another not question. 'Can you do that for me? That's great?'

Like, *totally*?

Was it wrong to have an almost unbearable urge to borrow Tufty's pepper spray and give her a damned good seasoning?

Tufty made a little squeaking noise as he put on his lanyard. 'This is *so* cool!'

'I know, right? I *love* working here?' She actually did a couple of hoppity-skippity dance steps. 'Come on, guys, follow me to where the magic happens?' Avril led the way to the main doors, holding them open and wafting them through into a wide room, decorated to look like an opulent cinema foyer.

Film posters lined the walls, the floor dotted with display cases full of movie props, awards, and trophies. A big mahogany-and-chrome reception desk dominated the space, with an old woman lurking behind it. Huge and pasty, with a round happy face, unnaturally brown hair. Arms like ham-hocks. Clutching a copy of *Hello!* magazine in her sausagey fingers.

Avril bounced around in a circle. 'You should've been here last week, we had *Joanna Lumley* and *Hugh Grant* in for pickups?' She put a hand on her heart. 'Career highlight?'

The old lady looked up from her magazine. 'Hey, Misty.'

Avril / Misty beamed at her on the way past. 'Hey, Mrs Clark, got the boss-man's visitors for him?' She pointed at them. 'You want anything from the canteen when I'm done?'

A big smile dimpled Mrs Clark's cheeks. 'Wouldn't say no to a Tunnock's or two.'

'You got it!' She pushed through a set of double doors, disappearing. Then poked her head into the room again. 'Come on, guys?'

Yeah, *definitely* far too perky.

They followed her into a bland corridor, magnolia paint slapped on breeze-block walls, the polished concrete squeaking under Misty's trainers. Grey doors lined the space, each one with a job or department title on a white plastic plaque. It all looked very … Hollywood.

Misty looked over her shoulder at them as she bounced along. 'Mr Clark's got a video conference with New Zealand at eight forty-five, so don't be offended if I have to throw you out then? Nothing personal?'

At the end of the corridor, she swiped her ID through a card reader and ushered them into a cavernous space. You could've stored a jumbo jet in here and still had room for a dozen double-decker buses. The walls were that eye-nipping shade of green they used for special effects, but the space in between was filled with big chunks of scenery – what looked like the inside of spaceships, space stations, grungy futuristic street scenes and a weird red forest thing.

Misty marched them past a prison block to where a large man stood, facing the other way, hands on his hips as he watched a team of overalled techs dismantling some kind of fighter cockpit. Tall and wide with it, broad shoulders and a Peaky Blinders haircut styled into a greying shark's-fin quiff. 'Be careful with that, Quin! I don't want to have to start again from scratch if this turns into a franchise.'

One of the dismantlers gave him a thumbs-up.

Misty pounced to attention beside the big man. 'Mr Clark? I've got your visitors?'

He turned, a smile dimpling his cheeks. Definitely his mother's son. Except he had a Vandyke with an elongated white goatee and red-framed glasses. 'Logan McRae! As I live, breathe, and exude sheer sexual chemistry.' He stepped forward and swept Logan up in a bear hug, lifting him off the ground. 'How are you? God, that thing last year! Completely gobsmacking.'

Barbed wire twisted beneath the skin of Logan's stomach, digging its metal spikes deep inside.

He had to force the words out between gritted teeth: 'Let me go, let me go, let me go!'

'Oh, yes, the stabbing! Sorry.' Mr Clark let go and stepped back, grimacing. 'Are you OK? Do you need something?'

Logan bent double, one hand pressing against his midriff, hot air burning in his lungs as he swallowed a couple of deep breaths.

'I've got painkillers! Naproxen, Tramadol, Co-codamol, you name it.' Mr Clark waved at their perky guide. 'Misty, grab some Vicodin and a bottle of water, would you, honey?'

Logan raised a hand. 'I'm OK, I'm OK.' He straightened up, slow. Hissing all the way. 'You caught me off guard, that's all.'

Misty perkied at him. 'It's no trouble, really? I can *totally* go get you some?'

'No. No drugs. Thanks. I'm good.' Liar.

'OK.' She did a couple of bounces for Mr Clark. 'I'm getting your mum some Tunnock's? You want?'

'Can't: diet.'

'All-righty then.' She turned and skipped off, back the way they'd come.

Weirdo.

Mr Clark put a hand on Logan's shoulder and steered him past a killer robot as Tufty scurried along behind. 'Oh, Logan, Logan, Logan...' The hand squeezed. 'Anyway, about last year: you haven't done anything about the film rights yet, have you?'

'Well, serving police officers can't really—'

'I'm thinking a hundred-and-twenty-minute thriller with David Tennant playing you. Well, it's him or Ewan McGregor.'

'It's just we're not allowed to—'

'What do you think about Tilda Swinton for Steel?' They passed the weird red forest, with its asymmetric leaves and twisted scarlet branches. 'Too tall? I think she's too tall. It's so great to *see* you again!'

Logan cleared his throat as they made for the nearest exit. 'I didn't get to thank you for the fruit baskets. They were—'

'I *love* Helen Mirren, but then she brings all that *Prime Suspect* baggage to a crime drama, doesn't she?' Mr Clark pushed open a bland grey door and propelled them into another magnolia breeze-block corridor. Only this one was lined with whiteboards, covered in scrawled schedules and bits of storyboard. More grey doors. 'Or how about Michelle Gomez? Because Steel's got that...' He made a theatrical gesture with one hand. 'You know?'

No. Logan most certainly didn't.

'I really—'

'There's something a bit *sexy* about her, isn't there? She's got that frisson of something almost *animal* in her magnetism.'

Don't think about her naked. DON'T THINK ABOUT HER NAKED! Too late – the image was seared across the back of his mind again, in hideous pink-o-vision. And after all the effort he'd gone to, trying to forget...

Logan shuddered. 'I've never noticed.'

Through another door into a stairwell. Up they went.

Tufty's voice echoed in the enclosed space. 'I noticed once. In the pub. But then she beat me about the head and neck with a packet of Quavers and that was that.'

Mr Clark gave Logan's shoulder another squeeze. 'And we'll need to invent a good sidekick for you. It's a trope of the genre, after all.'

'Ooh, ooh!' Tufty scurried up alongside. 'I'd make a great—'

Logan jabbed him with an elbow. 'Thanks for agreeing to help us find whoever posted that first tweet, Mr Clark.'

'It's *Zander*, Logan. Zander. You know that.' At the top of the stairs he pushed out into another corridor, but a much fancier one this time: plastered and decorated, carpets on the floor, pictures on the walls. 'And if Golden Slater Productions can help, it's my pleasure.' Zander opened a door marked 'VISUAL FX' and swept them into a large room, broken up into cubicled workstations.

No two were the same, as if there'd been a competition to see who could customise theirs the most. A pirate ship, a jungle, cowboys, aliens, My Little Ponies, cavemen...

Post-it notes and lines of coloured string covered the walls, intermingled with schedules, storyboards, concept sketches... Another display case full of awards over by the fancy coffee machine. A big screen nearly covered the end wall, filled with some very plastic-looking figures lumping their way through a scene. Like a really cheap video game.

Half a dozen people in shorts and assorted geekdom T-shirts were gathered around the storyboards, another four poking away at their computers.

Zander leaned in close to Logan, dropping his voice as if he was about to impart a state secret. 'You've timed it well – we finished post-production on a hardcore sci-fi serial-killer thriller, last week. Spectacular stuff, redefines the genre.'

Oh ho.

Logan raised an eyebrow.

Zander rolled his eyes. 'Not *that* kind of "hardcore".'

Tufty wandered off, peering into the trophy cabinet, like Charlie getting his first glimpse of the Chocolate Factory.

And no, that wasn't a euphemism.

Logan pointed at the computers. 'So...?'

'We've just started pre-viz on a steampunk blockbuster – which will *completely* blow both your socks off, then come back for your toes – meaning I've got about thirty / forty servers sitting idle you can play with. State of the art. Spared no expense.' Then he turned, raising his voice so it carried across the room. 'Hoshiko? Got a minute?'

A short, middle-aged woman in an American baseball shirt, jeans, and trainers looked up from where she was working on the storyboards. The slightest hint of a Japanese accent as she looked Logan up and down. 'This them?'

Zander nodded. 'Yup.' He gave Logan a wink. 'Hoshiko's worked for Hayao Miyazaki, Peter Jackson, *and* Katsuhiro Otomo. I was *so* lucky to get her!'

She didn't smile. 'Damn right you were.' Then she stuck her hand out to Logan, palm up. 'You got an algorithm for me?'

'Tufty?'

'Hmmm?' The daft wee sod was still staring at the trophies. 'Are these *really* AVN and XBIZ awards?'

Zander popped his eyebrows up, and gave his head a little waggle. 'Far be it for me to blow my own you-know-what, but there's a fair few Prowlers and F.A.M.E.s in there as well.'

At that Hoshiko *did* smile. 'We wiped the floor, every year we entered.'

'Of course, that was back when we still had *time* to make adult films.' Zander smiled at Tufty. 'If you're a big porn fan, I can probably dig you out a few comps on DVD if you like?'

Tufty spun around, face going a hot shade of pink. 'Me? *Porn?*

No, no, I was... I like to keep up with social trends and... Ahem...'

'Nonsense, no trouble at all.' He whipped out his phone and poked the screen. 'Misty? Can you find me a copy of *Crocodildo Dundee* for one of our police officer guests, please?'

'That's really not... It...' The blush had officially gone nuclear. 'But...'

Now, the *kind* thing to do would be to change the subject and spare the wee lad any more embarrassment.

Nah.

Logan grinned. 'Say "thank you" to the nice gentleman, Tufty.'

It looked as if the tips of his ears were about to combust. 'Thank you?'

Zander spread his arms wide. 'My pleasure. Now, Hoshiko?'

She hooked a thumb over her shoulder at a vacant workstation. 'Come on, Porno Boy, we'll get you set up, then you can tell me about this algorithm of yours...'

Zander's office was huge – the meeting table that ran down the middle big enough to seat twenty. It was lined with movable electronic whiteboards and flipcharts, displays plastered in yet more storyboard drawings. He perched on the edge of a fancy-pants desk, with a large leather chair behind it, a couple of monitors on cantilevered arms, some flowers in a vase. The whole thing reeked of power.

A pair of small raggedy cats chased each other across the meeting table. Pausing every now and then to stare at Logan as if he might be edible.

But by far the most impressive thing about the room was the floor-to-ceiling window that made up one entire wall, overlooking Soundstage 1 in all its gloomy glory.

Zander caught one of the cats as it battered past, holding it against his chest so it could chew at his goatee. 'When the oil industry took a tanking, I was able to get this whole thing for a song. Had to soundproof everything and expand out the back, but still. *Much* better than our last place.'

Logan looked down through the huge window. 'Do you still see DI Insch?'

The dismantlers were loading the chunks of fighter cockpit onto trolleys and wheeling them away.

'What, *David*? Oh yes. He's off doing second unit scouting for the new film. Iceland.'

Logan nodded. 'Tell him I said, "Hi," OK?' Seemed a bit inadequate after all these years, but what else was there?

Zander's reflection stepped up beside Logan's in the glass, one of the cats perched in his arms, on top of his belly. 'You think whoever sent that first tweet abducted Professor Wilson?'

'Maybe. Whoever it was, they knew he was missing a day before we did, so...?'

'Hmmm. It's a shame Wilson was such a tit.' A sigh. 'You know, when I first came up to Aberdeen, I had a boss who called me an F.E.B. for two whole years. "I don't know, ask the FEB.", "Hey, F.E.B., get the teas in, yeah?", "You know, Zander, you're my favourite F.E.B."'

Nope. Never heard of that one.

'F.E...?'

'"Fucking English Bastard".' Zander shook his head. 'Said it was "only a bit of banter". You try replacing "English" with "black", or "Jewish", or "gay" and see how bantery it feels then. Hate's hate.'

'Sounds like a lovely man.'

Zander waved that away. 'Oh, I rose above it. Showed him there were no hard feelings last year by buying the company and firing him.' A smile. 'I know it *sounds* vindictive, but he was stealing equipment and sexually harassing the young man on reception. Only had himself to blame, really.'

Down below, the last chunk of cockpit was wheeled away for storage.

'So how did you know Professor Wilson?'

'Is he really dead?'

Logan shrugged. 'Hope not.'

Zander rubbed his goatee on the cat's head, setting it purring. 'Made the mistake of hiring Professor "Acquired Taste" Wilson for *Witchfire*, thought it'd be good to have a genuine constitutional scholar involved: bring a bit of authenticity to the way society operated in the film. Just because it's alternative-history, doesn't mean it has to be fake nonsense.' His expression soured. 'What a pain in the arse that man was.'

'Yeah, I'm hearing that a lot.'

'Could start a fight in a bowl of soup. And not lumpy soup either: consommé. I bet you could boil socks and he'd—'

Logan's phone burst into 'If I Only Had a Brain' again, and he slumped. Pulled the damn thing out. 'Sorry, I'd better...' He answered it. 'Rennie, if you've called up to nag, don't. We'll be in when we've—'

'Boss, there's a package turned up at the BBC. You need to get over there, ASAP!'

Yes, because *that* didn't sound like he was being set up for something horrible, did it?

'What *kind* of package?'

'Didn't say, but I know King's on his way now. Lights and music, so it must be a biggie!'

A package delivered to BBC Scotland. Well, if King was hotfooting it over there, then it had to be connected to the Professor Wilson Case. And if it *was* connected, then Logan had to get there sharpish too. Because the scapegoat's scapegoat had no intention of letting the original-issue scapegoat screw things up and land him in it.

'OK, OK. I'm on my way.' He hung up and slipped the phone back in his pocket.

Zander's shoulders curled forward, the cat clambering up onto them. 'I'm guessing Gilbert and Sullivan had it right about a policeman's lot?'

'Got to go. Can you...?' Pointing through the door and down a bit, where the Visual FX department probably was.

'Don't worry, I'll look after the little lad for you. Make sure he stays out of trouble.'

'Yeah, good luck with that.' Logan made for the door. 'And don't let him have any more caffeine!' After all, things were bad enough as it was.

12

A large Jiffy bag, torn open at one end, sat on the desk. And not just any old desk, this was the one used for on-camera interviews. The one with a grainy out-of-date photo of Aberdeen in the background – the ugly warty lump of St Nicholas House still clearly visible in the shot, even though it'd been torn down years ago.

The tiny studio was barely bigger than a single bedroom, with ancient audiovisual equipment piled up against the walls, filling the space behind the remote-operated camera where it couldn't be seen. Lights hung from a ceiling rig, all of them angled to point at the Jiffy bag, making it glow against the grey Formica. A sickly shade of yellow-orange.

Logan had a squint at the address label, laser printed onto a plain white sticky square:

Professor N Wilson,
C/O The Muriel Kirk Show
BBC Scotland
Beechgrove Terrace
Aberdeen AB15 5ZT

Muriel Kirk adjusted the sunglasses perched on top of her greying hair and bounced from foot to foot, as if she was about to climb into the ring and punch someone. A visual reinforced by the trainers, joggy bottoms, and 'I RAN THE MELDRUM MARATHON!' T-shirt. Not an ounce of fat on her.

Her producer was a saggy man with a receding hairline, grey beard, and blue cardigan – even in this heat. Sweat shone on his top lip as he fiddled with his cardie pockets.

King popped an extra-strong mint, crunching as he stared at the package. 'And no one else has touched this?'

Mr Cardigan shook his head. 'It came in the morning post, but it was addressed to Muriel and she's not on air till one, so—'

'Yes.' Muriel Kirk rolled her shoulders. 'It'll have been touched by the postie, Al on reception, Graham here, and me.' Her eyes shone. '*I* was the one who opened it.'

Logan got out his notebook. 'Right, well. We'll have to take statements and—'

'Hold on, I need to get Barry in here.' She stuck two fingers in her mouth and whistled: deafening in the small space.

The heavy studio door creaked open and in came what had to be Barry, a camera on his shoulder, one eye pressed to the viewfinder, the other screwed shut as he framed the shot. 'And we're rolling.'

Muriel turned to the camera and pointed at the Jiffy bag, putting on a voice that was nearly an octave down from the one she'd just been using. A lot more refined too. 'When this package arrived at the BBC Scotland studios in Aberdeen earlier today, everyone thought it was simply another piece of mail.' She reached for the package. 'But when I opened it—'

'Wait, wait, wait, wait!' King barged in front of Barry, blocking the camera. 'What do you think you're doing?'

'You're kidding, right?' Muriel bounced on her feet again, limbering up. 'This is going to be the lead story on the lunch-time news. We're—'

'No. No you're not. This is an ongoing investigation!' He stuck a hand in the middle of Barry's chest and pushed him towards the heavy door. 'Come on, you: *out.*'

Barry peered from behind his camera. 'Muriel?'

King jabbed a finger at her and Captain Cardigan. 'You two as well. This is a police matter. Off you go.'

She curled her hands into fists. 'But this is *our* studio. It was addressed to *me*!'

'And I want to thank you on behalf of Police Scotland for bringing it to our attention.' He gave Barry a shove, sending him staggering backwards. 'Now: out.'

'Graham, are you going to let them throw us off our own story?'

Cardigan fluttered his hands. 'Perhaps we should all calm down a bit and discuss this like—'

'Quite right.' Logan pulled on his best all-in-this-together voice. 'That sounds like an *excellent* idea. But first, can you do me a favour and dig up any CCTV you've got of the package being delivered? That'll be a huge help.' Ushering Cardigan out of the door. 'Thanks.'

'Oh. Yes. I suppose...'

Logan turned to Muriel. 'And Mz Kirk, I know it's hard, but we've got to be *extremely* careful about DNA and cross-contamination. I'll have a word with the Chief Superintendent and see if we can get you exclusive coverage, OK? OK.'

'But—'

Guiding her out. 'You're helping us make a *real* difference, thanks. That's great.'

Soon as she was outside, Logan pulled the door shut and snubbed the lock. Then frowned at the remote-operated camera facing the desk. Held a hand out to King. 'Give me your jacket.'

'What?'

'Your jacket: I need your jacket. Please.'

'Oh for...' But King shrugged his way out of it, showing off the stains beneath the arms of his shirt.

Logan draped it over the camera and dropped his voice to a whisper – in case they had the microphones activated. 'They were only doing their jobs.'

'Bollocks.' Not even trying to keep his voice down. 'God save us from *bloody* journalists.'

Then King snapped on a pair of blue nitrile gloves and turned the package on the desk, so the open end faced them. Reached inside.

No, no. no!

Logan grabbed his arm. 'What the hell are you doing? We're not exactly in sterile conditions here!'

'It's been opened at least once.' King shook his arm free. 'You really think they've not filmed the thing already?'

'Are you *insane*?'

King pulled something covered in crumpled tinfoil from the Jiffy bag: vaguely rectangular, four or five inches thick. Smears of dark reddish-brown on the shiny metal. Yeah, that was *definitely* blood. 'Twenty quid says they're through there, editing a piece starting with, "Some viewers may find this report distressing."'

The foil package had a curled edge at the top, like a Cornish pasty. King unrolled the first corner.

'Don't! If you compromise the evidence we'll—'

'What?' He bared his teeth, chest out. 'What do you care? This is my investigation, OK? MINE!' Spittle flying, deep creases around his pink eyes. 'You shouldn't even *be* here!'

Logan backed off a pace, sniffing. There was something there, beneath all the mint and the outrage. Something sharp and sour. 'Have you been *drinking*?'

'I'm on duty, you idiot! And I don't need Professional Standards sticking their nose into my case!'

Here we go.

'I'm not "sticking my nose in", I'm here to support you.'

'You're *what*?'

'They didn't tell you?' Oh great. Well that explained a lot.

'All hail the mighty *Inspector Logan McRae* and his *Queen's Medal*! What, you think just because you were stupid enough to get yourself stabbed—'

'Look, it wasn't my idea, OK? All I wanted was a nice straight-forward little investigation, ease my way into things, not ... this!'

King closed the gap between them. Poked him with a finger. 'I don't need supervised by some jumped-up—'

'I'm not supervising, I'm *assisting*.' Logan stared him down. 'And you can blame Jane McGrath, thank you very much. The brass wanted to fire you – this,' pointing at the pair of them, 'was all her idea. I could be in Bucksburn now, eating KitKats.'

King glared at him.

Sigh. 'Look: if we cock this up, they'll throw us *both* in the blender, OK? Career-and-jobbie smoothies for everyone.'

No response.

But at least no one had thrown a punch yet.

Logan softened his voice a bit. 'Now put the package back where it came from and let's try to *pretend* we have a clue about evidentiary procedure.'

King stared at him in silence, breath hissing in and out through his nose... Then he closed his eyes. Shook his head. And slid the tinfoil pack into the Jiffy bag again. Cleared his throat and looked away, the colour fading from his face. 'I need to solve this case, Logan. I need to solve it soon. The press are going to ... hammer dirty big nails into me if I don't, and our top brass are going to let them.'

'Not if I can help it.' He tried for a reassuring smile. 'Now come on, let's get that package to the mortuary. And cheer up: we've finally got some forensic evidence!'

Logan shifted in his horrible SOC suit, setting it rustling. A trickle of sweat traced its way down his spine and into his underwear.

Normally the mortuary was the only cool room in Divisional Headquarters, but for some reason, today it was like a toaster. Or perhaps it was just the horrible Tyvek oversuits, trapping his body heat, not letting any moisture escape in case it contaminated the evidence. Turning his pants into a sauna.

King was pink-faced and shiny next to him, glancing up at the clock every two minutes.

Creepy Sheila Dalrymple seemed comfortable in her own SOC suit, her white wellies shiny against the mortuary's off-grey tiles. A smile on her wide flat face that didn't go as far as the eyes hiding behind her spectacles. Her long thin fingers in constant motion at the end of her long thin arms, as if they lived a life of their own, independent to the rest of her. She must have caught King looking at the clock again, because she turned her hollow smile on him. 'Not long now ... gentlemen.'

Even her pauses were creepy.

Another trickle of sweat joined the first.

Logan rustled a bit more.

Harsh overhead lights sparkled from the stainless-steel cutting tables and worktops. Dented, but clean. A couple of laptops, screensavers birling away. The low growl of the extractor fans. The harsh scent of bleach and formaldehyde undercut by something dark and bowel-like. *Eau de Mortuary, pour cadavre*.

And then, bang on the dot of ten, the cutting room door opened and Professor Isobel McAlister lurched in. Her SOC suit stretched taut over her swollen bulge, face a bit flushed, welly boots turned out at the toes to compensate for the extra weight growing inside her. She didn't even look at Logan or King. 'Well?'

'All is prepared ... Professor.'

About bloody time too.

Isobel pointed at the Jiffy bag. 'Sheila, if you would?'

'As you wish ... Professor.' All she needed was a lightning flash and the sound of nervous horses. Lacking that, Sheila slunk over to the nearest worktop – returning with a stainless-steel tray that had a couple of scalpels, a pair of pliers, three tweezers, and a spoon on it. She placed the tray beside the Jiffy bag, then laid out the implements on the cutting table as if she was setting it for dinner.

She gave Isobel a small nod, then pulled on a facemask and reached into the bag, easing out the tinfoil package and placing it in the middle of the now vacant tray.

Isobel frowned at the package, then at the room with its grubby tiles and shiny worktops. 'Where's my photographer? I *specifically* requested a photographer! How am I supposed to carry out any sort of examination without it being properly recorded?'

'They haven't turned up ... Professor.'

'Well we're not going any further until they *do*.'

Logan groaned.

King shook his head. 'Not acceptable.'

She glared at him. 'A proper photographic record is vital. How am I supposed to present evidence in court without photographs?'

King held her gaze, then threw his hands up. 'Fine! Get the camera and *I'll* take the photographs.'

'This isn't a children's birthday party, you can't—'

'I did the SIO course refresher last week and they had a module on crime scene photography.' He stuck his hand out in Sheila's direction. 'Camera.'

Sheila looked at Isobel. 'Professor?'

'Very well, but if these pictures are of inferior quality it's *your* investigation you'll be ruining.'

Sheila rummaged in one of the cupboards and emerged with a chunky digital camera, turned it on, then presented it to King. 'You have to press this button here to—'

'I do know how a camera works, thank you.' He removed the lens cap, fiddled with the settings, and took a couple of test shots. 'Right: where's the scale?'

She clicked a black-and-white ruler down alongside the package.

King rattled off half a dozen more, prowling around the table to get a variety of angles. The camera's flash bounced off the shiny surfaces.

Isobel held out a gloved hand. 'All right, let's see what you've done.'

He turned the camera around and showed her the viewing screen.

'Acceptable.' She nodded. 'Sheila, proceed.'

Those thin fingers took hold of the crimped top of the tinfoil pasty and unrolled it, spreading the sides open. Revealing a pair of severed human hands. The skin was pale as candlewax where it wasn't clarted in dark red-brown stains.

They'd been put in the package one on top of the other, palms together, fingers interlaced. As if they'd been severed mid-prayer.

King lowered the camera. 'Bloody hell...'

The butcher's-shop smell of iron and bone joined the mortuary scent.

Isobel snapped her fingers. 'You did a course, remember?'

King puffed out his cheeks and snapped off a few more pics as Isobel leaned in and had a good sniff.

'Well, they're reasonably fresh – no discernible trace of cadaverine.'

Sheila produced a second tray and prised the top hand free. It made a sticky, crackling noise, like damp Velcro. She turned the hand, showing it off so King could get some shots, then did the same with the other one. As if she was modelling them for a catalogue. They both went palm-up, side-by-side, on the new tray.

'Hmmmm…' Isobel hunched over them, peering and prodding. 'The wounds imply the use of a short, tapered blade. Wedge shaped. Possibly a hand axe – if you'll excuse the irony. Two blows for the right hand, one for the left. Our perpetrator may have been getting his "eye in" with the first cut.'

Logan nodded. 'The blood in the kitchen.'

'I couldn't comment, because despite repeated requests we still can't get photographs out of … *that*.' She turned her sneer towards a computer, stuck on top of a stainless-steel worktop, that looked as if it might have been cutting edge sometime in the late Cretaceous Period. 'How many times do I have to tell Police Scotland and the SPA that *context* is key?'

King lowered the camera. 'Preaching to the choir, Professor.'

'Before this ridiculous centralised nonsense, we used to get glossy eight-by-tens of the crime scene. Now we're expected to work with low-resolution snaps on a low-resolution screen. We can't even zoom in!'

'Erm… Hold on.' Logan dug out his phone, unlocked it, and scrolled through the photographs to the ones he took in Professor Wilson's kitchen. 'Try these.'

She took the phone and squinted at the screen, then put her fingers on it and zoomed in. Out. In again. Swiped through to the next one and did the same thing, all the way through till: 'Now it's just pictures of your cat.'

'She's a very pretty cat.'

A raised eyebrow, then Isobel swiped through the photos of

Wilson's kitchen again. 'From the quantity of blood and the way it's pooled, I would say some sort of tourniquet was used. Otherwise you'd be looking at arterial spray all up the wall and probably ceiling too. Going by the state of the table, they must have used something as a chopping board, wedged it in under Professor Wilson's arms before the blow.' She returned Logan's phone, leaving little sticky red fingerprints on the screen.

Urgh…

King frowned at her. 'Hold on. Chopping board?'

'Well of course, "chopping board". If they didn't use one, there'd be deep gouges in the tabletop, wouldn't there? From the axe head.'

'Oh.' King pointed. 'What's the chance of surviving something like this?'

'A bilateral amputation proximal to the radiocarpal joint?' She pursed her lips, humming as she frowned at the stumps. Then: 'Under sterile conditions, with trained staff, proper equipment, and anaesthetic: almost guaranteed.'

Yes, but Professor Wilson hadn't had any of those things.

'Hacked off with an axe in a kitchen?' Isobel pushed the tray towards Sheila. 'You're opening yourself up to primary and secondary infection. Without some *very* strong antibiotics it'll be septicaemia, then sepsis, then septic shock, multiple organ failure, and death.'

Sheila picked the right hand up and scraped out the dirt beneath the index fingernail. 'Assuming he isn't … dead already.' She wiped the black gunge into a small glass container and moved on to the next finger.

Maybe Professor Wilson would be better off if the initial shock killed him? If it was that or slowly dying from the pus-filled wounds where his hands used to be, what would be kinder? Quick and painful, or slow, drawn out, and tortuous, praying for a rescue that never came?

And talking of where Professor Wilson's hands used to be…

'Hold on.' Logan pointed at the stained tinfoil package. What looked like a folded sheet of paper sat in a thick clotted puddle of congealed blood 'There's something else in there.'

'So there is.' Isobel picked up a pair of tweezers and leaned in. 'Presumably a message of some kind?' She unfolded it as King clacked and flashed. 'A4, white, probably laser-printer or photocopy paper. Heavily stained.'

But the words in the middle were still clearly visible: 'THE DEVIL MAKES WORK'.

King appeared from behind his camera again. 'What's that supposed to...?' Then it must've dawned, because his mouth clicked shut. 'Oh. Yes.' More photographs.

Logan tapped Isobel on the shoulder, then tipped his head towards the severed hands. 'Can we fingerprint those? I know they're probably Professor Wilson's, but just in case?'

'Sheila?'

'I'll fetch the Livescan machine ... Professor.' She did, returning with something the size of a box of cat treats. Switched it on. Bashed her palm against it a couple of times when nothing happened. Then smiled and pressed the scanner against the tip of the right hand's index finger. She did the middle finger and the thumb too.

The Livescan machine bleeped in Sheila's hand, then one of the laptops let out a tinny *ding*.

'We have a match ... Professor.' She fiddled with the laptop's keyboard. 'Hands belong to one Professor Nicholas Wilson. The prints are in the system marked, "for elimination" and "from the professor's study, bathroom, and bedroom".'

Shirley and her Scene Examiners ride again.

Logan huffed a breath on his bloodstained phone screen and scrubbed it against his SOC suit's sleeve. 'Whoever it was wiped the kitchen down with antibacterial wipes. No prints where it happened.'

'Then I think we can safely assume that the remains do indeed belong to Professor Wilson.' Isobel raised an eyebrow. 'Or, at least, the right hand does. Let's not make assumptions until we've checked them both.'

Logan shook his head. 'He's dead, isn't he?'

King grimaced. 'For *his* sake, I certainly hope so.'

13

Logan followed King out through the side doors and up the steps to the Rear Podium car park. Windscreens and bodywork gleamed in the blazing morning sunshine, but this part was painted dark with shadows. At least it cut the heat a bit.

King stopped at the top. 'So we'll be looking for a dead body in a couple of days.'

'If he's not already dead.'

'Because things weren't difficult enough.' King covered his face with his hands for a moment, curling forward from the waist. 'Hardie's going to pop an artery.'

'We can't *not* tell him it's probably murder.'

King stood up straight again, arms hanging loose at his side. Strings cut. 'Maybe we can tell him it's a *good* thing? Let's be honest: a dead Professor Wilson will kick up a lot less fuss than a live, angry, bitter one with no hands.'

Wow.

'You do know you said that out loud, right?'

'Oh come off it. The dead don't give press conferences telling everyone what a useless bunch of turds NE Division are.'

True. But still...

King checked his watch. 'Look, I've got to go brief the team. Any chance you can pop past Hardie's office and let him know?' Then without waiting for an answer: 'Great, thanks.' And with that he marched off, hurrying in through the station's back doors. They swung shut behind him with an ominous clunk.

Coward.

'OK, will do.' Logan stuck his phone back in his pocket and wandered into King's MIT office. Just in time to rake over the dying embers of the team briefing.

King was at the front of the room, holding up a full-colour copy of the bloodstained 'DEVIL MAKES WORK' message, the whole team gathered around, staring at it. Well, everyone except for Heather, who was presumably off doing something important. Hopefully getting a round of teas in.

King lowered the printout. 'Soon as the media get hold of this you know what'll happen. It'll be like wading through a septic tank full of alligators. So go: achieve!'

Chairs squeaked as they rose and bustled out, faces grim, determined, until only Logan, King, and Steel were left.

As soon as the door closed, King sagged forward until he was nearly bent in two. Shuddered. Scrubbed his face with his hands. Mumbling through his fingers. 'We're completely and utterly screwed…' He looked up at Logan. 'What did Hardie say?'

'Detective Chief Inspector Hardie got dragged into a three-hour review meeting with Detective Superintendent Young about two minutes after I got there. So we've got a little breathing space.'

'At least that's something.'

Steel stuck her feet up on the nearest desk. 'Aye, well Horrible Hardie can poke it up himself if he thinks he's blaming *us* for this. We're no' the ones hacked Professor Wilson's hands off.'

King sagged even further. 'Try telling the media that.'

The door swung open and in strutted Heather, clutching an evidence bag, smiling like she'd just discovered quilted toilet paper. Nodding at them. 'Boss, Guv, Roberta.'

'*Please* tell me you've found something?'

She held up the evidence bag. 'Lab's been over the Jiffy bag: only viable fingerprints on the outside are the BBC receptionist, presenter, and producer. Everything else is too smudged.'

King sat up at that. Eyes wide, eyebrows up. 'But on the inside…?'

'None at all. And only the presenter's prints on the tinfoil package. Nothing on the hands themselves or the note. Our boy was bright enough to wear gloves. They've swabbed for DNA, but given the crime scene—'

'Aye.' Steel shook her head. 'You were right the first time, Kingy: you're screwed.'

He stared at the ceiling tiles, mouth moving as if he was swearing away inside his head.

'But I *have* managed to trace the package back to the Post Office it was sent from. First class, yesterday morning.' Hence the smugness.

'Pfff…' Steel had a big stretch, showing off a toad-belly pale slice of stomach. 'Aye, but they could've posted it from any postbox in the collection area. There could be thousands and thousands of houses covered by the one Post Office. No' to mention Happy Harry the Hand Hacker-Offer probably wouldn't use his friendly neighbourhood postbox. He'd drive somewhere out of the way and use theirs.'

Heather gave Steel's arm a little squeeze. 'No, dear, you're not listening: the hands were in the tinfoil palm to palm, yes?' She put the evidence bag down and gave them a demonstration. 'So that makes the package *too thick* to jam in through a postbox slot. You'd need to drop it off in person.'

Steel narrowed her eyes. 'Nobody likes a smartarse.'

'So I got on to a friend of mine who works at the Huntly depot and he traced the postmark for me.' She checked her notebook. 'Package was sent from the Westhill Post Office, yesterday, at nine twenty-three.'

King stared at her. 'Do they have…?'

'They're digging out the CCTV for us now.'

'Ha!' He punched the air. 'DS Steel: get a car. Heather: get—'

'Can it wait till I've given Gibbs his walk?'

'We're against the clock, H.'

'Well I can't leave him in the *car*, what if he has an accident?'

King screwed his face up for a breath. 'OK, OK. You stay here and coordinate things. I'll take Milky.'

'But—'

'You did great, H.' He gave her shoulder a squeeze. 'We're going to catch this bastard!'

Westhill shopping centre hadn't taken well to modernisation. The bulk of it was an old-fashioned grey-beige blockwork affair, with the shopfronts nestled in behind a covered walkway, but they'd bolted a knock-off strip-mall to one end, sticking out like a broken limb to line the far end of the car park.

A car park that was nearly solid 4x4s. None of which looked as if they'd ever been further off-road than the local Costco. Every now and then, a slightly older hatchback denoted some teenager's first car – usually complete with 'ironic' furry dice, oversized exhaust, and completely unnecessary ironing-board-sized spoiler. But mostly, it was 4x4s.

'...described it as a "terrible shock". We spoke to her soon after the grisly discovery.'

Milky pulled in next to a Range Rover, with a 'Bugger Off Brussels!' sticker in the rear window, as Muriel Kirk's voice purred out of the radio, in full-on presenter mode. 'We get a lot of fan mail at the Muriel Kirk Show, so I didn't think anything of it until I opened the package.'

King leaned forward in the passenger seat, staring at the radio. 'Don't say it, please don't say it.'

In the back seat, Steel nudged Logan. 'She's going to say it.'

'Inside was a tinfoil parcel.'

'Don't...'

'And inside that, was a pair of severed hands.'

'Told you.'

The car erupted as everyone had a simultaneous rant: 'For God's sake!', 'It's a murder investigation!', 'Don't tell everyone that!'

The original newsreader made a 'thinky' noise. 'And what did the police say?'

'Clearly they're playing it very close to their chests, but we need to *make sure everyone understands how serious this is. If anyone out there has any information that could help find whoever's responsible, please get in touch with either the police or the* Muriel Kirk Show, *on the air from one o'clock.'*

'Thank you, Muriel.'

Steel bared her teeth, sooking air through them. 'Oooh, that's no' good. Think they'll be dragging the Chief Superintendent out of his meeting now? He'll want to polish his arse-kicking boots.'

'Weather now, and this heatwave's set to continue on to the weekend at least, with temperatures—'

Milky killed the engine. 'I don't normally indulge in bad language, but as Heather would say, Muriel Kirk can … "sex and travel".'

King made a little growling noise, then hauled in a couple of deep breaths. Stuffing it down.

Couldn't blame him. Milky was right, Muriel Kirk really could 'sex and travel'.

Logan sighed. 'It was going to come out eventually. At least we've got a lead to follow, now.'

Steel reached between the seats and patted King on the shoulder, voice soft and kind. Completely unlike her. 'Laz is right. Come on, Frank: we can do this.' She checked her watch. 'Still got nearly two and a half hours: how hard can it be?'

Another deep breath, then King nodded and climbed out of the car. Stopped to look back inside. 'So what are you all waiting for?'

The Post Office was hidden away at the back of the local Co-op, just past the tinned vegetables and baby food. A bespectacled auld mannie with a baldy head and hairy ears sat behind the safety glass, watching with baggy eyes as a dumpy wee lady in a granny cardigan and fur-lined boots counted out a big pile of loose change onto his counter.

There was a queue: another pair of wee dumpies shuffling at the front of it, while a couple of spotty teenagers brought up the rear – the two of them fiddling with their phones and piercings.

King marched straight past the lot of them and up to the counter. Making friends as usual.

'Hoy!' One of the old ladies waved a bag-for-life at him. 'There's a queue!'

'You tell him, Babs.' Old Lady Number Three jerked her chins up. 'No swicking in, fatty!'

Logan squeezed past. 'Sorry about this. Police business...'

Steel and Milky followed him to the counter.

The lady counting out change didn't look up from her coins. Not even when King knocked on the safety glass.

'Hmm?' The auld mannie behind the counter blinked at them. According to his nametag – 'HELLO, MY NAME IS ANDREW' – they were supposed to 'ASK ME ABOUT TRAVEL INSURANCE!' He pursed his lips. 'I'm sorry, but there's a queue, so can you—'

King slapped his warrant card against the glass. 'I need to speak to the manager. *Now*.'

Mrs Bag-For-Life gave it another wave. 'Bloody disgrace, that's what this is!'

Mrs Chins nodded, setting her wattle swaying. 'We were here first!'

Andrew peered at King's warrant card, then over King's shoulder at Logan, Steel, and Milky. 'Oh. Right. I'll get Geraldine.'

Mrs Bag-For-Life raised a walking stick and took a wee hurpley step forward – brandishing it like a cutlass. 'Someone needs to teach you a bloody good lesson!'

'You tell them, Babs!'

Steel turned and smiled a cold hard smile. 'Hands up everyone whose road tax, council tax, and TV licence are up to date.'

Silence.

Then everyone developed a sudden and *profound* interest in whatever was on the nearest shelf.

Steel nodded. 'Aye, thought as much.' She leaned in close to Logan and dropped her voice to a whisper. 'Got that one from a Hamish Macbeth book.'

A row of small monitors took up most of the Co-op's CCTV room, mounted to the wall above a narrow workbench littered with paperwork and a rack of hard drives. Barely space for the single office chair, the woman sitting in it, King, and Logan. Steel and Milky peering in from the corridor outside.

The woman swivelled her chair and plucked a wireless keyboard from on top of the hard drives. Late thirties, with a fashionable haircut, suit and tie. 'HELLO, MY NAME IS GERALDINE' above the word 'MANAGER'. She poked at the keys and the screen in front of her jumped to a frozen shot of the shop floor, the camera pointing towards the front doors. Newspapers on one side, a display of fruit and crisps on the other, sandwiches in a chiller... 'I set it to play from when he comes into the store.' Geraldine tapped the screen, where a blurry figure was just visible through the automatic doors. 'This is the chap here.'

She pressed another key and the scene came to life: the doors slid open and in walked a man wearing the standard-issue hoodie-and-baseball-cap security-camera-avoidance outfit. He'd made the extra effort and donned a pair of sunglasses as well, for that exotic out-of-town look. So no way of making an ID of his face. The baggy grey clothes were pretty indistinct too. One thing was certain, though: whoever he was, the guy was *massive*. And it wasn't fat, either. Going by the way he moved, arms out from his sides, elbows turned, he was lugging a *lot* of muscle around. Broad of shoulder and short of neck. A Tesco carrier bag, with something bulky inside, dangling from one hand.

Geraldine moved her finger to where the sandwiches lurked. 'You can see Linda there, following him around.'

A security guard appeared from behind the lunchtime deals and followed Mr Hoodie towards the camera.

'Standard operating procedure for anyone dressed in this season's Shoplifter Chic.'

The pair of them disappeared off the bottom of the screen.

Click, they were caught on another camera, walking past the fruit and veg – Mr Hoodie acting all casual and calm, Linda, the security guard following at a discreet distance.

'Down fresh produce...' The camera jumped again. 'Past tinned fish...' Another jump. 'Dried goods...' One more. 'And into our Post Office zone.'

The camera was positioned behind the counter, catching Mr Hoodie as he stopped at the 'PLEASE WAIT HERE' sign.

An old man was being served – his moustache twitching with concentration as he filled out a form. The woman helping him was a furry blob in the bottom left corner, only the top of her head visible. And all the time, Mr Hoodie stood there, still as a lamppost. Didn't fidget. Didn't check his watch. Just stood there.

King folded his arms. 'Cool customer.'

Captain Twitchy Moustache handed over his form and shuffled away out of shot, then Mr Hoodie stepped up to the counter. Put the plastic bag down in front of him.

'We haven't got sound, I'm afraid,' Geraldine wrinkled her nose, 'but Shauna says he was definitely Scottish. Asked her to send the package first class.'

On the screen, Mr Hoodie's mouth moved in complete silence, then he placed the plastic bag on the scales. Took it off and slid it through the access window.

The woman-behind-the-counter reached for the bag. Opened it. Slid the Jiffy bag out onto the counter in front of her and applied the postage sticker.

'Clever boy.' Logan pointed. 'He never touches it.'

The woman crumpled up the plastic bag and passed it back through the opening, where Mr Hoodie stuffed it straight into his pocket. Leaving no physical evidence behind. Other than the Jiffy bag, which was, according to the lab, pretty much sterile.

He counted out a handful of pound coins and the woman scooped them up. Then he smiled at her, nodded, waved, turned and walked away.

Geraldine poked at her keyboard again, tracing his route back the way he'd come – camera to camera, the security guard following him at a discreet distance – to the front doors. They slid shut behind him and he was gone.

The security guard shrugged, then sloped off to lurk in wait for someone else.

'And that's it, I'm afraid.'

'Hmmm...' King scowled at the final image. Then turned to

the door, where Milky was still watching. 'Go round the other shops, hoover up all the security camera footage you can. Where's DS Steel?'

'Gone for a vape, Guv.'

'Oh for... *Fine*. Tell her I said she has to find out who's in charge of CCTV for the shopping centre. See if we can track this bastard to a car or something.'

A nod from Milky. 'Guv.' Then she scurried off.

Logan pulled out his notebook and wrote down the names of the security guard and the woman on the Post Office counter. 'We're going to need to talk to Linda and Shauna.'

'I thought you might.' Geraldine stood. 'They're in the break room, waiting for you.'

A colourful collection of watercolours dotted the three break room walls that weren't covered in beige lockers. Two round tables, some plastic chairs, a fridge, and a microwave. Nice. The air sweet-sharp with the scent of lemon floor cleaner.

Linda the security guard was squarer in real life, her shoulders and forehead making it look as if someone had built her out of Lego blocks. Shauna, the lady whose back had featured in the CCTV footage, looked different too. Going by the expression on her face, her front half hadn't enjoyed itself for *at least* the last thirty years.

The pair of them sat opposite Logan and King, Shauna picking her teeth, Linda folding and unfolding her arms, as if she didn't quite know what to do with them.

King doodled a circle on his notebook. 'And you didn't recognise his voice at all? Maybe he'd been in before and—' His phone blared into life and he dug it out. Frowned at the screen and grimaced. Then put it face down on the table. 'Sorry about that. Where were we?'

Shauna finally worked whatever it was free and pinged it away under the table. 'No, I didn't recognise him. We get a lot of regulars in, but he was ... a bit strange? Weirdly *still*, you know: immobile. Like he was made of plastic or something.'

'And he didn't say anything—'

This time it was Logan's phone, belting out its generic ring-tone. He pulled it out while everyone stared at him. The words, 'SUPT. BEVAN' sat in the middle of the screen.

Yeah. Thanks, but no thanks.

He pressed 'IGNORE' and switched his phone off.

King raised an eyebrow.

Logan shook his head.

King sighed.

Shauna wiped her damp finger on her uniform shirt. 'Look, can I go now? Only Andrew gets all stressed if he's left on the counter by himself.'

'We're done here anyway.' King's smile wasn't even vaguely convincing. 'Thank you both for your help.'

Their chairs' rubber feet *scronnnked* on the lino as they scraped them back and stood. A couple of awkward smiles. Then Shauna and Linda sloped off to work again.

Soon as the door shut behind them, King slumped. 'So close...'

Logan pointed at King's phone. 'Who was it?'

'DI Hardie. You?'

'Superintendent Bevan. So much for two and a half hours.'

'Yeah.'

Scronnnnk.

Logan followed him out into a bland corridor, the painted breeze-block walls scarred with scuffs and bashes. Past a couple of cages full of crushed cardboard boxes. 'We can say we had our phones turned off because we were interviewing witnesses. It's not lying, because mine is and we were.'

King's phone dinged, and he frowned at the screen. 'Voicemail.'

No doubt a message of encouragement from DCI Hardie.

They pushed through the double doors on to the shop floor. A handful of people were in filling their trolleys and baskets – one of the lippy auld wifies stocking up on cat food and spiced rum, while the other worried away at half a dozen scratchcards.

Logan and King didn't stop to say hello on the way to the exit. But as they passed the drinks aisle, King stopped. Patted his pockets.

'I'll meet you outside – want to get some more mints.'

118

And why did all those bottles of wine and spirits make him think of that?

Logan nodded, and walked out through the doors, pausing only to wave at Linda, on guard by the 'MEGA LUNCH-DEAL!' sandwiches, crisps, and drinks.

'Bloody hell...' The midday heat hit him like an iron, sizzling away at his eyes and ears. And that was underneath the covered walkway; in the full glare of the sun it would be unbearable.

He stuck to the shadows. Turned to look in through the Co-op window as a pair of kids rattled past on scooters. And there was King, marching towards the checkouts with two half-bottles of vodka in one hand and a four-pack of extra-strong mints in the other.

King froze, then juggled his purchases into one hand so he could dig out his phone and pull a pained face at the screen. Closed his eyes and moved his lips as if he was swearing away to himself. Then answered it.

Two half-bottles of vodka. Both the perfect size to hide in your jacket pockets if you were—

'Fit like, Limpy McMoans-A-Lot?'

Great. Steel.

Logan turned. 'Can you at least pretend you care about—'

'Guess what I've got, go on: guess.' She wiggled her eyebrows at him. 'Guess!'

'Worms?'

'I found a nice man called Johnny. Johnny works the security cameras for all the shopping centre's communal areas.' She pointed at one of the shiny black half-globes, protruding from the walkway's ceiling like a kraken's eye. 'Wave hello to lovely Johnny.'

She did, but Logan didn't.

'Aye, and guess what me and Johnny found when we went looking through yesterday's footage?'

Logan stared at her. 'You *didn't*.'

The grin turned a little bit obscene. 'We sodding well *did*!' Steel whipped out her phone and poked at it. 'Got him to email me the footage. Our boy might be able to manufacture a forensic-free abduction scene and Jiffy bag, but know what he didn't bank on?'

She turned the screen to face Logan.

On it, a muscle-bound lump of a man marched past Marks & Spencer, walking towards one of the cameras. Mid-twenties. Not the prettiest of guys, with a heavy forehead and wide jaw. Wearing a grey hoodie. Something in a plastic bag, tucked under his arm. He reached into his hoodie's pocket, took out a pair of sunglasses, put them on. Then did the same with a baseball cap. Pulled his hood up. And his transformation into Mr Hoodie was complete.

'They stuck a new security camera on the Citizen's Advice Bureau yesterday morning, cos some manky scummer keeps smearing shite all over their windows. If our boy, Chuckles, had posted those hands on Monday, he'd've got away with it.'

Logan looked up from the screen to the grinning Steel. 'I could sodding well *kiss* you.'

'Aye, well, better no'.' Deadpan. 'Don't want you undermining years of dedicated lesbianism.'

They had him. They had an actual face for Professor Wilson's abductor. 'We need to get this out to every station, in every division in Scotland.'

'No' be quicker doing a public appeal?'

She had a point.

'Maybe, but if we can find out who he is *before* the brass put on a press conference, we'll—'

'Your boy King might not get his arse handed to him in a damp paper bag?' She peered over Logan's shoulder at the Co-op. 'Ahoy-hoy, thar he blows.'

And there he blew – slouching out through the automatic doors with no sign of his vodka or extra-strong mints, still on the phone, one hand massaging his forehead. 'Yes, Boss, but— … I know that. … Yes. But if you'll just— OK…'

Steel leaned in closer to Logan, not bothering to whisper. 'Think he's getting a spanking? Sounds like a spanking to me.'

'Do you always have to make everything worse?'

'Part of my charm.'

King stopped. Sighed. 'Yes. ... I will. Yes.' Another sigh. 'Bye.' He hung up and thumped back against one of the walkway's pillars. Didn't look at them. '*Apparently*, the Chief Superintendent isn't happy about Professor Wilson's severed hands being all over the one o'clock news, so he kicked Superintendent Young's backside about it. And Superintendent Young kicked DCI Hardie's backside. And now DCI Hardie is kicking mine.' King deflated even further. 'God's sake...' He gave Logan a pained look. 'They're holding a press conference at four. Our attendance is mandatory.'

'No need to look so glum, Kingy-boy.' Steel slapped his shoulder. 'It's your lucky day: Roberta Steel to the rescue! *Again*.'

His eyes widened. 'You mean ... we got a *face*?'

'Now let's talk about the extra-large fish suppers you're buying us all for lunch. As a wee reward for my detectivey genius.'

14

The dual carriageway wheeched past the pool car's windows as DI King drove them into town, the soft comforting smell of hot batter and sharp-spined vinegar thick in the air, even with the windows open.

Milky leaned across from the passenger seat, a couple of golden chips in her hand. 'Sure you don't want any, Guv?'

He shook his head. 'Not hungry.'

Sitting in the back, Steel sooked her fingers sort of clean and dug her phone out. Squinted at the screen. 'That's Tufty sent the video out to everyone and her dog in Police Scotland.' A chunk of haddock went the way of all flesh as she chewed with her mouth open. 'Dirty wee scumbag says he's having beef Wellington in the studio canteen.' She stuffed in some more chips. 'All right for some.'

King nodded. 'Better make sure the media department get a "have you seen this man" done up before the press conference.'

Logan took a bite of pickled onion, chasing it down with a nugget of crispy batter. Whoever invented fish suppers was a genius. Sod haggis, *this* was Scotland's proper national dish, not some unmentionable mush of sheep innards stuffed into another bit of sheep innards, with four tons of herbs and spices added so you didn't have to taste what you were actually eating.

Haddock plus batter plus potatoes, plus salt, plus vinegar, equals genius.

He crunched through a perfectly golden finger of deep-fried potato, then leaned forward, into the gap between the front seats. 'There's something else we're going to need to talk about before the briefing.'

'It's not—'

'Just so we're prepared. There's no way Edward Barwell's going to pass up the opportunity.'

Milky dipped a chip in her little splat of mayonnaise. 'Who's Edward Barwell?'

King tightened his grip on the steering wheel. 'No one. He's—'

'Journo.' Little bits of batter fell down Steel's front as she chewed. '*Scottish Daily Post*. He's the one dug up that dirt on Kingy's Alt-Nat terrorist past.'

The only noises were the engine, the fluttering roar of air passing by the windows, and Steel munching.

Then Milky turned in her seat. 'He what? Wait: what terrorist past?'

King glared at Logan in the rear-view mirror. 'How did *she* find out? You're supposed to be—'

'Oh no.' Logan held up a greasy hand. 'Don't look at me!'

Steel smiled. 'Nah, I keep my ear to the grindstone, Kingy. Works wonders.'

More silence.

Milky stared at him. 'Guv?'

King took a deep breath, shoulders dropping an inch. 'I was going to tell you all before the briefing.'

'You were an Alt-Nat *terrorist*?' She hit him: not a playful slap – a full-on back-hand wallop, right in the chest. Voice hard and bitter. '*I'm* English! Yorkshire's in *England*, remember? And you want to chuck me out country?' She hit him again. 'Going to burn down me house as well?' Once more for luck, putting her weight behind it.

'Ow! Can we not do this now. Please?' Staring across the car at her. 'It was *nothing*. It was *years* ago. I never did *anything*.'

Steel stuffed in a mouthful of chips. 'That's the spirit!' She turned a mushed-potato grin on Logan. 'Glad I came now: Wednesdays are usually a lot more boring than this.'

The pool car rumbled up the ramp and onto the Rear Podium car park. Tucked around the back of Divisional Headquarters, the rectangle of tarmac was a suntrap, bordered on two sides by the bulk of DHQ, the mortuary on the third, and the rear of King Street on the fourth – a wall of dirty granite, punctuated by sash windows and black downpipes.

King took the only available space, next to the smokers' station with its overflowing bin, cigarette butts littered around it like tiny dead bodies after a massacre.

As soon as he hauled on the handbrake, Milky wrenched open the passenger door, face like a squeezed pluke, jaw clenched as she clambered into the sunlight.

King scrambled out after her. 'Oh, come on, Milky, it was years ago!'

She kept her face turned towards DHQ. 'If you'll excuse me, I've got a report to write.'

Milky marched across the shiny black tarmac to the building's doors, yanked them open and stormed inside.

Steel leaned across Logan, looking up at King. 'You made a right cat's arsehole of that one, Kingy.'

His mouth moved for a bit. Then he shrugged. 'She'll come round. Eventually.'

Milky reappeared in the doorway, grabbed the open doors and, turning inside again, slammed them shut behind her.

Steel sucked air in through her teeth. 'Aye, don't hold your breath.'

King hunched his shoulders. 'Is there any way we can speed up the ID process?'

Noticeboards lined the corridor, between the doors, covered in memos, thank you cards, and yet more bloody motivational posters. As if everyone working in Divisional Headquarters was hell-bent on doing a crap job, if not for a photo of some baldy

lump in a high-viz vest, grinning away beneath the words
'COMMUNITY FOCUSED!'

Steel sniffed. 'Public appeal.'

Not this again. Logan shook his head. 'We'll get swamped by
every well-meaning half-wit out there.'

'Aye, but it'd be quicker.'

King nodded. 'We need to...' He scuffed to a halt, staring
down the corridor.

DCI Hardie was standing in his office doorway, staring back
at them. Then he stuck out one hand and made a come-hither
gesture. His face a hard, angry scribble. 'DI King.'

A little groaning noise escaped from King, followed by a very
quiet, 'Crap.'

'A moment of your valuable time, please.'

King stood up straight. 'I was just—'

'In my office. *Now!*'

Steel patted him on the back. 'Been nice knowing you.'

A deep breath, then King raised his chin and marched off.

Hardie pointed past King at Logan and Steel. 'And you two:
go do something *useful* for a change!' Then he stepped aside,
so King could enter the office, gave them one last glare, and
slammed the door closed.

Steel puckered her lips. 'Yeah... He's dead.'

And then some.

'In the meantime...' Logan turned on his heel. 'Go chase up
the media department. And the other stations too. We need to
know who posted that sodding package.'

She made little wrinkles between her eyebrows, then
shrugged. 'Ah, why no'.' Stuck her hands in her pockets and
shoved through the double doors into the stairwell. 'Still say
we should do a public appeal!' And she was gone.

Right.

He took out his phone and sent Tufty a text:

Any news on that first tweeter yet?

No response.

A couple of uniforms giggled their way down the corridor,

clutching something in a brown paper bag. When they saw Logan the laughter died and they ramrodded past him, arms swinging as if they were expecting to salute a flag at some point. And as soon as they reached the doors at the far end, the giggling started up again.

Still nothing from Tufty.

'You better not be asleep, you lazy wee sod...'

He poked the 'CALL' icon and listened to it ring instead.

And ring.

And ring.

And ring.

'You has reached the Tuftinator! A message you may leave, after the bleep.'

'What's happening with that first tweeter – have you found anything yet, or are you sitting on your backside up there watching porn? Because if you are—'

'Guv.' Rennie appeared at Logan's shoulder. No noise, nothing. Just suddenly: Rennie, standing there with a blue folder under one arm.

'Gah!' Logan flinched. 'Are you on castors or something?' He hung up.

'They don't call us the Rubber Heelers for nothing.' A grin. 'Saw you pull into the car park. Quick heads-up: DCI Hardie is on the warpath, so steer clear, OK?'

'Too late.'

'Our beloved Superintendent Bevan has decided that since Professor Wilson's hands have turned up in the post, you could probably do with a ... well, you know: hand.' He snapped to attention and saluted. 'Sergeant Simon Rennie, reporting for duty!' Then slumped. 'Anyway, you wanna grab a coffee? I'm parchified. I can fill you in on Matt Lansdale on the way?'

Might as well.

Logan headed back down the corridor. 'Matt Lansdale?'

Rennie loped along beside him. 'Journalists keep asking about him? "Is Professor Wilson's disappearance linked to Matt Lansdale's?" You wanted me to look into it?'

Ah, *that* Matt Lansdale.

They pushed through into the stairwell and the smell of boiled cabbage, fried chips, and sweaty feet.

Rennie held up his folder. 'I dug out the files. Councillor Matt Lansdale was reported missing last Wednesday morning by one of his colleagues.' He opened it as they started down the stairs and passed a printout to Logan.

It was a photo of a saggy-faced man in his fifties, thinning on top and squidgy of nose. The kind of man who looked as if he'd knock back three pints of lager then start banging on about immigration.

'And I don't mean, like, *therapy* councillor, I mean town. Tory. Divorced last May, lives alone, one-bedroom flat in Kittybrewster.'

Logan handed the photo back. 'What's his connection with Professor Wilson?'

'When Lansdale didn't come in on Monday, they thought he was just having "one of those whisky-and-pity-party weekends". The head of a committee he's on tried calling him Tuesday, cos he'd missed a vote, but it went to voicemail.'

So far, so boring.

'Still waiting for a connection.'

They turned left at the next landing, making for the canteen doors.

'So the chairperson calls Lansdale's ex-wife. Turns out he was meant to pick up their kid for his regular every-other-weekend, but he was a no-show.'

A handful of officers were in, sitting in a clump at one of the tables, curled over plates piled high with stovies and mince and tatties and deep-fried things with chips. None of your salad nonsense here, thank you very much.

Wee Hairy Davie stood behind the counter in his tabard, wiping the surfaces with a blue cloth. Whatever nature had intended for Wee Hairy Davie, it probably should have quit while it was behind. The unfortunate results made a *very* convincing argument for birth control and spaying your pets.

Rennie wandered into Wee Hairy Davie's domain. 'See, Lansdale *kinda* disgraced himself with a sext scandal last year.

Sent pictures of his "electoral mandate" to someone on the Accounts Oversight Committee. Hence the divorce and the whisky-and-pity-parties.'

'I'm not kidding, Rennie.' Logan pointed at the array of stainless-steel cutlery poking out of a grey plastic tray, sitting next to the cash register. 'I'm going to grab a fork and stab you with it, if you don't get to the point.'

'Oh, yeah, right: the connection.' He waved at Wee Hairy Davie. 'Large cappuccino with a shot of hazelnut, chocolate sprinkles, and semi-skimmed, please, Davie.' Then turned to Logan. 'Guv?'

Logan grabbed a fork and brandished it. 'You were warned!'

'Eek! Give him something decaf!'

'The *connection*.'

Hands up. 'Lansdale was chairman of "No To Independence" and a big pro-Brexit campaigner. Massive.'

'Is that it?' He lowered the fork.

'I'm not the one saying their disappearances are linked, am I? You know what the press are like: someone farts on a Tuesday, by Thursday it's "Ebola panic grips nation!"'

'What about his house: any sign of forced entry? Blood?'

'Don't think anyone looked.' Rennie shrugged. 'I can probably get the keys if you want? You know, if we're after an excuse to make ourselves scarce before Hardie comes looking for us?'

Ah... Yes, the happy DCI Hardie.

'Not a bad idea. And I'll have a macchiato.'

'Kinda thought it'd be grander than this.' Rennie curled his lip and turned on the spot, no doubt taking in the glory of Councillor Matt Lansdale's living room.

It was nearly all taken up by a single black leather couch, a glass coffee table, and a huge wall-mounted TV. No bookshelves. No pictures. Only one thing stopped it being the perfect bachelor pad: it didn't have a poster of that tennis player scratching her bum. Lansdale had missed a trick there.

Logan peered out through the blinds at the block of flat's car park, two storeys below. It was the usual collection of Aberdeen hatchbacks and 4x4s, with an identical Monopoly-hotel-inspired block of flats on the other side. 'Just because he's pro-Brexit and pro-union, doesn't mean he's been snatched.'

'To be honest, after the sext scandal, no one's really all that surprised he did a runner. Probably embezzled a heap of cash too. You know what politicians are like.'

True.

Logan stepped out into the tiny hallway – barely big enough to hold the five doors leading off it: living room; bedroom; kitchen; bathroom; and a small coatrack, festooned with jackets, next to the front door.

There weren't any scratches around the Yale lock, the glass panel was intact, and the door frame wasn't splintered. 'No sign of forced entry.'

Rennie shrugged. 'Ah, but there wasn't at Professor Wilson's, was there?'

Also true.

Logan snapped on a pair of gloves and went through one of the jackets' pockets. 'Imagine living the kind of life where no one cares if you disappear or not.'

'You know,' Rennie leaned against the wall, a big sappy smile on his face, 'I never thought I'd say this, but I'm really enjoying PSD.'

Aha...

Logan pulled a set of keys out of the pocket and held them up. 'Car keys.'

'I always thought Professional Standards were a bunch of sinister bastards – same as everyone else does – but it's really cool, isn't it?'

'Course he might have a spare set...' Next up was a patched leather jacket that smelled of fried onions. 'Maybe not a spare wallet, though.'

It was a small brown leather job, scuffed and battered. Logan opened it and flicked through the contents: sixty quid in cash, two credit cards, a debit card, some receipts, and a handful of business cards.

Rennie nodded. 'Let's face it, we, we brave few, we band of *sinister* bastards, we keep the whole thing going, don't we?'

So wherever Lansdale went, he went without any cash.

'I mean, if you don't have PSD, you've got no one keeping the system honest.'

Logan dug into the next coat.

Frowned. 'More car keys.'

So no cash, and no car.

Rennie followed him into the flat's bathroom. 'Cos if the system isn't honest, then everything falls apart, doesn't it?'

No way that bath was big enough for a grown man to lie down in, but there was a shower mounted on the wall above the taps... No shower curtain, though. A *rail*, but no curtain.

Mind you, that was the least of the room's problems. A thick layer of grey fur coated the top of the cistern, and the back of the pan, where the hinges were. More dust on pretty much every other surface. The carcasses of shampoo bottles littered the edge of the bath, empty boxes of paracetamol and effervescent powders, empty toothpaste tubes, and a squirrel's nest of used dental floss heaped up by the overflowing bin.

But there should've been mould, shouldn't there? You can't fit in the bath, but there's no shower curtain so if you have a shower the water would spray everywhere. Soak things. And those things would go mouldy...

Logan stared up at the dust-free stainless-steel rail that went from wall-to-wall above the bath. 'What happened to the shower curtain?'

'Maybe he didn't get around to putting one up? These crazy bachelors and their lack of personal hygiene, eh?'

'He got the curtain *hooks* up.' A whole row of them: plastic circles with nothing held in their grasp.

'I went a whole term at university eating every single meal out of a cereal bowl with Tony the Tiger on it. Only bit of crockery I owned.'

'Kitchen.' Logan led the way, but there wasn't room for Rennie to follow.

It was even smaller than the bathroom. Not so much a galley

kitchen as a dinghy. Everything was crammed in. No room to eat. Barely room to turn around. It had the funky, gritty smell of mould that had been missing in the bathroom... And a quick glance into the sink showed why: a couple of plates, a bowl, and a mug sat in the bottom, crawling with furry black and green growths.

The only concession to washing up was the single whisky tumbler on the draining board.

A trio of hairy takeaway containers lurked beside the microwave – what was left inside all green and sprawling. As if Lansdale had got a curry in, woke up the next day, and decided to walk away from his flat and his life.

Rennie poked his head in from the hall. 'Anyway, yeah, so *we're* the ones that keep everything working. Without PSD there'd be no rule of law.'

A fridge sat under the tiny worktop. Logan squatted down and opened it. Milk and beer. Butter and cheese. Some unidentifiable green sludge in the salad drawer. A packet of sausages on the shelves two days past its sell-by date.

'The law only exists as long as the general population have faith in it. We're the ones maintaining that faith.'

He tried the washing machine, rearing back as the hard sharp stench of wet clothes left in there too long jabbed out. 'Urgh...' He clunked the door shut again.

'Yeah, I hate it when the towels go all widdly like that. Who wants to dry themselves on something that smells like a tramp's peed on it?'

The cupboard next to the washing machine was full of whisky bottles, the vast majority of which were supermarket own-brand, all of them cheap looking, and none of them with more than a dribble left in the bottom.

Logan stood. 'What's your impression of DI King?'

'Oh yes.' Rennie rolled his eyes, then put on a decent impersonation of King's Highland burr. '"Sergeant, there's *five hundred and thirty-three* English MPs and only fifty-nine Scottish ones."' He wrinkled his nose. 'What a shock: England gets more MPs than we do. There's ten times more people living

down there than live up here, what do you expect? Pfff...
Man's a broken record.'

Logan closed the cupboard door. 'Last room.'

The flat's only bedroom wasn't exactly huge. A wall of mirrored
wardrobes did their best to make the place look larger, but it
was an uphill struggle. A double bed took up most of the floor,
the only other bit of furniture being a chair in the corner covered
in discarded clothes. There wasn't even space for a bedside
cabinet.

Logan pointed at their reflections. 'Check the wardrobe.' Then
dug into the pile of clothes, fabric squeaking against his nitrile
gloves. Socks, pants, trousers, shirts, all needing a wash.

'So, where was I?' Rennie went for a rummage. 'Ah, right:
without Professional Standards you get anarchy, rioting, looting,
chaos, dogs and cats living together...' Silence.

'What?' Logan looked over from the pile of rumpled clothes.
'Find something?'

'Nah.' Rennie's reflection frowned back at him from the
wardrobe door. 'You know what I think?'

'Suicide.' Was the obvious conclusion.

'Only we've not had any John Does turn up at the mortuary.
I checked.'

'You try the hospitals?'

His head disappeared inside the wardrobe again. 'If I said yes,
would you believe me?'

Nope.

Logan dumped the last shirt on the floor, then heaved up
the corner of the mattress and peered underneath. Nothing. He
let it fall back again with a spring-echoing whump. 'Let's go
see if we can find Councillor Lansdale's car.'

You had to be a special kind of soulless monster to work in the
Aberdeen Planning Department – it was the only explanation
possible. Surely no human being would've granted permission
to build houses and flats this bland, depressing, and lifeless.

A few forlorn trees wilted in the heat, leaves curling at the edges. The tiny squares of grass, little more than yellowy scrub. Nothing in the car park outside Lansdale's building responded to the fob on his car key.

Logan pointed it at the other side and tried again. None of the lights flashed.

Rennie ran a finger around the collar of his black T-shirt. 'God it's boiling...'

OK, time to try the street.

Logan walked out into the middle of the road and pressed the button.

Still nothing.

'Urgh...' Rennie fanned himself with his peaked cap. 'Remember the good old days when it got warmer gradually and you had the chance to acclimatise?'

Other side of the road.

Yet more nothing.

Maybe Lansdale had parked somewhere else? Got drunk and took a taxi back to the flat?

'Nowadays: today it's hot, tomorrow it's cold, then tepid, then baking, then cold again. How are you supposed to get used to that?'

Logan turned the corner, where the depressing flats gave way to depressing houses – all tiny and squeezed in.

Rennie scuffed along beside him. 'Scotland's not meant to have twenty-five-degree heat, it's not natural. We're a race of gingery people! Anything past eighteen degrees and we melt.'

One last go.

Logan held up the fob, pushed the button, and an old, black, Ford Mondeo flashed its lights in reply. Bingo.

He marched over and peered in through the window. Lansdale's car was a lot tidier than his flat.

Rennie kicked the front tyre. 'Well, at least we know he didn't perform the old hose-from-the-exhaust trick.'

'Just to be on the safe side.' Logan unlocked the Mondeo's boot and popped the lid... Holy mother of *stink*! A rancid tsunami crashed out of the boot, the sweet stomach-churning stench of rotting meat burying him as he staggered backwards, waving a hand in front of his face, the other clutched over his nose and mouth. It was so strong you could *taste* it – bitter and rancid.

Rennie blanched. 'Oh no… It's not a dead body, is it?'

'Jesus…' Logan blinked, turned his head away for a clean breath of air, then tried again.

Asda carrier bags filled the Mondeo's boot, their contents slumped and oozing. What was left of a free-range chicken clearly visible in all its swollen mouldy glory. 'He's left his weekly shop in the boot, in this heat, for a week.'

Rennie took one look, gagged, then retreated. 'Ooh, I'm gonna be sick.'

Logan clunked the boot closed again. Backed away. 'Check the hospitals.'

15

Grey granite buildings slid past the Audi's windows, sparkling in the sunlight. The people, not so much. Oh, they'd embraced the summer with T-shirts and shorts, but seemed to have forgotten the sunscreen. It was like driving through a city populated by lobsters.

Sitting in the passenger seat, Rennie nodded. 'OK, thanks. Bye.' He stuffed his phone in his pocket. 'No sign of Councillor Lansdale anywhere. The only John Doe I could find in the northeast was an auld mannie who got hit by a bus in Elgin.'

'Well, maybe we—'

Logan's phone launched into 'Space Oddity' and seconds later 'BEHOLD THE GREAT TUFTINO!' appeared on the centre console, as the hands-free kit connected.

What?

Why 'BEHOLD THE GREAT TUFTINO!'? Pretty certain the wee spud was filed under 'Tufty' in his contacts list.

Logan shook his head and thumbed the button on the steering wheel. 'Tufty? Have you done something to my phone?'

His voice boomed out of the car's speakers. *'Loop quantum gravity's even weirder than I thought, it's totally awesome. I has a fascinated!'*

He had an idiot, more like.

'Have you found out who sent the first tweet yet, or not?'

'Oh, the tweet: *no. No, we're still running that.'*

Some days, people just begged for a kick up the backside. 'Have you done *any* work at all?'

'*See, diffeomorphism invariance and background independence mean there's a definable minimum size to things like time and space and—*'

'How long?'

'*Ten to the minus thirty-five metres, but the smallest* volume *is ten to the minus hundred and five cubic metres, and that means—*'

'No, you idiot, how long before you find out who sent that tweet?'

There was a pause as more Lobster People from the Planet Too-Ginger-To-Be-In-The-Sun went by.

'Tufty?'

'*No way of knowing. We've got forty-two* massive *servers churning their way through Twitter and Facebook and Instagram. But it could take months.*'

'Oh for... *Months*? How can it take months? Get your finger out!'

Lazy little sod.

A sigh hissed out from the speakers. '*About six thousand tweets get sent every second, that's five hundred and eighteen million, four hundred thousand a day. Fifty-five million Facebook updates. Ninety-five million photos added to Instagram. Every – single – day.* That's *why months.*'

Logan pulled up at the traffic lights, drumming his fingers on the steering wheel while a Lobsterwoman wheeled a buggy across the crossing, fag poking out of the corner of her mouth, phone in one hand. Ignoring her Lobsterchild as it hurled a crisp packet out into the sunshine, followed by a Capri Sun and what was left of a Mars Bar.

No way they could wait months for a result.

Fifty-five million Facebooks. Ninety-five million Instagrams. It was too much.

'*Sarge?*'

'Fine. Ditch Facebook and Instawhatsit. If our boy's tweeting about Professor Wilson's attack, he's tweeting about other things too. Focus there.'

'*Pfff... OK, OK: I'll reconfigure the search.*'

'And soon as you've set it up, get your bum back to the station. We're not paying you to sit about talking nonsense with film people.'

'But physics isn't nonsense, it's—'

Logan thumbed the button again, hanging up on him.

Rennie smiled. 'Bet you're glad you got yourself a top-of-the-range Simon Rennie sidekick, now, aren't you?'

Swap one idiot for another.

'Get a lookout request set up for Councillor Matt Lansdale. Maybe he hasn't killed himself, maybe he's done a Reginald Perrin?'

'Already done it. Top-of-the-range, remember? Doubt we'll get anything back, though. After all, who cares about a disgraced middle-aged missing city councillor?' Rennie sniffed. 'Could be anywhere by now.'

Look at the state of this shitehole.

Haiden kicks a lump of plaster, sending it skittering away like a rat across the bare floorboards. A crappy old room, the lathe sticking out of the crumbling walls like bones. Peeling wallpaper, the ugly pattern lurking beneath blooms of fungus-black and mildew-grey. Childish crayon drawings of crude stick-figures humping. Two windows, with chunks of broken glass poking out of their frames like jagged teeth. Letting the sunlight slash in. Casting thick dark shadows.

Bet there's rats in here. Big ones.

The five dirty-white chest freezers make a line from the door, most of the way round the room, each one marked with red spray paint that's run and dripped like blood: 'THREE MONKEYS', 'THE DEVIL MAKES WORK', 'SPITE', 'JUDAS', and 'WALLACE'.

A little green light glints in the gloom as the compressor on 'THREE MONKEYS' kicks in again, humming away to itself. It's the only one that's turned on, cos there's no point wasting electricity, is there? Environmentally responsible and all that.

Streaks and splots of rusty brown stain the white plastic surface around the lid.

Should really clean that up, but sod it.

The chest freezer next to it has the same kinda stains, but no rattle and hum. Instead, the sound of sobbing jags out into the hot stale air. Ungrateful sod should be *thanking* him. He propped the lid open, didn't he? Wedged a bit of skirting board in there so there's a wee gap for air to get in.

OK, so there's a thick chain and heavy padlock stopping it from opening any further than about ten mill, but hey, it's better than nothing, right? Any wider and the rats might get in.

Fat bluebottles waltz through the gap, their heavy bodies glowing in the sunlight.

Haiden kicks 'THE DEVIL MAKES WORK' with the side of his boot, hard enough to rock the whole thing on its feet.

A cloud of the little buzzing fatsos erupt from the gap, accompanied by a muffled scream.

Better.

He takes off one of his gloves and stuffs it in his pocket, pulls out his phone instead – thumbing through to the camera app. Unlocks the padlock.

The chain hits the floorboards with a clattering rattle as he yanks the chest freezer's lid open.

More bluebottles, swarming up from what's left of the man inside, bringing with them the cloying scent of stale meat, sharp piss, and dirty-brown shite.

Haiden holds his phone out, filming as Professor Wanky Wilson cowers away from the light. Not nearly enough space for him to stretch out, so he's curled up on his side with his knees against his chest, wriggling around, onto his back.

Not so big now, is he? Lying there, bawling like a bairn, snot and tears all over his face, piss stains on his trousers, crap in his pants. Ankles and elbows tied with thick blue string. Bandages round the stumps of his wrists, darkened with dried and fresh blood.

Suppose it's no wonder he's shat himself.

Course, he's not wearing a blindfold, but he's got his bloodshot eyes screwed shut as he blubbers. 'Please! Please, I haven't seen *anything*! I can ... I can just go away, forget this ever happened. Please!'

Aye, right.

Haiden moves his phone closer, filling the screen with that terrified face.

'You don't have to do this! I'll do whatever you want!' A sob wracks him, making his chest jerk and spasm. The words short and breathless between tattered breaths. 'I'm ... sorry! Whatever ... I did, I'm ... I'm sorry! ... Please ... please let me ... go. ... PLEASE!'

No chance, pal.

Haiden slams the lid down again and inside, Professor Wanky Wilson screams.

Tough.

Doesn't take long to padlock the freezer again, making sure he doesn't get fingerprints on anything. Cos he's not stupid.

Then out – through the crappy hallway and into the fresh air.

Eyes closed, face turned to the warm sun.

Got to love summer...

Still, better get back to work.

He pulls the front door shut, all those brand-new Yales locking with a clunk. Leaves the crappy old house, with its second skin of ivy and brambles. Marches across what's left of the front garden – if you can call a collection of rambling broom, nettles, and gorse a garden – to the ancient white Nissan Micra that's parked next to a battered grey Transit. The van's paintwork filthy and streaked with rust.

Haiden pops open the Nissan's driver's door and digs out his phone again, turning the brightness up so the video is visible out here.

Wanky Wilson's voice crackles out of the phone's speaker. *'Please! Please, I haven't seen* anything! *I can ... I can just go away, forget this ever happened. Please!'*

He looks even smaller on the screen. More pathetic as he begs for his worthless lying little life.

'You don't have to do this! I'll do whatever you want!' Then the sobbing. *'I'm ... sorry! Whatever ... I did, I'm ... I'm sorry! ... Please ... please let me ... go. ... PLEASE!'*

139

Perfect.

Haiden nods. Smiles. Sticks his phone in his pocket. Gets in behind the wheel and pulls out onto the rutted track.

Wanky Wilson's about to go viral, and it serves him bloody right.

— sins of the father, sins of the son —

16

The word *'Enter'* grudged itself out through the wood.

Logan let himself into Hardie's office.

The room had probably been designed to give an authoritative air of efficiency and probity, with its six filing cabinets, six whiteboards covered in ongoing cases, a top-spec computer, and a portrait of the Queen, but it came off a bit ... sad instead. Lacking in character. Oh, he'd added some personal touches – a couple of citations, three or four photos of Hardie with various bigwigs... But they always seemed staged and uncomfortable, as if they were trying very hard to remember his name and whether or not he owed them money.

King glanced over his shoulder from one of the visitors' chairs, wearing that same uncomfortable look. He gave Logan a quick grimace, then faced front again. Sitting in the other chair, Jane McGrath *humphed* at him.

Logan nodded at the florid-faced Hardie, sat behind his desk like an angry toad. 'You wanted to see me, Boss?'

Mr Toad glowered. 'Where have you been?'

'Following up some leads.'

'How am I supposed to strategise for this sodding press conference with you off gallivanting? You're meant to be *supporting* this investigation.'

Tosser.

'That's exactly what I *am* doing.' Logan closed the door and leaned against it. 'So go on then: "strategise".'

Hardie pointed at Jane. 'Well?'

She folded her arms. 'We need to get our statement out about DI King's involvement with his terrorist cell.'

'It wasn't a terrorist cell!' King turned to face her. 'And I *wasn't* involved, I went to a couple of meetings to impress a girl. That's all.'

'I still can't figure out why the *Scottish Daily Post* didn't expose you yesterday ... but I can assure you they're going to do it today. We need to break this before they do. Steal their thunder.'

Logan made a rocking gesture with one hand. 'Maybe. But I don't think Barwell's going to drop that bomb today.'

They all stared at him as if he'd grown horns.

Then Hardie put on a speaking-to-stupid-people voice. 'Professor Wilson's hands turned up in the post, Logan.' He held his own up and wiggled the fingers. 'His *hands*.'

'Yes, but we've got a suspect: we've got CCTV footage of the man who posted the hands to the BBC. We're making progress.'

Jane sighed. 'That doesn't change—'

'If you're Edward Barwell, when are you going to put the boot in: when the investigation's making progress, or when it's stalling? Because all investigations stall at some point, we all *know* that. It's how things work.'

She nodded at Hardie. 'Even more reason to get it out there now, while we're on top of the news cycle – not being buried by it.'

'Hmmm...' Mr Toad steepled his fingers. 'Detective Inspector King?'

'I didn't *do* anything.'

Logan shifted against the door. 'We're trying to find out who this guy is, but it wouldn't hurt to put out his picture and an appeal for witnesses.'

'Witnesses?' Jane scowled at him. 'Now you're just changing the subject!'

'Exactly.'

There was silence as, hopefully, they let that sink in.

Then Hardie sat back in his chair. 'You said you were following up leads. What leads?'

'I've got Tufty trying to ID whoever sent that first tweet, and Rennie and I have been looking into Councillor Matt Lansdale's disappearance. See if it's linked to Professor Wilson's.'

'And is it?'

'No. Lansdale's divorced, disgraced, and depressed. Chances are he's either embezzled council cash and done a runner, or tried to end his own life. Maybe succeeded, but the body's not turned up yet.'

'Hmm...' Obviously not convinced.

'There's no sign of a struggle at his flat – no forced entry, no blood – and if he'd been abducted, his hands would've turned up in the post by now, wouldn't they? Professor Wilson's did.'

Jane poked Hardie's desk. 'This doesn't help us with the current news cycle.'

'No, but it means we can eliminate him from our inquiries and journalists can stop asking stupid questions that make us look like idiots for not considering it.'

Silence, as Hardie swivelled in his chair. Then he nodded. 'We keep our statement about DI King in reserve for now. But at the very first sign of things "stalling", you tell me and we release it, understand?' He pointed at Logan and King. 'Understand?'

'Totally.'

'Yes.'

'Good.' Hardie checked his watch. 'It's three oh seven. Press briefing is at four. And if either of you even *thinks* about disappearing off on a sudden "urgent mission" I'll slap a formal complaint on your record before you're halfway out the door.' He jabbed a finger at the door. 'Now go. Do something useful.'

The canteen's dishwasher chugged and churned away to itself, the only other sound coming from the vending machine as a spotty support officer got it to give up a can of Irn-Bru. *Buzzzzz, clang, rattle. Tsssssst. Glug, glug, glug. Belch*. Then she gave Logan and King a wave, before sloping her way out of the canteen again.

King folded over his wax-paper cup of coffee and puffed out his cheeks. 'You would've thought he'd be happy, wouldn't you? We've got a suspect. On camera!'

Logan shrugged. 'That's what happens when you climb the greasy ladder – every rung is slick with politics and blame and potential career-ending slip-ups. Not saying that's an excuse, mind.' He took a sip. 'Where do you want to start?'

'Urgh...' King stood. 'Suppose we should check on the idiots interviewing Professor Wilson's colleagues.'

'Probably.' Logan followed him out into the stairwell. 'Maybe we'll get lucky and they've already talked to our Jiffy-bag posting scumbag?'

King grunted. Shook his head. 'When do I *ever* get lucky? I tell you, it's—' His phone launched into 'Fairytale of New York' and his whole body caved in on itself, as if someone had let the air out of him. Shane MacGowan's booze-soaked voice echoed in the stairwell.

'You going to get that?'

'Gah...' He yanked his phone out. 'WHAT? ... No, I don't have to, Gwen. I don't have to at all. You lost that privilege when—' He turned away from Logan. 'Over my dead body!'

The sound of feet clattered down the stairs from somewhere above.

'No, Gwen, *you* listen to *me* for a change: I paid for that flat and you— ... Oh for God's sake.'

The feet got louder.

'You know what? I don't *care* what your friends say.'

Rennie burst around the corner, battering towards them from the floor above, clutching a file to his chest, pink cheeked, a big grin on his face, eyes wide. 'We got him, we got him, we got him!'

Logan stared. 'No.'

King turned. Lowered the phone. 'Sergeant Rennie, did you just say what I think you said?'

'We got him.'

'YES!' King poked at his phone's screen, then stuffed it in his pocket. 'Where?'

'Ah... Not *"got him"*, got him, but we know who he is. A sergeant from Highland and Islands called – recognised the guy in the hoodie from that video we sent out.'

Silence.

Logan hit him. 'Any chance you could actually tell us?'

'Our boy's one Haiden Lochhead, twenty-six, Aquarius.' Rennie held up the file. 'Form for assault, drugs, robbery, and demanding money with menaces. And he's on the lam – ram-raided a jewellery shop in Elgin, got six years. Did a runner from the work placement programme a month ago.' Eyebrows up. 'And get this: his dad? *World-famous*, violent, independence-at-any-cost dickhead, Gareth "Gaelic Gary" Lochhead!'

King frowned. Leaned back against the wall. 'Like father, like son.'

And finally they had somewhere to start looking.

If Haiden Lochhead's dad was a violent Alt-Nat tosser, maybe King was right. Maybe Haiden was just carrying on the family business?

Logan pointed. 'Rennie: get a lookout—'

'Already got one. Kinda redundant as our Haiden's on a recall order, but "a belt-an'-braces stop yir brikks fae fa'in doon", as my dear old nan used to say.'

King had his phone out again. 'What about Gaelic Gary?'

Rennie reached into his folder and produced a sheet of paper with a magician's flourish. 'One address. For I am a top-of-the-range sidekick, remember?'

King grabbed it. 'Get a car, we can—'

'No.' Logan dug his keys from his pocket. 'We'll take mine it'll be...' The media briefing. Four o'clock. Sodding hell. 'We *can't*. Press conference is in twenty-three minutes. You heard Hardie.'

King doubled over and strangled a scream.

Couldn't blame him.

Logan poked Rennie. 'Get on the grapevine – I want everything you can find about Haiden Lochhead: last-known address, acquaintances, access to property, past associates, everything. Talk to whoever did him for the ram-raid, his CJ social worker, and anyone else you can think of. And do the same for his dad too.'

'Guv.' Rennie turned tail and scurried away up the stairs.

'HOY! LEAVE THE FILE, YOU TWIT!'

'Oops.' He scurried down again. 'Sorry.' Handed it over. Pulled a face. Then set off on scurry number three.

Swear that lad had been dropped on his head when he was wee. Several times.

Logan opened the folder: printouts and forms with a single photo lurking behind everything else. A mugshot from Peterhead police station, going by the ID number on the magnetic board Haiden Lochhead was holding, complete with his full name and the date. *Definitely* the same man from the security footage.

'Here.' Logan handed the photo to King. 'Think this'll put a smile on Hardie's face?'

'Let's go find out.'

The briefing room was packed, every seat in front of the dais stuffed full of journalists, the back of the room a dark forest of camera lenses. All of them staring at Hardie as he did his little turn. Which, thankfully, meant they weren't all looking at Logan, or King, or even Jane McGrath with her perfect makeup, hair, and suit. Her professional smile was a bit pained, though.

Someone had set up a projection screen behind the podium, showing off the Police Scotland logo as Hardie soldiered on. '... confirm that the human body parts delivered to the BBC Scotland offices this morning do belong to Professor Wilson.'

The hungry hordes shifted in their plastic chairs, licking their lips. Getting ready for the feeding frenzy. No wonder they called it a 'press pack', they looked desperate to separate someone off from the herd and tear them apart.

And knowing Logan's luck, it wouldn't be Detective Chief Inspector Hardie.

Look at him, sweating away up there on his hind legs, regurgitating the same bland nonsense they vomited out at every press conference: 'We are appealing for anyone who may have seen this individual to come forward.'

That mugshot of Haiden Lochhead, from Peterhead station, appeared on the screen behind him, but cropped so you couldn't see the board with his name on it.

The pack breathed in, tasting the air.

'If you do see him, do not approach him. Call nine-nine-nine.' Then Hardie nodded and sank back into his seat.

Jane stood. 'Thank you, Detective Chief Inspector.' She looked out at the salivating animals. 'Any questions?' A flurry of hands shot up and Jane pointed at one of them. 'Yes: Anne.'

A young woman with curly blonde hair lowered her hand. 'Anne Darlington, BBC. Do you have a name for the individual you want to talk to?

'We do, but we're not releasing it at this time. Donny?'

Donny looked as if he'd dressed in the dark, forgotten to shave, and might have died sometime in the last thirty-six hours. 'Donald Renlinson, *Scottish Independent Tribune*. DCI Hardie, is it true that Professor Wilson's disappearance is linked to that of sext-scandal councillor, Matt Lansdale?'

Hardie pulled up his chin. 'Our officers have looked into this and we can confirm that there's no connection between the two men. We are, however, concerned for Councillor Lansdale's safety and urge him to get in touch.'

And then Edward Barwell raised his hand, a smug smile on his smug face. It went with his smug haircut and Rupert Bear waistcoat. *Everyone* on the dais stared at him.

Jane cleared her throat and moved her finger somewhere less dangerous. 'Yes: Muriel.'

If being passed over bothered Barwell, he didn't show it. If anything, his smile got smugger.

Yeah, that wasn't a good sign.

'Muriel Kirk, BBC Radio Scotland.' She'd swapped her joggy bottoms and 'I RAN THE MELDRUM MARATHON!' T-shirt for a sober suit. 'There was a note with the hands, "The Devil makes work". Have you identified why the killer included it? What was the significance of sending Professor Wilson's hands to me at the studio?' Milking it.

King took that one: 'We think it was to gain as much media

attention as possible. So I think it's safe to say that you've helped him achieve his goal.'

Muriel narrowed her eyes at that. But before she could open her mouth, Jane's magic finger had moved on again:

'Yes: Phil.'

'Phil Patterson, Sky News.' Small and hairy, like someone had shrunk a Royal Navy Action Man in the wash, only without the baggy sailor suit. 'Can you tell us if this individual has killed before? Is he a danger to the public?'

'We can't comment on any previous convictions.'

Hardie nodded. 'But I would like to repeat – if you *see* him, do not *approach* him, call nine-nine-nine.'

Barwell still had his hand up.

Jane sighed. 'Edward?'

Here we go...

'Edward Barwell, *Scottish Daily Post*.' Dramatic pause. 'DCI Hardie, clearly the investigation is going well. Does this mean that Detective Inspector Frank King has your complete confidence and support?'

Silence from the table. Hardie shifted in his seat.

Yeah, because that didn't speak volumes, did it?

Barwell raised an eyebrow. 'Detective Chief Inspector?'

Logan poked his elbow into Hardie's side, hissing the words out the side of his mouth as quietly as possible. 'Say something!'

Pink flushed across Hardie's cheeks. '*All* my officers have my confidence and support, Mr Barwell. What a ridiculous question. Now, if you'll excuse us, we have an investigation to run.' He stood, motioning for Logan and King to join him as he marched away. Throwing a 'Thank you' over his shoulder at the assembled journalists.

Jane clapped her hands together. 'Thank you, everyone. See me after for photographs of the man we want to talk to.'

The squeal of seats scraping against the grey terrazzo floor filled the room as people got to their feet, conversations breaking out between the press pack, everyone staring at Logan and King and Hardie as they pushed through the door into the police-only part of the station again.

Soon as the door shut, Hardie curled his hands into fists, keeping his voice down, even though they were the only ones in the corridor. 'Bloody hell!'

Logan leaned against the wall. 'Not wanting to criticise, or anything, but there's no way they're not going read volumes into that big long pause.'

His cheeks darkened. 'Well what was I supposed to do?' Then Hardie stomped away a couple of paces, turned around and stomped back again. 'That wee shite Barwell was *playing* me! I don't signal my support, I'm undermining King and the investigation. I do and he can batter us about the head with it when he makes his big terrorist-cell reveal!'

King grimaced at the ceiling tiles. 'It wasn't a terrorist cell!'

Hardie stared at him. 'I think you're probably best keeping your mouth shut at this moment in time, don't you?' A deep breath. 'Logan, we need to find this Haiden Lochhead and we need to find him *now*. I'll free up more men. You can have an extra block of overtime, but – I – want – him – found!' And with that, Hardie stormed off, muttering to himself.

A uniformed PC stepped out from one of the doors further down the corridor, right in front of him.

Hardie threw his arms in the air. 'Out the bloody way!'

The PC flattened herself against the wall, forcing an ingratiating smile as Hardie stormed past and out through the doors at the far end. Soon as they'd slammed shut behind him, she turned to Logan and King, hooked a thumb at the closed door, and made a wanking gesture with her other hand.

Then her eyes went wide, presumably because she'd finally realised who Logan was, and making wanking gestures about senior officers was *probably* frowned upon by Professional Standards. 'Sorry.' She made herself scarce.

'Arrgh...' King covered his face with his hands. 'Hardie's right: it *was* a trap.'

Of course it was.

'Then let's finish this thing before he springs it.' Logan turned and marched off in the opposite direction to Hardie. Through the double doors and into the stairwell.

King followed him. At least, he did as far as the gents' toilet. Stopped outside with one hand on the door. 'I'll catch up. Nature calls.'

Nature, or the two half-bottles of vodka he bought in Westhill? Logan shook his head and kept walking.

17

North Anderson drive crawled past the Audi's windows. Half four and the rush hour was already in full swing. What the hell happened to people working till five o'clock? Lazy sods should still be hard at it, not clogging up the bloody road system.

Was going to take forever to get to Dyce at this rate.

King scowled out from the passenger seat, crunching his way through yet more extra-strong mints, his face a little pinker than it had been back at the station. Eyes a little pinker too. 'And you know what makes it even worse?'

Oh God, not this again.

'You've got to let it go, Frank, there's nothing you can do about it.'

'What makes it worse is that *now*, if we put out the statement, it'll look like we're only doing it because Edward Barwell's got us scared.'

They crept forward another car's length.

'He *has* got us scared.'

'That's not the point, he's—' The opening bars from 'Fairytale of New York' burst out of King's pocket and he bared his teeth. Let the song belt out for a bit. Then sighed and answered it. 'Gwen.' He screwed his face closed, one hand coming up to cover his eyes. 'Oh you have got to be *kidding* me. ... No. ... No, I didn't. ... Because I didn't.'

Yeah, it wasn't easy pretending not to listen in, because what else was Logan supposed to do – get out and walk?

Mind you, might be quicker than sitting in rush-hour sodding traffic.

Anyway, don't look at him. Eyes on the road.

'For God's sake, Gwen, I'm at work! ... No! ...' Getting louder. 'You know what? I'm not the one having the bloody affair, that's why!' He jerked the phone from his ear and hammered his finger into the screen. Slammed the phone down on the seat between his legs. Fumed at the passenger window.

She was having an affair. Well that explained all the angry phone calls.

Logan kept his voice neutral. 'You want to talk about it?'

Please say no. Please say no. Please say—

'No I sodding don't.'

Phew.

The car crawled forward another couple of lengths. Six more and they'd get their turn at the Horrible Haudagain Roundabout.

King rolled his shoulders. 'She's sleeping with someone at work. And not someone at *her* work, someone at *mine*. Which she takes great bloody pleasure telling me at every bloody opportunity.'

Ooh... Ouch.

'Any normal woman would run off and be with lover boy, but apparently that's not vicious enough for her!' He smacked a fist down on his leg. 'No, it's *much* more fun to call me up every five minutes and jab it in my face.'

'Do you know who she's—'

'I don't know and I don't care. Whoever they are, they're welcome to her.'

Fair enough.

According to the sign out front, Ravendale Sheltered Living Facility was 'A HOME FROM HOME, WHEN PEOPLE NEED A HELPING HAND'. With its bland grey-and-brown blockwork and patches of beige harling, it looked more like a cross between a primary school and a bus station. The car park was 'surprisingly' free of cars, as if the residents' relatives didn't actually *need* to visit, because, you know, it wouldn't do to interfere...

Logan pulled into a parking space as far away from the handful of other vehicles as possible. No point risking someone scratching his Audi's bodywork with a carelessly opened door. That was the thing about car parks – people turned into animals.

He pulled on the handbrake, killed the engine, grabbed his peaked cap and Rennie's file, then climbed out into the roasting sunshine. Within two breaths, sweat prickled across his shoulders, the heat grabbing at his lungs.

All that time spent moaning about last winter and all the ice. Could do with some of that now. Be nice to feel a bit less like a sodding ready meal.

He closed his door as King got out.

'You OK to do this?'

King didn't look at him. 'I'm *fine*.'

Aye, right.

'Because I can easily—'

'I said I'm fine!' And he marched off, across the car park to the reception doors. Yanking them open and barging inside.

Great.

Logan puffed out a long breath, grimaced, then followed him.

Ravendale's reception area was every bit as bland as its exterior, only with more pot plants. The sound of some moronic game show oozed out through an archway marked 'RESIDENTS LOUNGE', showing a woeful ignorance of the possessive apostrophe. Someone else that looked as if they suffered from the same affliction sat behind the reception desk. Bland and grey, like the room, in a baggy cardigan and a comb-over that wasn't fooling anyone but its owner.

He looked up and smiled a denture-perfect smile. 'Welcome to Ravendale. How can I—'

King slapped his warrant card on the desk. 'I need to speak to Gary Lochhead.'

Captain Comb-Over spluttered and fidgeted for a bit, squinting down at the ID. Then, 'Ah. Right.' He pulled on a pair of glasses and peered at it. 'He'll probably be in the residents' lounge, so...' His mouth closed with a plastic-on-plastic click as King marched off. 'Oh, you're going to see yourself there. Right.'

Logan gave Captain Comb-Over an apologetic wave and followed King into the residents' lounge.

They'd clearly tried to tart the place up, make it homely and welcoming, but it hadn't really worked. Horrible paintings besmirched the magnolia walls, created by someone with about as much artistic talent as a drunken horse. A beige carpet, mottled with stains. Dusty plastic pot plants. A ceiling-mounted projector casting a slightly fuzzy game show onto one wall, the red and green not really lining up the way they should – subtitles barely legible. The cloying scent of air freshener trying to cover something sharp and yellow. The unmistakable hot wintergreen scent of Ralgex chewing at the edges.

About two dozen residents were more or less present, none of them a day under eighty-five. Some trembling away in wheelchairs, others hooked up to oxygen tanks and/or drips, bags dangling from their chair frames. A woman in the corner was busying herself at an easel, daubing it with oil paint, no doubt producing another 'masterpiece' for the lounge's walls. A bald man weeping into his knitting. A balding woman shouting the answers at the fuzzy projected contestants. 'Lusitania, you moron! Lusitania!'

King raised his voice over hers, 'Gary Lochhead?'

The woman committing art crimes waved at them, then pointed her brush at a hunched figure in an electric wheelchair parked over by the windows, his back to the room.

King marched over. 'You Gary Lochhead?'

No reply.

Logan joined them, looking out across the road, through the chain-link-and-razor-wire fence at the gubbins of Aberdeen Airport. On the far side of the runways, the control tower was barely visible. A big orange 737 taxied past in the middle distance.

He put a hand on the old man's shoulder. 'Gary? We need to talk to you about Haiden.'

A tremor ran through the saggy skin as Gary Lochhead turned

156

his face towards Logan. He'd been a big lad, once, you could see that in the length of his limbs and span of his shoulders, but the arms and legs had withered to sticks, his chest and stomach swollen up so they poked out of his dressing gown. Surgical support stockings. Baldy head playing host to a couple of white tufts in need of a trim. He blinked at Logan, the oxygen line taped to his nose shifting as his dry lips twitched. When the words appeared, they were strangely high and effeminate. 'You want to talk about Haiden?'

Logan nodded. 'Yes.'

'Then you can sod right off, can't you?'

King pulled out his warrant card again. '*Police.*'

'Yeah, believe it or not, your big-eared mate's uniform was kinda the giveaway there.' His throat twitched, his face darkened, then a gargling cough rattled his whole body, shaking it back and forth as he hacked away. Then spat something dark into a handkerchief, clutched in one shaking liver-spotted hand. Emerging breathless at the other end. 'I don't ... know ... where ... he is. ... I don't know ... what he's doing. ... And I don't ... care.' Sagging into his chair.

Logan tried for supportive and understanding. 'He's your *son.*'

'Tell *him* that. Ungrateful wee sod's never been to see me. Not in prison, not here.' The other hand came up, curled into an arthritic claw. 'Far as I'm concerned, Haiden can go to hell and stay there. And so can you.'

King opened his mouth, but Logan shook his head at him and he shut it again.

Gary Lochhead glowered out at the 737 as it pulled away and roared up into the bright blue sky. 'Eighteen years I was banged up. Eighteen years for what?'

'You executed a property developer in the Inverness Asda car park.'

Gary waved that away with his claw. 'He wanted planning permission to build three hundred houses at the Peel of Lumphanan. Bloody cultural vandalism.'

Nope, no idea. And going by the expression on King's face, he didn't know either.

A sigh as Gary looked at them in turn. 'It was where Macbeth died, you ignorant tossers. The real one, not the regicidal monster from Shakespeare's play – lying Tudor propaganda-spreading bastard. It's part of our cultural *birthright*, and they were going to build three hundred houses on it?' He curled his lip. 'That's the trouble with you kids today: you don't learn your country's history. It's all World War One poetry and crop rotation in the sixteenth bloody century. You know why? Because the *English* control the curriculum and they don't want you to know we used to be a proud, independent nation!'

He jabbed at his wheelchair's controls, sending it lurching around through 180 degrees, then whirrrrring off towards the exit at a sedate walking pace.

They followed him.

Logan checked Rennie's file. 'What about that heist in Edinburgh? Two point six million in gold bullion, you and your mates got away with, wasn't it?'

A smile. 'No idea what you're on about. I was never charged with that and neither was anyone else.' The smile grew. '*Shame.*'

The old man with the knitting lowered his needles and embarked on a maudlin tune in a thin wobbly baritone. 'Oh my love is lost to me, my heart is nevermore…' Then trailed away into silent tears again.

Logan cleared his throat. 'Would you say Haiden was a bright lad, Gary?'

The wheelchair came to a sudden halt. 'With the amount of weed his mother smoked when she was pregnant with him?' Another bout of coughing left him gasping. 'Look … at this … hovel. … Four months … to live … and *this* is where … they stick me. … What's compassionate … about that?'

King looked across Gary's bald head. 'This is a waste of time.'

'Wait a minute.' Gary Lochhead narrowed his eyes, squinting up at King. 'Do I *know* you? You look … familiar. And I never forget a—'

'I'LL KILL YOU!' An older man in a blue cardigan launched himself across the lounge at the crying knitter, fists swinging. He battered into him, tipping Knitter's chair over backwards, the pair of them hitting the beige carpet in a barrage of snarling. Balding pates shining in the sunlight as they punched and bit and kicked. Hard and fast.

The woman with the paintbrush screamed.

Logan snapped his mouth closed and charged over. 'STOP! POLICE!'

King was faster, launching himself into the melee, grunting as a cardiganed elbow caught him in the face. Logan grabbed Knitter, pulling him away – still kicking and screaming.

'YOU'RE AN ARSEHOLE, BILL! YOU'VE ALWAYS BEEN AN ARSEHOLE!' Blood popping from his split lip and scarlet mouth.

'YOU STAY AWAY FROM MY ZOE!' Cardigan struggled in King's grip, lashing out with a foot – the slipper on the end flying off to bounce in the middle of an out-of-focus gameshow contestant.

'Enough!' King hauled Cardigan away.

Two burly women in pink scrubs burst in through the archway, the pair of them looking as if they could probably bench-press Logan's Audi.

The bigger of the two pointed at Cardigan. 'Mr Barnes! What have we told you about attacking Mr Foster?'

And at that, Knitter went limp and dissolved in tears once more.

Cardigan looked around, frowning. As if trying to work out where he was.

The nurses led the pair of them away.

Gary Lochhead shook his head. 'Silly sods. They're at it two, three times a week. Fighting over a woman who's been dead twenty years. That's dementia for you.' He started his wheelchair up again, following them out through the archway.

Left, past reception and into a bland corridor lined with beige doors that matched the beige linoleum. Plaques on every door with things like, 'Mrs S Blake ~ "The Laurels"' and 'Mr H Pearson ~ "Duntaxin"' on them. More horrible oil paintings.

Logan caught up with the wheelchair. 'It's really important we talk to Haiden, Gary. Any help you can—'

'What's he done?'

'Sorry?'

'You wouldn't be here if he hadn't—' Another coughing fit wracked that barrel chest. 'What's ... he ... done?' Lochhead howched up something brown and spat it into his handkerchief. 'You know ... what? ... Don't ... care.'

He turned his wheelchair hard right, bumping open a door marked, 'Mr G Lochhead ~ "Saor Alba"'.

The room was small but clean, the open blinds flooding the room with light. A hospital bed took up most of the available space, leaving just enough for a couple of plastic visitors' chairs and a tiny bedside locker. A wilting bunch of flowers sitting on top.

A big oil painting had pride of place on the wall opposite the bed. Big. At least four foot across, maybe more: a recumbent stone circle, surrounded by pine trees, in vibrant tones of green and blue and purple. And about a million times more accomplished than the rubbish hanging outside in the corridor and residents' lounge.

Lochhead's wheelchair buzzed to a halt in front of the window, so he could scowl out at another view of Aberdeen Airport's back end.

Logan stared at the painting. The more he looked at it, the better it got. The texture in the brushstrokes, the way the light dappled the trees, the subtle shades and forms... 'Don't think I know that stone circle, but the colours are—'

'If you're thinking we'll bond over art appreciation, you can save it.' Lochhead whacked the arm of his wheelchair with his claw. 'Yes, I painted it. No, I don't want to be your friend. No, I don't trust you.'

Logan pointed. '*You* painted this?'

'The only good thing about doing sixteen years is Barlinnie's got an excellent arts programme and there's plenty of time to practise.' The claw came up again, trembling in a small circle. 'Now go away. I haven't seen Haiden and I don't want to.'

King prodded at his left cheek, the skin already beginning to swell where Cardigan's elbow had made contact. 'He's involved in the abduction of someone from Aberdeen University.'

Silence.

Then Lochhead turned his wheelchair around, a smile pulling at his sallow cheeks. 'It's that prick Wilson, isn't it? The professor with the hacked-off hands?'

'It's vital we speak to—'

'Haiden did that? Good.' His voice swelled with pride. 'Might be some hope for the wee shite, yet.' Followed by a hacking laugh. 'You can bugger off then. Even if I knew anything, no way I'd tell you now.' Lochhead's wheelchair burrrred around to face the window again.

Their audience was over.

18

After the relative cool of the care home, the car park outside was like being wrapped in a freshly boiled duvet. Sunlight jabbed back from car windscreens; Logan pulled on his peaked cap, but it didn't really make much difference.

Gah... Whose bright idea was it to ditch the white shirts for black T-shirts? Did they all sit around trying to decide how to make life worse for police officers? Bet they were the ones responsible for the official-issue itchy trousers, too.

King loosened his tie. 'Well that was a waste of sodding time.'

'Look on the bright side – we've got a new mystery.'

'We've got bugger all.' He pulled out his mobile.

'If Haiden's as thick as his dad thinks, how come he managed to abduct Professor Wilson without leaving a single forensic trace? How did he manage to hack off, package, and post Wilson's hands to the BBC and not get a single bit of his own DNA on any of it?'

'He got caught on CCTV at the shopping centre, so he's not that bright.'

'Yes, but the camera he got caught on was only installed the *day before*. I'll bet he chose that route to the Post Office because he'd scoped it out in advance. That sound like a moron to you? He's methodical. He's planned all this out.'

But King wasn't listening, he was wandering off, phone to

his ear. 'Milky? Where are we with that lookout request? ... Come on, I *said* I was sorry, didn't I? ... No, I *don't* want to drive the English out of Scotland, I just want to know where we are with the lookout request. ... Uh-huh. ... Uh-huh.'

A familiar gravelly voice growled out behind Logan. 'Speaking of "morons".'

Steel was lounging against someone's Range Rover, her jacket draped over the bonnet, rolled-up shirtsleeves showing off the kind of pasty white flesh only achievable after *many* generations of Scottish ancestors. She licked a dribble from the side of what looked like a strawberry Mivvi.

'What are you doing here?'

She took a big bite. 'Might be playing hookie and eating iced lollies. Or I might be using some of that world-renowned initiative of mine.'

One of those hessian bag-for-lifes sat open at her feet.

Logan peered at it. 'Got any more lollies?'

Steel reached into her bag and pulled out a box of six. Sooked the last chunk off her lolly stick and pinged it in through the Range Rover's open sunroof. 'Depends.'

Typical. He pulled on his most deadpan of voices. 'Oh, do *pray* demonstrate the fruits of your world-renowned initiative, Detective Sergeant.'

'That's more like it.' She unwrapped a blackcurrant one – already starting to sag in the heat. 'Haiden Lochhead was done for ram-raiding a jeweller's shop in Elgin, right? Do you know why he did it?'

'The money.'

'You know that statue of the Duke of Sutherland the Alt-Nats are always moaning about? A *teeny-weeny* birdy tells me he was after buying an arse-load of explosives to blow it up. Never came out at the trial, shock horror.'

'Then how do *you* know?'

'Initiative.' She took a big bite, getting purple melt on her chin. 'I called up HMP Grampian and spoke to one of Haiden's cellblock buddies. Seems the wee turd was forever banging on about how much he hated the English.'

'And, let me guess: your teeny-weeny birdy didn't like that. Because he was English?'

Steel smiled and held out the box. 'Good boy. You may have a lolly.'

'Ta.' He took one and unwrapped it. The pineapple coating was melting, but the ice cream inside was still cold and delicious. 'And did Teeny-Weeny Tweetie Pie say anything else interesting?'

'Oh yes. He said our boy Haiden had a regular visitor.'

King reappeared, no sign of his phone. 'Who had a regular visitor?' He stopped and frowned at Steel as she sooked an escaped dribble from her forearm. 'Why are you here? Thought I gave you work to do!'

'Well, if you don't want me using my initiative...' She dumped the lolly box in her bag-for-life and sauntered off. 'Give my regards to DCI Hardie, next time you see him.'

King made a worried face at Logan, then hurried after her. 'OK, OK, I'm sorry. Tell me about this visitor.'

She grinned at him. 'We'll take Laz's car.'

Vast swathes of brittle-looking barley spread out on either side of the Audi as Logan hammered up the A90. Steel slouched in the passenger seat, picking at her teeth with a scarlet fingernail.

King leaned through from the back. 'You know what bugs me?'

She pulled her finger out. 'Tough: I called shotgun.' Then went in for another dig.

'*No*. What *bugs* me is that we've not had a ransom note. "The Devil Makes Work" doesn't count – where are the demands?'

True.

Logan accelerated, pulling out to overtake a milk lorry on a lovely long straight bit of road. 'Maybe he doesn't want anything.'

'Of course he *wants* something. Everyone wants something. He didn't abduct Professor Wilson for fun.'

Steel gave up on her molars. 'Hate to say it, but I think

164

Kingy's right: our boy wants something. It's just not something we can give him.'

That was true too.

Logan pulled into the left-hand lane again. 'I know we can't negotiate with—'

Steel reached across the car and punched Logan on the arm. 'Don't be *damp*. I'm no' meaning that. He's an Alt-Nat-Nut, right? What he wants is to punish the English for being English. He wants his wee campaign to be on the news. He wants English people worrying they might be next. He wants fear.'

'He's not doing too badly, then. And stop hitting people.'

'There won't be a ransom note, because he doesn't need one to get what he's after, he just needs to do horrible things and for everyone to talk about it.'

King nodded. 'Which is why he sent Professor Wilson's hands to the BBC.'

'Aye.' She stuck her finger in for another rummage, the words coming out all misshapen and slushy: 'So the real question is: what bit is he going to send next?'

Logan pulled the Audi into a space in the far corner. The car park was bounded on one side by the high stone wall that enclosed the old Victorian lump of Peterhead Prison. A much higher metal barrier ran along the opposite side, surrounding the newer HMP Grampian, which looked more like a secondary school than a state-of-the-art penal institution.

Good view from here, though. Well, as long as you enjoyed supply boats, warehouses, a patch of scabby grass and the North Sea. Which, today, was a deep shade of sparkling sapphire, beneath a lid of glowing blue.

Steel sniffed. 'Could you have parked further away from the entrance if you tried?'

Nope.

'Walk will do you good.' He grabbed his peaked cap and climbed out into the roasting heat. You'd think there'd be a sea breeze or something to cut it down a bit, but it was stifling.

Like wading through burning treacle. Which the car park tarmac was beginning to resemble.

It *screlched* beneath his feet as he marched towards the entrance, Steel and King lumbering along behind him.

'Urgh...' She caught up, both arms held out from her sides. 'Going to be Sweat Central under my boobs in five, four, three... Oh there it is.'

King grimaced. 'Do you *have* to?'

Logan shuddered. '*Please* don't talk about your breasts in the prison. People here are suffering enough.'

'Cheeky sod.'

The entrance was a huge wall of tinted glass, with 'HMP & YOI GRAMPIAN' in white letters above it. Very grand. The main door slid open and a young man wheeled a pushchair out into the glaring sunlight. He had tattoos up his neck, a spider's web by his eye, bruising all over his face, a toddler in the chair and a three-year-old on reins. Sniffling back tears as he marched past them.

Logan turned to watch him go. Then stepped through into the blissful embrace of air conditioning.

The reception area was double height, complete with balcony, a waiting room off to one side, a bank of lockers, a wooden-slatted desk like the prow of a square ship flanked by matching pairs of turnstiles, airport-security-style X-ray machines, and metal-detecting arches. One set marked 'STAFF', the other 'VISITORS'. Two prison officers sat behind the desk: an angular woman reading a manual, while her lumpy male colleague slurped tea from a 'WORLD'S SEXIEST GRANDAD' mug.

A tall thin man leaned against the 'STAFF' turnstile – pastel-yellow shirt, dark-blue tie, grey suit trousers and unbelievably shiny shoes – smiling as he walked towards Logan and his dysfunctional little team. There was something weirdly cat-like about him. Maybe it was the almond-shaped green eyes, or maybe it was the pointy sharp-toothed smile. Hopefully he'd leave off purring and licking his own bum until they'd gone.

He stuck his paw out for shaking. 'Inspector McRae? Daniel

Sabre, *such* a pleasure. I followed your story in the papers – I hope you're feeling better now?'

'This is DI King and DS Steel.'

Sabre let go of Logan's hand and took Steel's instead. 'Yes, we spoke on the phone.' He did the same with King, then turned and gestured towards the metal detectors. 'Shall we? I just need you to empty your pockets for security first...'

The Main Street rang with the sound of prisoners moving from one part of HMP Grampian to the other. A clattery rabble of men in their uniform blue sweatshirts and navy joggy bottoms slouched past on the lower level – Sabre leaned over the safety rail and waved. 'Archie!'

A spotty man with a cratered face and Incredible Hulk muscles stopped and looked up at them. Raised a hand of his own. 'Mr Sabre?'

'Congratulations on your National Five English! Very proud of you.'

A big grin. 'Cheers, Mr Sabre.'

They kept going, past a couple of inmates touching up scuff marks on the walls with lime-green paint.

Sabre shook his head at Logan. 'Haiden's disappearance was completely unexpected – which, I know, goes without saying. If we'd expected him to run off we wouldn't have allowed him out on work placement. But still...' He waved at a wee scrote with one leg in a cast hobbling along on a pair of crutches. 'Afternoon, Jimmy, how's the leg?'

'Aye, no' bad, Mr Sabre. Itchy, like.'

And they were past.

'What's worse is that Haiden had been doing so *well* up to that point. Model resident, never on a charge, went through the in-house catering programme with flying colours. Could whip up a broccoli-cheese soufflé you'd give your mother's ears for.' Sabre shook his head. 'We got him on a work programme – three days learning how to make pies and pasties at a local baker's – and boom: disappears through a back window. No trace.'

Sabre led them off the Main Street into a more modest corridor. Through a security door. 'To be honest, I was shocked Haiden could even *fit* through the window. Like many of our offenders, he spent most of his spare time in the gym, bulking up. Came in a twelve-stone weakling, went out looking like Arnold Schwarzenegger.'

Another corridor, this one a plain magnolia.

'What's *really* strange is he'd made it halfway through his six-year sentence without a single incident. He was eligible for early release on licence in September – that's why he was on the bakery programme – so why throw it all away for the sake of six weeks?'

Maybe he found out about his dad dying of lung cancer?

But then, Gary Lochhead said Haiden hadn't visited him in years. Not in prison, not in Ravendale.

Assuming "Gaelic Gary" Lochhead was telling the truth.

Have to get someone to look into that.

One last turn and they stood in front of a closed office door. 'This is us.' Mr Sabre unlocked it and ushered them inside.

A medium-sized room, with two desks against opposite walls. The ubiquitous filing cabinets. One motivational poster with a mountain top and 'TAKE IT ONE STEP AT A TIME AND YOU CAN SCALE ANY PEAK!' on it, and another with a kitten in a teacup: 'YOU'RE DOING GRRRRREAT!'

Wankity, wank, wank, wank.

The window overlooked the exercise yard, where a trio of topless inmates were picking up litter in the sunshine. Arms, chests, and backs turning an angry shade of scarlet.

Sabre pointed at a couple of ratty plastic chairs. 'Sit, sit.' He pulled out a swivel chair and parked himself on it as King and Steel sank into the creaky plastic ones. Smiled. 'Now, you wanted to know about Haiden's visitors. I checked the logs and, other than his Criminal Justice Social Worker, only five people have come to see him since he arrived here.' A photo appeared from Sabre's in-tray. He handed it to Logan – a smiling wrinkled face, with bright-yellow hair and a two-inch line of grey roots. 'One was old Mrs Hogarth – she likes to adopt a different offender every year. Knits them things. Comes in once a month. Between you and me, she's been lonely since her husband died.'

Another photo – this one a boot-faced woman in her mid-twenties, red hair pulled back from her face in a punishing ponytail. A big wide face and ruddy complexion, scowling at the camera as if the photographer had just insulted her dad's tractor. A proper farmer's quine – big and bracing. 'Haiden's wife and son visit from time to time, though, to be honest, they act more like complete strangers than family.'

Photo number three: An old man with very little hair on the top of his head, but lots poking out of his nose and ears. 'He's an ex-teacher of Haiden's. Comes here every couple of months to express his disappointment at the way Haiden turned out.'

Strange.

Logan frowned down at Captain Hairy Nostrils. 'Why did Haiden put up with that?'

'Said something about it "only being fair". No idea why, though.' Sabre dug out a young woman. The word 'mousy' could've been invented specially for her. Dishwater-blonde hair, glasses, grey cardigan, a crucifix on a chain, not making eye-contact with the camera, but looking off to one side with worried little creases between her pale eyebrows. If Haiden's ex was angry at everything, this one was scared of it. 'By far Haiden's most frequent visitor: Mhari Canonach Powell. That's "Mhari" spelled the Gaelic way. She was here once, sometimes twice a week.'

Steel leaned forward in her chair, making it creak. 'Bit of a mouthful.' She snatched the photo from Logan's hands. 'I'm all for playing Kinky Librarian and the Overdue Book, but there are limits, eh? Mind you,' she nudged King in the ribs, 'bet she's a *filthy* minx when she lets herself go. That sort always is.'

Mr Sabre retrieved the photo. 'Quite. I took the liberty of calling up the security footage from her last visit before Haiden disappeared.' He fiddled with his computer, setting a video playing on the screen, then scooted his chair to one side so they could get a better look.

The camera must've been ceiling mounted, going by the angle, looking down on a small round table, with four chairs arranged around it. Haiden was facing the camera, staring straight across at his visitor as if he was a starving Labrador and she was a whole packet of pork-and-stilton sausages. Mhari Canonach Powell's pale-beige hair hung in a veil in front of her face, and she tucked it behind her ears before lunging forward to snog the living hell out of Haiden. Full-on face-eating snogged him.

Steel grinned. 'Told you: Julie Andrews in the streets, Stormy Daniels in the sheets.'

Then a prison officer moved in to break it up, making them sit in their respective seats.

Sabre pointed as Mhari composed herself again. 'It's the oldest trick in the inmate handbook. Significant other pays a visit, concealing drugs about their person. Passes it over during a passionate kiss, and the offender either swallows it or palms it – hand into the pants, and up his, or her, bum it goes for retrieval later.'

Steel winked at King. 'That's called "cheeking" in polite society.'

'Only, every time we strip-searched Haiden, he was clean. They weren't passing contraband, it *genuinely* was just kissing.' A shrug. 'Now that might not seem like a big deal to you, but I've lost count of the number of mother-son tonguing sessions we see on a weekly basis. So it rather stood out.'

King produced a Police Scotland business card and snapped it onto Sabre's desk. 'Can you email that footage to me?'

'Of course.' He pocketed the card. 'Now, is there anything else we can help you with? At HMP Grampian we believe in—'

'Fairytale of New York' blared out of King's pocket. 'Oh for God's sake, what now?'

Sabre stared at him, mouth pinched. 'You're not supposed to have that in here: *all* phones have to be left at reception. I told you that when we came through security!'

'Sorry. Sorry.' He dug it out and killed the call. 'I didn't mean to—'

'We take security *very* seriously here! It's a *prison*.' Voice cold and aloof, nothing like the man who'd congratulated Archie on achieving a National 5.

King put his phone away, pink rushing up his cheeks. 'I must've grabbed it from the tray after the X-ray machine. Force of habit.' A pained smile and a shrug. 'Sorry.'

Logan tried hard not to sigh. 'Do you have an address for Mhari?'

Sabre produced a sheet of A4 from his in-tray. 'I took the liberty of listing everyone's addresses from the visitors' book.' He gave the printout to Logan and a withering look to King. 'Now, if you'll *excuse* me, I'll get someone to escort you back to reception. I have *work* to do.'

And it had all been going so well.

19

A large prison officer waved them off, as Logan, King, and Steel stepped out through the front doors and into the early evening sun.

The only sounds were the raucous skirl of the seagulls and the drone of supply vessels making for the harbour exit.

King stopped, throwing his hands out to the sides. 'I forgot I had it on me, OK?'

Steel shook her head. 'Kingy, Kingy, Kingy...'

Which was a lot more polite than Logan would've been. He pointed at her. 'Go run a PNC check on Mhari, see if she's got prior with Haiden. And then get on to the care home – I want to know if anyone matching Haiden's description has visited Gary Lochhead in the last couple of weeks.'

'Gah...' She stomped off, pulling out her phone. 'Slave-driving tosspot cock-muppet...'

Logan marched back to the car.

King hurried to catch up. 'Honestly, it was a simple mistake anyone could've made.'

You keep telling yourself that.

Logan checked the printout. 'Closest is the old lady, lives locally. The schoolteacher is just outside Fraserburgh. Ex-wife's in Stonehaven. Girlfriend's in Pitmedden.'

'Only one worth rattling: the girlfriend. Think our boy Haiden's hiding out at her house?'

'Only if his dad's right and he really *is* an idiot. Always bound to be the first place we'd check...' A shrug. 'Worth a go, though. But if there's even a tiny chance he's there, we have to call for backup.'

'True.' King turned to squint out at the huge orange-and-white supply vessels. 'Mind you, if he's bright enough to leave a forensically neutral crime scene, is he *really* going to be moronic enough to hide out at his girlfriend's? Be a huge waste of time and resources getting a dog team and OSU and all the rest involved. Never mind the paperwork.'

'You want to risk it? Because speaking as a member of Professional Standards...'

'Yeah. You're probably right.' King dug out his contraband phone and poked at the screen, wandering onto the yellowy grass as he held it to his ear. 'Milky? ... No, it's me. ... How many times do I have to say I'm sorry? ... Milky— ... No, Milky— ... Look, can you get me the number for Ellon police station. ... Please.'

Yeah, good luck with that. Knowing Milky, she wouldn't be letting him in off that particular high ledge for a *long* time. If there was one thing Yorkshiremen and Yorkshirewomen excelled at, it was holding a grudge.

Steel wandered over, her shirt unbuttoned down to the bra line, flapping both sides to get some air circulating around her...

Logan closed his eyes and shuddered. Best not to think about it. When he opened them again she was standing right in front of him, still flapping.

She nodded at King – pacing about in the middle distance. 'Can you *believe* that numpty?'

'What did the Police National Computer say?'

'Imagine smuggling a phone into prison. Everyone knows heroin's where the big money is. Lot easier on the bumhole too.' She raised her eyebrows. 'Any idea how hard it'd be to get a charger up there?'

'Leave DI King alone, he's having a hard enough time as it is.'

'You meaning the Alt-Nat terrorism thing, or the cheating wife thing?'

How on earth did she know?

'Oh don't look at me like that.' Steel untucked her shirt and gave the sides an extra-strong flap, exposing pale belly skin as well. 'I used to be a Detective Chief Inspector, remember? Course I know things.' A couple more flaps. 'PNC says: Mhari Canonach Powell, twenty-two, arrested during an anti-Trump rally in Newcastle last year.'

'Which one?'

'Who can remember? Got off with a fine in any case. Other than that, she's a model citizen. DVLA says she's got an ancient white Nissan Micra registered at her address in Pitmedden – never had a speeding or parking ticket.' An unwholesome smile slithered its way onto Steel's shiny face. 'Too good to be true, to be honest. Needs dirtying up a bit.'

'Just don't, OK?' Logan pulled his peaked cap down, shading his eyes. 'What about Gary Lochhead's visitors?'

'Didn't have any. Not a one. Well, no' unless you count his CJ social worker, but she's a woman and she's only been twice. And before you ask – no, it wasn't Haiden in a dress. Gaelic Gary's got nae mates.'

So they were no further forward on the 'why now?' front.

King returned from his sticky tarmac pacing. 'Sergeant Winston can give us a patrol car now, but if we want an Operational Support Unit we're going to have to wait till nine at the earliest.'

Nine?

'Suppose we *could* hang around till then.' Not exactly ideal, though. Logan unlocked the car and climbed in. Cranked up the air conditioning.

King got in the back. 'What if he's been and gone, by then? What if he hears we were at the prison?'

'He'll do a runner. Unless we go down there and stake her house out? Assuming he's even there.'

Steel groaned her way into the passenger seat, shirt held open over the blowers as they pumped cold air into the car. 'You lumpies are kidding, right? We're no' sodding about outside some manky wee house in Pit-bloody-medden till *nine*!'

'At the earliest.' King fastened his seatbelt, voice dripping with condescension. 'This is what *police work* is like, Detective

Sergeant Steel. Waiting. Watching. *That's* how we *catch* people.'

She curled her lip at him. 'Don't patronise me, Kingy. I was running murder investigations while you were still in short trousers, sucking your mummy's—'

'All right,' Logan held up a hand, 'that's enough. We're staking out Mhari Powell's house till backup arrives, and that's an end to it.'

'Nooo...' She slumped in her seat. 'Nine o'clock...' A groan. 'For the record: I hate the pair of you.'

In the rear-view mirror, King scowled. 'Join the queue.'

Logan pulled up, two doors down, behind a half-empty skip, and killed the engine. Mhari Powell's house was a bland cut-and-paste bungalow, hidden away in a curling cul-de-sac on the outskirts of Pitmedden. Brown-grey harling on the walls; grey, lichen-acned tiles on the roofs; satellite dishes like drooping mushrooms; backing onto woods and flanked by fields of brittle yellow barley.

King peered through from the back seat. 'Which house?'

'Number sixteen.' Steel pointed. 'The one with the dog rose and all the heathers.'

'Hmm...' He sniffed. 'What kind of car was it again?'

'God's sake, *try* and pay attention, Kingy. White Nissan Micra.' She swung her finger around to point at a rattletrap speckled with dents, parked on the lock-block drive. Orange-brown patches blistered through the paintwork all around the wheel arches. A 'DON'T BLAME ME, I VOTED SNP!' sticker on the boot. 'That one. Now, does anyone have any more stupid questions?'

Logan checked his watch. 'Ten past seven.'

'Urgh...' She slumped. 'Two hours...'

'At the *earliest*.' King gave her a cold smile in the rear-view mirror. 'Settle in, Sergeant, we're here for the long haul.'

And at that, Steel curled forward and *thunked* her head off the dashboard. 'Knew I should've gone into organised crime instead of the police.'

Logan thumped her arm. 'Don't whinge, we're all doing it, aren't we?'

'Urgh!'

'Oh let her sulk.' King sat back again. 'I wonder what happened to the rest of the bullion Gaelic Gary and his mates nicked. Two point six million... Course, you'd probably have to deduct the thirty-two grand of heroin they were going to buy machineguns with.'

'If I'd gone into organised crime, I could be breaking someone's kneecaps right now. Or snorting coke off a stripper's pert buttocks.'

Logan stared at Steel. 'Hello? Professional Standards, remember?'

'Oh, like you've never dreamed about it.'

'Certainly not.' Well, that was at least *half* true.

King kept muttering away to himself. 'Call it another eight grand in sundry expenses...'

'OK, forget the cocaine.' Steel waggled her eyebrows. 'Have you ever dreamed about licking *cheese spread* off Ginger McHotpants's pert buttocks?'

'No! And stop calling her that.'

'Primula's good. But no' the stuff with ham or prawns in it. The wee bits get places you're no' supposed to have wee bits.'

'Can you *please* stop talking now?'

King chuntered on in the ensuing silence. 'Even then, that leaves two point one million pounds. Wonder what that'd be in today's money?' He got his phone out and fiddled with it.

'OK, so you're no' into squeezy cheese. How about Nutella? You could—'

'No!'

'Gah!' Steel folded her arms. 'Two hours stuck in a car with Police Scotland's answer to root-canal surgery.'

More silence.

'Wow... It'd be worth over eight million today.' King leaned through from the back again and tapped Logan on the shoulder. 'And they never found it? Not *any* of it?'

'Not a penny.'

'Well, if I'm no' allowed to talk about squeezy cheese, buttocks, or Nutella, why don't we discuss how much of a waste of my sodding time it is sitting in this car with you pair of bumnuggets?'

King glowered at her. 'Detective Sergeant Steel, if you're not prepared to behave like an *adult*, why don't we all just sit here in awkward silence?'

'Suits me.'

Oh joy.

Pff...

So far, the only exciting thing that'd happened was a little old lady taking her Great Dane for a walk. Other than that, sod all for the last – Logan checked his watch – thirty-five minutes? Was that all? It felt like hours. And hours. And hours.

Steel was slumped in the reclined passenger seat, eyes closed, mouth open, making the occasional snuffling grunt.

King loosened his tie and sighed.

Thirty-five minutes.

Logan turned and stuck a hand between the front seats at King. 'Lend us your jacket, Frank: I'm going to check on our backup.'

There was a pause, then King shrugged, picked up his jacket and passed it forward.

Steel didn't even open her eyes as Logan climbed out into the evening warmth: 'Get me some fizzy juice while you're out. And crisps. And some sort of dirty magazine!'

No chance.

Logan clunked the door shut.

A lone buzzard screamed out its cry overhead, circling in the rich blue of the sky.

He pulled King's jacket on, hiding the Police-Scotland-issue black T-shirt with its epaulettes and inspector's pips. Not the greatest of disguises – a bit baggy and long in the sleeves, to be honest – but it would do.

Not walking too fast, or too slow, as if he was just an ordinary member of the public, out for a stroll in an ill-fitting borrowed suit jacket.

He took a left at the end of the street, onto another road

lined with bungalow clones in shades of brown and grey. Not rundown yet, but heading that way.

A Yorkshire terrier scampered past, going in the other direction, chased by a young boy with his hair in pigtails, an X-Men T-shirt, and a cape that looked as if it'd been improvised from a bath towel.

Odds on, Tufty dressed like that most weekends.

A right at the junction with the main road and there was the patrol car Ellon had lent them. A pair of uniforms were relaxing in the front seats, stabproofs off and piled up in the back with their equipment belts, windows rolled down, one scoofing from a tin of Irn-Bru, the other eating a chocolate bar.

Nice for some.

Logan knocked on the car's roof, then peered in through the passenger window. 'You lot Sergeant Winston's?'

The guy in the driving seat lowered his Fruit & Nut. 'Oh aye. Inspector McRae? I seen youse in the papers.' A toothy smile. 'Fit like the day?'

'Not meaning to be funny or anything, but if our boy's not home already, do you think he's going to toddle past you pair without noticing? In your big shiny patrol car? With the big lights on the roof? And the word "Police" down the side in big shiny letters?'

Pink rushed up PC Fruit & Nut's cheeks. 'Ah...'

His partner in the passenger seat shook her head. 'Told you.'

'Sorry, Inspector.'

She waggled her can at him. '"Shut up and drink your Irn-Bru." Remember that?'

'Shut up!' PC Fruit & Nut leaned across from the driver's seat and grimaced up at Logan. 'We'll go park somewhere a wee bittie less oot in the open.'

'You do that. Thanks.' He patted the patrol car's roof, then turned and walked back the way he'd come as they pulled away.

Pair of Muppets.

The rich smoky scent of a distant barbecue wafted in through the open window, curling its way around Logan's nose, making his stomach growl as he reclined his seat a bit and put his peaked cap over his face. Replacing the scent of burning sausages with the musty-hair smell of the inside of his hat.

No one ever washed police hats, did they? Not as if you could chuck one in the washing machine, was it? Or could you? Have to check the instructions.

He stretched out his legs and crossed his arms, vampire-style across his chest.

Comfortable and warm.

Could go a snooze right now.

Well, he could if King and Steel weren't still nipping at each other like a pair of yappy dogs:

'That's no' what I said, I said, "These Alt-Nat nutjobs need castrating." No' the same thing.'

A contemptuous snort from King. 'You Unionistas are all the same.'

'Hoy! I voted "Yes", thank you very much! Unionista, my sharny arse!'

'Then why are you so anti-independence?'

'I'm no' *anti-independence*, I'm anti-people-being-dicks-about-it. I'm anti-harassment. Anti-burning-people's-houses-down. Anti-blowing-stuff-up. Anti-hating-people-just-because-they're-English!'

Pause.

'Oh. That's OK then.' King poked Logan in the shoulder. 'What about you?'

Logan stayed where he was. 'No politics in the car. No religion either. Go back to playing I-spy.'

Something that sounded suspiciously like ... rummaging came from the passenger seat. No way Logan was taking the hat off his face to see what she was up to, though. Seen quite enough of her bra-fiddling to last three lifetimes, thank you very much.

King sighed in the back, the *pik, pik, pik,* of his mobile phone marking time with him sending a text or something.

'Girls Just Want to Have Fun' bounced into the car, getting louder and louder, then it fell silent, replaced by Steel's gravelly tones: 'Who dares disturb my rummaging? ... Uh-huh. ... Uh-huh.' Sniff. 'And why didn't you phone *him* instead of *me*? ... Oh, I see. ... No, you're a coward. ... Yeah, I suppose he is a bit Nosferatuy. You're still a coward, though.'

Logan raised his peaked cap a bit and peered out. 'Who's "Nosferatuy"?'

'That was Sergeant Winston from Ellon station: we've lost our backup.' She put her phone away, then dug a hand into her pocket, far deeper than it should have been able to go. 'They've had a shout on a grade-one flag: on their way now with lights and music blaring. Apparently some auld wifie's tried to kill her husband three times this year, and she's hoping fourth time's the charm.'

'Great. And what are *we* supposed to do?'

Steel stuck her tongue out one side of her mouth. 'On the bright side...' Her hand re-emerged, clutching a packet of Polos, bringing a small cascade of fluff with it. 'We now have sweeties! There's a hole in my pocket, so they were stuck down in the lining. Bit hairy, but still sookable.'

King's left hand appeared between the seats, holding a full packet of extra-strong mints. 'You should have said: I've got about three packets of these.'

'Oh for...' She slammed her hairy Polos down on the dash-board. 'Why didn't you tell me?'

Logan settled back and put the cap over his face again. 'No eating in the car.'

Rennie's voice groaned in his ear. 'Sorry Guv, haven't had time yet. And it's my turn to pick Donna up from swimming. I'm kinda running late as it is.'

Logan sighed. 'OK. But do it first thing tomorrow.'

'Guv.'

He hung up. Shook his head. 'So we *still* don't have Haiden Lochhead's known associates.'

Steel tutted. 'Cos Rennie, and I mean this with all due respect, is goat-buggeringly useless.'

Harsh but true.

Logan adopted his snoozing vampire position once more. Well, it passed the time...

Maybe he should take his hat to the dry cleaner? That would get rid of the slightly funky smell, wouldn't it?

Still, it was better than making conversation with Captain Broken Record and Her Royal Wrinkliness.

King was on the phone again, sounding as if he'd just slammed his willy in the car door. '*How* long? ... Oh for goodness' sake! ... No, I know. ... OK, well, do what you can. ... Yeah. Thanks.' A growly sigh, then a thud.

The passenger door clicked open and clunked shut as Steel got back in again. 'I miss anything exciting?'

King gave a little strangled scream.

Steel did some sniffing. 'Laz hasn't farted again, has he?'

A finger jabbed into Logan's shoulder. 'Sergeant Winston says we've lost our Operational Support Unit too. They've been rerouted to a bar brawl in Peterhead. Going to be at least another hour and a half.'

Great. Wonderful.

Another hour and a half with the Chuckleless Brothers.

He pulled the hat off his face. 'Well, what choice do we have?'

Steel's face darkened, mouth working on something bitter. Then, 'No. Sod that. Sod them. And sod this whole sloth-buggering *wankfest*.' She clambered out again, slamming the passenger door behind her.

Logan sat up, staring as she marched off, past the skip and down the road towards Mhari Powell's bungalow.

King poked him again. 'Logan, Logan, Logan!'

Oh no. She wouldn't.

Would she?

She bloody well would.

20

They scrambled from the car, Logan plipping the Audi's locks as they hurried after her.

Not fast enough, though: Steel had too much of a lead. She banged through the garden gate and was reaching for Mhari Powell's doorbell by the time King caught up with her.

He grabbed her arm. 'Don't!'

But she jammed her thumb down on the bell anyway.

King hauled her back a step. 'Are you *insane*?'

She looked down at his hand, then up at his face. 'You can either move that, or I'll make you glove-puppet yourself.' Voice cold and level. 'Right up to the sodding elbow.'

Logan pushed himself between them, forcing them apart before the punches started. 'All right, that's enough. You're both supposed to know better!' He turned to Steel. 'And you're...'

The front door opened and there was the small mousy woman from the prison photo. She peered up at them through a curtain of dishwater hair, shoulders hunched, her posture meek and subservient. Cowed and nervous. Which might have had something to do with the bruising at the corner of her left eye. Her voice wobbled. 'Yes?'

King stood up straight. 'Mhari Canonach Powell?'

And she shrank a bit further into herself. 'Have... Have I done something wrong?'

'It's OK.' Logan gave her the most reassuring smile he could muster. 'You've not done anything wrong, we just want to ask you a few questions, that's all.' He pointed past her into the bungalow. 'Can we come in?'

'I ... no.' She clutched the door. 'The house is a mess. I'm...' Her eyes turned away. 'What's this about?'

King loomed. 'Your boyfriend, Haiden Lochhead. Where is he?'

'I don't...' She shrank away from them. 'I have to go.'

She went to close the door, but Logan got his foot into the gap before it could shut.

'You're not in any trouble, I promise.'

'Please, I have to go.' On the verge of tears. 'I haven't *done* anything.'

Steel elbowed Logan and King out of the way. 'Shift it, you pair of turdhats.' Then shrugged at Mhari Powell. 'Never mind them, they're men. And men are morons.' She turned and made shooing motions. 'Bit of privacy while we girls have a chat?' And when they didn't move, 'Go. Away. Sod in the direction of off.'

As if she was somehow the saviour in the cock-up *she'd* created.

Logan sighed, shook his head. Then walked down the path to the pavement.

It took a couple of beats before King did the same.

Steel leaned in close to Mhari Powell for a muttered conversation that was too quiet to make out from the roadside, nothing but the vague tones of consolation, resignation, and wheedling.

King kept going, across the road to the other side, out of earshot. Stood there, gesturing until Logan joined him. Kept his voice down and nodded towards the house. 'Did you see those bruises?'

'Maybe Haiden's a *hands-on* kind of boyfriend?'

'She definitely knows something she's not telling us. Along with everyone else.' King pulled out his phone and poked at it. 'Heather? It's Frank. Get someone to look into Haiden Lochhead's known associates. ... Uh-huh. ...' He wandered off, feet scuffing along the kerb. 'How about Milky, is she still sulk—

... Thought she might be. ... I apologised! ... Uh-huh...' Voice fading as he disappeared behind the skip.

Logan turned and looked across the road, where Steel was still huddling with Mhari Powell and puffed out a breath. '"A nice easy case," she said. "Something to ease you back into work," she said. Aye, right.' He pulled out his phone and checked for text messages, scrolling through the usual barrage of rubbish from Tufty, Rennie, and—

A crash sounded somewhere behind Mhari Powell's house, wooden and splintery, with lots of swearing in a hard-core Ellon accent.

King poked his head out from behind the skip, stared at Mhari's house, then at Logan. Then he was stuffing his phone into his pocket as he sprinted across the road.

Logan limped after King, a small knot in his stomach hissing at him with every step. That was the great thing about stab wounds – the gift that kept on giving. He gritted his teeth and limped faster. Broke into a run.

King disappeared around the side of the bungalow and Mhari pushed past Steel, waving her hands at them. 'Where are you going? No! You can't go in there! You can't!'

Tough.

Logan pushed harder, squeezing the hissing knot down, bursting into the back garden just in time to see the last boards of what *used* to be a shed collapsing onto the grass.

Three paces and King launched himself at the fence. Scrambled up it. Looked left and right. Deep breath. 'STOP! POLICE!' He glanced over his shoulder. 'It's him!' Then King wriggled over the top and dropped down the other side, disappearing from view. '*I SAID STOP!*'

No way Logan was assault-coursing over an eight-foot fence.

He stopped at the remains of the shed: spade, rake, hoe, an open bag of potting compost, tiny orange Flymo... Ah, there!

Logan dug the stepladder out of the wreckage and clacked it open. Rammed the feet into a flowerbed and clambered up, one hand on the aluminium and the other on the fence. Paused at the top.

A weedy overgrown path ran along behind the gardens, between the line of fencing and a drystane dyke that marked the edge of a thin band of woodland with more barley on the other side. No sign of Haiden, but King was just visible – fading into the distance.

No ladder for the other side, so the only choice was...

Logan hopped over the top and dropped onto the path. That knot went from hissing to bellowing, coils of frozen wire jabbing all the way through to his spine. Yeah, let's not do that again.

Pulling out his phone, he run-hobbled after King. Breathing hard. Thumbing through the on-screen menus till he got to the contact entry stored as 'HORRIBLE Steel!' Poked the call icon. Ran past a slimy drift of grass clippings someone had dumped over their fence.

And *finally* she picked up. *'What the hell was—'*

'It's Haiden! Get your backside in the car and see if you can cut him off!'

'Sodding...' A *scrunch-whurch-scrunch* noise, which was probably her hurrying away from Mhari's house. *'Which way?'*

'Right, towards the main road.' The motion was doing his scar tissue a bit of good, loosening it up. That or it was the adrenaline.

The path turned, following the woods as it skirted the houses of the next street over. 'First left you can take!'

'OK, I'm at the car...'

Logan dodged another impromptu compost heap of rotten grass clippings and bits of hedge. A hard right as the path turned again. Every laboured breath tasted of dust. 'He's making for the ... for the main road! ... I think. ... If you hurry ... you can still catch him!'

'Where's the sodding car keys?'

'Oh you have got ... to be kidding me!' They were in his pocket. Of *course* they sodding were.

'You want me to break a window and hotwire it?'

'Don't you dare!'

Around another corner and—

Brakes! Brakes! Brakes!

Logan skidded to a halt, inches away from crashing into King. Silly sod was just standing there, panting, looking left and right along the line of painted fencing, where the path split in two, one side following the woods and drystane dyke, the other curving its way between two sets of rear gardens, disappearing into the overhanging darkness of spreading trees.

King grabbed his knees, hauling in breaths. 'I don't … don't know … which … which way.'

'You go left, I'll go right.'

A sweaty-faced nod and King puffed away, along the side of the woods.

Logan limp-hobbled down the other path, into the shadows cast by those backyard branches.

Steel's voice crackled out of the phone. *'Aye, wee word of advice?'*

As if he had enough breath for a sodding lecture. 'Can we not—'

'See if you do catch up with Haiden Lochhead? Let Kingy do the tackling, fighting, and arresting, eh? Haiden's liable to be violent and I'd rather no' lose my resident babysitter.'

This time, getting up any speed was a struggle. His legs were full of burning sand, feet full of concrete, lungs full of boiling mud. 'I'll … do my … do my … best…'

The path opened up and Logan burst out between the fences and onto a strip of short dying grass, then a path, then the main road. He stopped, both hands on his stomach, dragging in claggy evening air as he turned on the spot.

Nothing.

No cars, no people, and no Haiden Lochhead, just blue sky and sticky tarmac.

They'd lost him.

Logan limped down the road. Long shadows reached out from the houses on either side, the light growing gold and orange as the sun sank towards the horizon.

King joined him at the junction with Mhari Powell's street, hobbling along, one hand clutching his side, face all pink and sweaty where it wasn't smeared with dark brown and green. More on his shirt. He'd torn his trouser leg too. Breathing hard. 'Remind me *why* we thought it was a good idea to join the police?'

'Are you sure it was him?'

'Positive. Well, not positive. But ... kind of. I didn't see his face, but who else could it be?'

Logan wiped a hand across his forehead, it came away dripping.

They passed Logan's Audi, then the skip, emerging from the other side to a slow handclap: Steel was waiting for them at Mhari's garden gate.

'Oh aye. *Very* impressive. Well done.'

King's face darkened a shade. 'And where the hell were you?'

'I was supervising, Kingy.'

'We wouldn't be in this position if you hadn't gone off half-cocked in the first place!'

'Oh aye?' She stepped closer, chin out. 'Don't blame me. No' *my* fault you couldn't catch syphilis in a brothel.'

King's eyes bugged. 'In a...?' He threw his arms out. 'YOU BLEW THIS WHOLE THING! YOU SHOULD NEVER HAVE GONE TO THE HOUSE!' Then he shoved her, hard enough to send her staggering back a couple of paces. 'YOU SHOULD'VE STAYED IN THE BLOODY CAR LIKE YOU WERE ORDERED!'

Oh even more joy.

Steel surged at him, fists curled. 'That's it, you're getting—'

Logan stepped between them. *Again.* 'All right, enough!' He poked King in the chest. 'You: go stand over there and cool down.' Then poked Steel too. 'You're out of order, Detective Sergeant! Threatening a senior officer? Are you trying to get busted down to *constable*? Wasn't the last demotion enough?'

She glowered at him. Then at King. Then sniffed. Stuck her hands in her pockets and her bottom lip out. Looked away. 'He started it.'

'I don't care who—'

'He *pushed* me.'

'You're a police officer, not a six-year-old!' God's sake. Logan

187

marched up the path to the front door, where Mhari was still cowering just inside, one hand clutching her throat. Eyes wide as she bit her bottom lip.

He stopped in front of her and had a go at firm-but-reasonable. 'I don't want to arrest you, I really don't. But if you harbour an escaped prisoner...' Sigh. 'What am I supposed to do?'

Her face puckered, eyes shining as the tears threatened. 'I can't... I'm sorry. You don't know what he's like. *Please*.'

'Then help me to help you. He's violent, isn't he?' Because men like Haiden always were. 'He hit you – I can see the bruises.'

She lowered her eyes. 'He loves me.'

And you know what? Maybe he did. Maybe Haiden really *did* love her in his own twisted fashion. But that wouldn't stop him beating her to a pulp for looking at him the wrong way, or contradicting him, or burning the toast, or just because his football team lost. Dickheads like him thought it was their right.

'I know it's not easy, but there are things we can do: support, women's shelters. Better yet, we can put him in prison again, where he belongs.'

Tears spilled down her cheeks. '*Please* don't ask me that. I can't. I can't.'

And maybe next time Haiden would put her in the hospital. Or the mortuary.

God, this job was depressing sometimes.

Logan nodded, then slipped a Police Scotland business card out of his wallet – printing his mobile number in biro on the front. 'Here. You can call me any time, day or night. You don't have to live in fear of him, Mhari. We can help.'

She took the card, still not meeting his eyes.

'And if Haiden tries to get in touch again, tell him we're watching the house. That'll keep him away.'

She wiped a palm across her face, sniffed, then closed the door on them.

And that was that.

Logan turned away from the bungalow and marched over to where Steel was sulking. 'I can't even *begin* to describe how much trouble you're in right now.'

Steel shrugged. 'Come on, don't be like—'

'If you hadn't charged off on your own because you couldn't be arsed waiting, Haiden Lochhead wouldn't have got away!'

She just stared at him.

Well, you know what? She wasn't wriggling out of it this time.

'What do you think the media are going to make of it? What do you think the *top brass* are going to do?'

'I was only trying to—'

'Professor Wilson could die because of this!' Putting a bit of force behind it.

She pursed her lips. Stared down at her boots. 'I'm sorry.'

Yeah, that probably wasn't going to cut it this time.

21

Parched countryside rippled past the windows in shades of yellow and grey, the air shimmering above heat-hazed tarmac, as they headed towards town. Steel banished to the back seat, King sitting up front. Scowls and frowns all round.

King glowered at the rear-view mirror. 'I *still* say we should've arrested her.'

Steel snorted. 'Aye, and I still say you should ram it up your spudhole.'

'Sergeant—'

'All right!' Logan raised a hand off the steering wheel. 'All right. God's sake...' Why him? Why couldn't they bugger off and annoy someone else instead? 'We *couldn't* arrest her, because we couldn't prove she'd done anything wrong.'

King slapped a hand down on the dashboard. 'She was harbouring Haiden Lochhead!'

'And how are we going to prove that? You didn't even see his face, could've been any random numpty disappearing off into the sodding sunset.'

'It was Haiden!'

Of course it was. 'But we can't *prove* that. And if we've no proof, we can't arrest her.'

King's bottom lip pinched like a five-year-old told he wasn't allowed any more biscuits. 'Could've arrested her on suspicion.'

Steel poked her head through, between the seats. 'Pin your

lugholes in the upright and locked position, Kingy: you – can't – arrest – victims – of domestic – violence – for being – controlled – by their – abuser. Poor cow was terrified.'

'I'm not telling you again! We wouldn't *be* in this position if it wasn't for you.' He turned to Logan. 'We get an SE team and we swab her house for DNA. That'll prove Haiden was there.'

Surely a DI should be brighter than that?

Logan did his best not to sound as if he was explaining it to that biscuit-less five-year-old. 'Her lawyer will claim contact cross-contamination from when she visited him in prison.'

'Then fingerprints!'

'He's her boyfriend. He visited her before he went into prison.'

'What, and they're still there three years later? She hasn't cleaned since then?'

'Hoy!' Steel poked him. 'She's a woman so she's got to be a house-proud wee mouse, does she? Cleaning and polishing for some man?'

Logan scowled at Steel in the rear-view mirror. 'You would be *really* wise to stop talking right now. You're in enough trouble as it is.' He reached out and clicked on the radio and some bland happy-clappy pop tune jingled out of the speakers. 'Can we please sit in silence till we get back to the station?'

Steel thudded into her seat, face creased, arms folded. 'Fine.'

King turned to face the passenger window. 'Perfect.'

Logan just sighed.

A floor polisher made dubstep noises in the corridor outside DCI Hardie's office.

Still no sign of the man himself. Probably dragging it out, leaving Logan and King to stew in the juice of their own failure and await the coming bollocking.

King brushed a clump of dried dirt from his trouser leg. The pale beige lump burst as it hit the carpet tiles, turning to dust. He picked at another bit, not looking at Logan. 'What's going to happen to her?'

Good question.

'Disciplinary hearing. If she's lucky, she'll get off with a suspension. If not? Demotion, fine, maybe fired. If Professor Wilson dies, definitely fired. And maybe prosecuted.'

King nodded. Then scooted his chair closer to Logan's, keeping his voice down. 'Can't you just ... you know?'

Logan stared at him. 'No. I can't just *"you know"*.' Honestly... 'Doesn't matter how much I want to: if I do it for her – if I bend the rules for friends – I'm compromised. Can't be trusted. I undermine the whole system.'

Silence as King frowned at the rear of Hardie's monitor. Then a sigh. 'Yeah, you're probably right. But—'

'And why do you care all of a sudden? You've done nothing but moan about her since this started.'

'I know, but—'

The office door banged open and DCI Hardie stormed into the room. Face: red and sweaty. Shirt: stained down the back and under the arms. Eyebrows: furrowed. Teeth: bared. 'What the *hell* were you thinking?'

King sat up straight. 'It wasn't—'

'Letting Haiden Lochhead get away! Have you *any* idea what the media are going to do to us when they find out? Pineapples! Great big sodding pineapples!' He threw himself into his chair, the impact sending him and it trundling away, till they clunked into the wall. 'The Chief Superintendent isn't pleased. And when the man in charge of the whole *bastarding* division isn't pleased, *I* am not pleased. Because *he* seems to think *your* screw-up counts as *my* screw-up!' Spittle flying. 'AND I DO NOT SCREW-UP!' Glaring at them, eyes bulging in his flushed shiny face.

Logan cleared his throat. 'Maybe we should all take a deep breath and—'

'Don't interrupt me when I'm bollocking you!' Hardie slammed a hand down on the desk. 'Of all the half-arsed, incompetent, piss-poor excuses for police officers; you should've waited for backup!'

King pulled his chin up. 'With respect, Boss, we didn't have a choice. We *had* to move in when we did. I was watching the front of Mhari Powell's house when I saw Haiden Lochhead look out of the window and spot us. Ellon had pulled our patrol car off on another job, the OSU was an hour and a half away. If we'd waited, he'd have been long gone.'

You *what*?

Logan stared at him. Lying little sod. Well, lying big sod, but it was still a lie.

Hardie harrumphed, a bit of the fire fading from his cheeks. 'He's long gone now.'

'Yes. But at least we *tried*.' King nodded, agreeing with himself. 'We couldn't sit there and do nothing because we didn't have backup. Would you?'

The fire died, letting the steam leak out of Hardie in a slow disappointed hiss. He sagged in his chair. Rubbed a hand across his eyes. 'You're right, you're right. I'm sorry.' A big sigh. 'It's not going to make tomorrow's media briefing any easier, though. The press will spin it as a disaster and Edward Bloody Barwell will drop his bomb.'

King deflated too. 'Then my career's over anyway.'

Probably.

Hardie checked his watch, chewed on his lip for a bit. 'It's well past quitting time.' He pointed at Logan. 'Open the third drawer down, would you? "Historic Analysis of Traffic Offences 1985 to 1993".'

OK. Not entirely sure what double parking and driving without due care and attention had to do with Professor Wilson and Haiden Lochhead, but probably best to play along in case Hardie was still flammable.

Logan rattled open the filing cabinet drawer. Instead of hanging files, there was a cardboard box, about the size of the ones printer paper came in. He lifted it out and stuck it on the desk.

Hardie opened it, pulling out three crystal tumblers and a decanter half-full of amber liquid. He poured a stiff measure into one of the glasses and handed it to King. Then did the same for Logan. 'We'll issue the statement at the start of the briefing: get Jane to put a hard positive spin on it. Play up how you *almost* caught Haiden Lochhead today.' Hardie poured himself

193

one and pointed it at King. 'You got into a scuffle with Lochhead, right?'

'Scuffle?'

'The scrapes and dirt. You tackled him, but he escaped?'

King brushed away another clump of pale beige. 'Went hammering around a corner, slipped on a pile of lawn clippings, and collided with someone's fence. Then the ground. Think they'd been out with the hose earlier.'

Hardie's face fell an inch. 'Oh...' He shrugged and raised his glass. 'Jane will still be able to spin it. *Slàinte mhath*!'

King raised his. '*Slàinte mhòr*!'

Ah well, might as well join in.

Logan held his up too. '*L'chaim*.'

They clinked glasses, then King and Hardie took massive swigs while Logan barely sipped at his. A warm smoky wash of peat grabbed at his tongue, making the edges tingle and numb. Like drinking oak-aged Novocaine.

They both frowned at him. Probably wondering why he hadn't scoofed half the glass, like they had.

'Driving.'

Hardie shook his head. 'Leave the car here. We'll make a night of it. About time we did some team building!'

Yeah...

King whacked back the last of his whisky and raised the empty glass. 'I'll drink to that.'

Music blared through the open toilet door, loud and clear, then fading to a muffled thump-and-grind as the door bumped shut again. The sharp rancid-vinegar of a pub gents' mingling with the weird artificial-mango scent spritzing out of the air freshener mounted on the wall.

Logan's knees weren't working at full strength for some reason, making him wobble a bit as he directed the stream of wee after a lump of someone's discarded chewing gum – chasing it up and down the trough.

The newcomer took up position at the opposite end. Belched. Did a little wobble of his own as the sound of a zip joined them at the urinal. 'Can't remember...' Oh, it was King. He burped and wobbled some more. 'Can't remember the last time I went ... went out *drinking* with ...' another belch, 'anyone from work.'

'Nope.'

The chewing gum performed a little pirouette and headed off the other way. Slippery customer.

'That's the trouble ... with being an *inspector*, isn't it? When you're ... you're a *constable*, you're one of the gang. When ... you're a *sergeant*, you're the buffer between the dicks in charge and the constables, so everyone likes you.' His voice drooped like a sad willy. 'Then you get promoted and ... and suddenly *you're* one of the dicks in charge.'

'Yup.'

The chewing gum drifted to a halt – no more pee to push it.

Logan gave PC Naughty a shake and tucked him away again. Did his zip up and stiff-legged over to the sinks. No funny business, knees!

Now wash your hands.

King's back was reflected in the graffiti-scrawled mirror: broad shoulders and that thick mane of hair. Like he was in a commercial, or a cop show, or something. 'And it ... it wouldn't be so bad, if it was ... like the TV, or the books, and ...' belch number three, 'and you got to go running about interviewing people and cracking cases, but it's ... it's ninety percent paperwork and bloody meetings!' A lurching two-step to the left, quickly rectified. 'Briefings. Debriefings. Status reports. Stragety ... I mean, *strategy* focus groups. Statistics...'

Logan rinsed the soap off his hands. Took care over the words, in case they got a bit squished by all that lager and the whiskies. 'You lied to Hardie.'

'Did I?'

'You *didn't* see Haiden in the window.'

'Yes I did.'

He flicked water off his hands and onto the brown tiles. 'Steel knocked on Mhari Powell's door, because ... because she has the impulse control of ... a six-month-old Labrador. Not because Haiden Lochhead appeared.'

King shoogled his bum from side to side, probably finishing up. Sounding genuinely puzzled: 'You would rather ... you rather I landed her in it?'

'I'm not saying that.' He crossed to the hand dryer – a motion sensor setting it roaring.

'Then what...' King raised his voice over the blower. 'Then what's the problem? She screwed ... screwed up. *Everybody* screws up sometimes. God knows ... know I have. We all have! But ... but we deserve a second chance, don't we?'

'That's not the point.'

'It doesn't matter now. Far as Hardie's concerned: I saw Haiden, we went after him.'

It doesn't matter?

'He – got – away.'

King zipped himself up. 'And we're going to have to live with that.'

'Yes.' Logan wiped his hands dry on his trousers and headed for the door. 'The problem is: Professor Wilson probably won't.'

— dead letters and abandoned mail —

22

The voice belted out at full volume: *'Fit like, loons and quines?*
It's six o'clock, which means you're listening to OMG it's Early!, *with*
me, Rachel Gray. Glad you could join us.'

Gnnn...

Logan forced his eyes open, and blearied at the ceiling, one
hand searching for the bloody alarm-clock-radio.

'It's going to be another scorcher out there, so let's get in the spirit
with some Alicia Lewis, and "Summer's Ashes".'

Tara reached across the bed and hit him, voice mushy and
sour. 'Make it stop!'

'Take it away, Alicia!'

'Trying...' Where the hell was the button?

A horribly cheery hand-clap-and-guitar thing bounced out
of the speaker.

She hit him again. 'Makeitstop, makeitstop, makeitstop!'

'Baby, can't you see it's you and me, and we're burning?
It's time we—'

His finger found the button and blessed silence rolled back
into the bedroom.

Oh God...

Logan slumped. Groaned. Rubbed at his face. Ground the
grit out of his eyes.

Six in the sodding morning.

It felt as if someone had emptied a bin bag into his mouth and then set fire to it. The pounding in his head matching time with the lurching of his stomach.

Who the hell thought flaming Drambuies were a good idea at one in the morning?

He struggled his way out of bed and stood there, drooping, scarred and slightly out of focus in the bedroom mirror.

His reflection grimaced back at him. 'I *hate* mornings...'

Logan fastened the epaulettes to his T-shirt's shoulders on the way to the front door, then bent down and rubbed Cthulhu's head as she wound herself around his legs. Probably leaving a trail of grey and brown on his itchy police-issue trousers.

Still, at least the rest of him was clean.

She gave an extra loud purr as he got to her ears.

'Better be nice to Aunty Tara today, she's in a grump. And be nice to Daddy when he gets home too – it's going to be one of those days, if—'

His phone launched into its generic ringtone and when he pulled it out the words 'Supt. Bevan' loomed in the middle of the screen. Great. Because that was *bound* to be good news.

Logan groaned, then answered it. Doing his best to sound happy to hear from her. 'Boss, I'm on my way in. You need anything?'

Her New Zealand accent was slightly cooler than usual. '*I do indeed, Logan. You, in my office. Please.*'

Yeah, that didn't sound good. He stepped out of the front door. 'Be right there. Call it fifteen minutes if the traffic's...'

Buggering hedgehogs of doom.

Not even twenty to seven yet, and the driveway was flooded with sunlight, dappling its way through the trees to make leopardskin patterns on the lock block. Birds singing like sarcastic bastards in the trees. Mocking the big empty space where his Audi should have been. But wasn't. Because he'd left it at Divisional Headquarters last night.

Wonderful.

A strange cat sashayed along the top of the garden wall, as if it was wearing high heels.

He'd have to either get a bus into town, or wake Tara up and plead for a lift.

Oh, she was going to *love* that.

'Logan?'

'Sorry, Super, better make that half an hour.'

'I see.' A pause. 'And when you come in, remind me to discuss your timekeeping as well.' She hung up.

'Urgh...' He bent backwards, wincing up at the bright blue sky. 'I *really* hate mornings.'

Right, just had to hope that Superintendent Bevan was 'morally flexible' when it came to accepting caffeine-based kickbacks. Logan shifted both wax-paper cups of coffee into one hand and knocked on her door.

'Come in?'

He did, closing it behind him and placing one of the cups on her desk. 'Got you a latte, by way of an apology.'

'Punctuality matters, Logan.' She peeled back the plastic lid and peered inside. 'The shift starts at *seven*, and if you can't... Ooh, are those sprinkles?'

'*And* marshmallows.' He lowered himself into one of her visitors' chairs. 'You wanted to speak to me?'

'We don't approve of bribery in Professional Standards.' Bevan took a sip. Smiled. 'But I'll make an exception this time.' She pointed at a copy of the *Scottish Daily Post*, sitting next to her in-tray. 'Did you see the papers this morning?'

OK...

'Not yet. Why?'

'Still nothing about DI King's past.'

'Really?' He helped himself to her copy, flicking through it. Sex scandals, embezzlement, some footballer's drink-and-drugs shame, a banker caught with an underage girl, a politician caught lying – as if that was even news these days. But Bevan was right. Not so much as a whiff of King. 'That'll change. DCI Hardie's putting out the press release about it at the briefing today.'

Little wrinkles marred her forehead. 'Ah…'

'Put it this way: the story's a landmine. We don't know when we're going to step on it, but sooner or later we will. With any luck, a controlled explosion will put the damn thing out of commission.'

'The thing is – and I don't mean to cast aspersions here – but it might have been better if you *hadn't* let Haiden Lochhead get away.'

'We didn't "let" him anything. They pulled our backup and he did a runner. It was bad luck.'

The wrinkles deepened. 'I'm sure Professor Wilson will think so.'

'Yes, I said that.'

'And Detective Inspector King?'

Good question.

'I genuinely think he's doing his best.' A shrug. 'He can be a little preoccupied with his marriage breaking up, but his work doesn't seem to be suffering for it.'

'And yet…?'

'You know what the job's like. It's a pressure cooker full of raw sewage on cases like this.'

She smiled. 'This another one of your landmine metaphors?'

'Technically it's more of a simile.' Logan returned her newspaper. 'Does he have a history of anything … worrying on his service record that I don't know about? Something not in his official file?'

'Such as?'

'Something I should be looking out for, so I don't end up going down with the ship.'

The smile twitched. 'Landmines, pressure cookers, and shipwrecks. Chief Superintendent Doig never said you were such a clichémonger.' Bevan went in for a slurp of latte, giving herself a small creamy moustache in the process. 'I believe you when you say DI King's a good man, Logan. It's not his fault life's handed him this particular basket of ticking time bombs.' She shook her head. 'You've got *me* doing it now.'

Logan shifted in his seat. 'So, I'm putting my career on the line because…?'

'Keep me informed, Logan. I want this one to end well for a change.' She pulled over her keyboard and pecked away at it with a couple of fingers. 'And *please* try to be on time tomorrow!'

'Yes, Boss.' He gathered up his coffee and let himself out, before she changed her mind.

The PSD office was half-full – people on the phone, people hunched over their computers, people chatting. Shona battering away at the laser printer, using a ring binder as a cudgel. 'Work, you moronic, half-arsed, turd-fuelled excuse of a thing. Work!'

Clearly, now that all the birthday paraphernalia had been tidied away, it was business as usual.

Rennie backed in through the doors, carrying a tray laden down with greasy paper bags from the baker's. 'It's rowie time: get 'em while they're hot!'

Pretty much every phone conversation was brought to a rapid halt as the assembled horde swarmed Rennie and his offerings, helping themselves in a barrage of muttered thanks, before heading off to their desks to chomp and munch. Leaving no one but Logan and Rennie standing.

He proffered the tray in Logan's direction. 'Wasn't sure if you were coming in or not, but I got you a Cardiologist's Delight just in case.'

'Ooh, ta.' Logan helped himself to the bag with 'CD' scrawled on it, the paper nearly transparent with grease. He pulled out a pair of hot rowies with a slice of plastic cheese and two sausages sandwiched between them. It popped and crackled as he bit into it, mouth flooding with melted butter and porky goodness.

Rennie opened the remaining bag and produced two more rowies, twisting them apart to reveal the jam and butter liberally spread on the inside surfaces. 'Heard you were out on the lash with King and Hardie last night.'

'Don't remind me.' He grabbed the tomato sauce as they passed Shona's desk, applying a liberal squirting of crime-scene red. 'Last I saw of Hardie, it was gone midnight and he was spattering his shoes with an extra-large doner with chilli sauce and garlic yoghurt.'

'Ooh, *pukearama*.'

'Nope: too drunk to get much of it in his mouth.' Logan ripped another bite of his arterial monstrosity, the sweet tomato sauce rounding the whole thing out. 'Mmmmnngghhinn nnggggginggg?'

'Maybe?' Rennie settled into his seat and took a dainty bite, shoogling the mouse with his other hand to wake up his computer. 'I looked into Haiden Lochhead. Word is: that jewellery shop he ram-raided? Wanted the cash to—'

'Buy explosives so he could blow up a Duke of Sutherland statue?'

A disappointed pout. 'You knew.'

'Anything else?'

Rennie checked his screen. 'Grew up around Ellon, moved to Auchterless when he was eight and his dad got out of prison for the third time. Family holidays at Cruden Bay. Lost his wee brother in a fishing accident – boat sank, Haiden barely made it to shore alive. Took three days for his brother's body to wash up.' Another dainty bite. 'They let his dad out of Barlinnie for the funeral. Lochhead senior was doing a three stretch for breaking his lawyer's legs with a crowbar at the time.'

Logan wiped a dribble of sauce off his chin. 'To be fair, we've all fantasised about that.'

'Haiden dropped out of community college after a couple of months, went to work for his uncle Sandy's building company. Uncle Sandy's got form for aggravated assault, drugs, and was eventually put away for helping his brother, "Gaelic Gary" Lochhead, execute—'

'A property developer.' Another big bite.

That got him a look. 'What's the point my going digging, if you already know all this stuff?'

'Keep going, you're doing fine.'

'Uncle Sandy got into a fight with an ex-special-forces guy from Guildford for, and I quote, "being an English twat". So the aforementioned "twat" battered him to death in the prison laundry.' Rennie did some more nibbling. 'All in all, a lovely family. Bet they'd make a great episode of *Jeremy Kyle*.' He frowned as Logan stuffed in the last lump of Cardiologist's

Delight. 'You know what gets me about people like good old Uncle Sandy? Always banging on about Bannockburn and Culloden and the clearances. My great gran lived in Clydebank – World War Two, the Luftwaffe come over and bomb the crap out of the place. The only house left standing in the whole street is hers. Next night, they come back and finish the job. And is anyone suggesting we chuck the Germans out of Scotland? No. Because no one alive today was responsible for that.' He shook his head. 'We've forgiven *them* for what happened in 1941, but we're still holding grudges from 1314?'

Logan sooked his fingers clean. 'What about known associates?'

'Was going to do it this morning, but DS Gallacher says King's got someone on it already.'

'Fair enough.' A sigh. 'So, we're basically clueless until someone spots Haiden Lochhead.' Great. Unless Tufty had managed to find something online? And if not, a boot up the bum might motivate him. 'Grab your hat, we're off to see a weirdo.'

Rennie blew a short, wet raspberry. 'Be quicker getting out and walking.'

The rush-hour traffic crawled along Queen's Road, the trees hiding Rubislaw Quarry barely shifting in the passenger window.

Logan inched them forward another car's length. 'Don't whinge.'

'I said we should've gone Auchmill Road, but nooo, you said out to the ring road and back would be faster.'

'I can get another sidekick, you know.'

'What, like Steel?' Rennie smirked. 'Yeah, good luck with that. I'm the best of the best, the rest are just ...' a frown, 'something that rhymes with best, but means the opposite.'

Another car length.

'So – and I say this as the best sidekick you'll *ever* have – that team-building night you went on with DI King and DCI Hardie...'

Logan glanced at him. 'What about it?'

Pout. 'Why didn't *I* get an invite?'

'Because you're a soggy sack of sharny socks, that's why. And you're not of inspector rank, or above.' Not to mention being a pain in the hoop.

'Hmmph. You're the so-called "elite" Brexiteers are always going on about, aren't you?' One side of Rennie's face creased for a moment. 'Depressed? Obsessed? Molest?'

If this was a top-of-the-range sidekick, God knows what a bargain-basement one would be like.

A wail of sirens erupted from somewhere behind them, followed two seconds later by flickering blue lights in the rear-view mirror. The cars following Logan's Audi parted to let a patrol car through – blues and twos going.

Logan pulled over too, and as soon as they were past – pulled out after them, poking the switch that set his own lights and siren going. Raising his voice over the din: 'In case they need our help.'

'The rest are just a pest!'

Idiot.

The parting traffic meant he could finally put his foot down, accelerating to a heady thirty-five miles an hour.

'Get on the blower, find out what we're chasing.'

Rennie twisted around and fumbled at the back seat, coming out with a Police Scotland fleece in the usual shade of furry black. He dug an Airwave handset from one of the pockets. 'Alpha Whisky Six Three Two, to Control, safe to talk?'

A sigh gurgled out of the speaker. *'What can we do for you this time, Sergeant Rennie?'*

They burst out onto the roundabout with Anderson Drive, a pair of matching eighteen wheelers bookending the dual carriageways on both sides. Some idiot in a Lexus 4x4 tried to sneak out behind one of them, then slammed on the brakes as the patrol car zipped past. Did *exactly* the same thing a second later as Logan's Audi followed.

Why couldn't people learn to drive?

Rennie grabbed for the handle above his seat as they jinked onto Queen's Road again. 'We're following a patrol car down Queen's Road, looking to give assistance. Can you detail the shout?'

'Elderly I-C-One Male on Whitehall Place is hurling excrement at passers-by.'

Rennie grimaced across the car at Logan. 'And is it his own or...?'

'He's apparently got several large carrier bags with him, if that helps?'

'Ah. Yes. OK.' He pulled his eyebrows up and showed Logan all of his teeth. Mouthing, 'Do you want?' in silence.

Not a chance in hell.

Logan shook his head.

Rennie nodded and pressed the Airwave's talk button. 'Control? You know, I'm sure the first responders don't need Professional Standards muddying the waters. Right? Breathing down their necks.'

'More comfortable throwing it than having it thrown at you, eh?'

'You're breaking up, I can't ... it ... hello? ... hear...' He made hissing noises into the handset, then tossed it onto the seat behind him. 'Yeah, let's not do that.'

Logan killed the siren and flickering blue lights, as he merged with the slow-moving traffic again. 'Not that I wouldn't have helped out if I was needed.'

'No. No. Me too. Definitely.'

Big granite buildings crept past on the left. Mostly offices now, but the occasional one still kept as a private residence for people with utterly shedloads of money. Jammy sods.

Logan followed the Golf in front past one of the swanky boutique hotels. 'What happened about those lookout requests, by the way?'

'Lookout...' Rennie looked at him, mouth hanging open. Then, 'Oh, the ones on Haiden Lochhead! Aha. Yes.' A nod. 'From Land's End to Lerwick, we've had about sixty-four reported sightings. All of which will be from the kind of nutters who frequently mistake their own knees for Lord Lucan and Shergar.'

'Local forces looking into them?'

'And bitching mightily about it.' He gave a big pantomime sigh. 'I don't know why we bother asking the public stuff. Don't get me wrong: they're not *all* idiots, but it's a sodding large percentage. I tell you—'

His Airwave gave its three point-to-point bleeps and he jumped in his seat. 'Eek!'

A muffled, *'Control to Alpha Whisky Six Three Two, safe to talk?'* burst out into the car.

Rennie turned and fumbled for the handset, holding it like a pinless grenade as he took the call. 'If this is about the auld mannie with bags full of jobbies, I'm not interested.'

'Have you got Inspector McRae with you?'

A sly expression slunk its way across his face, making him look a bit like a sunburnt weasel. 'Depends. Who wants to know?'

'One: tell him to sign out an Airwave handset. I know he's been off on the sick, but that doesn't mean he's exempt from carrying one.'

Logan's shoulders tried to drag him down, along with the groan that accompanied it.

'Second: DCI Hardie says he wants to see him in his office ASAP. Only he used a lot more words than that, many of which I can't repeat in an open-plan office.'

Oh joy of fabulous joys.

'And thirdly: tell Inspector McRae it's nice to have him back. Even if he hasn't bothered popping past to say hello yet.'

Rennie nodded. 'Will do.' Then returned Satan's Telephone to his pocket with a grimace. 'Wonder what's crawled up Hardie's backside and set up base camp. Maybe he's got a hangover from going on the lash with you last night and wants to take it out on someone?'

'Try not to sound so pleased about it.'

'Pleased? *Moi?*' A grin. 'So, given the choice: being shouted at by Hardie, or helping out with that jobbie-flinging grandad, which one sounds better?'

Either way, he probably wasn't going to like what was thrown at him.

23

King's incident room felt a lot smaller today, which probably had something to do with the extra desks, chairs, whiteboards, and computer kit that had been squeezed into it. A row of support staff were battering data into the Home Office Large Major Enquiry System so it could churn out actions. Because following orders from DCI Hardie and all the monkeys further up the tree wasn't bad enough, now they got to do what a computer program told them as well.

A couple of plainclothes were on the phone, but other than them and the HOLMES team, most of King's new seats were empty.

He was at the front of the room, drawing up some sort of roster on the smaller of the assembled whiteboards.

Logan joined him. 'Nightshift make any progress?'

A grunt. 'Take it you saw this morning's papers?'

'No mention.'

King shook his head. 'Don't know if I should be pleased or not. This thing's been hanging over me that long...' A deep breath and a frown. 'Nah. If it's going to come out, better it's on *our* terms, not Edward Sodding Barwell's.' Sounding as if he was trying *really* hard to believe it.

Rennie slunk in, almost completely silent as he padded over to loom behind one of the plainclothes officers. The boy had definitely been practising that.

King picked up a copy of that morning's *Aberdeen Examiner* and slapped it against Logan's chest. 'What the papers *are* full of is Professor Wilson.'

Logan unfolded it, smoothing out the front page. A photo of Wilson at some white-tie do sat beneath 'WERE PROF'S MISSING HANDS DOMESTIC TERRORISM?' Logan shuddered. 'God, I hope not.' Clearing his throat and reading the article out loud. '"Prominent Leave and Unionist campaigner Professor Nicholas Wilson, brackets sixty-eight, may have been the target of domestic terrorists, says a source close to the investigation—"'

'Which is journo-speak for, "We made it all up, but let's pretend the police said it."'

Rennie leaned on the desk behind his victim. 'Ever notice how Brexiteers always seem to be hardline Unionistas?'

'Gah!' The plainclothes officer nearly jumped out of his seat, turning to stare at him. 'Where the hell did you come from?'

'I mean, don't get me wrong: I'm perfectly happy with us staying part of the UK, but even though Brexiteers think the European Union is undemocratic and crap, apparently the so-called *United* Kingdom is total peachy bananas. Scotland votes remain, England votes leave, and we all know what a gargantuan wank-shambles that turned into. How is it democracy when they don't give a toss what we think? No wonder the Alt-Nats hate them.'

A small smile twitched at the corners of King's mouth. 'Don't you have something useful to do, Sergeant?'

'Already doing it.' He stuck his arm out and made a big show of checking his watch, then raised his eyebrows at Logan. 'His Holiness, the Detective Chief Inspector of Hardie, requested the delight of your company ASAP, remember?'

Logan ruffled the newspaper. 'Look at it: they've got two pages of commentary on what the severed hands and "The Devil Makes Work" mean. Two pages. Everyone from a forensic psychologist to that knoblump off of *Big Brother*.'

'Ooh, Scotty Meyrick? I liked him on that.' Rennie poked Officer Jumpy. 'What was his catchphrase again?'

King shook his head. 'Apparently the Professor was meant

to be appearing on *Any Questions* at the end of the week, so, as you can imagine, the BBC are taking a particular interest in the case. Hardie's had to fend off the *Today* programme, the *World at One*, Jeremy Vine, and those shouty ones from Radio Five Live so far. I was on the receiving end of a twenty-minute rant about it after the morning briefing.'

That explained the summons.

'So much for last night's team-building, then.'

'Which is *exactly* why Haiden Lochhead sent those hands to the BBC studio.' King crunched his way through an extra-strong mint. 'He's got us under siege and eating our own young.'

Silence.

It wasn't that King was wrong, it was just depressing to hear it out loud like that.

Rennie did another checking-his-watch performance. 'Sorry, Guv, but you know what DCI Hardie's like. And if you're late, he might take it out on me, and none of us want that, do we?'

Logan settled back against the wall and folded his arms. 'It doesn't make sense, though. There's Haiden, apparently thick as a bricky's hod, but he's orchestrated all this like sodding Moriarty.'

Rennie lowered his arm. 'Maybe he's only been *playing* thick, lulling everyone into a false sense of security till … BAM!'

'Playing?' A snort from King. 'You know how they caught Haiden Lochhead for that jewellery shop ram-raid? Because instead of *stealing* a car to crash through the front window, like a normal person, he borrowed it from his aunt. Who wasn't best pleased when the cops turned up on her doorstep. The man's a moron.'

Yeah, Stephen Hawking he wasn't.

Logan puffed out a long breath. 'Maybe the *Aberdeen Examiner's* right: this really *is* domestic terrorism and Haiden's part of a cell. Maybe someone else, someone less thick, is telling him what to do?'

Rennie was mugging at his watch again. 'Terrible though that thought is, Guv, if you don't turn up at Hardie's—'

'What about known associates?' King frowned into the middle

distance. 'Not Haiden's, his dad's. Say he knew them from his old man's glory days, or he came into contact with them in prison? Someone with ties to the Alt-Nats?'

Worth a go. 'So we send someone up to dig through HMP Grampian's records for the three years Haiden was there.'

An evil smile took over King's face. 'And I know the *very* person.' He pulled out his phone and dialled. Listened to it ring. Then, 'Detective Sergeant Steel! You'll be delighted to know that I'm giving you a chance to redeem yourself for yesterday's fiasco. ... Yes, I thought you'd say that.'

Rennie shoogled his watch at Logan. 'Guv? Please?'

Suppose he'd put it off as long as he could.

'Might as well.' Logan slouched out through the door. 'It's not as if today could get any worse.'

Hardie was *still* banging on about Professor Wilson and the media and the top brass. Crumpled there, behind his desk, face like a wet flannel draped over an unhappy frog.

Logan did his best to look as if he was paying attention, nodding his head from time to time and throwing in the odd agreeing noise, while the self-pitying whingefest rattled on and on and on.

How could one man expend so many words on saying so little?

Then there was silence, Hardie staring at him, as if expecting an answer to whatever it was he'd been talking about.

Nope, no idea.

Only one thing for it: Logan narrowed his eyes and tilted his head a bit to the side. 'In what way, *exactly*?'

'Oh come on, Logan, you know he's going to—'

A tattoo of knocks rattled the office door. *'Sarge? You in there?'*

'Why me?' Hardie sagged even further. 'Come!'

The door cracked open and Tufty stuck his head in, flashed his teeth at Hardie. 'Sorry, Guv.' Then turned to Logan. 'Sarge, Rennie said you'd be in here and I wasn't to disturb you, but it's kinda urgent. Like super-duper card-carrying warp-factor-six-Mr-Sulu urgent.'

Hardie stiffened behind his desk. 'Is this meant to be some sort of joke?'

'Oh no, Guv, no joke here, no joke at all. Look!' He held out his phone. 'Someone posted a video online.'

Grainy footage filled the phone's screen: a man cowering in the bottom of what looked like a ... was that a chest freezer? The white walls were scraped and dented and smeared with what was probably blood. The man was curled up, lying on his side, because there wasn't room in there to stretch out.

Oh crap.

Logan grabbed the phone and stared at it.

'What?' Hardie sat forward. 'What is it?'

It was Professor Wilson: ankles tied together, elbows too, bloody bandages marking where his arms came to an abrupt axed end. Eyes screwed shut, as if he was afraid to see whoever it was filming him. Which would be Haiden Lochhead.

Wilson's voice screeched out of the phone's speakers. *'Please! Please, I haven't seen anything! I can ... I can just go away, forget this ever happened. Please!'*

The camera moved in, till his face filled the screen.

'You don't have to do this! I'll do whatever you want!' Sobs jerked through his body, making him twitch and writhe. *'I'm ... sorry! Whatever ... I did, I'm ... I'm sorry! ... Please ... please let me ... go. ... PLEASE!'*

Professor Wilson's face froze on the screen, streaked with tears and blood as the clip came to an end. It was replaced by a bunch of screengrabs for other videos: if you liked that, then you'll love this! According to the stats underneath it, the Professor Wilson footage had over thirty thousand views and six thousand likes.

Logan blinked. 'God...'

'What is it, Inspector McRae, I demand you tell me!'

He slid the phone across the desk and Hardie picked it up. Jabbed at the screen. Face crumpling as the video started playing again.

'Please! Please, I haven't seen anything! I can ... I can just go away, forget this ever happened. Please!'

Tufty's fingers curled in mid-air, as if longing for the return of his mobile. 'Twenty-six seconds long, posted at six fifteen this morning. It's going viral – people are sharing and reposting it *everywhere*.'

Because they weren't already screwed enough as it was.

'You don't have to do this! I'll do whatever you want!'

Logan scrunched his eyes closed and groaned.

He'd been wrong. Today *could* get worse.

24

Jane McGrath paced up and down the length of the meeting room table. 'This is bad. This is very, very bad.'

It was big enough for about twenty people, if you seated them around the outside of the doughnut of desks. More, if you made them sit in the middle too. Instead of which, they had to make do with a Superintendent Young – who looked as if he'd just discovered his mother doing unspeakable things with a goat, a Detective Chief Inspector Hardie – slumped in his seat like an abandoned beanbag, a Detective Inspector King – crunching his way through a packet of extra-strong mints like a reincarnated racehorse, and Logan.

Young held out a hand as Jane made another pass, blocking her way. 'Sit down, for goodness' sake. Wearing a groove in the carpet tiles isn't helping anyone.'

'I mean, it was very bad before, but now it's *thirty thousand* times worse!' She glanced at her phone. 'No, make that forty-two and a half *thousand* times. Forty-two thousand, five hundred, and eighty-nine views: how are people still "liking" this? Who the hell presses "thumbs up" on a torture video?'

Young glared at Hardie. 'I want that footage taken off the internet and I want it taken off *now.*'

'Oh, it's too late for that.' Jane poked at her phone. 'Right now it's getting shared and tweeted and posted to Alt-Nat message boards all over the sodding planet!'

Hardie straightened up a little. 'We're doing everything we can, but—'

'Then do more!' Young's jaw tightened. 'And this investigation requires direct supervision.'

'Exactly what *I* was thinking.' Hardie poked a finger in King's direction. 'I want hourly updates on your progress.'

But before King could complain, Young was giving them all the steely-eye. 'From this point, DCI Hardie will be taking over as Senior Investigating Officer.'

'Quite right. And progress needs to be...' Hardie's mouth clacked shut and his eyes widened, face going an unhealthy shade of puce. 'Wait, what?'

'This case has become too high-profile to have a DI in charge.'

Spluttering finally gave way to, 'But—'

'This is now the division's number one priority!' Young bashed a fist down on the tabletop. 'Clearly the Chief Superintendent has to retain a level of detachment, for the inevitable PIRC review, but if he was here,' getting louder with every word, 'I'm sure he would encourage me to start *kicking* people's *backsides* until something sodding *happened*!'

Silence.

King cleared his throat. 'We're doing everything we—'

'Oh no you don't.' Hardie stuck his nose in the air. 'If you and McRae hadn't let Haiden Lochhead escape last night, we wouldn't be sitting here!'

King just stared at him, eyebrows pinched up in the middle. The proverbial puppy given a kicking by its master.

'DCI Hardie, I'm authorising you to bring in a dozen officers from the rest of the division. More from other divisions if need be.'

King nodded. 'Thank you, sir.'

Which was when Young turned to face Logan. 'I'd expected more of you, Inspector McRae. I really had.'

Logan kept his voice as flat and level as possible. 'I think, given the circumstances, you and I should have a wee discussion in private, Superintendent. Don't you?'

Narrowed eyes and gritted teeth, then a forced, 'Fine.' Young snapped his fingers. 'The rest of you: out.'

There were a few shared looks and raised eyebrows, then one by one Hardie, King, and Jane slunk from the room, shutting the door behind them, leaving Logan and Young alone.

Young stood, flinging his hands out to the side. 'It's a complete and utter *bollocking* disaster!'

As if somehow that was all Logan's fault.

'When you were in Professional Standards, what would you have said if a senior officer threatened and bullied members of his command?'

'That's not the point!'

'That's *entirely* the point.' Logan put on his professional not-angry-just-disappointed voice. 'Ranting and raving at people – you know better than that.'

'Gah! This is what I get for letting you talk me into not firing King in the first place!'

'*I* talked *you* into it?'

Young crumpled into his chair again. 'The media are ripping holes in us that get bigger every day, Police Scotland are breathing down my neck, and the Scottish Tossing Government want an official briefing! And you know what *that* means.'

A sigh. 'You still can't go about bellowing at members of your team.'

'Do you have *any* idea how bad this makes us look?'

Logan turned the disappointment up a notch. 'Do you really think Police Scotland needs another bullying scandal? Have we not lost enough senior officers already?'

'WHAT AM I SUPPOSED TO DO?' Tiny dots of spittle flared in the sunlight.

'A couple of deep breaths might help?'

Outside, the sound of a patrol car siren wailed into life, then faded as they drove off to whatever emergency was underway.

The seagulls *cawwwwed*.

Someone outside in the corridor laughed.

Then Young slumped back in his seat. Looked away. 'Is he up to it? King, is he ... *unbiased*?'

'Look at it from his point of view – if he cocks this up, even accidentally, his career's over. He'll be pilloried in the media, probably never work again. He needs a result.'

'Well, that's something, I suppose.' A sigh. 'Did you hear about our beloved Chief Superintendent, Big Tony Campbell? He's retiring next month, and guess who he's passing the baton to?'

'I didn't know he was retiring.' Logan pointed. 'Are you...?'

'No. Apparently no one who's actually *worked* here is worthy. They're lumbering us with some high-flier from G Division.'

Of course they were. Because clearly, if you weren't from Clydeside, you weren't a real police officer. God forbid one of the parochial neeps got put in charge.

'Oh. Lucky us.'

Young grimaced. 'Her handover period officially starts next week. Might be nice if we had all this tied up before she gets here, don't you think?'

'We're doing the best we can.'

Young stood again, and put a paternal hand on Logan's shoulder. Gave it a squeeze. 'I know. I know. Just ... do it quicker.'

Logan scuffed along the corridor, heading for DCI Hardie's office. Why didn't they have air conditioning in here? OK, so it was Aberdeen and in the winter you needed sixteen jumpers, gloves, and a woolly hat, but still. Global warming meant—

His phone dinged and buzzed in his pocket – incoming text message.

According to the screen it was from 'CLAP HANDS, HERE COMES TUFTY!'

The little sod had done something to his phone, it was the only explanation.

> Sarge, Can I be in Mr Clark's new
> steampunk film? Can I? Can I? Hoshiko
> says I can be one of the baddy's techno
> henchmen! Can I? Can I? Can I? Can I?
> Can I?

Idiot.

He thumbed out a reply:

> No.

Before he got his phone halfway to his pocket it ding-buzzed in his hand again.

IT IS I, TUFFY!:

> Pleeeeeeeeeeeeeeeeeeeeeeeeeease? They'll
> even let me have lines! She says I'm a
> dead ringer for Baroness Grimdark's
> Henchman #3, AKA: Arachnox.
> Pleeeeeeeeeeeeeeeeeeeeeeeeeease?

Oh for God's sake...

> Why's my phone coming out with all these
> weird caller IDs? WHAT DID YOU DO?!?

SEND.

Hardie's office loomed up ahead.

The door was open, so everyone could see him: worrying away at his cheek with one hand, the phone pressed to his ear with the other. Face scrunched up. Teeny beads of sweat shining on his forehead, but maybe not from the heat.

His sidekicks were there: DS Robertson erasing things from one of Hardie's whiteboards, in all her dark-haired and jowly glory; while DS Dawson strutted about on his mobile, doing his best to look efficient, as if that would fool anyone. Big-nosed, hair-gel-wearing idiot that he was.

'Yeah. ... Yeah, I know that, but don't tell me, tell Superintendent Young. ... Yeah, I thought that might.'

The only one out of place was King. He heaved himself up from the visitor's chair, face all creased.

No one seemed to notice him leaving, not even Hardie – he just kept worrying away at his face, curling forward over his phone: 'I don't know, Stacy, as long as it takes, OK? ... Yes, I appreciate that, but look at it this way: you don't have a choice.'

King stepped out into the corridor and closed the door behind him. Slumped against it and closed his eyes. 'God...'

Logan went for cheery and upbeat. 'On the *bright* side, at least we're not the sole scapegoats any more.' That had to count for something.

'Oh, if I know Hardie, he'll find a way to Teflon anything bad so it lands smack-bang on me.'

Logan's phone ding-buzzed, yet again. Then again. And again. And again. And again.

Bloody Tufty wouldn't take no for a telling, would he?

King opened his eyes and pointed. 'You not going to get that?'

'It's just Tufty, wingeing on because I said he couldn't play a henchman in a film.' He turned and led the way down the corridor. 'And there's another bright side: now we *know* we were right about Matt Lansdale's disappearance. If Haiden had abducted him not only would Lansdale's severed hands have turned up, there'd be a video too.'

King took a deep breath and sighed it out, shoulders rounded as he scuffed along beside him. 'I suppose. At least that's something.'

Who said soon-to-be-murder investigations didn't have their lighter moments?

Beever popped a pellet of chewing gum, munching as she wheeled her postal trolley along yet another magnolia and glass corridor. Earbuds in, Green Day's *American Idiot* rocking out, cos everyone loves a bit of retro every now and then. Plus it was *way* political.

Gotta admit it was kinda cool – turning Marischal College into the council's main offices. The building was old as balls, all ornate and spiky granite, and *way* better than the ugly tower block thing they used to be based in. OK, so when she told her mates she was going to work here they all rolled their eyes so hard it looked like Sonja's were going to fall out of her ears, but you know what? While they were off doing their work placements in nail salons and hairdressers, Beever was *in the seat of power*. Where the city's cogs and wheels turned to make stuff happen.

And OK, so she was only delivering the mail, for now, but that's what internships were like, yeah? You worked your way up. And Beever was going *all* the way to the top, baby.

She had a *plan*.

The school's careers adviser said you had to dress for the job you want, not the job you got. So Beever turned up every morning, ten minutes early, in a smart-as-shit shirt and tie, neat black trousers, and tasteful trainers, cos who wouldn't want to promote that?

Oh yeah.

'Jesus of Suburbia' accompanied her around the Council Tax Department. 'Boulevard of Broken Dreams' was the soundtrack to dropping off a box from Amazon and a stack of brown envelopes for Trading Standards. 'Give Me Novacaine' for the Finance Department. 'Letterbomb' in the lift with Fat Doris – which wasn't her real name, it was really just Doris, but she was big enough for around eight people, stuffing a yum-yum into her gob and moaning on her mobile about how she couldn't get a date. 'Homecoming' for the trek to Customer Service. And by the time 'Whatsername' *dwannnnnged* to an end she was in the new councillors' bit. A bunch of temporary offices, squeezed into Marischal College while they sorted out the Town House's leaky sewage problem. Cos you can't run a city from somewhere that stinks like a greasy paedo's Y-fronts. Which meant, for now, *this* was where all the big decisions were made.

How cool was that?

Beever slipped her earbuds into her pocket and dumped her gum in the nearest pot plant. Slapped on the professional smile she'd been working on. Yeah, the braces were a bit of a drawback, but you couldn't be a politician without straight teeth, could you? Who wanted to vote for someone with a busted-piano-keyboard smile? No one, that's who.

She made her way from office to office, making polite chit and polite chat. Look at me! Look how young and keen I am! Why yes, I *am* planning on studying politics when I go to university. But *completely* not overplaying it.

Envelopes. Parcels. Jiffy bags. You name it: she delivered it.

No mistakes made here, thank you very much. Not on Beever's watch.

One more letter to go and she was done. Time for an ice-cold Diet Coke in the canteen with Lewis – who wasn't nearly as cute as he thought he was.

Beever held the final envelope up and bared her teeth at it. Ooh, that wasn't good. The address was written in green ink and you know what *that* meant: it'd been written by a nutter. Her dad swore on the *Sunday Post* that green ink was a clear sign of being dangerously fruit-loop mental.

Still, that was Councillor Lansdale's problem, not hers.

She knocked on the door, but there wasn't any answer.

No shock there. According to the papers he was totally the victim of some sort of Alt-Nat conspiracy, but Mrs Onwuatuegwu in Finance swore on a stack of *Take a Break*s that he'd done a midnight flit with one of the temps in Waste and Recycling. And apparently the temp was *twenty years* younger than him. Total shudderfest, right?

No wonder the dirty old pervert got mail from nutters.

Beever grabbed the green-ink envelope and let herself in.

Not a huge room. Kinda a slap in the face, to be honest, considering how nice some of the other temporary offices were. Didn't even have any pot plants or paintings – just a photo of Councillor Lansdale, standing there in all his saggy middle-aged glory, shaking hands with the Lord Provost.

Lansdale was one of those shirt-and-tie-with-a-jumper-on-top-under-a-suit-jacket kinda guys. Never met him, but he couldn't have looked more #MeToo if he tried. Bet he was the kind of guy who...

Beever stopped.

Sniffed.

What the hell was that funky *smell*?

She dumped the green-ink envelope on top of the pretty much overflowing in-tray.

It was, you know, like if you go away on holiday? Only you forget to empty the fridge, and when you get home the bacon's green and there's mould growing on the leftover corned beef?

A bunch of packages sat in the middle of the desk. Two Amazon boxes and a trio of Jiffy bags.

Big fat bluebottles crawled all over one of the bags, more feasting on whatever that brown yuck leaking out the bottom was, soaking into the leather desk blotter.

God, *complete* horror show.

She inched closer. Nostrils twitching.

That mouldy corned-beef stink was definitely coming from the Jiffy bag: rank and dark, catching in the base of her throat like she was going to blow chunks any minute – Weetabix and banana everywhere.

Whatever was in that bag it wasn't good. Wasn't good *at all*.

Beever swallowed hard. Then picked up the desk phone and called Security.

25

It was getting crowded in King's MIT office as Superintendent Young's promised extra bodies milled about, making the place look untidy. Far too many of them for the manky wee room. Which meant Logan had to squeeze and 'pardon me' his way over to where King stood staring at one of the two new whiteboards.

'God, it's like a rugby scrum in here.'

'Hmm?' King kept his eyes on the board. Someone had stuck photos of Professor Wilson, Haiden Lochhead, and his dad, Gaelic Gary, to the white surface with little magnetic dots in cheerful colours. Red lines connecting the three of them, a printout of the crime scene report, and lots and lots of question marks. 'Thing is, what if there *isn't* a connection?'

'The fact Haiden posted Wilson's hands to the BBC does kinda suggest there is.'

'Not what I meant.' King poked Haiden's photo with a finger. 'If he targeted Wilson just because he's a high-profile anti-independence figure, then there's no real *connection* connection, is there? Maybe they never met at all, and who Wilson *is* isn't as important as what he represents. He could be anyone. Haiden doesn't—'

'Boss?' It was Heather, mobile phone clamped to her chest. 'There's some woman downstairs in reception, won't give her name. Says it's urgent and she has to speak to you.' A shrug. 'Well, you or Inspector McRae.'

Interesting.

Logan raised an eyebrow at King. 'Perhaps we'd be better together?'

He got a scowl in return. 'I'm not going to dignify that with an answer.' King pushed his way through the crowd, making for the door. 'H: Make sure everyone's got something productive to do.'

'Boss.'

King stopped on the threshold and looked back at Logan. 'Well? Are you coming or not?'

Fair enough.

Logan skirted a knot of plainclothes officers and joined him. 'Wonder what this mystery woman wants.'

'Bet it'll be a waste of time.' King shoved the door open and they stepped out into the corridor.

And froze.

Steel was meandering away from them, mobile phone pinned between her shoulder and her ear, leaving her hands free for a big cup of coffee and a Danish pastry. Nibbling and sipping as she went. 'Did he? ... Yeah. ... Well, that's what happens when you smear Nutella on—'

'You!' King pointed at her. 'What the *hell* are you doing here?'

'Oops. Call you in a sec.' She balanced her Danish on the coffee's lid, stuck her phone in her pocket, turned, and graced them with a pastry-flaked smile. 'Just coming to see you, Guv.'

'You're *supposed* to be in Peterhead, interviewing Haiden Lochhead's cellmates!'

'No I'm not.'

King's eyes bugged. 'I *told* you to go!'

'No, you said "someone has to go speak to Haiden's cellmates", so I sent DC Harmsworth. He's a miserable git anyway, might as well give him something to be miserable about.'

He just stared at her.

Another nibble of pastry. 'I can start recording our conversations, if that makes things any easier?'

'*Fine.*' He marched past her, heading for the stairs. 'Then you can make yourself useful: with me. Now!' He battered through the double doors, leaving Logan and Steel alone in the corridor.

She puffed out her top lip and made a squeaky farting sound with it. 'He's always like this when he's not getting his leg over. See if you can talk him into having a surreptitious wank for all our sakes.'

Now there was a mental image *nobody* wanted.

'Do you have to wind him up the whole time?'

'Part of my roguish charm.' She fell in beside Logan on the way to the doors. 'So where we going?'

'Reception. Anonymous visitor.'

'Cool. You and Kingy go ahead and I'll stay here and finish up my—'

King's voice boomed out from the stairwell. '*I SAID* NOW, *DETECTIVE SERGEANT!*'

She squinted one eye shut. 'Or maybe we should just have him fixed? Our neighbour's Collie went from *The Hound of the Baskervilles* to *Lassie Come Home* when they whipped off his nadgers.'

To be honest, it was probably worth a go.

Mhari Canonach Powell was waiting for them by the 'HAVE YOU SEEN THIS MAN?' posters – Haiden Lochhead glowering out at her as she fidgeted with her lank off-blonde hair. She'd dressed in dowdy shades of beige and grey, and plastered her face with makeup – foundation, blusher, eyeshadow, and bright scarlet lipstick. The resulting mask *almost* managed to conceal the bruises that had been clearly visible yesterday evening.

Logan waved at her and she blinked back at him, eyes shiny and pink. On the verge of tears. Then the front door opened behind her and she flinched. Shuffled to one side, eyes down, as a grubby hairy man in a filthy pinstriped suit staggered in and lurched up to the desk.

Mr Pinstripe banged on the glass, his remarkably posh voice raised to a near shout. 'Hey! Hey you, there! Officer Woman Thing!' More banging. 'Some rotten bugger's stolen my script!'

Logan tried again. 'Miss Powell?'

'He's gone. Haiden's gone and it's all my fault!' She produced her phone and poked at it, then held it out so they could see the screen. Looked like a text message, but the text was too small to make out the words from here. 'You see? He's *gone*!'

King snatched the phone from her. Turning away as she reached for it. Reading out loud: '"Don't expect me home tonight: I'm in Dover. Gonna get the next ferry to France. You'll never see me again." Only he's spelled "France" with an "S".'

'Please, it's my phone...'

King scrolled to the next one. '"Why couldn't you back me up when the police came? Why didn't you send them away? Do you want them to arrest me?" All caps for that last bit and three exclamation marks.'

Mhari reached for her phone again. 'Please!'

'"After all I've done for you. I thought you loved me. You said you loved me. How could you let them nearly catch me?" Nearly with two "E"s.' King's finger scrolled and scrolled. 'There's a lot more where that came from.'

She scrabbled for the phone, but he held it up, out of reach. 'It's mine! Give it back!'

Steel sighed. 'Come on, Kingy, don't be a dick.'

'It's evidence. So—'

Logan yanked the phone out of King's hands and passed it to Mhari. 'I'm sorry. Look, we need to ask you some questions. Can we do that?'

She clutched the phone against her chest, and backed away from King. The first tear broke free and rolled down her cheek.

'Hey.' Steel held up her hands. 'It's OK, it'll be you, me, and the boy here. Detective Inspector King will wait outside.' Scowling at him. '*Won't* you, Detective Inspector?'

They stood there, staring at each other.

Logan put a hand on King's arm, kept his voice low. 'Come on, Frank, she's not going to tell us anything if you're there.'

King bared his teeth at Steel, then pulled out his own phone, turned, and marched away. Letting himself through the security door. 'Heather? Get on to Port of Dover Police and the Border Force – Haiden Lochhead's trying to hop a boat to France...' The door clicked shut, cutting the rest of it off.

Good riddance.

They were *definitely* going to have to have a chat about his behaviour before someone made a complaint.

But in the meantime...

Logan smiled at Mhari. 'Come on, we'll have a sit and a chat, and DS Steel will get us all a cup of coffee. And a nice pastry.'

A bluebottle buzzed against the room's window, banging its head off the glass behind the drawn blinds. Its big black body was a fuzzy silhouette against the glowing white, making it look the size of a small Labrador.

On this side of the blinds a row of locked filing cabinets ran along one wall, a small table, and four plastic chairs taking up the rest of the space – Mhari on one side, Logan opposite, Steel sitting between them. All with wax-paper cups of Wee Hairy Davie's best Colombian roast and a pastry on a napkin. Mhari's and Steel's were fancy apricot-and-custard-Danish concoctions, but Logan had been lumbered with an Eccles cake – because hell hath no fury like a grumpy detective sergeant sent to the canteen to fetch coffee and pastries.

Mhari fiddled with her wax-paper cup, sniffing back the tears. 'It was ... it was like we were two bits of Lego, you know? We clicked together like that and stayed.' She wiped at her eyes. 'We *love* each other.'

'Aye,' Steel nodded, 'I know the feeling. Me and Susan were the same.'

'I don't *mean* to annoy him, or make him angry, I don't. But sometimes I can't help it.'

Steel patted her arm. 'I'm sure none of that's your fault.'

'He loved me and now he's gone and I'll never see him again...' Bottom lip trembling.

'You know what? Some men are just like that.' She glanced at Logan. 'It doesn't matter how good you are, doesn't matter what you do, there's always going to be *something* that sets them off.' Another pat. 'It's not you. It's *never* you. It's something inside them.'

Mhari shrugged.

Logan had a go. 'Some men are always looking for an excuse to hit someone.'

Her hand fluttered up to the bruises beneath the caked-on makeup. 'I walked into a door. Haiden always says I'm clumsy...'

Logan glanced at Steel.

She shook her head.

He nodded back. 'Did Haiden ever mention Professor—'

His phone ding-buzzed in his pocket: incoming message. Then again. And again.

'Sorry.' When Logan pulled it out the caller ID 'IT'S-A ME, TUFTY!' sat in the middle of the screen. 'I should probably—'

The thing launched into 'Space Oddity' and 'BEHOLD THE MAGNIFICENCE OF TUFTITUDE!' replaced the last ID.

'Oh for God's... How is he *doing* that?' Logan pressed 'IGNORE' set his phone to silent and stuck it on the table. Smiled an apology at Mhari, tried to pretend he couldn't see Steel rolling her eyes. 'Where were we? Yes. Did Haiden ever mention Professor Wilson to you?'

'He ... didn't like him. Wilson was always in the papers, and on the telly, banging on about how Scotland couldn't survive without England.' She took a sip of her coffee, leaving a blood-red smear of lipstick behind. 'One time, Wilson was on the *Today* programme, saying Scotland should be grateful we're allowed *any* MPs in Westminster at all and Haiden ... I don't know. He *flipped*. Started screaming and swearing at the radio. Grabbed it and smashed it to pieces on the work surface. You know? Hammering it down, over and over again, shouting about how this is our country. Ours.'

Steel ripped a bite out of her pastry, setting free a little spray of flaky bits as she chewed and talked at the same time. 'Was that when Haiden went after him?'

'He...' Deep breath. 'He said he was going to teach Wilson a lesson. I thought, you know, he'll beat him up, or something. Show him what happens when you moan about Scotland like it's a diseased piglet hanging off the English teat.'

'When was this?'

She looked away. 'Sunday night. I ... I didn't hear him come in again, so it must've been late.'

'Notice anything different about him?'

'You don't understand: Haiden *had* to stop Professor Wilson spreading his lies. He's a propagandist for the Imperial Aggressors. It's people like him and the Unionist media that are holding this country hostage!'

Wow. All delivered with the unblinking zeal of a cult member.

Logan sat forward. 'Did he say where he'd been?'

'We have to rise up and be the nation again! They've kept us down for too long now. We can't let them...' She trailed off, staring at Logan's phone as it buzzed and skittered on the tabletop. The words 'It's Tufty-Time!' flashing on the screen.

'Sodding... Enough.' He switched the damn thing off and jammed it in his pocket.

King wouldn't be the only one getting a talking to about his behaviour.

Logan let out a long slow breath. Stuffed the anger down. Smiled at Mhari again. 'Do you have any idea where Haiden took Professor Wilson?'

She shook her head.

'Any idea where he's hidden him?'

More shaking.

'Any idea at all?'

'He wouldn't tell me.' The tears overflowed her eyes, little jagged sobs making her rock in her seat. 'And now ... now he never ... he never will!'

Logan punched the code into the lock for the door to reception, holding it open for Mhari to shuffle through.

She dug a hankie out of her grey sleeve, blotting her eyes and cheeks. Sniffing as she looked up at him. 'If you find Haiden, you won't tell him, will you? You won't tell him I told you where he was?'

'Promise.' Logan walked with her to the exit, Steel scuffing along behind. 'If you think of anything else, if you remember anything, doesn't matter how small, you can call me at any time.' He handed Mhari his business card. 'And if Haiden gets in touch, tell him he needs to speak to us, OK? We want to stop him getting in any more trouble.'

She nodded. Wiped her eyes again, apparently forgetting how much makeup she had on – the hanky removing enough foundation to reveal the skin beneath. The greens and purples of a well-established bruise. Then Mhari took a deep breath and walked out through the doors.

Soon as they'd closed behind her, Steel sagged. 'Pfff... Talk about drinking the Kool-Aid. I mean, I'm all for independence, but by the Sainted Crotch of the Hairy Jesus.'

'Think she knows more than she's saying?'

'Yeah. But what are we going to do, waterboard her?' Steel curled her top lip. 'Better no' say that too loud – don't want to give Kingy ideas.'

Outside, Mhari stopped, turned, and waved at them through the glass.

They waved back.

Her hand fell to her side, then she walked away. Down the stairs and off towards Broad Street. With her bruised face and bruised heart.

Logan sighed. 'Might be worth sticking a grade-one flag on the house.'

'Don't know about you, but see if I was Haiden Lochhead? No way I'd be coming back. Off to the land of burgundy, brie, and baguettes I jolly well sod.' Steel shook her head. 'Soon as that video hit? Welcome to Splitsville, man.'

'Splitsville?' He smiled at her. 'What on earth have you been watching?'

'I'm down with the cool kids.' A scowl. 'And speaking of someone who *isn't*...'

King barged through the door into reception, face dark and

twitchy as he hurried across the floor towards them. 'Nine-nine-nine call from Council Headquarters: there's a suspicious package at Councillor Lansdale's office.'

That was all they needed.

'Bomb threat?'

'Worse. It's postmarked last Thursday, the day after he went missing. And it stinks of rotting meat.'

And just like that, a bomb would've been better. 'Sodding hell.'

'And we all know what *that* means.' King pointed at Steel. 'You: get round there and take possession. I want it back here and analysed ASAP.'

She curled her lip. 'When you say "it stinks", do—'

'And no delegating! Take Milky with you: I want everyone who touched that package IDed, interviewed, fingerprinted. DNA if you can talk them into it. Every single one of them gets their alibi checked.' He paused, but she didn't move. 'Go!'

'Gah... Bloody hell.' Slouching away, muttering to herself as she pushed out the doors and into the sunshine. 'Arrogant, condescending, badger-wanking, cock-trumpet...'

The door thunked shut and King massaged his forehead. 'Does that woman *ever* do what she's told without a fight and a serious bollocking?'

'No. And there's someone else needing one.' Well, two some-ones, but they'd have to take turns. And right now it was DI Frank King's. 'What the hell is wrong with you? You can't seize someone's phone like that.'

'Those messages from Haiden—'

'She's a *witness*, we need her cooperation! This isn't a TV cop show: there are procedures, rules. And I don't care how much pressure you're under, you don't get to do whatever the hell you feel like! You want her phone? You get a warrant, or you ask her permission. You – don't – just – take – it!'

'I...' He pulled his chin in. 'Her phone's evidence in an ongoing—'

'No. You need to *listen* to me, Detective Inspector: your balls are on the chopping board with this case, all it'll take is one formal complaint from Mhari Powell for Hardie to cut them clean off.'

Pink spread across King's cheeks. He looked away. 'All right, all right. I get it.'

'Make sure you do. Now, if you'll excuse me, it's time for round two.' AKA: Tufty's turn. Logan pulled out his phone and turned it on again. Twenty unread text messages and four voicemails, all with the word 'TUFTY' in their caller ID. He pressed the 'CALL' button and walked away from King. Grinding his teeth as it rang and rang.

'Sarge!'

'Tufty! What in God's name do you think you're—'

'Sarge! Boss! Guv! I've—'

'I don't care if you've been offered the role of Leading Sodding Lady, you're supposed to be a police officer so start acting like one!'

'Leading…? No, no; it's—'

'This bumbling cutesy act has to stop! We're investigating a bloody—'

'WILL YOU PLEASE LISTEN TO ME!'

Right, it was time for a serious boot up the arse.

But before Logan could lace it up, Tufty was back again: 'I got a hit off my algorithm. I know who sent that first tweet about Professor Wilson.'

Oh for God's sake.

'It was Haiden Bloody Lochhead! We worked that out yesterday, you complete and utter—'

'It wasn't him.'

What?

Logan swallowed. 'It wasn't?'

'That's what I've been trying to tell you! I texted and I texted and I left messages and I texted again.'

'I swear to God, Constable Quirrel, if you don't tell me who sent that tweet, I'm going to hunt you down and stuff your—'

'It was Mhari Canonach Powell. Only she's not Mhari Canonach Powell. Not the real one, anyway.'

Logan stared out through the front windows, where Steel was marching off towards Marischal College. The same direction Mhari had disappeared in.

'Sarge, you still there?'

'How can she not be the real one?'

'I did a search. The real *Mhari Canonach Powell's* registered address is a residential psychiatric facility two miles outside South Shields.'

'So she's mentally ill?' Which explained the swivel-eyed Alt-Nat rant about Imperial Aggressors and the English teat. 'Give them a call, tell them she's escaped.'

'She's not a nutter, Guv, she's one of the nurses. Studying to be a psychologist. Hold on, I'll send you a photo from her Facebook.'

Logan's phone announced an incoming text from 'FEAR THE TUFTY!' It was a photo: a gaggle of women in their twenties, all wearing very skimpy tops, very short skirts, and very high heels. All making pouty duck-faces. If you screwed up your eyes, the one in the middle – wearing a sash with 'BIRTHDAY GIRL!' on it – sort of looked a *bit* like Mhari, but it clearly wasn't her.

'Maybe *she's* the one taking the photo. Did you think about that?'

Tufty's voice was thin and tinny through the phone's speaker. '*It was Mhari's twenty-third birthday party. In Newcastle. Last night. And here's one of her getting arrested at that anti-Trump rally...*'

Another text, this time from 'IT'S TUFTALICIOUS!' In it, the woman from the first picture was dressed in jeans and a 'NO TO FASCISM!' T-shirt, grinning at the camera as a police officer led her away in cuffs, surrounded by people with anti-Trump placards.

King tapped him on the shoulder. 'What's going on? Why do you look like something horrible's happened?'

Logan turned away from him, back on the phone again. 'Well ... maybe it's someone with the same name?'

'Yeah, if it was just "Mhari Powell", but with that *middle name? No chance. This is the real one: one hundred percent, stake my rubber duckie on it. And that's not a euphemism.'*

'Buggering...'

Logan barged out through the main doors onto the sun-baked concrete slabs outside DHQ.

He limp-ran to the top of the stairs, standing there looking down at Queen Street. The parked cars. The 'shoes of all nations' display in the windows of McKay's. The granite lump of Greyfriar's Church, up by the junction. The glittering spines and twirls of Marischal College beside it.

Where the hell was she?

King skidded to a halt beside him. 'What's got into you? Why are—'

'It's not her!' He hurpled down the stairs and along the pavement, heat pounding down on his black-clad shoulders. Came to a halt at the junction. A bus rumbled past, followed by a small flurry of bicycles. A crowd of office workers, bustling along the pavements, determined to spend as much of their lunch hour out in the sun as possible.

No sign of Mhari, or whoever the hell she really was.

King grabbed him. 'Will you tell me what's—'

'She's been *lying* to us the whole sodding time!' He did another three-sixty, scanning the crowds. 'Where did you go?' One more time around, but she was long gone. 'AAAAAAAAAAAAAAAAAAAAARGH!'

26

The only light in the room came from the bank of TVs that covered nearly a whole wall. All showing various views of Aberdeen city centre and the surrounding areas. A couple of CCTV operators sat at the central bank of controls, fiddling with joysticks to move the cameras, hunting for the con artist formerly known as 'Mhari Powell'.

Inspector Pearce – mid-forties with a haircut that was a bit too mumsy for her, or anyone else, come to that – pointed at one of the back-wall screens. It showed the junction between Queen Street and Broad Street as Mhari marched into shot. 'She crosses the road to here...' The inspector moved her finger to another screen, showing an alley lined with tall granite buildings – a pub, and some shuttered shopfronts. Mhari appeared again, a definite spring in her step. 'And *this* is waiting for her on Netherkirkgate.'

It was a rusty white Nissan Micra, last seen parked outside Mhari's house in Pitmedden. The car sat on double yellows in front of what used to be Craigdon Sports, facing the camera. Meaning the driver was clearly visible.

King whistled. 'Haiden Lochhead. Sodding hell.'

'He was parked there about fifteen minutes by the time she turned up.'

Great. Haiden Lochhead, the scumbag they'd set up a nation-wide manhunt for, had been sitting right there, barely a three-minute walk from Divisional Headquarters. That would go down well when the top brass found out.

Logan winced. 'You'd better get back to Port of Dover Police and tell them they can stop searching the ferries and docks.'

'Oh God...' King sagged against the wall. 'They're going to *love* that.'

Mhari jumped into the passenger seat and grinned across the car at Haiden, then pretty much leapt over the gearstick to give him a serious snogging.

Pearce sniffed. 'Any idea who she really is?'

'Not a sodding clue.'

Snog over, Mhari sat down again, scarlet lipstick all smeared. Then Haiden started the Nissan and drove off the edge of the screen.

'We pick the car up on Union Street.' Pearce frowned, naming the streets as the picture jumped from camera to camera, following the Nissan. 'Past Market Street, Trinity Centre. Right onto Huntly Street. Next time we see it it's on Carden Place.' The car chugged past and out of sight. She clicked a button and the screen went blank. A pained smile. 'Sorry.'

King stared at her. 'They can't just disappear!'

'There's only so many roads covered by CCTV and ANPR. We've got a flag out, though: if the Automatic Number Plate Recognition system picks them up, we'll know. Till then?' She shrugged.

Wonderful.

Logan groaned. King covered his face with his hands, swearing under his breath.

Pearce shrugged again. 'Nothing I can do.'

They were *so* screwed. 'She was right here and we let her walk out the front door.'

Pearce patted him on the shoulder. 'I can offer you a nice slice of coconut macaroon cake, if that helps?'

Yeah, it's a crappy wee car, but it's not so bad when you get used to it. Kinda fun, really. Maybe that's why he's in such a good mood? Or maybe it's cos they've put one over on those moron coppers.

Muppets.

Or maybe it's because he's with *her*.

Haiden smiles across the Nissan Micra at Mhari. God, it's amazing how she does that – one minute she's looking like a librarian spinster, the next like she could suck a golf ball through a garden hose. Sexy and beautiful and smart as a whip.

What she sees in a lump like him is anyone's guess, but by Christ he's gonna enjoy it while he can.

She reaches out and puts her hand on top of his as he changes the gears. All it takes is that one wee gesture, and his cock's like a crowbar.

He grins at her. 'We did it!'

'No, Haiden, *you* did it.'

'No, *you* did it.'

She squeezes his hand, then reaches further and puts her hot little hand on his thigh. 'You were right, baby: they think you're in Dover, on your way to Calais, and we, my dear Haiden, are *free*!'

Damn right.

'Nothing we can't do, cos we're a team.'

Her hand drifts up. 'Go team us!'

Oh yeah. 'Go team us.'

This time, when she moves her hand, she cups his erection through his jeans. That little bit of pressure making him moan.

Then Mhari turns and looks over her shoulder at the rear seat. Rubbing him as she does. 'Have you got the...?'

Focus, Haiden. Don't disappoint her. 'In the boot: two rolls of duct tape, six foot of electrical cable, box of gloves, decorators' masks, overshoes, paper oversuits. And check the glove compartment.'

She does, keeping her other hand at its business as she rummages through the usual driver's manual and service history crap. Then pulls out the carrier bag, opens it, and peers inside. 'Ooh, pretty.'

'Knew you'd love it.' Soon as he saw it, he knew. Cos he's a damn good boyfriend, no matter what his bitch ex-wife said.

Mhari lets go of his cock to slip the hunting knife from its sheath. Eight inches long, serrated down one side and polished to a glittering shine. She grips it in her left hand and takes hold of him again, licking her cherry-red lips. Squeezing and rubbing till he's breathing heavy. 'Baby, we're going to have *so* much fun tonight!'

Oh yes, they definitely are...

Logan found King out front, perched on one of the grimy concrete wall / planter things that lined the stairs down to Queen Street. Sitting there, with his back to the station, face to the sun. Shoulders slumped, face hanging. He didn't look up as Logan sat beside him, just sighed. 'Well, that's it, we might as well march ourselves up to Hardie's office and resign now.'

Logan brushed little bits of coconut off his black T-shirt. 'It's not our fault, how were we—'

'Get it out of the way before the press conference...' King's face crumpled, both hands curling into fists. 'The sodding press sodding conference!' He sat up straight, putting on a revoltingly chipper voice, complete with cheesy fake smile. 'Hey, everybody, did you know DI Frank King used to be in a terror cell? Well yesterday he allowed *Haiden Lochhead* to escape, and today, instead of arresting Mhari Powell, he watched her waltz right out of Divisional Headquarters. Isn't that *super*?' He sagged again. Groaned. Scowled at Logan. 'I told you we should've confiscated her phone, but would you listen?'

'How were we supposed to know she wasn't the real Mhari Powell?'

'Do you think anyone will care? They'll just see me letting two Alt-Nat nutjobs get away with murder.' A big shuddering sigh. 'I'm royally and utterly screwed. And so are you.'

The scapegoat's scapegoat.

'It's not our fault! We did a PNC check, we got her DVLA records. Everything said she was who she...' Logan stared off into the distance. They couldn't, could they? Maybe they *could*. He stood, a grin spreading. 'Mhari Canonach Powell – the *real* one. She was arrested at an anti-Trump rally in Newcastle.'

King didn't sound in the least bit interested. 'Good for her.'

Logan poked him. 'If they arrested the real Mhari Powell, they took her DNA. So what we need is a sample from the fake one!'

'How are we supposed to…'

But Logan was already hurrying toward the main doors.

King's voice rang out behind him. 'Logan! Oh for God's sake.'

Logan burst in through the doors, scrabbling for purchase on the floor as he took the corner too fast, trying not to collide with a middle-aged balding bloke in a three-piece suit and a screeching toddler on a leash.

'Hoy!'

'Sorry!' He kept going, almost slamming into the door through to the side of reception. Fumbling with the keypad entry system as King skidded to a halt behind him.

'What on earth are you doing?'

Logan wrenched open the door and burst into the corridor. Skittered to a halt, staring at the cleaner's cart parked outside the little side office where he and Steel had interviewed the Mhari Powell who wasn't. 'No!'

He barrelled over to the open door. A large woman in a blue tabard and baseball cap stood in the middle of the small space, just about to tip the wastepaper basket into a black bin bag.

'STOP!'

She turned and stared at him. 'What? I empty bins.'

'No. Please, put it down, OK?' Hands up, as if he was negotiating with a gunman. 'Put the bin down and step away from it. It's all right, you're not in any trouble.'

Her eyebrows went up. 'But I *always* empty bins.'

'Not this one you don't.' He eased forwards and took it from her hands. Clunked it down on the table. Then took a pair of blue nitrile gloves from his pocket and dipped inside. The first three goes of the lucky dip produced some used tissues, a crisp packet, and a banana peel. All of them got dumped in the cleaner's bin bag. The fourth go produced a wax-paper cup from the canteen, still smelling of the coffee it'd contained… Sod. There was lipstick on it, but it was the wrong colour. But lucky dip number five was the winner: one wax-paper cup complete with bright-red lipstick smear.

Logan held it up like the Holy Grail and beamed at King. 'We DNA test this, maybe we can find out who Mhari Canonach Powell *really* is!'

A polished plastic rubber plant loomed in the corner of the room, its leaves thick, green, and shiny. Logan and King sat in a pair of matching arse-achingly hard chairs. Waiting for the office's owner to appear.

One wall was taken up by a massive whiteboard – covered in technicians' names, with a list of case numbers under each of them. The single desk faced a large window, looking out over the Nelson Street lab, where every single workstation was personned by someone in a white SOC suit. Taking samples. Sticking things into machines. Battering away at keyboards. Writing things down on clipboards...

King puffed out his cheeks and pulled out his phone. Thumbed away at the screen. 'Dr McEvoy's doing this on purpose, you know. Making us wait.'

Logan shifted his grip on the brown paper evidence bag in his lap and had another look at the whiteboard. 'Have you seen how many cases they're working on?'

'Not the point.'

Logan faced the front again. 'While we're waiting, what was that with Mhari Powell? Taking her phone.'

'She's not Mhari Powell, remember?'

'That doesn't make what you did OK, Frank. As far as you knew, she was just a member of the public and *probably* a victim of domestic violence.' Logan shook his head. 'You need to do something about your temper, or it's going to get you into trouble.'

King actually laughed at that. 'Are you remembering they're going to stand up at the press briefing in ...' he checked his watch, 'fifty minutes and tell everyone I used to be in a so-called "terrorist cell"? If whoever "Mhari Powell" really is wants to make a complaint, she can get in sodding line.'

Sigh.

'Frank, I'm Professional Standards. I can't just let you—'

The office door banged open and a short spiky woman in an unbuttoned old-fashioned lab coat bustled into the room. Bright-yellow shirt. Dark hair greying at the temples, pulled up in a bun and trapped within a blue hairnet. Severe glasses. Nose like an old-fashioned tin opener. She pointed at the evidence bag in Logan's hand. 'Is this it?'

He passed the thing over. 'As soon as possible would be good.'

She arched an eyebrow and grunted, then snapped on a pair of purple nitrile gloves from the dispenser on her desk and opened the bag. Pulled out the wax-paper cup inside. Grunted again. Then returned it to the bag.

Logan tried an ingratiating smile. 'Right now, if you can?'

'You *are* joking, I take it?' She pointed at the window and the bustling techs behind it. 'These arson attacks have got us at full capacity for about the next three months.'

'This takes priority, Dr McEvoy.' King folded his arms. 'And before you complain: check with DCI Hardie, Superintendent Young, or even the Chief Super. All the same to me.' A shrug. 'Young's got his hobnail boots on for this case, so I see no reason why *our* backsides should be the only ones getting kicked.'

Dr McEvoy stiffened. 'You people think we're like Santa's little helpers, don't you? I'm at my overtime limit as it is. We can't just—'

King's phone sang in his pocket and he grimaced. 'Sorry.' He stepped away and answered it. 'King. ... OK. ... But— No.'

Time to try a more diplomatic approach.

Logan settled on the edge of her desk. 'It's important, Lesley. This case? Hugely high profile. Everyone from Sky News to the Chief Constable is waiting for us to screw it up and there's a man's life on the line.'

She turned to face the window, looking out at her bustling minions. 'I still can't magic personnel out of thin air.'

'Professor Wilson will *die* if we don't find him soon. He'll die.'

Dr McEvoy groaned again, her reflection in the window

rolling its eyes. 'All right, all right. I'll see what I can do...' She stomped over to the whiteboard and stared at it for a moment, then nodded. Back at her desk, she reached past Logan to poke a button on her big grey landline phone. 'Jeffers, come to my office, would you?'

Her words were clearly being relayed through speakers in the lab, because they were just audible, muffled by the glass, with a half-second delay.

As one, all the technicians looked up from their lab equipment to stare through the window at the office, followed by a chorus of 'Ooo-ooo-ooh!' as one of their number slumped, then marched towards the door.

Logan nodded. 'Thanks, Lesley.'

Over by the plastic rubber plant, King had one finger in his other ear. 'Why is she— OK. ... Yes.'

There was a knock on the open door and the sacrificial Jeffers lurked on the threshold. His SOC suit wasn't as pristine white as his colleagues', instead a grimy grey patina smeared the end of his sleeves and his chest. Blue biro pen marks around his mouth. 'Boss?' Fidgeting with a fat round brush as he peered at them through little round glasses.

Dr McEvoy waved him into the room. 'You've done your DNA training, haven't you?'

'Well, yeah, but I'm really more of a fingerprint—'

'Excellent. Stop what you're doing and get this analysed.' She handed him Logan's evidence bag. 'I want it sequenced, checked, and back here ASAP. ASABP if possible.'

Jeffers peeked into the bag, worrying away at his bottom lip with his teeth. 'Er... Is that a *coffee* cup? What if the coffee's degraded the sample? What if I can't—'

'I have every faith in you. Now,' she clapped her hands, 'chop, chop.'

A little defeated noise escaped from his mouth, then he sighed. 'I'll see what I can do. But it'll take a while to get the sample run against the database. Gimme ... an hour?'

Dr McEvoy looked at Logan. 'There you go, can't say fairer than that.'

'Thanks.'

King abandoned the fake greenery. 'No, I understand. We'll be right there.' He hung up and hooked a thumb over his shoulder. 'We're needed at the mortuary.'

Logan stared at Jeffers. 'We've got a press conference at two o'clock. *Please*: try and find something before then.'

All he got in reply was a shrug.

Which meant they were probably doomed.

27

Logan pushed through the door into the cutting room… Paused – King bumping into him as he stood there, sniffing.

Something rancid and rotten. A burst bin-bag stuffed with off meat. The extractor fans were going full pelt, but the stench was still eye-watering.

Isobel and Creepy Sheila stood in the middle of the room, arms folded, scowls on their faces as they glared across a cutting table at Steel. They were in scrubs and wellies, ready to go, but Steel was in her civvies, hands in her pockets, whistling something jaunty.

A Jiffy bag sat on the table between them, its underside discoloured and soggy looking.

Isobel raised her chin at Logan. 'About time too!' She jabbed an imperious finger in Steel's direction. 'Will you talk to your subordinate officer, Inspector McRae? She won't sign the chain of evidence!'

'Aye, I will.' Steel held out her hands to Sheila. 'Come on then; haven't got all day.'

Sheila whacked a clipboard down on the cutting table and Steel signed it with a flourish and a biro. 'See, no' so hard, was it?'

King marched past Logan, into the room, looming over her. 'What the hell are you playing at?'

'They wanted to open the package without the two of you, Kingy. I said no. See? Team player, me.'

Isobel snapped on a pair of purple nitrile gloves. 'Sheila, tell Mr Black we're ready for him. The rest of you can suit up if you wish to remain.'

Steel held a hand up. 'Don't worry your pretty little head about it, Sheila. Your Aunty Roberta will get the nice Mr Black for you.' Then she turned and marched for the cutting room door, booted it open and stuck her head out. Deep breath. 'GAV! GET YER ARSE OOT THAT CHUNTY, IT'S CLICKY-SNAPPY TIME!'

A deep crimson blush bloomed across Sheila's cheeks as she handed Logan and King a set of Tyvek coveralls, dumped another one on the worktop, then bustled off in the other direction.

Steel swaggered over and struggled her way into the spare suit. 'They never make these things long enough in the crotch.' Hauling at it. 'Like I'm sitting on a cheese wire.'

A wee round man appeared in the doorway, in full SOC getup, a huge digital camera strung around his neck. 'I would just like to say that I wasn't in the toilet, I was finalising a crime scene report!'

Logan pulled on his hood and zipped himself up. Tried not to smile.

Steel helped herself a pair of purple gloves. 'Oh, aye? You left the bog like a crime scene? Filthy wee bugger.'

'That's not what I—'

'Bet you didn't flush either.' She wiggled her way into blue plastic booties, grinning at Isobel. 'Men, eh?'

Sheila returned with a couple of trays and some tools, laying them on the cutting table beside the Jiffy bag like last time. 'Ready, Professor.'

'Everyone: masks and safety goggles.' And as soon as they'd complied, Isobel pointed at the photographer, snapped her fingers, then pointed at the Jiffy bag.

Gav harrumphed, then fired off a couple of shots. 'I *wasn't* in the toilet.' He checked the camera's screen. Nodded.

The camera clacked and bleeped as Isobel slit the bag open along the bottom and tipped the Jiffy bag up. A carrier bag slithered out onto the tray – the plastic filthy and dripping, sitting there, oozing brown watery liquid. The rancid meaty bin-bag smell increased about twentyfold. A stench so thick it was *chewy*.

Logan backed off a couple of paces, wafting a hand in front of his face. It didn't help. 'God...'

Steel curled her head away from the bag, voice choked: 'Bet you're glad I made them wait, now.'

King shuddered. The sliver of skin between his mask and the goggles was getting paler, little beads of sweat shining on his cheeks, the camera's flash bouncing off his plastic goggles.

'The bag has been knotted by its handles.' Isobel pointed with a purple finger. 'There may be some viable DNA inside the knot where it's been kept away from the decomposition products, so I'll make my incision here...' She slit the bag open along its base, then tipped the contents out onto the tray.

King's cheeks bulged and he gagged. 'Oh ... *Jesus!*'

Steel hissed, retreating to the other side of the room, one hand clasped over her facemask.

Logan's stomach tried to claw its way up his throat and out of his body. He swallowed the bitterness down, but it tried to escape again.

Five ... *things* sat on the tray, surrounded by their little stinking lake of yuck.

Isobel leaned in closer, her fingers smeared with brown and black as she teased the things apart. 'The two flattened hemi-spheres are, or used to be, ears – the cartilage is still intact. This larger lump was a tongue.' Then she prodded what looked like a pair of deflated testicles that had been marinated in HP Sauce. 'And these were eyes, though clearly they're in an advanced state of putrefaction.' She looked up. 'Mr Black, you're supposed to be documenting this.'

'Sorry.' The flash clacked again, searing the slimy blobs of horror onto everyone's retinas.

King's cheeks bulged again. He tore off his facemask, turned, and ran from the room.

Isobel watched him go. 'Well, that wasn't very professional.' Then prodded the remains again.

'Urgh...' Steel sidled up to Logan, keeping well away from the slithery mess on the tray. 'Don't know about you, but I'm going vegetarian for dinner tonight.'

Gav lowered his camera and peered at the Jiffy bag. 'Professor? There's something else in there.'

'Is there indeed?' Isobel reached in to pull whatever it was out. Shook her head. 'It's stuck to the lining.' So she picked up her scalpel again and sliced the bag along the other two sides. When she folded them out of the way, it revealed a sheet of A4 paper – like the one that had come with Professor Wilson's hands, only soaked through and filthy.

Whatever was printed on it wasn't readable from where Logan was, and there was no way in hell he'd be wading over there to look.

Isobel frowned at the sheet, wrinkles deepening around her eyes. 'I *think* it says ... "three monkeys".'

A nod from Steel. 'See no evil, speak no evil, hear no evil.'

Oh great.

Logan cleared his throat. 'The bits: are they ... human?'

'A reasonable question.' Isobel prodded the squelchy lumps again. 'Given the morphology, I'd be surprised if they weren't, but we'll need to run some tests to confirm it.'

Today just got better and better.

He nodded at the tray's contents. 'If someone did *that* to you, what's the chance you'd still be alive afterwards?'

'Unknowable.'

Creepy Sheila shrugged. 'The ears and eyes would cause a degree of blood loss, but the tongue would bleed a *lot* when you cut it out. There are women in India whose dickhead husbands have mutilated them like that for trying to escape abusive marriages, and they've managed to survive. Aren't men just *great*.'

Steel rocked on her heels, hands in her pockets again. 'Which is why you should ask me about my radical lesbian feminist agenda.' A nod. 'I should get that on a T-shirt. "Ask me about my radical lesbian feminist agenda". Save a lot of time at parties.'

Logan looked down at the stinking remains. 'So Councillor Lansdale could still be alive?'

'It's—'

'Unknowable.' Isobel raised a hand. 'Now, can we get back to examining the evidence, please? Some of us have children to pick up from school today.'

'Gah...' Steel shuddered on her way through the rear mortuary doors and into the sunshine. 'Well that *was* fun!'

'Whose fault's that?' He followed her up the stairs. 'Yours, is whose.'

'Don't take this the wrong way, but you and Kingy are completely and utterly *comprehensively* buggered. And I mean massive-great-big-strap-on buggered.' She held both hands out, about two foot apart to show how massive-great-big it was. 'With lumps on.'

'You didn't sign the paperwork because you wanted us to smell that, didn't you?'

Steel got to the top and turned a grin on him, blocking the way. 'Team player, remember?' She dragged out her e-cigarette and vaped up a big cloud of strawberry-and-lime. 'Mind you, it's a shame you convinced Hardie to stick his neck out, last press conference, and tell everyone Councillor Lansdale's disappearance had sod all to do with—'

'Yes, thank you; the thought had occurred.'

'Rookie mistake, Laz. Never admit to anything, never confirm anything, and never volunteer for anything.'

'You're not helping.'

She patted him on the shoulder. 'Look on the bright side: as a lowly DS I'm out of the spatter zone. All the jobbies will be flying in you and Kingy's direction.' A wink, and she sauntered out onto the Rear Podium car park.

The tarmac gripped at Logan's feet, sun-softened and sticky as they made their way over to where DI King was bent double behind one of the patrol cars, hands on his knees.

He'd managed to wriggle free from the top half of his SOC suit, the empty arms dangling around his ankles.

Steel produced another bank of strawberry-and-lime fog. 'Hope you're no' spewing your ring there, Kingy. Bunnets get enough puke to clean up as it is.'

He straightened up. Wiped his mouth with the back of his hand. Looked over Steel's head at Logan. 'This press briefing is going to be a disaster.'

'Oh aye.'

Logan glanced up at the bulk of Divisional Headquarters, glowering down on them in the blistering sunshine. 'Who knows, maybe we'll get lucky and the building will burn down first?'

King paced from the filing cabinets in Hardie's office to the whiteboard, to the filing cabinets, to the whiteboard. Hardie slumped behind his desk, hands covering his face.

Jane McGrath stared at Logan as if he'd just slapped her, then curled up in the other visitors' chair, knees against her chest, arms over her head. 'Noooo...'

Hardie peered out between his fingers. 'So, let me get this straight: *yesterday* we told the world's media that there was *no connection whatsoever*, and *today* Councillor Lansdale's eyes, ears, and tongue turn up in a Jiffy bag?' He covered his face again and muffled a scream. 'For Christ's sake!'

Jane sagged in her seat. 'They're going to eat us alive, they really are.'

'I think we're well within our rights to not tell them about it.' Logan shrugged. 'It's an ongoing case. We haven't even confirmed the body parts are his yet.'

Hardie peeked out again. 'How could they not be his? They delivered them to his sodding office!'

King paused on the way past. 'Are we *sure* we want to go out with the statement about my past now?'

'Absolutely not.' Jane shook her head. 'I'm pulling the plug on that one. No statement.'

'I think that's—'

'Hold on!' Hardie lowered his hands. 'We agreed this was the right time.'

'It was the right time when we were ahead of the investigation! When we had a *suspect* and *information* and didn't look like a bunch of utter morons.'

Bit harsh.

Logan turned to her. 'We don't look like—'

'We told them there was no connection!' She banged her fist off Hardie's desk.

'Because you *swore* there wasn't!'

'As far as I knew, there wasn't! We didn't know about the parcel. How were we supposed to know about the parcel?'

'Don't try to obfuscate this. You're—'

'Oh, what, we're supposed to be psychic now? They sent Lansdale's ears, eyes, and tongue to an *empty office*.' Getting louder and louder. 'It's not my fault Mhari and Haiden are morons!'

They glared at each other for a couple of breaths.

Then Jane threw her hands in the air and treated the ceiling tiles to a rattling snarl. Then sagged in her seat again. Shook her head. 'It's too late to put a statement out. We should've done it right at the very start when I *said* we should. Now we'd need a breakthrough of massive proportions before we go anywhere near King's past!'

Hardie grimaced. 'Or a sodding miracle.'

As if they could ever be that lucky.

Reporters and cameras packed the press briefing, every chair taken, with more standing along the far wall and down both sides, all staring up at the podium as Hardie finished the official update.

Behind him, the screen displayed a pair of photographs – one of Haiden Lochhead, and one of whoever 'Mhari Powell' really was. 'If you know these individuals, or have any information about their whereabouts, please: get in touch. You can make a real difference.' Hardie nodded at Jane and sat down as she stood.

Her smile didn't exactly look genuine. To be honest, she looked as if she was about to stab someone. 'Now, any questions?'

An explosion of hands shot up, their owners shouting over

each other, questions reduced to little more than a barrage of noise by the time they reached the podium.

Jane looked even more stabby than before. 'One at a time! One at a time!' She pointed. 'Yes: Alan.'

The wee teuchtery man raised his iPhone. 'Aye, fit aboot that video showing Professor Wilson in the chest freezer. Hiv you foond oot fa posted it?'

King stuck his chin out. 'We are investigating that at the moment.'

'OK, who's next? Phil?'

'Philip Patterson, Sky News. Sources tell me a suspicious package was delivered to Councillor Matt Lansdale's office last week and that you've seized it as evidence. My source says it stank of decomposing meat. Does the package contain Councillor Lansdale's severed hands?'

His fellow journalists turned to stare at him, hungry. Then back towards the podium in anticipation of a feed.

Hardie folded his arms. 'I think we'll let Inspector McRae answer that one.'

Rotten sod.

Logan frowned, as if considering the question. Also known as stalling for time. There had to be a way to wiggle out of this … Aha! 'A package *was* recovered from Councillor Lansdale's office this afternoon. Its contents are being examined at the moment, but I can confirm the package does *not* contain Councillor Lansdale's hands.' Which had the benefit of being one hundred percent true and completely misleading. 'I won't expand on that any further for operational reasons.'

The room exploded again – questions making a wall of jagged sound.

'Anne Darlington, BBC. You claimed yesterday that Councillor Lansdale's disappearance wasn't linked to Professor Wilson's. Are you now admitting you were wrong?'

'We aren't issuing any further comment on this aspect of our investigation for the time being.'

She narrowed her eyes. 'Why are you so afraid of the truth, Inspector?'

'We're not "afraid of the truth" we're doing our job. Next question.'

In the middle of the press pack, Edward Barwell stood, a big smile on his smug face. 'I've got one for DI King.'

Oh God, here we go...

'What do you think Professor Wilson's family will say when they find out what you did?'

An audible 'Oooo...' went through the assembled journalists. Microphones, cameras, and phones swung around till they all pointed at Barwell.

King just stared.

'What's the matter, Detective Inspector: terrorist got your tongue?'

Fidgeting in the ranks.

You could taste the anticipation in the air – sharp and metallic. Everyone waiting for Barwell to stick the knife all the way in and twist it.

A deep breath, then King got to his feet. Cleared his throat. Looked out at the assembled ranks of cameras and microphones. 'I have a statement I wanted to make before we started the briefing today, but it was felt that it might detract focus from the investigation.' His right hand trembled. He clasped it in his left. 'When I was sixteen, I did something very stupid in order to impress a girl...'

Barwell sat back down and *grinned*.

28

King drooped in his seat, arms hanging limp at his sides, looking as if someone had shot his puppy and made him eat it.

The waiting room outside the Chief Superintendent's office wasn't ostentatious – clearly Big Tony Campbell didn't feel the need to flaunt his authority – nothing fancier than a desk and a couple of chairs, a pair of suspiciously healthy-looking house plants, and a spud-ugly assistant hammering away at a keyboard.

King gave another long, hissing sigh as the sound of raised voices came from behind the closed office door again.

Couldn't make out any words, but the tone was clear: not – sodding – happy.

Logan thumbed a text message into his phone:

> Jeffers – where are my DNA results? I told
> you we needed them ASAP!

SEND.

King turned in his seat, fixing Logan with those shot-puppy eyes. 'I think that's the most humiliating thing I've ever had to do in my life.'

'Hmm?' He pulled a face, hamming it up. 'Try changing a screaming toddler's nappy, when you're dressed as a "Silly Pirate" and she's got explosive diarrhoea.' A shudder. 'I *still* get flashbacks.'

'They're going to fire me, aren't they?'

'Bright orange, and it went *everywhere*. Like one of those dye-packs going off in a duffel bag full of stolen money.'

That almost earned him a smile. 'I know what you're doing.'

'How one wee girl managed to produce so much ... liquid *horror* is beyond me. I swear to God, she pooped three times her own body weight in about fifteen seconds.'

Back to staring straight ahead. 'Just because my career's drowning, doesn't mean yours should get dragged down with it.'

That's the spirit.

'They're not going to fire you.'

'I'm serious, Logan. *Listen* to them.'

More angry voices. What sounded like someone bashing the tabletop with a fist.

Logan put his phone away. 'It was the *smell*, though. You think it was bad in the mortuary today? Four showers later and I could still smell it. Had to burn that pirate costume in the end.'

This time King really did smile, but it was a sad one. A 'thank you for trying, but it's terminal' smile.

And he probably wasn't wrong.

Hardie's office had all the fun and joy of a wee-free funeral. He was sprawled in his seat, staring at the ceiling tiles, the desk in front of him littered with paperwork. King was curled over in one of the visitors' chairs, with his head in his hands. Jane in the other one, massaging her temples, mouth downturned and moving, as if something alive was trapped inside. Leaving Logan to lean against a filing cabinet, scrolling through the home page of the *Scottish Daily Post*'s website.

Outside the window, a patrol car's siren wailed into life. Then faded as whoever it was drove away from DHQ.

Lucky sod.

King looked up at Hardie. 'But they're *supporting* me? You're sure?'

'For now.' Hardie's face soured. 'And only because Jane convinced them it'd look even worse to fire you.'

She held up a hand before King could say anything. 'And don't bother thanking me: I only did it because we can't have people thinking we've been blindsided by this. We'd come across as weak and incompetent.'

King nodded, staring at his hands as Hardie sat forward.

'But you have to understand, Frank: you're no longer on thin ice here – you've gone crashing straight through. Right now you're treading freezing water and the sharks are circling.'

A grimace from Jane. 'And Edward Barwell is gleefully hurling chum into the water.'

Not exactly a heart-warming metaphor, but it summed things up pretty well.

A small awkward silence settled onto the room.

Finally Jane broke it. 'What I don't understand is why he sat there grinning through the whole thing. Surely Barwell should've been furious – he's not printed his story yet, but there's DI King telling the whole world, blowing his exclusive. But Barwell just sits there and *grins*.'

Logan clicked through to the next page. 'He's got something else. Has to. Something worse.'

She stared at him, rabbit-in-the-headlights style. 'Oh God.' Pointing at the phone in Logan's hand. 'Has he...?'

'No, they've published the same front page they sent us.' Logan turned the phone so she could see the web page, even if it was too small to read from there. 'Went live on the website soon as the briefing started.'

'It was premeditated, then. Soon as we screwed up, that was it.'

'Arrrgh...' King covered his face with his hands again. 'I *said* we should've put the statement out first!'

Jane curled her lip at him. 'Don't be a revisionist dick, Frank. We're the only friends you've got right now.'

Oh the delights of a happy team.

Logan put his phone away. Had a bash at soothing the waters. 'Look, this was always going to come out sooner or later. We knew what we were dealing with.'

Hardie sat up and glared at King. 'What does he have? What's worse than this?' Banging on the desk. 'What did you *do*?'

Everyone stared as King wrapped his arms around himself, rocking back and forward in his seat. Back and forward. Back and forward. Back and forward. Shaking his head. 'I don't know Nothing.'

There was a knock on the door and a spotty PC stuck her head in. She threw a pained smile in Hardie's direction. 'Boss? The Chief Superintendent wants to see you in his office again. Said it was kinda urgent.'

'Urgh...' Hardie scrubbed his face with his hands. 'All right.' A big sigh, then he levered himself out from behind his desk and towards the door. Pausing to pat King on the shoulder as he passed. 'If I was you, I'd get out of here before the top brass change their mind. Go see if you can achieve something.'

'Thanks.' King waited till Hardie's footsteps faded down the corridor, before standing. He turned to Logan. 'I'm going to the toilet, and then, assuming I don't drown myself or slit my wrists, we'll grab a car and go speak to Haiden Lochhead's ex-wife.'

'OK, I'll go chase up our DNA results.'

Soon as King had shut the door behind him, Jane collapsed in her chair like a dropped jellyfish. Dangling there making groaning noises. '*Utter* disaster.'

'I don't see what your problem is. Barwell was always going to publish his story, we knew that. It's why I was assigned to support DI King. None of that's changed. And King's doing a good job.' Actually, it *might* be best not to permanently nail his colours to that particular flagpole. Reel it back a bit. Logan shrugged. 'You know, under the circumstances.'

She smiled and sat up. 'Inspector McRae, I say this with the utmost respect, especially given your heroism last year...' She took hold of his hand and gave it a squeeze, gazing deep into his eyes. 'You're an idiot and no one cares what you think.'

Logan stepped out into the suntrap masquerading as the Rear Podium car park. No sign of King yet. So he pulled out his phone and dialled Jeffers' mobile. Listened to it ring for a while as he picked his way across the sticky black tarmac to his Audi.

Then, finally, the lazy sod picked up. *'I didn't forget, I swear, I've been doing them!'*

That would be a first.

'And?'

'Er... Sorry?'

'No, you numpty, what are the results?'

'Oh, yes. OK, so I managed to isolate a good sample and I ran it through the database.'

Why could nobody get to the bloody point?

'And what was the result?'

Silence.

Two seagulls fought each other for what looked like a puddle of dried sick behind a parked patrol car. Someone emerged from the mortuary and sparked up a cigarette.

And still no reply from the Nelson Street lab's resident idiot.

'Jeffers?'

'Nothing. Sorry, I mean, there's no match in the system.'

'Oh for... Nothing *at all?'*

'Not even a cocktail sausage. Whoever she is, her DNA's not on our database.'

'She has to be! You don't go from law-abiding citizen to Alt-Nat torture groupie in one easy step. She's in there somewhere, so run it again. And keep running it, till you find something.'

'Erm...' His voice took on an even more ingratiating tone. *'I'm more of a fingerprint kind of guy, to be honest. I'm really good at fingerprints! If you want fingerprints doing, I'm all over it.'*

Well, at least that was something. 'So what happened when you ran the fingerprints on the cup?'

A pause. Then, *'But you said to do the DN... Ah.'* He cleared his throat. *'OK. Right. I ... see what I did there. Sorry?'*

'Find something.' Logan hung up, pinched the bridge of his nose.

Morons. Why was he always surrounded by—

'Thought it was you.'

When he turned, there was Rennie, standing right behind him, wiggling his eyebrows. Proving the point.

Rennie pointed at the slab of concrete and glass over his shoulder. 'Saw you from the office window.'

Swear that boy was on sodding castors.

'*Please* tell me you've got some good news.'

'Kinda. At least now we know Haiden's not a serial killer.'

What?

'Are you insane?'

'Nah, look at it. "The Devil makes work": you chop off the hands.' Rennie mimed it. '"Three monkeys": see, hear, and speak no evil; you cut out the eyes, ears, and tongue.' Another mime, then a nod. 'Serial killers don't do "themes", do they? They don't re-enact grisly murders from the Bible, or the Spanish Inquisition, or *Pingu*. That's just books and TV. *Real*-life serial killers fantasise about one thing, then spend the rest of their lives practising and refining it. Trying to make it perfect.'

'And this helps us *how*, exactly?'

A shrug. 'Well, if Haiden's not a serial killer, he's doing all this to make a point. Killing people who oppose Scottish Independence. That's your basic domestic terror—'

'No, no, no, no! We do *not* use the "D.T." words in this Division. Say it too often and poof: SPEVU appear.'

Rennie scrunched up one half of his face, as if there was a bee trapped inside his hollow-point skull. 'It's a terrible name, isn't it? SPEVU. Should be EVPUS: Extremist-Violence Prevention Unit, Scotland. They should've asked someone good with words to name it for them.'

Morons, morons, everywhere, with not a brain to think...

Logan folded his arms. 'Haven't you got anything useful to do?'

'I could get cracking on Haiden Lochhead's known associates, if you like? See if anyone's heard from him, or knows where he'd hide out?'

'Thought King had someone doing that already.'

'Actually, yeah. Not so much.'

'But I *heard* him tell DS Gallacher to do it.'

'Trouble is she delegated the job to Detective Constable Anthony "Spaver" Fraser, renowned moron of this parish, who decided it was a waste of time talking to anyone from more than three years ago. And as Haiden's been in HMP Grampian for the last three years...?'

'Oh for God's sake.'

'Sorry, Guv.' Rennie shrugged. 'Face it, not everyone's got a Top-Of-The-Range Simon Rennie Sidekick like you do.'

'Fine. Go. Talk to them. But take someone with you for corroboration. Tufty could probably do with the exercise.'

Rennie groaned. 'Not *Tufty*! He's such a dweeb.'

'Fine. Take Steel instead.'

He opened his mouth. Then closed it again. 'Ah... Have I mentioned how much I like Tufty? Good officer. Excellent work ethic. Fascinating conversationalist.'

Aye, right.

'And while you're at it, go through Ravendale's visitor's log, talk to the receptionist. I want the names of everyone who's been to see Gary Lochhead since he got there.'

Another groan, this time accompanied by a rolling of the eyes in proper stroppy teenager fashion. 'Guv.'

King shoved out through the back doors, popped a mint in his gob and crunched it as he made his way over. Face a bit pinker and shinier than it had been in Hardie's office. Eyes a bit more bloodshot. He nodded at Logan. 'You ready?'

Rennie stood up extra straight. 'Caught your statement at the press conference, DI King. Very good.' He raised a fist in salute. 'More power to your elbow.'

'I *beg* your pardon?' King's face darkened. 'Are you taking the piss, Sergeant?'

'Nope.' He backed away, hands up. 'I'd better be... Yeah.' Then turned and legged it as King stood there and glowered after him.

Logan took out his keys. 'Think I'd better drive.'

The car dealerships on Wellington Road slid past on either side as Logan took the dual carriageway south.

King, in the passenger seat, crunched his way through yet another mint. Barely five minutes out from DHQ and he'd polished off nearly a whole packet, rubbing at his chest as if he had heartburn. 'I checked with Inspector Pearce – still no sign of Mhari's white Nissan Micra on the ANPR. So either they haven't left Aberdeen, or they've got another vehicle.'

Of course they had.

Logan tightened his grip on the wheel. 'See, *this* is why I was against going public about Mhari. Soon as it's all over the media, she knows we're on to her. But no, Hardie has to have something positive to tell the press.'

Another mint disappeared. 'Because he knows this is going to come back and bite someone on the arse and he sure as hell won't let it be him.'

'What I don't get is: why didn't they post a video of Councillor Lansdale on the internet? Haiden and Mhari did one of Professor Wilson, so why not Lansdale?'

'Far as Hardie's concerned, we're expendable.'

Logan overtook an eighteen-wheeler labouring up the hill past the half-arsed Aztec pyramid that doubled as Shell's headquarters. At least for now. 'Maybe Lansdale didn't survive, so they dumped his body and tried again with Professor Wilson?'

King sighed. 'I meant what I said about not dragging you down with me.'

'I know. But I'm not—'

'Fairytale of New York' blared out from King's pocket. Again. He screwed his eyes closed. 'Leave me alone!' The song played and played and played. King groaned, sagged in his seat. 'Used to think that was the best Christmas song ever.' A bitter laugh. A sigh. 'I met Gwen in New York, Christmas Twenty-Twelve, at a charity bash for the NYPD. Got married six months later and picked this for our first dance.'

His hand drifted to an inside jacket pocket – not the one Shane MacGowan was currently singing in – and stroked something. Maybe that was where he kept his half-bottles of vodka?

A sad smile. 'Thought it was romantic and ironic. Never guessed it would be so sodding prophetic.'

The song faded away, leaving them in silence.

Aberdeen had thinned out a bit, trees taking the place of warehouses and office blocks.

'Eight point one *million* in stolen bullion.' King let his hands fall into his lap. 'You think it's still out there?'

Logan frowned across at him. 'I thought they only stole two point six?'

'If they didn't cash it in, if it's still lumps of gold, then it's worth eight point one now. Perhaps Gary Lochhead's still sitting on it. You heard him – they never charged anyone for the robbery, and they never recovered a penny of it either.'

'If I was dying of lung cancer in a ratty wee care home, I'd be out there spending it. Not rotting away like a plastic bag full of body parts.'

King shook his head, eyes wide. 'Eight point one million. The things you could do...'

They took Stonehaven Road at the next roundabout, the grey-brown bulk of The Aberdeen Altens Hotel slipping past on the left – looking more like a prison than HMP Grampian did. Then Cove went by the window.

King broke the silence, obviously doing his best to sound casual. 'You heard anyone boasting about shagging a married woman?'

'No.' Logan put his foot down as they finally passed through the limits, joining the main road south. 'Would it help? To know?'

Yet another mint met its fate. 'Least then I'd know who to *punch*. And—'

His phone launched into 'Fairytale of New York' again.

'AAAAAAAARGH!' He yanked it out and jabbed his thumb down on the red 'Ignore' button three or four times, before switching his phone off and ramming it back into his pocket.

Maybe, just once, Logan could be partnered with someone who wasn't suicidal, homicidal, or some combination of the two?

But he wasn't going to hold his breath.

29

Logan parked in front of number sixteen. Not the prettiest bit of Stonehaven, by any stretch, but not the worst either. Boxy, hutch-like houses faced off across the road – two down, one up, going by the windows, with linked garages joining the whole lot together, making a string of slightly grubby harling with steep, peaked, grey pantiled roofs. It looked a bit like a Toblerone that'd been left in the fridge too long.

Number sixteen's garage was surrounded by scaffolding, its brand-new pitched roof featuring a man in green overalls nailing pantiles into place. The up-and-over door was gone, the hole where it'd been now filled by studwork for a door and a window, all filled in with builder's paper.

Stepping out of the Audi's air-conditioned interior was like being grabbed by a very large hot fist. And squeezed.

King blinked in the punishing brightness, then pulled on a pair of sunglasses, hiding those bloodshot eyes. The front door was tucked away at the side of the building, near the garage. He marched down the driveway to it, squeezing past a blue people carrier, and rang the bell. Turned to Logan. 'How much you want to bet she's got tattoos on her neck and—'

The door opened, and a middle-aged woman scowled out at them with hostile eyes and red hair. She looked them both up and down. Curled her lip as if she didn't like what she'd seen.

'You took your time, didn't you?' She hauled in a deep breath and bellowed back into the house. 'CINDY!'

Logan tucked his peaked cap under his arm. 'Did we?'

'Should've been here, telling *us* before you told the rest of the sodding world.' Another deep breath. 'CINDY!'

A voice boomed out from somewhere inside the house. 'WHAT?'

'DOOR!' Mrs Shouty folded her arms. 'What if that moron, Haiden, tries to abduct his little boy? What if he tries to murder us all in our beds? What about that?'

'Has he?' King stepped forward, eager. 'Have you seen him? Has Haiden been in touch?'

'That's not the *point*. You police don't care, do you? You swan in here and—'

'What?' The grumpy woman from the prison photographs appeared behind her, little flecks of yellow on her broad face that looked disturbingly zit-like against the flushed cheeks. More paint on her orange overalls. Her hair – red like Mrs Shouty's – was mostly hidden beneath a Rosie-the-Riveter headscarf. She scowled at them in exactly the same way her mum had. 'Oh it's *you*, is it?'

Logan stuck out his hand. 'Cindy Lochhead?'

Mrs Shouty stuck her chin out. 'It's Cindy *Norton*, thank you very much. She gave up that moron's name when she divorced him. And good riddance.'

'Quite right too.' King poured on the charm. 'Mrs Norton, I know it's a pain, but I don't suppose there's any chance of a cup of tea, is there?'

'You're trying to get me out of the way, aren't you?'

A you-got-me shrug. 'Well, we—'

'Let me tell you: that boy was nothing but trouble for my Cindy! She was a good girl before he came along. Everything that went wrong in her life was *his* fault.'

Cindy Norton rolled her eyes. 'Mum—'

'She was going to go to *university* for God's sake, till he got his grubby...' a little shudder rippled through Mrs Shouty, '*seed* inside her.'

'Mum, please, I can—'

She raised a hand. 'Oh, I love my grandson, don't get me wrong. I love him like he was my own, but Cindy had a future! She—'

'MUM!'

That produced an outraged look.

Cindy waved her away. 'Go on, sod off for ten minutes and let me speak to them, OK?'

A withering silence, then, *'Fine.'* She turned and stomped away, nose in the air. 'But I'm not making tea for useless, lazy policemen!'

Probably just as well. That would be the kind of tea that came with a free order of sputum.

Cindy sniffed at them, grimaced, then turned and marched off down the corridor, leaving the door open. 'You can have ten minutes. That's it.'

They followed her along the hall, past the open lounge door where an older man slumped in T-shirt and shorts on the couch, watching a daytime soap on the telly. He didn't look up as they went by.

Into the kitchen – small and bland, with fitted units that looked as if they were the height of fashion sometime in the seventies. Mrs Shouty stood by the fridge, glowering at them as Cindy opened the back door and ushered King and Logan out into the garden.

Big bushes, a plum tree in the corner laden with unripe fruit, yellowy grass. Everything wilting in the heat.

Cindy made for the side of the scaffolding-shrouded garage.

Logan caught up with her. 'Has Haiden been in touch?'

She ducked through a sheet of plastic strung between two scaffolding poles and disappeared.

So much for cooperating with the police.

He ducked in after her.

They'd divided the inside up with plasterboard walls, but hadn't got around to the doors yet, leaving a tiny kitchen, wetroom, and living room on show.

'Miss Norton, can we please...'

She kept going, into the living room. A ladder was fixed to the far wall, leading up to a hatch in the roof, where, presumably there was an attic bedroom. Because otherwise there'd be nowhere to sleep.

It wasn't the only ladder in here – a stepladder sat near one wall, a large pot of paint set on top of it.

Cindy picked up a brush and dipped it in the pot. 'Don't mind Mum, she's just pissed because they'd nearly finished paying off the house and now, instead of a new kitchen, they've had to extend the mortgage to pay for all this.' The brush left a thick, warm yellow line across the white plasterboard. Not quite the same colour as in Logan's house, but close enough.

He had another go: '*Has* Haiden been in touch?'

'I saw he'd escaped. Did a runner from some prison-programme bakery thing? He never could stick at anything.'

'Your mother seems to think he'll try to abduct your son.'

'Haiden?' A small laugh. That got bigger. And bigger. Till she was bent double with it, paintbrush dripping onto the chipboard at her feet. Then she sighed, straightened up, and wiped the tears from her eyes. Stuck her brush in the pot again. 'He wouldn't dare. Wouldn't even care. He's never shown any interest in Marty.'

King folded his arms, chest out, feet apart. 'Do you know where he might be?'

Another sigh. 'I really loved him, you know? At first. Two years older than me, had a motorbike and a job and cash to throw about. Thin as a whippet, but not in a weedy way: like he was tightly coiled and ready to spring. A greyhound. *Always* had the best weed.' More paint on the wall.

Logan watched her block out a ragged rectangle of indoor sunshine. 'It's important, Cindy.'

'Mum thinks I was driven snow, till Haiden came along. He wasn't the first boy I let finger me after Geography. Or the first one I went shoplifting with. Or got stoned with. Or...' A very dirty smile spread across her face, then she filled in a bit of plasterboard she'd missed. 'Course, the longer I was with him, the more the veneer wore off. It's all well and good shagging a bloke who's a bit thick, but when you've finished you want someone who can engage you intellectually. You know? All he could ever talk about was "English imperialism" and how we needed to "take our country back".' Cindy shook her head. Slapped on more paint. 'And they weren't even *his* opinions, they were his dad's. You couldn't even debate him on them.'

King tried looming again. 'So you haven't seen Haiden.'

'Not since Marty got into my handbag and ate all my birth control pills, because some idiot at school said it'd get him high.' She jammed the paintbrush in the pot then punished the wall with it. 'After I'd finished making Marty puke them up, I stuck him in the car and we went right up to Peterhead so he could see what happens to stupid boys who don't *think*.'

Nothing like growing up in a happy family where the parents loved each other, was there?

Logan raised his eyebrows at King, who nodded.

Cindy turned and stared at them, paintbrush raised like a knife. 'Look, Haiden married me because I *made* him. Because I was pregnant. He bailed on us because he's a dick. The only use that man is to Marty is as an object lesson.'

Well, it'd been a longshot anyway.

Logan dipped into his pockets for a business card and wrote his mobile number on it. 'If Haiden gets in touch—'

'I won't have Marty making the same mistakes I did. Mum's right, I was going places. Doing well in school. Next thing you know, I'm a teenaged mother without a standard grade to my name. Now I'm going to evening classes, getting my qualifications.'

King tilted his head on one side. 'Did Haiden ever mention Professor Wilson, or a woman called Mhari Powell?'

The red of Cindy's cheeks darkened. 'Mhari? Never heard of her.'

Yeah, that was a lie.

'Are you sure?' Logan pulled out his phone, flicked through to the photo of Mhari Powell they'd shown at the briefing earlier. He held it out. 'You don't recognise her at all?'

Cindy barely looked at it. 'Said so, didn't I?'

'Maybe you heard Haiden talking about her?'

She stabbed the paint and assaulted the wall. 'I – don't – know – her!' Bash, slash, bash. 'Jesus…'

'OK.' King nodded. 'What about Councillor Matt Lansdale?'

She paused. Frowned. 'Lansdale… Wasn't he that tosser who was big in the local "No" campaign? All condescending and slimy about how Scotland isn't big enough or clever enough or hard-working enough to go it alone?' A snort. 'Yeah, now I think about it, Haiden's dad hated the guy. Was going to send him a bomb in the post, but they banged him up for shooting that property developer, didn't they?'

King's face sagged a bit, probably realising that this'd all been one huge waste of time. 'Is there *anything* you can tell us? Anything about where he might be hiding? Any favourite haunts?'

'Pfff… I remember him wanking on about family holidays in Cruden Bay? And they went to Loch Lomond to see some folk festival every year too. And stone circles. The whole bloody family was obsessed with stone circles.' She put the brush down. 'He's killed them, hasn't he? Haiden's killed Wilson and Lansdale. I always knew he'd end up killing someone.'

'So he was violent, then?'

Another laugh. 'What, to me? I'd have ripped his nuts off and made him eat them.' She shook her head, as if trying to dislodge the ridiculous image. 'No. Haiden would never hit a woman. Not a chance in hell. Wouldn't dare.' She picked up the brush and got back to work. 'His harridan mother beat that shit right out of him when he was wee.'

Logan started the Audi's engine and they sat there as the air conditioning's cooling fingers massaged the oppressive heat away.

Cindy's mum, Mrs Shouty, stood in the doorway to number sixteen, glaring out at them.

'What do you think?'

King fastened his seatbelt. 'She's definitely lying about not knowing Mhari.'

'Yup.'

'Jealous Haiden's found someone else? You know what women are like.'

Logan frowned at him. 'Bit misogynistic.'

'You've never been married, have you?' He pulled out his phone and turned it on again. 'OK, *you* explain it.'

'Maybe she and Cindy were friends? Want to nip out and see if the mother recognises her?'

'Not really.' But then his phone started to ding and buzz as all the texts, voicemails, and emails that'd been sent since they drove out of Altens arrived in a rush. A grimace, then he dumped it on the dashboard and produced a 'HAVE YOU SEEN THIS WOMAN?' poster from his jacket pocket. Got out of the car. Then clomped over to where Mrs Shouty stood and held it up.

Logan dug out his own phone and gave Rennie a bell.

'Wassap, boss man?'

'How you getting on with Haiden's associates?'

There was a disappointed hissing noise. *'Imagine a sleeping bag full of angry bees and you're not far off it.'*

'They not cooperating?' Suppose that was only to be expected. Haiden's mates were hardly likely to be the most civic-minded members of the local community.

'Not so you'd notice, no.'

Outside, at number sixteen, it looked as if Cindy's mum was giving DI King a bit of a shouting at.

'How many more have you got to go?'

'Pffff… About a dozen? Everyone says they've not seen him in ages. Even before he went to prison.'

'Hmmm… What about Ravendale?'

There was a pause, and what sounded like muttered swearing. Then, *'Just on my way to do it now, Guv.'*

Yeah, right. And the moon was made of marshmallow.

King clearly thought he'd been shouted at enough for one day, because he about-faced and stomped towards to the car, ramming the poster into his jacket. Face like a ruptured haemorrhoid.

Suppose they should really head back to the office now and…

Logan frowned. Hardie was probably right about steering clear of Divisional Headquarters until they'd actually achieved something. 'Rennie? Email me the list and who you've seen so far. Might try one or two on our way in.'

'*Will do.*' Then he lowered his voice to an angry whisper. '*And may I just say, before you go, that I owe you one for saddling me with bloody Tufty!*'

That was worth a smile. 'It's good for you. Builds character.' He hung up as King yanked the passenger door open and threw himself into the seat. 'Let me guess...?'

'Never seen her, we're all a bunch of useless bastards, and we should be ashamed of ourselves.' He hauled on his seatbelt. 'Why do we bother?'

Logan frowned at the house, fingers drumming on the steering wheel.

'Well?' King clipped on his seatbelt. 'What are we waiting for?'

'Seems a bit ... odd, doesn't it? Haiden's ex says he would never hit a woman.'

'So?'

'How come Mhari Powell has a black eye?'

'Because people change. Because he's spent three years in prison. Because he's a violent dickhead.' King stared across the car at him. 'Or maybe Mhari bastarding Powell lied about that as well? She lied about everything else.'

True.

Cindy's mum was still glowering at them from the open front door. She must have seen Logan looking, because she raised both middle fingers in the Audi's direction, teeth bared in a snarl.

He pulled away from the kerb, making for the main road north again. 'I love it when members of the public help with our inquiries. Makes me feel all warm and fuzzy inside.'

30

King looked up through the windscreen as Logan parked in front of the block of flats. 'This us?'

Whoever built it either didn't have much of an eye for architecture, or hated buildings and everyone who lived in them. Four storeys of bland grey harling, punctuated with white-framed windows and a flat roof. The only decorative touch was the narrow concrete portico that sulked above the entrance. Not exactly welcoming.

Logan checked Rennie's email. 'Robert Cockburn, AKA: Gonorrhoea Bob. Previous for drugs and assault. Did six months in borstal with Haiden. Not long finished a two stretch for a racially motivated attack.'

King got out of the car. 'Want to bet *he's* got tattoos on his neck?'

Turned out King was right: 'Gonorrhoea Bob' had a thistle on one side and a spider's web on the other. Daggers, skulls, and saltires on the back of his hands. Probably a ton more lurking beneath his crisp white shirt, black tie, suit trousers, and trainers. Hair Brylcreem-oily and parted on one side. Looking so buttoned-down he was liable to pop at any moment.

His flat was the kind of spotless that usually came with a diagnosis of OCD, every surface gleaming, the air thick with the sharp plastic smell of lemon-scented polish. The mismatched collection of charity-shop furniture had probably never been cleaner in its life.

Gonorrhoea Bob nodded and blinked at them. 'I know, and I'm sorry, but I was a different person then. The man that I was died when I accepted Jesus into my heart.'

King settled onto the couch. 'You kicked an Asian shopkeeper half to death for having a "Better Together" sign in the window.'

'And I'll have to live with that till the end of my days.' His Adam's apple bobbed like a vulture's beak. 'All I can hope is that I get the chance to redeem myself before I stand in front of Saint Peter.'

Logan pulled out his notebook. 'When did you last see Haiden Lochhead?'

Tears sparkled in Gonorrhoea Bob's eyes. 'I don't see *anyone* from those days any more. That was the old me. I changed when—'

'When you let Jesus into your heart. We know.'

Sun sparkled on the surface of Duthie Park's boating pond, the water a good bit greener than the River Dee on the other side of the road. A handful of couples were spread around the outside of the pond, chucking torn-up bits of sliced white while the ducks cackled their Sid James laughs. Bullying their way to the soggy morsels.

Ian McNab slouched on a bench, in black tracksuit bottoms and a replica Aberdeen Football Club shirt. *Peaky Blinders* haircut. Big rampant lion tattoo all the way up one arm. Fag in one hand, the other rocking a pushchair back and forward a few inches – its occupant asleep. A small child hurtled around and around the bench, shrieking and waving his arms, dressed as a mini version of his dad, only without the tattoo.

McNab looked up at Logan and King, then shrugged. 'Yeah, I saw Haiden on the telly.' He pointed at them with his cigarette. 'He was on this screen thing behind you pair of poofs. Mind? You were sitting there like someone just shagged yer mum wi' a flagpole?'

King tried his looming trick again. 'Has he been in touch?'

It had the same amount of success on McNab as it had on Cindy Norton. Sod, and indeed, all.

'In touch wi' me? *Naw*, Officer, I'm no' allowed to consort wi' known criminals, am I? Condition o' ma release. Staying oot a prison for ma bairns, like.' Sounding more bored than contrite.

The kid made another circuit. 'Look at me, Daddy! Look at me!'

McNab didn't. 'Aye, very good, Timmy.' He took a long drag on his cigarette and blew the smoke at King. 'Anything else I can help you poofs with?'

Logan had a go. 'If Haiden went into hiding, where would he hide?'

'Naw, that'd be *cheating*. First rule of hide and seek: naebody likes a clype.' McNab closed his eyes, tilted his head back, and smiled at the sun. 'Now be good wee poofs and bugger off. I'm trying tae work on ma tan here and yer blocking the light.'

Jacob McCain ran a hand over his shaved head – not so much a fashion statement as an unavoidable necessity, going by the paucity of blue stubble up there – and loaded another box of cheese into the chiller cabinet from the cage at his side. He wore a long-sleeved high-necked white T-shirt beneath his blue stripy tabard, twin bands of tattoos just visible in the gap between his cuffs and his thick black gloves. Not the tallest of men, and not the broadest either. But there was … something *imposing* about him. Something dangerous. As if asking where the hummus was might get you stabbed.

King held out Mhari's picture again. 'Come on, Jacob, at least *pretend* to look at her.'

McKinnon's Family Market – 'Bargantuan savings since 1998!' – on Holburn Street wasn't going to challenge Asda, Tesco, or Sainsbury's any time soon. It was more of a strip-light and tin-can, pile-'em-high and sell-'em-for-a-moderate-markup kind of place. Somewhere you could get knock-off Lithuanian KitKats and Tundidor's Tasty Caramel Wafers, all in lookalike packaging.

Jacob dumped another thing of Bulgarian cheddar on the shelf. 'Don't need to. I know the bitch.'

Finally: someone prepared to admit it.

'You know her name?'

'Mary. Only she spelled it the Gaelic way, with an "H" and an "I".' Armenian Edam joined the ranks of cheese. 'Was a fashion for that, back in the good old days, yeah? Gaelic-ing up your name so you'd look more committed to the cause. Driving the English out.' He shook his bald head. 'Utter bitch, like.'

Logan handed him the box of Spanish Bleu. 'Did Mhari say anything about herself. Where she came from?'

'Only met her once.' He slit the box open with a Stanley knife and banged the contents one by one onto the shelf. 'Went up to visit Haiden in Peterhead, didn't I? Took him some fags. And there she was, the sainted sodding Mhari.'

A young-ish guy in a shirt and stripy blue tie stalked around the end of the aisle, holding a clipboard to his pigeon chest. Pale and clean-shaven. Like an intestinal parasite that had landed a middle-management job. He raised his voice, scowling along the dairy aisle at their bald informant. 'Is there a *problem*, Jacob?' Sounding about as friendly as prostate cancer.

Jacob shook his head. 'No, Mr Cousins.'

'Then why are *the police* in my store, Jacob?'

Logan raised a hand. 'We're in getting some supplies for the station. Jacob here was advising us on organic versus nonorganic dairy products.'

'Oh.' Pause. 'Well, that's all right then.' He stood up to his full wormy five nine and fixed Jacob with what was probably meant to be a steely gaze. 'Soon as you've finished here, get around to Cleaning Products and Pet Food. Someone's dropped a litre-bottle of fabric softener and it's all over the aisle.'

Another nod. 'Yes, Mr Cousins.'

'Good.' He turned and marched off, heels clicking on the linoleum floor.

Soon as he'd gone, Jacob's hands turned into fists for a moment. 'Wanker.' Keeping his voice low as he hammered cheap smoked cheese in plastic casings in beside the pre-grated mozzarella. 'Rip your bastarding arms off and make you eat them...' Then Jacob seemed to remember that he was standing there with two police officers, because he cleared his throat and looked away. 'Just a joke, like.'

Not given Jacob's record it wasn't.

Logan picked up a packet of Cheese Rope. 'So you actually *met* Mhari?'

'What? Yeah, the fags. She wouldn't let me give him them. "Haiden's giving up," she says, "he's getting healthier for the cause," she says.' A wee growl, then a sniff. Then Jacob went into the cage for a box of Cheerful Cattle Spreading Triangles. 'Next thing you know, I'm not allowed to visit him any more. Bitch said his old mates were a bad influence. We're—'

Mr Cousins' voice battered out through the supermarket's PA system, echoing and distorted. *'Jacob McCain to Cleaning Products and Pet Food. Clean-up on Cleaning Products and Pet Food.'*

'Gah!' He hurled the box back in the cage and slammed the grilled front shut. 'See if I wasn't on licence?' Then took hold of the cage and stomped off, pushing it in front of him as he went, the wheels squeaking like tortured gerbils.

Logan watched him go. 'Five quid says Mr Cousins comes to some sort of very unfortunate and painful accident before too long.'

King leaned in closer. 'And, to be honest, he'd sodding well deserve it.'

Couldn't argue with that.

Tartan Tam's was the kind of establishment that gave old-fashioned Scottish pubs a bad name. Small; dark; with a short bar featuring four pumps, a line of greasy optics, and a bored-looking woman hunched over a *Scottish Daily Post*. A puggy machine dinged and wibbled away to itself by the bar – enough flashing lights on it to give half the city seizures as it offered them nudges, lucky sevens, and lemons.

There wasn't a surface in the pub that didn't look sticky. That included the table Logan and King stood in front of, staring down at a guy with a teddy-boy quiff, pint of Guinness, a packet of dry-roasted, and a 'F*CK THE ENGLISH!' T-shirt.

He slouched in his bench seat, arms along the back. 'So?'

King leaned his fists on the tabletop, trying for another loom. 'Look, Mackers, have you seen Haiden or not?'

A shrug. 'I've seen his handiwork. Get it?' A smile and a wink. '*Hand*-iwork? Cos he chopped off that professor tosser's hands?'

Logan pulled out his notebook. 'You *saw* him do it? You were there at the time?'

'Naw, in the *papers*, like.' He took a swig of Guinness, chased it down with a couple of peanuts. Talking before he'd finished chewing them, grey and white residue sticking to his teeth. 'Good for Haiden, though. Them Unionistas need a short sharp shock. With any luck he'll go after the papists next. Then the immigrants: Pakis, Poles, and Darkies. Purge the whole fucking lot of them. Scotland for the Scottish!'

Rush-hour traffic filled the road before them, slowed to a crawl as they waited in the long, *long* line for Mounthooly Roundabout.

King was about as slumped as he could be without actually slithering into the passenger footwell. Looking out of the window as Aberdeen's only pagoda crawled past. 'God, that was depressing…'

'Lovely people, Haiden's friends.'

He scrubbed at his face with his hands. 'Not everyone who wants independence is like that, Logan. Some of us just want a fairer country to live in. One that makes its own rules instead of having to bow and scrape to a parliament in Westminster we didn't elect.'

'Yes, well, technically we *do* elect them. United Kingdom, remember?'

King waved it away. 'Rennie was right: all that talk about a "democratic deficit" during the EU referendum – that's all we've had up here for sodding generations!' He turned in his seat. 'The last hundred years: do you know how many times England has picked the UK government? Every single time, but three. Three times we got the government we wanted and they didn't. And even then it was because they couldn't make up their minds who to put in power.' A short bitter laugh. 'And do you know how long one of those three times lasted? Six months – 1974.'

Great. A lecture.

Logan reached for the radio. 'Told you before: no politics in the car.'

Something drive-timey rocked out of the speakers, completely at odds with the slug's pace the traffic was actually moving at.

Closer to the roundabout. Closer. Closer...

King turned the radio down. 'How did you vote in the referendum?'

'What, the completely secret ballot that I don't have to disclose to anyone?'

He curled his lip. 'Yeah, I thought so. You're a sodding *Unionist*.' Imbuing the word with all the warmth of a puddle of yesterday's cat sick.

'Don't be a dick.'

'Logan, there's *five hundred and thirty-three* English MPs and only fifty-nine Scottish ones. They could get together tomorrow and decide to rename Scotland "Whingey Tartanbaws McJockland" and there's sod all we could do about it.'

Seriously?

'They're not going to change "Scotland" to—'

'It's just England pushing us around! Us and Wales and Northern Ireland.' King's face got more and more flushed with every declamation. 'Making all the big decisions. Telling us what to do. Ordering us about. The West Lothian question's a joke: they outnumber us nine to one!'

'You finished?' Preferably *before* you have an aneurysm.

King thumped back in his seat. 'The UK isn't a partnership, it's an abusive relationship.'

— the blade, the reality-TV star, and the screaming —

31

King checked his watch, then nodded at the assembled officers. 'So I want you in here, seven sharp tomorrow. Till then, try and get a decent night's sleep – no boozing it up. I need you all at your best.' He pointed at the door. 'Off you go, then.'

Most of the team stood: some trying to look grim and determined, the rest clearly delighted at getting to go home at last. Support staff, plainclothes, and uniform, all bustling out through the door. Leaving only Milky, Steel, Tufty, Heather, King and Logan as it swung shut again.

Briefing over, King slumped down on the edge of a newly vacated desk, as if he'd been wrung dry. 'Sodding hell...'

Steel popped her feet up. 'Everything's going great, then?'

He turned to Rennie. 'And you didn't find *anything*?'

All the way through the briefing and he hadn't made eye contact with Logan once. Had barely spoken to him since the 'Parliamentary Arithmetic' rant in the car.

Rennie shrugged. 'Between us we've covered all of Haiden's known associates and none of them have a clue where he is. Or if they do, they're not telling.'

Sitting beside him, Tufty nodded. 'There's two worth keeping an eye on, if that helps? Really shifty when we spoke to them. Lots of tattoos too.'

Must be this season's Alt-Nat look.

Logan pulled out a chair and sat. 'Jacob McCain said he

wasn't allowed to visit Haiden in prison any more, because,' making quote bunnies, '"Mhari" wouldn't let him. She thought Haiden's old friends were a bad influence.'

'Pfff… She's no' exactly a wee fairy princess herself!'

'Does sound like a pattern of control, though.'

There was a single clap and they all turned to look at a smiling Rennie.

'*Speaking* of Fairy Princesses, and straying off topic for a moment, are you all remembering it's Lola's big birthday party this Saturday? Everyone's invited.' He looked at them in turn, eyebrows raised. No reply. 'Anyway, Mistress Fizzymiggins wants to know how many people want to make their own magic wand and fairy wings, so she can get enough glitter in.'

King pinched his face closed for a moment. 'Can we stick to the abductions and attempted murders for now? Please, Sergeant? Can we do that?'

'Ah. OK.' Doing his best to sound casual. 'I suppose that's sensible.'

Milky filled the ensuing silence. 'Harmsworth and me didn't get anything from the guys on Haiden's cell-block either. Half wouldn't know Wednesday from a line of coke, and t'other half wouldn't talk to us if their mum's life depended on it.'

'Aye, naebody likes a clype.'

Logan frowned at Steel. 'Not you too. Got enough of that from Ian McNab.'

'Before we drift too far from the point, *again*,' Heather checked her notebook, 'we should concentrate on the local Alt-Nat groups. Someone's bound to know something.'

'What about tracking down our fake Mhari Powell?'

Tufty: 'I know! I know! We could go through all those social media accounts my algorithm found – the ones she's posting from under aliases and stuff – see if we can figure out where she works, who her friends are?'

'Good.' King nodded. 'Make that your number one tomorrow. I want a list of people to interview. Maybe they'll be a bit more forthcoming than Haiden's criminal mates.'

Steel: 'Search her house too. Bound to get a warrant now we know she's a faker.'

'Then that's *your* number one. And make sure you've got a dog unit with you.'

'Hey!' Heather. 'What about my Alt-Nat theory?'

'Definitely. Take Milky and hit them up tomorrow. I want a list of groups on my desk by nine. Then go speak to everyone you can ID.'

She looked at Milky, then sucked on her teeth for a bit. 'Yeah... Might not be the *best* of ideas, Boss. Alt-Nats tend not to like the English very much, and Milky is a bit...' Heather made a seesaw motion with her hand, 'let's call it "ethnically distinctive".'

Milky laid it on thick: 'Gi'oar, ya daft apeth!' Then an evil smile. 'If they don't like the English, I'll bloody well give them English.'

'That's settled then.' Steel stood and stretched, showing off the pasty dead thing passing for her stomach. 'Are we done now, oh Great Mint-Scented Leader? Only some of us have wives to get home to.'

A pause as something pained scratched at King's features. He shook it off. 'Yes. Fine. Go. All of you.'

She shot him with both finger guns. 'Later, lumpty-numpties.'

Tufty, Rennie, and Milky scuffed out after her, Heather bringing up the rear.

The door clunked shut behind them and King shook his head. 'Well, *that* was a fun day.'

Logan stood and had a stretch of his own. 'Look on the bright side: up till now, Mhari Powell, or whoever she is, has been playing us all for idiots. At least now we know.'

'Excuse me if I don't throw a parade.' King picked himself off the edge of the desk, still not making eye contact. 'I spoke to Inspector Pearce: no sign of the white Nissan Micra.'

'They'll have seen the media coverage, dumped the car somewhere, and got the hell out of Aberdeen. You'd have to be thick as mince to hang about after all this.'

King scrubbed at his face, shoulders bowed. 'Maybe France

was a double bluff? They make us think Haiden's running away to Calais on the ferry; only they know we'll find out it's all fake, because he's sitting in her car on Netherkirkgate, right in front of a security camera; so *we* think they'll never really sneak across the Channel; when, in fact, that's exactly what they're planning to do?'

'Bit convoluted, isn't it? Anyway, Mhari didn't know we were on to her until Hardie made his idiotic announcement at the press conference. Far as she was concerned, they were getting away with Plan A.'

He sagged a bit further. 'True.'

Outside, the wailing cry of another siren on its way to something horrible faded in the distance.

Logan stepped in front of King. 'Are you sulking with me, because I won't tell you how I voted in the referendum?'

He still wouldn't look at him. 'Course not.'

'Because that would be childish, and *really* counterproductive given all this Alt-Nat nonsense flying around.'

'I know, I know. It's just...' And finally, King met his eyes. 'It's just with Gwen, and the case, and Edward Bloody Barwell, and Hardie...' A sigh. 'Sorry.'

'Are you sure you want to keep going with this one? You could recuse yourself, if you like. Tell them you're stepping down to avoid distracting from the investigation. Take some time and sort things out at home.'

'They'd never let me run another high-profile case if I did that.' He rubbed at his face again. 'And what's left to sort out? Gwen hates me, Logan. I mean she really, really loathes me. You've seen how often she phones to have a go. Gloating about her affair. Telling me how she's turning the kids against me. Making sure I suffer...' There was a tiny, unhappy laugh. 'I can't even leave her: I've got nowhere to go.' His whole body deflated a bit, as if someone had let the air out of his life. A deep breath didn't seem to help. 'Pub?'

'Can't.'

'Come on, let me buy you a couple of pints as an apology for calling you a Unionist.'

'Love to, but I'm babysitting the monsters tonight.'

'Yeah. Raincheck.' King shrugged as if it didn't bother him one way or the other. 'You're right, by the way: Hardie's press conference was pretty much guaranteed to set them running. The man's an idiot. Haiden and Mhari will be miles away by now.'

Haiden runs his hands across the dashboard again, fingers skimming the glove compartment's latch. Nice wee car this. Bigger than it looked on *The Italian Job*. Shame it's a bit manky.

But when you're stealing something from long-term parking, you can't go nicking a flash motor. Nah, you want something that'll go unnoticed.

He grins across the car at Mhari, who, let's be honest, is bloody stunning. She's swapped her mousy-librarian costume for a tight pink T-shirt and sexy low-rise jeans, flashing a strip of beautiful tanned stomach that makes his groin tighten every time he looks at her. Those little leather driving gloves she's got on, gripping the steering wheel like it's his cock and he's been naughty. She's done that thing with her hair as well, from lank to exotic and oooh...

He adjusts himself through his trousers.

She smiles. 'Steady, Tiger.'

Oh yeah, they are *so* going to do it later.

But for now, concentrate on the mission, Haiden. Make sure she knows you're not just a pretty face. 'Where we going to send the package this time?'

She thinks about it as the backwoods of Aberdeenshire slip by the car window. 'The BBC worked wonders with Wanky Wilson. Let's send it there.'

'Yeah.' He nods. 'But *maybe* we should try ITV this time? Or Channel Four? Sky? You know, whip up a bit of competition?'

She reaches across the car and squeezes his leg with those leather gloves. 'Genius. See, that's why you're in charge, Babe.'

Squeeze higher, Mhari. Please, squeeze higher...

But she doesn't. The hand goes back to the steering wheel instead.

Ah well. Just have to wait till later and hope his balls don't explode before then.

Haiden reaches into the footwell and picks up the claw hammer. Bit rusty, but it'd do the job. Slaps it against his palm. Frowns at it. 'You know, we should've done that with Lansdale. Sent his bits to the media.'

'How were we supposed to know no one would open his post? Politicians are meant to have assistants, or a secretary, or something.'

'Yeah… Shame he died before we could film him, though. Jesus, the state of his *face*! Would've frightened the crap out of them Unionist bastards.'

'Hey, we learned, didn't we? We *learned*. And this next one?' She squeezes his thigh again. 'Going to be perfect.'

Bloody disaster, that's what it was. But, then, had it ever been anything else?

Frank unscrewed the cap again and took a swig from his halfy of Co-op own-brand vodka. It went down like burning petrol, spreading its fire.

He'd actually found a parking space outside the flat for once. Not that it would be his flat for long. The lights were on up there. Flat 2R, with its sodding dreamcatcher in the window and the double glazing that needed replacing, and the rusty bracket where the last lot's TV aerial used to be. The dirty granite strung with black cables, because BT couldn't be arsed wiring the place up properly. And *her*…

Here's to Mr and soon-to-no-longer-be-Mrs King.

He toasted the window and took another swig. The blaze spread, numbing the base of his skull in the way only vodka could.

'Home, sweet sodding home.'

Should really go in. Been out here long enough, stoking the boiler. Getting ready for the inevitable fight.

Maybe he should—

His phone rang in his pocket. Not the dreaded 'Fairytale of New York', but the bland, generic ringtone that came as default.

Frank pulled it out and squinted at the screen, still sober enough to read it with both eyes: 'UNKNOWN NUMBER'.

Hmph.

He answered it. 'King.'

A small pause, then a familiar voice slithered its way into his ear. *'Detective Inspector King, it's Edward Barwell.* Scottish Daily Post.*'*

Of course it was. After a day like today, how could it not be? One last kick in the crotch before going home to the wife.

Well, you know what? He'd had enough. 'Bye.'

He was halfway to hanging up, but Barwell wasn't giving up that easily – voice thin and tinny through the speaker. *'Sure you don't want to give your side of the story?'*

'I did that at the briefing, remember? Now, if you don't mind—'

'Oh, you got your "I was just there trying to impress a girl" thing out, but that doesn't really cover what you did, does it?'

Course it did.

Didn't it?

He put the phone against his ear again.

'See, I know way *more about you than you think. And I'm betting way more than your colleagues do.'*

Frank turned in his seat, searching the street. A long terrace of flats, most of them the same shade of dirty granite as his own. A builder's merchant opposite, all dark and plastered with warning signs. Parked cars crammed along both sides of the road. The shadows starting to lengthen, but the sun still hot enough in the sky to make the air above the bonnet shimmer.

Was Barwell out there? Watching him? Some paparazzi scum sitting next to him taking shots with a telephoto lens? 'DISGRACED ALT-NAT COP'S SECRET ALKIE SHAME!'

He looked down at the bottle in his hand. Too late to worry about it now, then.

Frank gave them something to photograph: gulping down half the bottle. Let loose a little hiss as the numbness turned to tingling.

'Don't know what you think you've got, but it's a lie.'

'Sure you don't want to say a few words to the great unwashed? How about to Robert Drysdale's family? Want to say something to them?'

What?

'Who the hell is … Drysdale?'

He swallowed.

'Well, well, well: is that the sound of a penny dropping, I hear?'

'No idea who you're talking about.'

A laugh. 'You keep telling yourself that. Meanwhile, I'll be telling everyone the truth.'

Frank bared his teeth. Sat forward in the driver's seat, half-bottle clenched in his fist. 'Then I hope you've got a bloody good lawyer, cos I'm going to sue your rag for every penny it's got!' He jammed his thumb on the 'End Call' button. Slammed the phone down on the passenger seat. Bellowed out a howl of rage – flecks of spit spattering the windscreen.

He knocked back a hefty swig of vodka. And another one. Then another, draining it.

Screwed the top on like he was throttling that rancid wee shite, Barwell. Twisting the black metal till Barwell's eyes popped out of his greasy little head. Banged the empty bottle down beside his phone.

Hauled himself out of the car and slammed the door hard as he could.

Stood there staring at it for a moment.

You know what? No way he was suffering an evening with Gwen nipping at his head the whole time. Not without a *lot* more vodka inside him.

And that's *exactly* what he was going to get.

32

Logan hung up his fleece, took off his boots, and put a hand on the banister, looking up towards the top floor. 'Hello? Anyone home?'

No reply.

'Cthulhu?' Sing-songing it out. 'Where's Daddy's favourite kittenfish?'

Still nothing.

Hmph.

He wandered through into the living room. No sign of anyone there either. 'Hello?'

A muffled shriek from outside.

Ah, that explained it then.

Logan stepped out through the open patio doors, onto the patio – the paving slabs warm beneath his socks.

Tara stood in the middle of it with her hands over her eyes. God knew why, but she was wearing a ridiculous homemade tiara that looked as if she'd cobbled it together from half a ton of pipe cleaners, three gallons of glitter, and enough tinsel to strangle fifty department store Santas. 'Eighty-five, eighty-six, eighty-seven.'

Logan waved at her, even though she couldn't see him. 'Hello.'

'Eighty-eight, eighty-nine, ninety.'

'Is no one happy to see me at all?'

'Ninety-one, ninety-two, ninety-three.'

Typical.

Welcome home, lovely Logan. How great it is to see you. Pfff...

Cthulhu padded out from under a bush, tail in the air.

'Ninety-four, ninety-five, ninety-six.'

He squatted down and Daddy's Favourite Kittenfish bumped her head against his knee, purring and prooping. Doing the LOVE ME dance with her big fluffy white paws. 'At least you're happy to see me.'

'Ninety-seven, ninety-eight, ninety-nine.'

'Unlike the rest of these bumheads.'

'One hundred!' Tara snapped her hands down and span around, staring out at the trees and shrubs. 'Here I come, ready or not!'

Logan scooped Cthulhu up, turning her tummy-side-up as she stretched out her furry arms and legs. He raised an eyebrow at Tara. 'Do I even get a hello?'

'Don't distract the Seeker! I'm hunting ... *monsters*!' And with that, she charged off into the garden, growling.

They were all off their tiny rockers.

More shrieks from the undergrowth, then Naomi charged out, wearing a pirate costume and a ridiculous homemade tiara of her own, both arms in the air, waving a water pistol around in one hand and Captain Bogies in the other.

Tara lumbered after Naomi, not going anywhere near fast enough to actually catch her. 'Bwahahahahahahaha!'

And neither of them bothered to even *look* in his direction.

'Fine. I'm going to get a beer and you can all go poop yourselves.'

He carried Cthulhu inside, through to the kitchen, and plonked her down on the table. Opened the fridge – setting the huge collection of kids' drawings pinned to it flapping – and dug out a tin of Stella.

Had to admit, the room had turned out better than expected: granite worktops, a good gas cooker, decent units, nice tiles. Head and shoulders above the bargain-basement kitchen he'd

DIYed into place at the Sergeant's House in Banff. Even if the worktop by the microwave *was* almost buried under an assortment of metal coat hangers, packs of multicoloured pipe cleaners, balls of tinsel, and jars of glitter.

He cracked the tab on his tin and froze.

Was that giggling?

He turned. Hunkered down. And peered in under the table.

Jasmine stared at him, eyes glittering, both hands over her mouth. Shoulders jiggling from the effort of keeping the giggles in. And *her* tiara was the most OTT of them all.

'Evening.' He pointed at the monstrosity on her head. 'Why are you wearing a—'

'Shhhh! You can't tell Aunty Tara where I'm hiding!'

Not her as well...

Logan held up a hand and backed away. 'I know, I know: "naebody likes a clype".'

Tara stepped up behind him and wrapped her arms around his chest. Warm against his back in the sunshine as he finished off his tin of Stella. Naomi and Jasmine thundered about in the garden, Cthulhu sitting on a garden chair by the patio doors – staying well out of it.

Logan put his tin on the windowsill. 'I take it you rotten sods have eaten?'

'Don't sulk.' She kissed his neck. 'I saved some tuna casserole for you.'

'Should think so too.'

Naomi and Jasmine battered past, holding their oversized wobbly tiaras on top of their heads.

He turned and frowned at the lurid concoction sitting on top of Tara's. 'OK, I'll bite: what's with the fancy headgear?'

'Rennie's daughter's birthday party this weekend: it's BYOT.'

'Ah, so *that's* what it stands for.'

She smiled. 'Don't worry, we made one for you too.'

Why did that sound like a threat?

*   *   *

The bedside clock glowed '21:00', but even with the curtains drawn, daylight crept in around the edges. Jasmine and Naomi, in their respective jammies and beds, clutching their respective stuffed animals – Captain Bogies the filthy octopus for Naomi, Mr Stinky the threadbare bear for Jasmine.

Tara leaned against the door frame, wearing a huge smile. Probably very pleased with herself for talking him into wearing the monstrosity she and the kids had made. Which looked a bit like a cross between an explosion in a pipe-cleaner factory and a prolapsed Christmas tree. The others had been over the top, but his was definitely the over-the-topiest of them all.

Everyone stared at him as he turned the page and hoisted the pirate accent up a couple of yardarms.

'So Skeleton Bob grabbed hold with both hands,
And decided that this was a *ludicrous* plan,
The Kraken, you see, didn't mean to eat Dave,
Or chew through the ship as it sailed through the
    waves,
The truth was the Kraken was just a bit lonely,
And that's why it ate those three whales and the pony,'

Naomi's eyes widened. 'Ooooooh...'

'A bus full of people, a bear, and a goat,
Six taxis, a church, Captain Dave, and the boat,
Now, inside its tummy, they'd all been condemned,
To be mushed up and chewed to a sticky brown blend,
And that's where we'll leave them, and call this...'

Everyone joined in for the last bit, even Tara: 'The End!'

Logan closed the book, stood and kissed Jasmine on the head. 'Night Monster Number One.' Then did the same with Naomi. 'Night Monster Number Two.'

She held up her grubby octopus. 'Don't forget Captain Bogies!'

'OK.' Captain Bogies got a kiss on his head too. 'Night Monster Number Three.'

He stopped in the doorway – ducking a bit so he didn't lose his tiara on the architrave – and clicked out the light, leaving them with the rotating glow of a wee planetarium globe thing. Well, that and the sunshine oozing in around the curtains.

Tara blocked his way out, so he kissed her as well. She tasted of cherries. 'Monster Number Four.' That seemed to do the trick, because she backed away far enough to let Logan close the door behind him.

She reached up and adjusted his tiara. 'Very fetching.' A lopsided smile. 'You make a good dad, you know that, don't you?' Then closed one eye and chewed on the inside of one cheek for a bit. 'Maybe it wouldn't be such a bad idea after all?'

Oh-ho.

'Well, there's nothing to stop us getting a bit of practice in.' He wrapped her up in a hug, complete with *very* wandering hands. Getting a laughing shriek for his troubles as she grabbed hold of his bum for a revenge grope.

Jasmine's voice barged through the closed bedroom door: *'GOD SAKE, YOU TWO. GET A ROOM!'*

Which wasn't a bad idea...

Sylvia's voice purred in his ear. *'And the sell-in's great, Scotty. We're talking potential top ten bestseller here.'*

Scott grinned. A top ten bestseller: how cool was that?

Wait a minute... 'Sylvia, does that mean we have to give the guy who wrote it more money?' He stuck the phone on 'Speaker' and dropped it into his top pocket, freeing both hands to tip the remainder of his pear and Roquefort tarte tatin into the food recycling bin – well, you never knew when something like *The Great British Bake Off* might come calling. And lesser mortals than him had parlayed that into a lucrative media career, so why shouldn't he?

'You let me worry about that. Your name's on the cover, you get all the fame and ninety-nine percent of the cash.'

'Less your fifteen percent.'

A laugh. *'Hey, a girl's gotta eat, right?'*

The kitchen, let's be honest here, was an absolute triumph

– lots of chrome and brushed steel appliances. A dark-maroon statement wall for the range cooker to sit against. *Mahoosive* fridge with separate wine cooler. But then the whole house was a monument to his superior taste, thank you very much.

Shame no one had thought to get in touch with *Grand Designs* when he was having it built. Could've been great on that.

'And have you thought any more about: you – know – what?'

'Yeah...' He sucked a breath in through his teeth. 'I'm not sure *Strictly* is a good fit for me. What about the charity single idea? Or ... presenting something on TV, you know? Something with a bit of gravitas?' He pulled the bag out of the recycling bin and tied the top edges together.

'Scotty, you can't just coast into a cosy media career off the back of four weeks in the Big Brother *house any more. It's not 2002 and you're not Jade Goody.'*

Damn right he wasn't. 'How about *Celebrity Mastermind*? I could—'

'Are you insane*? No one in the history of* ever *got a career boost from* Celebrity Cocking Mastermind, *have you seen the Z-list nobodies they have on that show?'*

He carried the bag out into the hall – big, atrium style, with an Italian marble floor, huge rubber plants and citrus trees and the like. All of which had cost a small fortune. As had everything else in here, including the state-of-the-art home cinema setup in the lounge.

'Listen to me, Scotty: you want the TV show and the turn on Desert Island Discs*? You gotta do* Strictly.'

Groan.

'And while we're at it, have you done that opinion piece for the Telegraph *yet?'*

'I'm a bit... Look, Sylvia, are you sure this is the right direction for me? My dad's SNP and he's still not speaking to me after the last one I wrote.' Scott walked through the porch. Smaller in scale – so you'd get the wow factor stepping out of it into the hall: see, he knew what he was doing when he briefed the architect – but still pretty damned grand as far as designs went.

'Don't be daft: "Why Scotland should be scared to go it alone" was terrific. Best thing in the whole paper.'

'But—'

'Scotty, darling, trust me. That "Tackling the Tartan Menace" shtick plays very well down here. London loves it. And where do you think all the casting decisions are made?' She left an expectant pause, but there was no point answering the question, because they both knew it wasn't Scotland.

'OK, OK, I'll write the piece.' He checked his reflection in the gilt-edged mirror – not bad – unlocked the front door and stepped outside. 'But if my dad disowns me, it'll be your fault.'

A proper gravel driveway led down to the large wrought-iron gates, bordered by waist-high drystane dykes that cost an eye-wateringly large amount to put in.

The sun caressed the horizon, painting the sky with purple strokes, a smattering of clouds flaring fluorescent pink as the switch to twilight came... Hey, that was pretty good: 'Painted the sky with purple strokes.' Have to remember it for later, write it down when he got back inside.

Maybe he wouldn't need someone to write the next book for him? Couldn't be that difficult, could it? All you did was stuff one word down after the next till a book plopped out the other end. Any idiot could do that.

'Now, about Strictly...?'

The gravel crunched beneath his feet as he made for the gates, skirting the brand-new, dark-blue, BMW Z4. 'Not convinced.'

She put on her patient voice. 'Scotty, darling, let me explain Agent Sylvia's patented Showbiz Hierarchy of Needs. I'd love to get you a presenting job, but to do that I need to get you on Strictly first. After that we go for a guest spot on Corrie, then EastEnders, Doctors, Casualty. How about Saturday Kitchen? You like your food, right?'

'Oooh, I could do that.' He pulled the little remote from his trouser pocket and pressed the button. The gates swung open on silent hinges.

'TV exposure is the oxygen our entertainment ecosystem thrives on. The more of it you breathe, the more of you they want.'

'And what about *Celebrity Pointless*?'

A thinking sound, then, *'Liking it.'*

He dumped the bag in the green recycling bin. Straightened up.

Frowned.

Was that...?

'Hold on, Sylvia.'

A sound. Sort of scuffing, like someone trying to hide their footsteps?

He stood there, head cocked to the left, listening...

The sun was setting, but it'd be twilight for at least another hour yet. Longest day – wouldn't be properly dark till after eleven. And yet ... the shadows gathered. Deep blues and purples, reaching out from the drystane dykes, blurring the detail. Hiding things.

Somewhere, off in the distance, a fox yowled.

'You still there?'

Nah. It was nothing. Badger or a vole. That kind of doodah.

He shut the recycling bin's lid. 'Then there's radio work, right? Bound to be *something* we could pitch to Radio Four.'

'Not as good as TV, but all exposure is good exposure when you're Feeding The Beast.'

Scott started up the drive again, clicking the remote over his shoulder as he crunched across the gravel. The gates swung shut with a reassuring *clang*.

'And there's always my charity single idea! How does...' He froze. There it was again. The scuffing noise. He inched his way around till he was facing the gates again, every single hair on his head standing to attention.

'Scotty, you OK?'

'Thought I heard something.' He raised his voice at the growing shadows. 'Hello?' Trying to keep the tremor out of his voice. 'Hello? Is anyone there?'

Give Sylvia her due, she had his back, without so much as a pause: *'Do you need me to call the cops?'*

Silence.

Not even the fox.

Oh, what was he *doing*?

A laugh bounced its way out of him. OK, it was a bit high and nervous sounding, but if you can't laugh at yourself being an idiot, who could you laugh at?

He shook his head and hurried back to the house. Not running, but not dawdling either.

'Honestly, I *genuinely* terrified myself then.'

Soon as he was inside, he locked the front door, double bolted it and put the chain on too. Gave himself a little shake. 'Sorry, sorry. What were we talking about again?'

'*Brainstorming PR opportunities with my very favourite client.*' Bet she said the same thing to *all* her clients. But it was still nice to hear.

Scott pushed through into the atrium – which, let's face it, sounded so much better than 'hall'. There was a bottle of Courvoisier XO in the kitchen. Big glass of that would go down very nicely indeed. Well, he deserved it, didn't he? After nearly scaring himself to death.

'Right, yes: so my charity single idea. I was thinking we could—'

A dull *thunk* reverberated around the inside of his skull and the room rushed at him like the incoming tide. Ringing in his... Knees buckle, not straight... Floor rushing up to meet him.

Darkness.

33

Sylvia frowned at the phone, sitting in its cradle on the kitchen countertop – hands-free, so she could enjoy a nice large Pinot Grigio and a dish of Kalamata olives. 'Scotty?'

A *thunk* from the phone's speaker, then a groan.

She rolled her eyes and popped another olive.

Honestly, why did male clients have to be such a pain in the proverbial? I want more exposure! I want on BBC *Breakfast*! I want on the *One Show* – though why anyone would want *that* was absolutely beyond her – *Bake Off*, *Strictly*, *MasterChef*, *I'm a Celebrity*, *Saturday Kitchen*, wah, wah, wah, why aren't I more popular?

But when you've recently bought a two-bedroom flat in Kensington, you do what you have to in order to pay for it. Even if it meant polishing the egos of whiny wannabes like Scott Meyrick.

Sylvia took a sip of Pinot and frowned at the phone as scuffing and grunting came from the other end. He better not be having a phonewank at her...

'Hello? Scotty?'

Some muffled rustling noises, then another groan.

Swear to God, if it wasn't for her *staggeringly* huge mortgage she'd dump his whiny Z-list arse in a shot.

'Very funny, Scotty. Now, can we get on with business?'

Then a woman's voice, hard and Scottish: *'Grab his legs.'*

Sylvia sat up, put the wine glass down and turned the volume up. Pressed the 'RECORD CALL' button. 'Scotty? Is everything OK?'

'Right, you little bastard.'

A ... what was that? It was too muffled to make out. She grabbed the phone, pressing it against her ear.

The next voice was a man's, a thicker, coarser version of Scotty's accent. *'He's coming round.'*

There were people in her client's house.

Oh – my – God...

And she was getting it all on tape.

'SCOTTY!'

'You hear that? It was a... There: in his shirt pocket?' The man's voice got louder. *'Oh shite, he's on the phone with someone!'*

'So what? Let them listen. All publicity's good publicity, right?'

'LEAVE MY CLIENT ALONE!'

Laughter.

Then moaning. A confused, *'Wmnnnnghh... I...'* Scotty's mumbling snapped straight to pure terror. *'Who the—'* whatever he said next was muddy and indistinct, as if someone slapped their hand over his mouth.

The Woman: *'So Scotland's a "half-arsed nation of chippy wee wannabees", is it?'*

A metallic sound. Followed by muffled pleas.

The Man: *'Spite's a terrible thing, Scotty. Real terrible.'*

The Woman: *'Hold him still.'*

A scream belted out of the speaker, high-pitched and terrified and wine-curdling. Sylvia wrenched the phone away from her ear, knocking over her glass. It shattered against the worktop, Pinot Grigio going everywhere as the screaming went on and on and on and on...

She dug her other iPhone from her handbag and dialled 999.

Come on, come on, come—

'Emergency services, which service do you require?'

'Police! Get the police out there now!'

*   *   *

Mhari pulls down her facemask and grins at him.

Haiden checks his own white oversuit – speckled with tiny red dots, but hers is caked, bright scarlet all the way from her gloves to her elbows. More on her chest.

His stomach does a wee spin to the left, then the right, but he swallows it down.

Jesus…

She snatches a fancy-looking bottle from the kitchen countertop, twists off the top with her bloody gloves, raises the brandy in salute. 'Slàinte mhath!' Then swigs straight from the bottle. Holds it out to him.

Yeah, maybe not.

'He got any whisky?'

She jerks her head towards the open kitchen door, where the lower half of Scotty Meyrick is slowly inching past, legs barely moving as he tries to crawl away. Not getting very far. Leaving a thick smear of scarlet on the marble floor. 'He's a Unionist wanker, course he hasn't.'

Mhari wiggles the bottle at Haiden and he shrugs, then takes it. Lowers his mask.

'Slàinte mhòr.' He takes a big scoof of brandy. Shudders as the sweet grapey liquid hits the back of his throat. Forces it down. 'Gah…'

Mhari puts her bloodstained hand on his white-suited chest. 'Oh, baby, we're nearly done. We're *so* close.' Then she steps in close and kisses him, her breath like petrol from the brandy. 'Soon we can do *anything* we like.'

Now that's more like it. He smiles, slow and sexy. 'Anything?'

She laughs, then grabs him and kisses him again – deeply this time, with lots and lots of tongue. Breaks for air and stares through the open door at Scotty Meyrick's half-arsed escape crawl. 'But first we have to take care of our new friend, before the cops get here.'

34

Two patrol cars sat on the wide gravel drive, blocking in a fancy BMW Roadster. The one nearest the massive, garish, house still had its blue-and-whites on, the flickering disco of misery reflecting back from the wall of glass that fronted the property.

The sign by the gates was a slab of granite with 'CAIRNHARN COTTAGE' on it, which was a bit of an understatement. Scotty Meyrick's house was huge. One of those places that got featured in property supplements as 'HOME OF THE WEEK!' – had to be *at least* five bedrooms in there; landscaped gardens; the edge of a tennis court poking out behind one corner of the house.

Logan pulled his Audi into the only gap left and climbed out.

Not often you got to describe a night in Aberdeenshire as 'sultry', but this probably qualified. The air, thick and sticky. Smelling of dust and something … chemical. Like the warm verruca-plaster scent of chlorine. Which probably meant there was a pool as well.

A pair of security lights cracked on as he crunched his way to the house, flooding the gravel with their harsh white glare.

Logan stopped outside the front door, pulled on a pair of nitrile gloves, and let himself in.

Big porch, a line of jackets on a row of hooks. Large mirror on the wall opposite, because God forbid you should step out of your front door looking anything less than your fabulous best.

The porch opened on a *massive* hall, more like a hotel lobby than someone's house. The marble floor was speckled with dark red, a pool of it in the middle of the room. Bloody handprints. Bloody footprints. Not as much as there'd been in Professor Wilson's kitchen, but still...

Whatever Mhari and Haiden had done to Scotty Meyrick wasn't good.

A thick streak of scarlet stretched away towards the cavernous living room, as if their victim had tried to escape, but barely made it to the open doors.

A lone PC stood with her back to the room, all done up in the full stabproof-and-high-viz kit, talking into her phone. 'No, there's no sign of the householder. Dundee Bill and Smithy are out searching. ... Uh-huh. ... OK.' She groaned and sagged. 'Inspector *McRae*? Why do we need some Professional Standards toss—'

Logan cleared his throat. Nice and loud before she could hang herself.

She froze. 'Oh God, he's behind me, isn't he?'

'He is. And since we've got off to such a great start, perhaps you can tell me why there's no one out there stopping every Thomas, Richard, and Harold barging into our crime scene?'

'Got to go.' She hung up and turned, pulling on what was probably meant to be an ingratiating smile. It didn't go with her wide turnip face. 'Inspector McRae! Great to see you up and about again. You know, after what happened last year.'

'I want this scene *secured*, Constable.'

'Ah... Well, the thing is, we don't even know if it's a proper crime scene yet, because—'

'Scott Meyrick, who's been quite clear about his anti-independence stance, was abducted while on the phone to his agent.' Logan counted the points off on his fingers: 'She heard screaming, the floor's covered in blood, and, let me guess, he's nowhere to be found?'

Pink rushed up Constable Turnip's cheeks. 'Yes.' The pink darkened. 'I mean, yes, sir. Boss. Guv?'

'Good. Now we've got that cleared up, get this sodding crime scene secured!'

She scurried off towards the front door, phone clamped to her ear again. 'Guthrie, whatever you're doing, stop it and get back here. Nosferatu's Ninjas have arrived...' Banging the door behind her as she vanished into the porch.

Unbelievable.

OK, so giving her a hard time wouldn't exactly help to dispel Professional Standards' reputation as 'a bunch of sinister bastards', but if you presented your backside for kicking you couldn't complain when someone took a run up and planted their boot square between your cheeks.

And where the hell was the cordon? The bloodstains on the floor should've been taped off by now. Sodding amateurs.

He squatted down a couple of inches past where the splatter ended. A lot of blood, but not a life-threatening amount. Well, at least not bleeding-to-death threatening.

Maybe Haiden and Mhari had planned something more, but had to cut it short? After all, according to Scotty Meyrick's agent the two of them knew she was on the phone, listening as they did whatever it was they were doing to him. Knew she'd phone the police. Knew that patrol cars would be racing over here, lights and sirens blaring. Knew their time was running out...

Logan stood and followed the blood smear to the lounge door.

This room was massive too: the front wall, solid glass, looking out at the patrol car and its flashing blue-and-whites. A big sound system against one wall, a collection of tan leather couches, a big glass-and-chrome coffee table, far more pictures of the house's owner than was healthy – even for a committed egomaniac.

'Ostentatious' was the word that sprung to mind.

The only things spoiling Scotty Meyrick's nouveau-riche narcissistic look-at-me-I'm-famous theme were the St Andrew's cross spray-painted across a large projection screen in dripping blue aerosol and the word 'SPITE!' graffitied on the opposite wall, taking in several of the ego-photos.

They knew the police were on their way, but they still hung around to do that...

Foolhardy, reckless, or maybe they just didn't give a toss any more? Not now Hardie had outed them to the whole world. And there was no way that didn't make them a lot more dangerous.

Hardie was such a stupid—

'For God's sake!' DI King's Highland accent boomed out in the hall. *'Get out my bloody way!'*

'Please, Guv: I've got to do crime scene management or Inspector McRae will have my ovaries.'

See? Applying boot to backside had the desired effect.

'Oh for...'

There was a pause – presumably that would be PC Turnip making King sign in – then the man himself lurched into view. He wasn't his usual dapper, if slightly sweaty self. A bit rumpled, to be honest.

King stopped in the doorway to the living room, rubbing a hand across his blue-stubbled jaw as he frowned down at the blood smear. His suit looked as if he'd slept in it, purple bags under his pink eyes. He stuffed a mint into his mouth, crunching it down with a grimace. 'Got here as soon as I could.'

A waft of aftershave made it across the room to where Logan stood. Sharp and overpowering.

Logan backed away a couple of paces, but it followed him. 'Scott Meyrick. That's three Anti-Nat, Pro-Union figures missing in eight days. I think Haiden and Mhari are escalating.'

King rubbed at his stubble again. 'We're going to have to wait at least two hours for a Scene Examination team. Had to draft one up from Tayside, because all ours are out at another sodding arson attack.'

'Thought we had top priority? They *told* us we had top priority!'

'A man died, Logan. Burned to death in the flat above his pub.'

'Bloody hell...' No wonder they couldn't get anyone out here.

'Yup.' King puffed out his cheeks and took another look at the smeared blood. 'Think Scott Meyrick's hands are going to turn up in the post? Or his cock?' King gave a small lurch to the side. He caught it fast enough, but it was still visible. 'Or Christ-knows what.'

Maybe that explained all the aftershave?

Logan stepped in closer and sniffed. There was something underneath it. Something sour, lurking between all those extra-strong mints. 'Have you been *drinking*?'

Those pink eyes narrowed. 'I had *one*. One drink, with my wife, over dinner.'

One drink? With the wife that completely hated him? Yeah, that sounded plausible.

King stuck out his chest. 'What?' Then he shook his head and marched into the room, pretty much collapsed into one of the leather couches. Scowled up at the vandalised projection screen. 'We've got two options. One: Haiden and Mhari are abducting their victims, mutilating, killing them, and dumping the bodies. Two: they're actually trying to keep them alive for some reason.' The words were slow and crisp, as if he was forcing the slush out of them first. But not quite managing.

One bottle, more like.

'They sent us a video of Professor Wilson pleading for his life in a chest freezer, remember?' Logan sighed. 'This is probably the most high-profile case you'll ever work on, Frank. The media are picking over every single thing we do and so are our bosses. You can't turn up for work with a drink in you. Not *now*, not ever.'

'Oh come on! How was I supposed to know I'd get dragged out here at...' he peeled back his sleeve and peered at his watch with one eye – the other squeezed shut, 'eleven o'clock?'

'Suppose not.' But that didn't make it right.

King gave himself a bit of a shake. 'So where are they keeping them? Where do Mhari Powell and Haiden Lochhead have access to?'

Oh for God's sake.

'We're looking into that, already, remember?'

'Urgh...' He scrubbed at his face again.

Maybe more than one bottle. And probably something a lot stronger than wine.

'Go home, Frank, you're not helping the case or yourself by being here.'

King wouldn't look at him. 'Robert Drysdale.'

'What about him?'

A long pause while King pursed his lips and frowned, as if he was working up to some big secret. 'He's... Yeah.' Whatever it was, the moment passed. 'Don't suppose it matters now.' King sagged back and stared at the ceiling. 'You ever think about jacking it all in, Logan? About marching up to Hardie, Young, and all the rest of those useless tossers and telling them where they can stick this buggering job?'

All the time. *Especially* today.

Logan hooked a thumb at the patrol cars outside. 'Come on: go home. I'll get someone to drive you.'

'Doesn't matter what I do, I'm screwed. Can't erase the sins of the past.' He covered his face with his hands. 'They're going to tear me apart, Logan. They're going to crack open my bones and feast on the bloody marrow.'

Probably.

'We're doing everything we can.'

'I was doomed from the moment I decided Cerys was the one for me. My first real love... Sixteen years old and that was my life. Ruined.'

Logan helped him up. Close in, like this, the smell of alcohol was eye-watering. 'It'll look better in the morning.'

'No. No, it really won't.'

Logan sat back on the sofa and stifled a yawn.

Tayside's Scene Examination team had cordoned off the blood spatters in the hallway, and now half a dozen of them were giving the crime scene laldy, all dressed in their scrunchy white SOC suits. Fingerprinting, swabbing, and photographing things.

For some reason, their Transit van – parked right outside the living room window – wasn't the usual filthy grey with obscene slogans written in the dirt. Instead it was a pristine shade of recently cleaned white. They'd have to watch that, if any of the other divisional SE teams found out, they'd get drummed out of the Scene Examiners' union.

Another yawn.

Urgh...

Should've gone home when King did. Or at the very least, when the Tayside team finally turned up. No one could say he hadn't showed willing.

One of the SE team ducked out from under the tape cordon and padded across the marble on his blue-bootied feet. Stopped right in front of Logan, still wearing the full goggles-facemask-and-gloves outfit. Nodded back towards the bloodstains. You could've cut marmalade and sawn through jute with his accent: 'Got some good fingerprints off the floor around where the body was.'

'Body?'

'Aye, body. You can tell from the blood patterns.' He pulled down his facemask and gave Logan a lopsided smile. 'I love blood patterns, me. Every little scarlet dot, shimmering like a ladybird, tells a story. You just have to ken how to read it.'

Logan smiled. 'I know a forensic soil scientist you'd love.'

'Ace.' A nod. 'So, I'd say our victim was standing when they were hit first – there's fine particulates on the wall and the rubber plant at head height. Then he hits the floor – more blood, but radiating outwards, a few stray hairs caught between the tiles. Some smearing. And that's when they cut him.'

'They cut him?'

'Oh yeah. He's lying on his back, right? And they have a go at his face with something. You can tell, cos it's quite a gusher to start with, so his body's acting like a stencil. He tries to haul himself in here, see the slug trail?' Pointing at the drag marks. 'Then they haul him to his feet and frogmarch him out. By then it's more dribbling than anything, so they've maybe packed the wound with something? You can see the foot-scuffs in the dribbles. And it's definitely dribble, not flobble, cos it's come straight down with a wee splash.'

Logan stared at him.

'What?'

'Normally, I have to batter Scene Examiners over the head with a stick to get even the vaguest predictions out of them.'

'Oh, the *official* report will be full of caveats and bet-hedging, but we're all mates here, right?' He rocked on his blue-bootied heels. 'So, Scotty Meyrick, eh?'

Had to hand it to Haiden Lochhead and Mhari Powell – to break in, overpower their victim, mutilate him, vandalise the living room, and vanish into the night taking him with them, before the police could turn up... That took skill. And planning.

The tech sucked on his teeth. 'Never really liked him on the telly, bit too slick, aye? But he talked a lot of sense in them *Telegraph* articles. The trouble with Scotland is a bunch of numpties saw *Braveheart* and now they think if we could only sod about the hills in kilts all day, flashing our arses at the English, somehow everything will be all right.'

Logan stood, checked his watch: twenty to three. 'How much longer do you think?'

'I mean, Scotland voted to stay in the EU because we know it's better to be part of something bigger, right? So why the hell would we want to leave the UK? Bigger's always better.' A cheeky wink. 'Ask any woman.'

Logan blinked at him. Then handed over a business card. 'If anything urgent comes up, call me.'

'Will do, Chief.' He gave himself a wee satisfied chuckle as he wandered off towards his precious bloodstains. '"Ask any woman." Priceless, Leonard, priceless.'

Looked as if Tayside's policy on hiring weirdos was every bit as robust as Aberdeen's.

Logan picked his way past the cordon and out into the night.

No moon. Nothing but the glow of every light in Scott Meyrick's house blazing away beneath a blanket of indifferent stars. The Dundee lot had marked out a common approach path with blue-and-white 'POLICE' tape, and Logan followed it as far as his Audi, bypassing one of the white-suited team, on their hands and knees in the gravel, working away with a high-powered torch.

Logan pulled out his phone, one finger hovering over the

contacts list. Not even three o'clock yet. It wasn't really fair to call Jane McGrath this early.

Then again, why should he be the only one up and worrying about this stuff?

He poked her name and his mobile rang, and rang, and rang, and rang, and rang and—

'Gnnnn...? Wh... Urgh. Do you know what time it is.'

'Yes.' He leaned against his car. 'The press are going to find out about Scott Meyrick soon. No way we can keep this quiet.'

'I'm not an idiot, Logan, I'm well aware of that.' A sort of half-yawn-half-gurgle noise came down the line. 'His bloody agent held a press conference about thirty minutes after she called nine-nine-nine. It's all over the twenty-four-hour news outlets.'

'Oh for God's sake...'

'So you woke me up for nothing. And I've got to be on the BBC in... Aaaargh! Four and a bit hours!'

'Sorry.' No he wasn't, but at least she couldn't see him grinning. 'Jane ... off the record ... hypothetically speaking—'

'What?' And just like that she sounded a lot more awake. 'OK, you're worrying me now!'

'Have you ever heard of someone called "Robert Drysdale"?'

'Who's Robert Drysdale?' An edge of panic was creeping in. 'Why should I have heard of him? Has something happened?'

'Call it "idle speculation".' All innocent.

'Oh great. Thank you very much. How am I supposed to get back to sleep now?'

'Well it's—'

'Going to be up all night worrying about Robert Bloody Drysdale! Gah!' And with that, she hung up.

It was hard not to grin, it really was. After all, a problem shared...

Logan climbed into his Audi, clicked on the lights, and drove off into the night.

— in case of emergency: break glass —

35

The last bars of something *far* too raucous for this time of the morning screeched and hollered out of the car radio as Logan turned onto Queen Street. Sunlight glittered on the granite buildings, made the concrete glow, sparkled in the looming windows of Divisional Headquarters. A handful of miserable people trudging along the early morning pavements on their way to work.

The DJ laughed. *'I know, I know, but it's growing on me. Got the news, travel, and weather coming up at seven. And we'll be going live to Aberdeen Divisional Headquarters for a special exclusive report on Scotty Meyrick's abduction last night.'*

'Oh ... sodding hell.'

'If you're out there listening, Scotty, everyone here wants you to know we're thinking of you at this difficult time. Stay strong!'

'Yes, because that'll do him a *huge* amount of...'

The armada of journalists who'd gathered outside DHQ hove into view – doing their early morning bulletins to camera. Serious faces for a serious story.

Logan slowed to have a bit of a nosy.

A big BMW van was parked just ahead, splattered with Sky TV branding, a paddling-pool-sized satellite dish on the roof. The side door rattled open as he passed and that wee hairy Philip Patterson hopped out, tissue paper stuffed into his collar so he wouldn't get however many tons of makeup he was wearing on his shirt. A camerawoman clambered out after him, jostling up the walkway to the Front Podium.

Be sure to get a shot with the Police Scotland signage in the background, don't want people to think you're not really here...

'Great.'

'Anyway, you're listening to OMG It's Early!, with me, Rachel Gray. And now, here's an oldie but a goodie: The Eagles and "Hotel California". This one's for you, Scotty!'

Yeah, not exactly appropriate.

PC Ugly was behind the desk outside the Chief Superintendent's office again, hammering away at his keyboard as if going for a new world record.

King lowered himself into the seat one down from Logan's, clean shaven, Hollywood hair slicked back, suit, shirt, and tie immaculate. As if he hadn't turned up half-cut at the crime scene last night. He dug into a pocket and waggled a roll of extra-strong mints in Logan's direction. 'You look rough.'

Cheeky sod. But Logan took a mint anyway, sticking it into his cheek like a hamster.

King put the packet away. 'They give you a time for the press briefing yet?'

'No. You?'

'Why would they tell me? I'll be fired by then.'

Welcome to the Friday-morning pity party.

'They're not going to fire you just because Scott Meyrick got abducted. That wasn't our fault.'

'You've not read the *Scottish Daily Post* this morning, then?'

Logan turned in his seat. 'Didn't have time. You?'

'Didn't need to. I *know* what's coming.'

Wonderful. So he'd been right yesterday – there *was* worse on its way. 'What has Barwell—'

The office door opened and Superintendent Bevan stuck her head out. The smile she flashed wasn't a hopeful one. 'Ah, Logan. Good. Can you join us inside, please?'

He and King stood, but she waved at King to sit again. 'Sorry, Frank, I need you to wait here for now.'

King's smooth shaved cheeks darkened. 'I see. That's how it is.'

Logan patted him on the shoulder, then followed Bevan inside. Closed the door behind him, shutting out King's hurt wee face.

Big Tony Campbell's office was done out in the same Spartan fashion as the reception area outside. The only nods to decoration were the framed photos of Big Tony with various local VIPs and a couple of First Ministers. No whiteboards, no filing cabinets, no pot plants – just a big-ish desk with the man himself, Chief Superintendent of all he surveyed, glowering away behind it, a coffee table, and half a dozen comfy chairs. Only one of which was unoccupied.

Bevan settled into it, between Superintendent Young, and Jane McGrath: who looked at Logan as if he was something needing biopsied. Hardie sat on the other side of the coffee table with an unknown woman: grey-streaked shoulder-length hair, a proud chin, superintendent's crowns on the epaulettes of her dress uniform.

Scowls and frowns all round. And not one of them could look him in the eye.

Fair enough, it was going to be one of *those* meetings.

Logan nodded at each of them in turn. 'Boss, Guv, Chief, Super, Jane...' He raised an eyebrow at their mystery visitor. 'Ma'am?'

She nodded at him.

It was Big Tony Campbell who broke the ensuing silence. 'Three pro-union public figures in less than a fortnight, Logan. *Three.*'

Let the bollocking commence.

Logan put on his best reasonable voice. 'We're not the ones abducting them, Boss.'

'Is that supposed to be funny, Inspector?'

'We've got lookout requests on the go, Mhari and Haiden's photos distributed to every force in the UK, three teams going door-to-door, we're doing a fingertip search of—'

'And then Jane comes in and shows me this!' He slapped a hand down on a printout. 'Well?'

Nope. No idea.

Jane leaned forward, waving a copy at him. 'Robert Drysdale? You giving me insomnia at two in the morning, remember that?'

'I remember, because I wasn't in bed, I was still working.'

Bevan cleared her throat, little wrinkles furrowing her brow. 'Logan, how did Robert Drysdale's name crop up in your investigation?'

'Why? Who is he?'

Everyone turned to look at the newcomer.

She nodded. 'Very well.' Slightest hint of a Glaswegian accent, hidden under a public-school upbringing. 'But this goes no further than this room, am I clear?'

Now they were all looking at *him* instead.

Yeah, whatever this was, it wouldn't be good.

'OK...'

'Robert Drysdale was a member of the People's Army for Scottish Liberation, twenty-nine years ago. He went missing in November that year and his body turned up a week later in an abandoned bothy outside Strichen.' A dramatic pause, as if what she'd just said meant anything to Logan. 'Someone had hammered thirty galvanised clout nails into his arms, legs, chest, and head. They were seventy-five millimetres long, so they went in a fair distance.' She reached into a leather satchel at the side of her chair, coming out with a series of photographs. Handed them to Logan.

The first picture showed a dark, manky little room, with holes in the plaster, another in the ceiling, dust and dirt, streaks of bird shit on the walls. A naked man filled the middle of the shot, strung up by the neck from an overhead beam, arms tied behind his back. The photographer's flash had caught the nail-heads, making them shine like stars against his blood-darkened skin. Whoever took the shot obviously had a flair for the dramatic, because they'd caught the graffiti on the wall behind the body in perfect horror-film style.

One word, in dripping red paint: 'JUDAS!'

The next six shots were close-ups of the bruises and contusions, the rope around his neck, the nails... They stuck out about five or six millimetres from the flesh, the nailheads on top of their shiny metal stalks like sinister mushrooms.

Last one in the set: an abandoned bothy on a mountainside somewhere. Broken windows, guttering hanging off, rough stonework, corrugated steel roof. The landscape smothered in snow.

He flipped back to the first shot. 'There are definitely similarities. Scott Meyrick had "spite" painted on his living room wall, "the Devil makes work" was on the note with Professor Wilson's hands, and Councillor Lansdale got "three monkeys".' Logan frowned at the newcomer. 'You think Mhari and Haiden are taking inspiration from a thirty-year-old murder?'

She shrugged. 'When your Media Liaison Officer,' pointing at Jane, 'mentioned Robert Drysdale this morning, I recognised his name from a cold-case review Strathclyde ran not long after I joined.'

'Let me guess: Drysdale informed on one of his fellow PASLers? "Gaelic Gary" Lochhead found out and they made an example of him.'

'Robert Drysdale's real name was Detective Sergeant Martin Knott. He joined the PASL as part of Operation Kelpie.'

A murdered undercover cop.

Great: things weren't just worse, they were a *hell* of a lot worse.

Bevan sighed. 'So you can see why, when his name came up...?'

Big Tony stuck a fist on his desk. 'If we've got a chance to put someone away for DS Knott's murder, I want to know about it.'

'We're doing everything we can, Boss.' Logan had another squint at the photos. 'But until we find out where Haiden and Mhari are hiding, or where they're keeping their victims?' Why did Drysdale have to be an undercover cop? Come on: options. Think. How do we work through this one? 'We ... can try fronting up Haiden's father again? Give him a grilling about the murder? If he was involved, maybe he'll want to boast about it?'

'Why on earth would he do that?'

317

'He's got less than four months to live, Boss. What's he got to lose?'

Hardie clearly felt it was time to make his presence felt, crossing his arms and nodding as if he'd been in charge all along, instead of sitting there like a sack full of damp pants. 'Good. Go. Keep me informed. But be back here by twelve – we'll have to brief the press about Scott Meyrick.'

Logan turned to Superintendent Bevan and raised an eyebrow. She nodded.

'Will do.' He'd almost made it to the door, when:

'Inspector McRae?' The new superintendent was staring at him. 'You didn't say *how* Robert Drysdale's name came up.'

Ah. No, he hadn't. And it would have been nice if no one had spotted that little omission.

'I can't remember. Someone must have mentioned it last night.' Liar. But DI King was in enough trouble already, without Logan pouring unleaded on the fire. An innocent shrug. 'It was pretty late.'

She pointed at the door. 'OK, then.'

Big Tony's voice boomed out as Logan slipped into the reception area: *'And make sure you find something!'*

Logan clicked the door shut and... Where was King?

The row of seats was empty, just Mr Ugly The Receptionist in here, clattering away on his keyboard.

Logan waved at him. 'What happened to DI King?'

'Phone call.'

Either that or he'd gone AWOL with a half-bottle of vodka...

DHQ wore the muffled silence of early morning – ten to eight, so dayshift uniform were all out keeping Aberdonians from doing horrible things to other Aberdonians. All the major teams had done their daily briefings and sodded off, leaving the place to the support staff and the handful of officers who'd found an excuse to hide inside rather than go traipsing about in the blazing sun. Which would be tempting, if it wasn't for Chief Superintendent Big Tony Campbell's parting words.

Logan was reaching for the door to the MIT incident room

when it banged open and Tufty bustled out into the corridor, a pink folder tucked under one arm.

'Sarge!' He flashed Logan a smile and a wee wave. 'Cool. About Mr Clark's steampunk film, are you one hundred percent definitely certain I can't be in it?' Making with the big puppy eyes.

Not *this* again.

'You're a police officer.'

'Yeah, but I could go to Comic-Con and be on panels and people would dress up like my character and I'd be completely funky and I'd never ask for anything else ever again! *Promise.*'

Logan stared at him.

'Oh noes.' His shoulders sagged. He shuffled his feet. Cleared his throat. Then raised his folder. 'Well, suppose I'd better get this over to the media office then.' And scuffed away, like a kicked dachshund. 'Pity poor Tufty...'

Bless his little Starfleet socks, but that lad was a complete and *utter* weirdo.

Logan let himself into the incident room. It was probably the only busy office in the whole building – phones ringing, support officers answering them, overlapping conversations as details were taken and notes made. The HOLMES team busy hammering data into the system, the printer in the corner churning out action after action. Milky had perched herself on the edge of someone's desk, flipping through paperwork on a clipboard while Heather commandeered a whiteboard – humming 'Uptown Girl' to herself as she printed the names of Alt-Nat groups on it in big red letters.

Steel lounged in an office chair, feet up on the desk, a butty in one hand and a wax-paper cup in the other. A little island of laziness in an ocean of police work. As usual.

Logan marched over there and loomed at her. 'Thought you were searching Mhari Powell's house?'

She didn't bother swallowing or covering her mouth as she chewed. 'Waiting on a dog unit.' Steel dipped her butty in her coffee, and took another bite. 'Think you could stop with the abducted Unionists now? Only every time we make any progress on this sodding case, you turn up another one.'

He gave her leg a smack. 'Feet off the desk. Supposed to be setting an example.'

Dip. Munch. Honestly, she masticated like the back end of a scaffies' wagon. The only things missing were the mechanism for tipping wheelie bins into the hopper and the smell of split bin bags. 'Aye, that'll be shining.'

Hopeless.

Logan had another look around the office. 'Where's King?'

Steel dipped her butty again, a broad smile on her face. 'I've never had one of these before. Very nice.' Then crammed a soggy brown lump of it into her gob. 'Did you meet her then? The new head honcho. Or is it honchesse? Honchetta?'

'Nope.' He dug out his phone and gave King a ring.

'Superintendent Pine, from G Division, AKA: Darkest Strathclyde, AKA: The Evil Empire. Kinda shaggable if you've been on the razz all night, and don't mind the greying hair and Jimmy Hill chin. No idea what her arse is like, though.'

Grey-streaked hair, proud chin, superintendent's crowns...

'Was that her?' Suppose it had to be. 'Didn't seem too bad to me.'

Still no response from King.

'Word is she can unhinge that huge bottom jaw of hers and swallow babies whole.' Steel tried to do much the same thing with the last chunk of her butty, all drippy with coffee. Cramming it in. Grinning as brown dribbled down her chin.

Urgh...

He was about to hang up when, *'King?'* crackled out of the phone at him.

Logan turned his back on Steel, before she did anything else revolting. 'Where are you?'

'Calling to give-me the bad news, are you? How long have I got to clear out my desk?'

Steel nudged Logan with her foot. 'See, what I like is the way the silky hazelnut coffee complements the crunchy-chocolatey-soft-buttery-bapness of the KitKat butty. That's Heston-Blumenthal level genius, that is.'

He moved out of range, lowering his voice so Madame Lugs

wouldn't hear. 'Will you get your arse in order, please? I'm not carrying this sodding case all on my own!'

No reply. Just silence.

'Where are you?'

Still nothing.

The office door opened and in scuttled Tufty, rubbing his hands together. 'Did I miss anything?'

'Frank?'

'They're not firing me?' Finally.

'We need to speak to Haiden's dad again. Something's come up.'

'Are they really not firing me?'

'Really. Now can we go do our jobs?'

'Erm... OK. I'll ... meet you down the Rear Podium?'

'Good.' Logan hung up. Hissed out a sigh. 'Offering support' wasn't supposed to be the same thing as babysitting.

Tufty settled down behind his laptop, looking around as if he'd lost something. Patting his paperwork. Frowning. Lifting things up and putting them down again.

'Aye well...' Steel sooked her fingers and stood. Stretched her full length like a very manky cat. 'Suppose I'd better be offski. Time and search-trained canines wait for no woman, no matter how sexy she is.'

Logan leaned against Tufty's desk. 'Have you found anything?'

He didn't look up from his rummaging. 'They were right here. I'm *sure* they were.'

'Mhari Powell, Tufty: concentrate.'

'Hmm? Oh right.' He opened a desk drawer, pouted at the contents then closed it again. 'I'm still going through all the social media accounts she's been posting from, but I've IDed three Facebook friends who interact with her on a regular basis. Or, at least, they interacted with one of the people she was pretending to be. None of them with the same pretend person, though.' Tufty pulled a printout from his in-tray and handed it over – a list of three names and addresses – then rummaged through his desk some more. 'Still working on the rest.'

'Hoy!' Steel stopped in the doorway, turned, clacked her heels together and gave Logan a sarcastic salute. 'Don't forget: no more deid bodies while I'm out!' And with that she was gone.

Logan pocketed Tufty's list. 'Keep at it. I want to know who "Mhari Powell" really is by the time I get back.'

'Mmmm? Yeah, OK, Sarge...' He went back to searching his desk. Raised his voice to address the whole room: 'Has anyone seen my KitKat butty or hazelnut latte?'

Detective Sergeant Steel strikes again.

36

Ten past eight in the morning was *not* the best time to be driving across town to Dyce. The morning rush hour was like a diseased thing, crawling along on its belly, belching noxious fumes into the hot summer air.

Speaking of which: sitting in the passenger seat, King crunched down one more in a long line of extra-strong mints. A newspaper open in his lap, his window cracked open an inch – letting the scent of diesel exhaust invade the Audi's interior as they followed a bus along Westburn Drive.

Logan inched the car forward another couple of feet. 'Where did you disappear off to?'

A grimace. 'Gwen called. Again. She's got herself a lawyer and they're citing my "unreasonable behaviour" as grounds for divorce.' He gave a short, bitter laugh. '*My* unreasonable behaviour? I should be the one suing her: she's the one having the affair! She's the one been *torturing* me with it!'

And speaking of torture: 'Robert Drysdale.'

King froze for a beat, then looked out the passenger window again. 'What about him?'

'That's what *I* want to know.'

The Audi crawled forward a whole car length.

'Why didn't they fire me?'

'Frank, I'm serious. Who was he?' AKA: here's some rope, please don't hang yourself.

323

'Hmph…' King's jaw tightened. 'I grabbed a copy of this morning's *Scottish Daily Post* on the way out the station.' He picked the paper off his lap and opened it, stared down at the front page. A posed publicity shot of Scott Meyrick smiled back at him under the headline 'FEARS GROW FOR REALITY TV STAR'.

'I can't help if you don't talk to me, Frank!'

'Edward Barwell's "exposé" got bumped to a two-inch sidebar with "continued on page eleven".' King crumpled the paper into his lap again. 'Nothing about Robert Drysdale.'

Silence.

Up ahead, the lights went red, as if anyone was moving fast enough to have to stop.

More silence.

Oh for goodness' sake. 'Was Robert Drysdale in the PASL when you were?'

King waved a dismissive hand. 'There were lots of different cells, that was the point: so there wouldn't be cross-contamination. We didn't exactly get together for coffee mornings and bake sales.' A sigh. 'I'm tired of being a whipping boy for everyone and their hamster.'

'*Cells*? And you say it wasn't a terrorist organisation?'

This time the sigh brought with it a sad little smile. 'I used to love being a police officer… Out on the beat, keeping people safe, banging up crooks and thugs. Now look at me.'

'If you're going to keep up the self-pity all the way to Dyce, you can get out and walk.'

'It's all right for *you*: you're a decorated police hero with a Queen's Medal, a hot girlfriend, a family, and a big house. All I've got is a cheating soon-to-be-ex-wife and a career circling the U-bend.' He nodded. 'Should march into Hardie's office, hand in my resignation, and walk.'

OK, enough.

Logan thumped him on the arm. 'What's the point of running away? If people are picking on you: stand up for yourself!'

King turned to look out the window again. 'Hmph.'

'I'm right here with you, aren't I?'

A long, slow breath. 'I'm not going to survive this one, Logan. Be lucky if they just fire me. I'm done.'

Finally the lights turned green and they could crawl forward another car's length.

'In the words of Detective Chief Inspector Roberta Steel, as was,' Logan put on the voice – gravelly and gin-soaked, '"You'll no' see the bright side with your heid jammed up your arse."'

'Yeah.' King sagged in his seat. 'She should hire herself out as a motivational speaker.'

Sunlight cascaded in through Ravendale's windows, making the reception carpet glow with garish shades of brown, pink, and green. As if someone had gorged themselves on chocolate pudding, Ribena, and guacamole, before being copiously sick all over the care home's floor.

The radio was on, playing something cheerful and bland as the same bland old man in his bland old cardigan behind the bland old desk hummed along, worrying away at a Sudoku book.

He looked up as Logan and King walked in and the smile of greeting faded from his face. 'You again.'

King opened his mouth, but Logan got there first: 'We'd like to speak to Gary Lochhead, please.'

'Ah... Mr Lochhead isn't having one of his better days, today.'

'I'm sorry to hear that, but we still need to talk to him.'

'The pain's so bad we've had to up his morphine.' The receptionist looked left, then right, then over his shoulder, as if the KGB might be lurking nearby ready to steal his secrets. He lowered his voice to a whisper. 'You didn't hear this from me, but the medical staff aren't very optimistic about his prognosis. With patients in palliative care...' A shrug. 'We see a lot of this towards the end.'

Logan nodded. 'We wouldn't ask if it wasn't important.'

A pause, as Mr Bland chewed at the inside of his cheek. Then a nod. 'Well, you can talk to him if you promise to keep it brief. He might not make too much sense though.' Mr Bland picked up the desk phone and dialled. 'I'll get Denzil to see you through.'

* * *

The corridor outside number nineteen was a patchwork of light and shadow as the morning sun seared through the skylights.

King leaned back against the wall opposite Gary Lochead's door. 'What do you think, Good Cop, Bad Cop?'

Genuinely?

Logan frowned at him. 'He's *dying*, Frank. What are we going to threaten him with?'

'True.' He tilted his head to one side, eyes narrowing. 'You know what? Maybe we could—'

The door opened and Denzil poked his hairy wee head out, bringing with him the sound of a radio tuned to the same station as the one in reception. A small, compact man, with powerful furry arms and a warm smile that faded into a concerned look. 'OK. He's stable, but he's been in a lot of pain, so—'

'Morphine.' King loosened his tie. 'We know.'

'Right. Well, don't tire him out, and I'll be right here outside if … he needs anything. Or stops breathing. Or something like that.'

King pushed past him and into the room.

Logan gave Denzil an apologetic smile. 'Been a long week.' Then followed King into Gary Lochhead's room.

The blinds weren't quite fully drawn, and a shaft of sunlight fell across the hospital bed. A wall-mounted reading light was on, pointed towards Gary's painting of that stone circle in the woods, making the colours glow. Shame it couldn't do the same for the bloke who painted it.

He was slumped against his pillows, skin pale and shiny – like butter kept in the freezer. A full oxygen mask covered his nose and mouth, the clear plastic misted with vapour, and an IV line reached from a bag of something clear, through a feeder box, and into the cannula in the back of Gary's hand. That would be the morphine, then. His NHS-blue blankets were rucked up at one side, showing off a liver-spotted leg, wishbone thin.

The cheery song on the radio burbled to an end, replaced by the kind of teuchter accent you could cut concrete with. '*Aye, Aye, loons and quines! Gid Mornin' Doogie's got a wee bittie traffic update for yis. The A-berdeen bypass is closit Eastbound atween Parkhill and Blackdog fir a three-vehicle accident. So dinna ging that wye if yer—'*

King switched the radio off and loomed over the bed. Voice hard and sharp. 'Gary. We need to talk to you about Haiden.'

'Gnnnnnghnnnph?' Gary Lochhead's head turned in trembling jerks and pauses, his pupils big as buttons, the mask muffling his words. 'Haiden? Is that...?'

'Sorry, no, it's not.' Logan pulled up one of the visitors' chairs, positioning it level with Gary's elbow, so he could see who he was speaking to. 'Hi, Gary.'

'Haiden, is that you?'

'It's not Haiden, it's the police, we were here on Wednesday, remember?'

A shaky hand reached for Logan's. 'Haiden, they wanted me to clype on you, but I wouldn't do it. I kept our secrets. I kept them...'

Oh, ho?

King widened his eyes at Logan, eyebrows up. Then he grabbed the other chair and squealed the rubber feet across the floor to the opposite side of the bed, sat, and pulled on a reasonable mid-Aberdonian accent. 'Dad?' He took hold of Gary's other hand. 'Dad, I'm sorry I couldn't come sooner.'

What?

Logan glared at him, making throat-slashing 'Stop it!' gestures.

But King turned the accent up instead. 'Had to dodge the cops, yeah? You know how it is.'

A nod. 'Buncha stupid bastards.' Gary reached up with his free hand and slipped the breathing mask off, so it cupped his chin. Then trembled that hand down over King's, making it the filling in a hand sandwich. 'Is your mother OK, Haiden? You'll look after her, for me, won't you?'

'Course I will, Dad.' The lying sod was nearly squirming in his seat with excitement. 'I did what you wanted. Got Councillor Lansdale, Professor Wilson, and Scott Meyrick.'

Logan leaned towards him, teeth bared, voice a hard hissing whisper. 'This isn't *right*!'

Gary gave King a shaky smile. 'You're a good boy.'

'I took them out to the place, Dad. You remember the place? The place you told me to take them?'

'I want to go home, Haiden.'

'I know you do, Dad. I know. Shall we go past the place first? You remember the place?'

What started as a gurgling wheeze turned into a ragged coughing fit, painting the old man's face an angry shade of purple as he rocked against his pillows, tears rolling down his cheeks. Until it finally hacked itself out in a painful mix of wheezing and groaning.

Logan's whisper got louder and harsher. 'Detective Inspector King, I'm warning you – this isn't appropriate.'

King answered the same way: 'You want Professor Wilson to die? That what you want?'

'You *know* I don't, but—'

'Then shut up and let me do my job.'

The morphine pump bleeped and whirred, making Gary sag further into his pillows, the creases easing from his face a little. Breathing a little better. 'I miss ... I miss the family ... holidays the most. ... We should ... we should do that ... again.'

'Yeah, totally, Dad. But we'll go to the place first, right?'

The wobbly smile returned. 'You were so happy, running ... up and down the beach with ... with your kite. ... Remember Scruffy? You loved that wee dog.'

'Describe the place to me, Dad, so I know you remember it.'

Logan stood. 'OK, that's *enough*.'

'Come on, Dad, they say you've forgotten, but I know you remember it.'

'And we'd have barbecues and ... your mother would make potato salad ... and Scruffy would always get the first sausage...'

'Dad, *focus*.' Voice harder now, running out of patience. 'Where is the place?'

'You used to love those summers, Haiden. ... You and Scruffy and Mum and me.'

'I'm not warning you again, Detective Inspector!'

'Gah!' King pulled his hand away from Gary's, wiped it on

the blankets. 'This is a waste of time, anyway.' He stood, kicking his chair away as he buttoned his suit jacket and glared at Logan. 'We can't afford to sod about here any more. Wrap it up.' Then he turned on his heel and stormed off, barging out through the door.

It banged shut behind him.

It wasn't the sort of thing a member of Professional Standards was supposed to say about a fellow police officer, but DI King really was a *massive* arsehole.

Logan shook his head. Sighed. Looked down at what was left of "Gaelic Gary" Lochhead. 'I'm sorry. If you want to make a formal complaint, we—'

'Do you remember … when that dead porpoise washed up … on the beach and Scruffy … Scruffy found it and rolled in it? God, the *stink*…'

Ah well, before he left, might as well have a bash at what they came here for.

Logan settled onto the edge of the bed. 'Gary, can you remember someone called Robert Drysdale? He was in the People's Army for Scottish Liberation, same as you. Do you remember him?'

Gary reached for Logan's hand – the skin hot and papery to touch. 'Those summers were magic.' His eyes glittered with unshed tears. 'Look after your mum, Haiden.'

Even after everything he'd done, it was hard not to feel sorry for a dying old man.

Come on, what harm would it do?

Logan nodded. 'I will … Dad.'

'Maybe we can go to Uncle Geoff's house again next summer? You, me, your mum, and Scruffy…' He gave Logan's hand a squeeze. 'You always loved that house.' Gary's eyes drifted up towards the stone circle. 'It's a beautiful country, Haiden. Scotland is the best … it's the best country in the world.' He blinked away the tears. 'Put down your roots and keep them here. We *are* this land. Never … never let them take it away from you.'

*   *   *

Logan shoved out through the front doors, into Ravendale's car park. Where the hell was...

There – over by the care home's battered minibus. Detective Inspector King. On his phone, pacing up and down with one finger in his other ear. 'Have you spoken to those Alt-Nat groups yet, H? ... Well why not? Get your sodding finger out!'

Logan marched over, the heat of the morning just adding to the fires. 'What the bloody *hell* was that supposed to be?'

'Hold on, Heather.' He put a hand over the phone's microphone. 'I'm doing my job.'

'Lying to a dying old man?'

King's face darkened. 'Lochhead *knows*, OK?' Jabbing a finger towards the building. 'He – knows!'

'SO DO YOU!'

King retreated a step, pulled his chin in. Clearly not expecting a shouting at. 'I don't—'

'Robert Drysdale. He was in the PASL when *you* were, wasn't he? He wasn't in a "different cell". You knew what they did to him.'

He licked his lips, then raised the phone to his ear again. 'Heather, I'll call you back.' Put his phone in his pocket. 'Look, I never had any—'

'Then why bring him up? Why pluck *that* name at random from the ether?'

'I...' King puffed out a breath. 'OK: Edward Barwell calls me up last night, after work, and says he's going to tell everyone about Robert Drysdale. That I should take the chance to set the record straight before he did.'

'*What* record? What did you do?'

'Nothing! I hadn't even heard of Drysdale till then. I had to google him.'

Logan stepped closer. 'Then why does Barwell think you were involved?'

'I... I don't know.' King can't have liked the scowl that got him, because he held his hands up. 'I don't! He's trying to make it look like I'm involved in some way, but I wasn't. I didn't even know who Drysdale was till last night!'

They stood there, in silence.

Then Logan turned his back and walked to the edge of the car park, where an eight-foot-high chain-link fence separated Ravendale Sheltered Living Facility from the airport.

A Puma helicopter taxied into position, readying for takeoff. Ferrying those still lucky enough to have a job offshore, away for another stint on the rigs. Which, let's face it, *had* to be easier than trying to hunt down violent Alt-Nat nutjobs.

Logan pulled out his phone and scrolled through the contacts till—

What the buggering hell?

The person he'd been looking for was now listed as, 'THE TERRIFYING TUFTYSAURUS REX!'

Rotten little... He stabbed the button and listened to it ring.

'*Sarge? Got another name for you. He was going as "Inde-pun-dancer", but his real—*'

'What the hell did you do to my phone?'

'*Your phone?*' If that was meant to be an innocent voice, it needed work. '*Why would I have done something to your—*'

'You know what, I'll bollock you later. Right now I want you to look up Gary Lochhead's wife. Where is she?'

'*Aha, so, we're playing "Hunt the wife", are we? Let's see what we can see...*' The sound of a keyboard being punished rattled down the line. '*Aha: Tufty wins! You want me to text you the address?*'

'Is it near?'

'*Two miles outside Fyvie: Clovery Woods of Rest. They buried her there six years ago.*'

So much for that.

'OK: give me Gary Lochhead's known associates. Not just the recent ones – go all the way back about thirty years.'

'*Yes, Sergeant, my Sergeant.*' More keyboard noises. '*Did you know someone stole my KitKat butty and hazelnut latte? Bloody police station is full of... Got it.*'

'I want someone called Geoff, could be either spelling.'

'*No Gee-offs or Jeffs. But I have a Jeffrey, if that helps?*'

Might do. 'Does he own property in Cruden Bay?'

'*Let's have a look.*' He bashed his keyboard again. '*Jeffrey*

Moncrief. Jeffrey, Jeffrey, Jeffrey, wherefore art thou Jeffery...? Oh. He's currently doing life in Barlinnie for stabbing an English shopkeeper sixteen times then setting fire to the remains. This was in Argyll and Bute. No chance of parole, because he keeps attacking prisoners born south of the border, down Englandshire way.' A pause. *'He's what we, in the law-enforcement trade, call "a total dickhead".'*

There was a shock.

'What about property?'

'No mention on the Police National Computer.'

Sod.

'Well ... can we get the Land Registry to rush through a search?'

'Maybe. Or...' More keyboarding, this time accompanied by a hummed version of the *Countdown* clock theme tune. *'Woot! We're in luck! But only because I has a genius.'*

Whatever came next was drowned out as the helicopter's engines roared. It pulled forward, gathering speed, then heaved itself into the air on a rib-shaking clatter of blades – the whump-whump-whump fading as it climbed and turned, heading out over Dyce towards the sea.

'Sarge? Hello? I said, "Aren't you going to ask what flavour of genius I has?"'

'Is it my-boot-up-your-bum flavour?'

A sigh. *'You get more like her every day, you know that, don't you? No, it's searching-for-incident-reports-involving-Jeffrey-Moncrief flavour. And amongst the hundreds of entries, there's sixteen call-outs to the same address in Cruden Bay. And yes, you* may *compliment the chef.'*

'You, my little fiend, have earned your bum a reprieve and a bag of Skittles too.'

'Woot!'

'KING!' Logan ran for the Audi. 'GET YOUR BACKSIDE IN THE CAR – WE'VE GOT SOMETHING!'

37

Fields and fences flashed by the Audi's windows as Logan roared along the back road towards Balmedie. Lights flickering, siren wailing. He yanked the car out onto the wrong side of the road, changed down a gear, and stuck his foot hard to the floor, overtaking a little grey Skoda with what looked like nuns inside it.

Sitting in the passenger seat, King grabbed the handle above his door, phone in his other hand – pinned to his ear. Belting it out: 'What? ... Heather? ... No, I can't hear you!'

Logan slowed for a sharp bend, throwing King against the door with the change of direction, then hit the accelerator again.

Flames of broom and whin crackled along the drystane dykes. A flickering strobe of fluorescent yellow and dark green.

'What?' He stuck the phone against his chest and grimaced at Logan. 'Can we switch the siren off? Can't hear myself think!'

'You want to end up dead? Because if you do I can switch the lights off as well.' They flew past a couple of tiny cottages.

'Told you we should've taken the bypass!'

'Eastbound's closed for a three-vehicle RTC, remember?' He slammed on the brakes at the T-junction, slithering to a halt on the double dotted lines. Then nipped out ahead of a muck-encrusted Transit, shifting through the gears like a rally driver. Slammed on the brakes again for a hard left, almost bouncing King out of his seat.

'Gah!' King braced his legs in the footwell. 'Speak up H. ... No. ... I know I said that, but I need every hand we've got out to Cruden Bay.' He glanced across the car. 'ETA...?'

'Twenty, twenty-five minutes.'

A nice long straight bit – the needle hitting ninety-six as Logan floored it. Swathes of barley whipping past. Nipping out to overtake a tractor.

'Call it twenty-five minutes, H. But sooner you lot get there the better.'

A farmyard lunged up on the left – a huge eighteen-wheeler was in the process of pulling on to the road, the driver's eyes going wide as he spotted them, his lorry juddering to a halt, air brakes squealing.

Logan jerked the Audi around it.

'Car. Car! CAR!' King scrunched his eyes shut and had a wee scream to himself.

He jinked the Audi back onto their own side of the road, about six foot away from ploughing straight through the Range Rover coming the other way.

A deep, shuddering sigh from the passenger seat. 'OK, leave the siren on.'

'We need to do a risk assessment. And see if DS Gallacher can get us a canine unit, OSU, firearms team: the works.'

'There isn't time for that!' A frown. 'Do you think there's time for that?'

'No, but we need to *ask* for all that stuff so at least we can say we tried if everything goes horribly wrong.'

'Sodding hell...' King switched his phone to the other ear. 'Heather? I need you to see about backup: Dogs, Thugs, Guns, and anything else you can think of. ... Uh-huh. ... Uh-huh. ... Hold on.' He stuck it against his chest again. 'How sure are we?'

Cows stopped doing cow things to stare at the car as it howled past.

'Eighty percent. Maybe seventy.'

Yeah, King didn't look convinced by that.

Have another go: 'OK, fifty / fifty?'

Another conflagration of gorse, the flowers a searing shade of molten gold.

King nodded, then stuck the phone to his ear again. 'Call it forty / sixty, H. But it's the best lead we've got. ... Yes, I know it's the *only* lead we've got. Heather, get it done, OK? ... Thanks.' He hung up and bared his teeth in a pained wince as they wheeched through an avenue of trees. 'It's more like thirty / seventy, isn't it?'

'Better than nothing.'

A short row of bungalows on the left as they flew into Belhelvie – Logan standing on the brakes to take them down to a more sedate forty. In case someone's cat had a death wish. Or child. Or grandparent.

Another T-junction, this one marked with a set of signposts. Left: 'POTTERTON', right: 'BALMEDIE B977 1½', a huge green and white CLAAS tractor rumbled across in front of them, hauling a trailer behind it. Soon as it'd passed, Logan nipped out, overtook it, then put his foot down again. 'Maybe twenty / eighty.'

The A90 should've been quicker: after all, it was nowhere near as twisty-turny as the wee side roads, but there were a hell of a lot more vehicles on it. Some of which were *clearly* being driven by morons WHO WOULDN'T GET OUT OF THE BLOODY WAY!

Like the one right in front of them. And it wasn't as if Logan could overtake them, not with all the traffic coming the other way.

He stuck his hand on the horn and held it there – blaring away in addition to the siren – until the moron in question finally took the hint and pulled their manky BMW over to the side of the road.

King took a deep breath as Logan hammered the speed up again. 'OK, so what's the plan?'

'We get there, we wait for backup.'

'And what if Professor Wilson, or Matt Lansdale, or Scotty Meyrick dies while we're sitting on our thumbs?'

Good question.

Logan overtook a removal van. 'Yes, but what if we barge in there, getting them *and* ourselves killed?'

'Suppose.' King looked over his shoulder, at the back seat. 'What kit have you got in the car?'

'What do you mean, "kit"?'

'Taser, stabproof vests, extendable baton, pepper spray?'

'It's my *car*, not the Batmobile!' Using the opposite lane to leapfrog a Citroën, a Kia, a Vauxhall, and a Transit with 'EAT MAIR FISH!' on the side.

'You've got blues-and-twos.'

'A couple of LED lights and a siren don't make this an assault vehicle. And they only fitted *them* because it was cheaper than buying another pool car for Professional Standards.' He roared past a filthy Toyota Hilux. 'I've got a couple of high-viz vests, if that helps?'

'What are we going to do, Health-and-Safety Mhari and Haiden to death?' He scrunched his face up. 'Come on, Frank: *think*.' A pause as they slowed for another bout of traffic coming the other way. 'OK. OK. No equipment. What about ... a crowbar: something we could lever a door open or hit people with?'

'Probably a wheel brace in the boot.'

'OK, so that's—' His phone launched into something upbeat. He pulled it out and answered it. 'Heather! Talk to me, H, what's—' A wince. 'Oh for God's sake.' He turned to Logan. 'Firearms team are stuck at the Bridge of Don – eighteen-wheeler from Peterhead hit a builder's truck. Smoked haddock and scaffolding pipe all over the bridge. Fire Brigade and Air Ambulance on the way. Our Guns are backtracking round to Gordon Brae.'

'What about our Operational Support Unit?'

'H: what about our Thugs?' He sagged a good three inches. 'Couldn't get any. Or Dogs. They're all busy dunting in a dealer's door outside Stonehaven.'

Of course they were.

'Remember that risk assessment we should've done?'

'Well it's too late now, isn't it?' King turned away and focussed on his phone. 'Where are the rest of you? ... Uh-huh. ... Uh-huh. ...' A sigh. 'Well, do your best, OK?' He hung up and slumped in his seat. 'You want the bad news, or the worse?'

'Gah...'

'The only ones that made it across the bridge before the crash were Steel and Tufty. And they're about as much use as a Plasticine bicycle.'

The traffic thinned out a bit and the speedometer needle crept up to ninety again.

Right, no way they could do this without backup. They'd have to find bodies from somewhere else and hope they'd be enough.

Logan poked at the dashboard's console – bringing up the address book from his phone. 'Scroll through that lot till you get to "Stubby".'

King did, then poked the call button.

Ringing belted out through the speakers, competing with the siren's din.

Until, finally: *'Whatever it is, I didn't do it.'*

'Stubby? It's Logan.'

'I know who it is: the name "Sinister Bastard" came up on my—'

'I need backup, ASAP. My firearms team is stuck in Bridge of Don behind twenty tons of smoked haddock and a mangled builder's truck.'

'Firearms? Can't give you Guns, but I can give you Thugs. Where and when?'

Logan hauled the brakes on, slithering to a halt at a junction marked 'Bridgend ¼ ~ Cruden Bay 2'. More morons on the other side of the road, heading south, completely ignorant of the fact that flashing lights and a bloody siren meant GET OUT OF THE WAY.

He looked at King. 'How do you pronounce the cottage?'

'"Kee-ow-nn-tri-ey." Ceann is "head" in Gaelic, and tràigh is "sand", or "beach". So Beachhead, give or take.' King checked his phone. 'GPS is showing three point one miles.'

'You get that, Stubby? Ceanntràigh Cottage, south end of Cruden Bay. ASAFBCWP!'

Finally, a minibus coming the other way slammed on its brakes and flashed its lights. Logan held up a hand in thanks and roared across the junction, picking up speed.

'*FB* and *CW? Wow. OK, we're on our way.*'

'Thanks, Stubby!'

'*Glen: grab Ted and the wee loon, we're—*' She hung up.

The Audi shot past not so much a village as a tiny collection of houses, then out through the limits into open countryside. Yellowy grass in parched fields, miserable sheep lolling about in the morning sun. All very flat and open.

Logan overtook a fat man on a scooter. 'Peterhead station's about … fifteen minutes north? Ten if they really go for it.'

King looked up from his phone and pointed. 'Right, there!'

He wrenched the car into the turn, the rear end skittering out on the dusty tarmac, and onto a single-track road. The sign said 'WEAK BRIDGE', the narrow road hemmed in on both sides by waist-high stone walls. The Audi got some air in the middle … bumping down on the other side.

King bounced in his seat. 'You want to wait for this "Stubby" person to show up?'

A hard ninety-degree left, between what looked like a school and a farmyard.

'We'd be insane to go charging in without backup. Haiden's built like a pit bull, only without the winning personality. *And* they're armed.'

A graveyard, its serried ranks of granite headstones glittering in the sunshine.

King shrugged. 'Just knives.'

'Trust me: knives are bad enough. I should know.'

'Fair enough. Left, here.'

Another ninety-degree turn, swiftly followed by a hard right.

King checked his phone again. 'Not far now.'

They flashed across a junction, and onto another single-track road. Golden swathes of wheat pressed in on the tarmac. A sliver of North Sea visible on the left where the land dropped away.

Logan accelerated up the hill. 'So, it's agreed: we get there, we block the road and we wait for Stubby.'

'OK.' A nod. Then King's eyes bugged, free hand grabbing at the dashboard. 'Sheep! Sheep!'

Logan stamped on the brakes, wheeching around the big fat ewe wandering down the side of the road.

'*Jesus*, that was close.'

The words, 'NELSON ST. LAB' appeared on the dashboard screen a second before the Audi's hands-free kit rang.

King let go of the dashboard to press the green button. 'Hello?'

'*Inspector McRae?*' Jeffers, their three-quarters-useless DNA analyst.

'He's driving.'

Logan shook his head. 'We're a bit busy, Jeffers!'

The car crested the brow of a small hill, and the jagged boundary between land and sea was laid out before them. Sunlight sparkling on the bright blue water.

'*I lifted a perfect thumb and forefinger off that coffee cup, but there's no corresponding prints in the system.*'

'Literally *right* in the middle of something.'

King pointed through the windscreen at a tiny bungalow perched on the headland near the cliffs, down a dead-end dirt track. 'Ceanntràigh Cottage. That's us!' It sat near the end of Cruden Bay beach, well away from anything else. Isolated. The perfect location for laying low and hiding the people you'd abducted and mutilated. A rusty Mini was parked out front.

Logan slowed to a crawl. 'You sure?'

'Look, there's a car.' King licked his lips. 'Do you think it's them? I think it's them.' A grin. 'We've got them!'

The dirt track petered out in front of the cottage, with its grey slate roof and dirty harling walls. A whirly washing line with no clothes on it. What probably used to be a garden, but had turned into a wobbly rectangle of parched grass and dande-lions. No other way in or out.

'*Anyway,*' Jeffers's voice crackled out of the speakers again, '*so I had a word with Dr McEvoy about the DNA, and she showed me how to expand the search parameters against the national database.*'

Blah, blah, blah.

Logan pulled on the handbrake. 'Can this wait?'

'*Well, it could, I suppose, but thing is: now we know who Mhari Powell really is. Well, we do and we don't, but it's a result, isn't it?*'

Logan raised an eyebrow. 'Come on, then: who is she?

There was a pause. Then, '*You're probably not going to like this…*'

38

Oh man...

Haiden rolls off Mhari and lies there, breathing hard, sweat cooling in the air.

Jesus. Yes. Hoo...

Wow.

He grins at the ceiling.

Aye, the room's a bit twee, but then what do you expect? Place is ancient. With its lace doilies, old-fashioned furniture, wooden walls in need of a paint – chipped and scarred from, like, *decades* of use. Bed's good, though.

He reaches out a hand and pats Mhari on her naked stomach. 'That was ... that was ... bloody great!'

'You're welcome.' She wipes between her legs with his T-shirt. To be honest, it needed a wash anyway. And let's face it, no way he could grudge her, not after that.

'Wow...'

She climbs out of bed and pads over to the window, looking up the hill. You could *never* get tired of ogling that pert round arse, or the firm high tits, or that wee tufty triangle between her legs. Where the magic happens.

He stretches, all the knots and aches and worries of the last two weeks melted away. 'God, I wish I still smoked.'

'It's not good for you, baby.' She slips on her pants – red with wee black hearts on them – then wrestles herself into a black bra. How come bras were so difficult to put on? See if it was men had to wear them? We'd sort that shit out so it's comfy. No twisting your arms behind your back like you're being handcuffed by the cops. She smiles at him, and honest to God he can feel the warmth spreading through his cock again. Cos she can do that.

He adjusts himself under the duvet. 'We got any beer?'

'You lie there and I'll go see.' Mhari gets dressed: tight pink T-shirt, camouflage cargo pants, sitting on the end of the bed to pull on her socks.

'Oh, and if there's any of last night's pizza in the fridge...?'

'Course, baby.' Soon as she's got her boots on, she's standing in front of the window, looking up the hill again with a strange wee smile on her face. Then Mhari nods and walks out of the room, on a mission for her man.

Her man.

God, imagine that... All the guys in the world, Mhari could have her pick, you know? And she chooses *him*.

He grins at the ceiling again. 'You're a lucky sod, Haiden.' Has another stretch.

Lot to do today: make a video of that tit Scotty Meyrick and get it online. Think about who's gonna be next. Who's gonna get themselves an all-expenses-paid trip to Chest-Freezer City. Maybe that git on the *Scottish Daily Post*? Bet they could do something special with him. Turncoat wee bastard. How do you go from, 'a once-in-a-lifetime opportunity to seize our country from the Westminster elite, to reclaim our soul and our destiny' to 'independence will destroy Scotland'? Just cos some English wanker buys the paper you work for? That's your thirty pieces of bloody silver, right there.

Oh aye, Edward Barwell could be their Judas.

Yeah, Mhari would like that.

And there she is, standing in the doorway, holding last night's greasy pizza box in one hand and a cold tinny in the other. She's put on her hoodie and a waterproof jacket – like it's going to rain. No way. Forecast is balls to the wall sunshine for at least the next week. Women, eh?

She passes him the box and he opens it. Not a lot left, but enough for a post-humping snack.

'Cheers, Mhari.' Big mouthful of ham and mushroom with extra mozzarella, all salty and earthy. Chewing with his eyes closed, it's that delicious. Yeah, the base is a bit soggy, but in a good way, you know? He swallows and winks at her. 'Early morning shag, a beer, and leftover pizza. A guy couldn't get a better girlfriend. No way. Not possible.' Another huge bite, talking through it, 'Mmm, think I actually love this stuff even more the next day.'

She settled on the end of the bed and looked at him, head on one side. 'Do you think we've made Dad proud?'

'Whose dad, my dad?' He sticks his hand out for the lager and she clicks open the ring-pull, takes a wee swig, then hands it over. Gotta love Tennent's: it tastes of school holidays and Saturdays with Mum, and fizzy happiness. 'Oh aye. Dad hates them English bastards more than he hates his lung cancer.' Poor old sod, lying there in his hospital bed, dying. Haiden puts the tin down. Sighs. 'Wish I could go see him…'

'You know you can't do that. I *told* you: it's what the police expect. The care home would tip them off soon as you walked in the door, and that would be it.'

'Yeah…' She was right. She was always right. Didn't make it hurt any less, though.

She pats his leg through the duvet. 'Besides, I passed on his messages, didn't I? Like a good big sister?'

He polishes off the last crust of pizza and washes it down with a scoof of lager. Stuffs down the belch that comes free with it. 'But I wish…' Hang on a minute. 'Big sister?'

She points at the window. 'Come look at this.' Then stands, makes her way over there and leans on the sill.

'No, wait, what? I don't *have* a big sister. Had a wee brother, but he drowned. They found him three days later, down the coast from here.' All pale and wrinkled. Wee black holes where the fish and crabs had been at him.

'Come on, Haiden. Indulge me.'

Yeah, cos how can he ever refuse her. It isn't possible.

He wriggles out of bed, and joins her at the window, takes a sip of his tinny. Course some blokes would be self-conscious, standing there like that, stark-bollock naked with everything on show, but not him. Nah, you spend as much time in the prison gym as he had, you wanna show that bad boy off. Brad Pitt's a podgy slob in comparison. Aye, and that's *Fight Club* Brad Pitt, too.

She points up the hill, where a white Audi's parked, blocking the track down to the cottage. 'You see that?'

'How come you said "big sister"?'

'That's the police. They've come to get us.'

'The *what*?' Oh sodding hell. The police. She's right; who else would block them in like that? Any minute now they'll be booting in the door, and it'll be all helicopters, and dogs, and big bastards with batons and guns. Escape! Make a run for it. Go. Go. GO. 'We've got to—'

Something thumps into his back. Not as hard as a punch, more like a...

Then a crackling, ripping noise and shards of white-hot glass tear through his stomach and spine. Oh God...

Mhari leans in and kisses his neck, breath warm against his skin. 'There we go.'

Everything tastes of hot batteries and raw meat as his throat fills, little red dots on the window as the bubbles pop between his lips.

Oh God...

He grabs for the windowsill and his tin of Tennent's bounces off the floor, spilling out its contents in a froth of white-edged gold.

'See, Haiden, they had me too young, Mum and Dad. She couldn't cope, so I had to go live with her sister in Canada. Then they had you and suddenly they *could* cope. Strange that, isn't it? How a wee boy is more "worth the effort" than a little girl?'

Oh God...

His knees don't work any more. They give up and he hits the carpet next to the emptying tin. Only now the carpet's slick with red. That's not coming from inside *him*, is it? It can't be: there's way too much of it. Can't be him. Please. Please don't let it be him. 'I didn't... It...'

'Shhh...' She squats down beside him and strokes his head, like he's a puppy. 'It'll all be over soon. OK?'

'Why...?'

'I'd love to stay and keep you company, but...' She sucks air through her teeth. 'Police.' A smile. 'It's been fun catching up, though.' Then Mhari stands, wipes the hunting knife on the duvet cover, slips it into its sheath as she walks from the room.

'Don't ... don't leave ... me.'

Oh God...

Haiden forces himself over onto his front and grabs at the bed's legs – dragging himself across the sodden carpet to the door. Following her.

The back door's open, letting sunlight spill into the kitchen.

Come on, Haiden, you can do it.

He hauls himself along the wall.

Closer.

Come on, you're not a quitter, are you? No. You're Haiden Bloody Lochhead!

Oh God...

Can't feel his fingers.

Every breath stinks of raw meat.

Come on, Haiden.

Into the kitchen, inching his way across the grubby cracked lino to the open door. Getting slower with every heave. Heavier. Till he can't move any more.

Mhari's there – marching across the patch of grass that separates the cottage from the cliffs. Not huge cliffs, safe enough to play on with your wee brother: soldiers, storming the gun batteries. She looks over her shoulder and waves at him, then disappears, swallowed by the boiling clouds of broom and gorse.

Please don't leave me...

But she's gone.

And he's all alone.

And soon he'll be dead.

— broken promises, windows, and bones —

39

Logan stared at the dashboard display. 'She's his *what*?'

'*Sister.*' It sounded as if Jeffers was doing his best to sound all authoritative and reliable, but couldn't pull it off. '*The woman you know as "Mhari Powell" is Haiden Lochhead's sister and "Gaelic Gary" Lochhead's daughter.*'

King looked from the display to Logan, mouth hanging open. 'But ... we saw her get into the car with Haiden and snog the arse off him. It was all caught on CCTV. And the visiting room at HMP Grampian. They were all over each other!'

'*We couldn't get an exact match, because she's not on the system, but soon as I opened the search up I found the familial ones. You see, I don't really do DNA, I'm more of a—*'

'Fingerprint man. Yes.' Logan reached for the button to end the call. 'Thanks, Jeffers: you did good today.' He hung up. 'She's Haiden's *sister.*'

King whistled. 'Wow. Talk about the family that plays together, lays together, and slays together.'

'It doesn't change anything, though.'

'I mean, everyone knows the PASL, SPLA, SFFRF, and the rest of them were kinda incestuous, but Gaelic Gary's kids are *humping* each other? No wonder we never get independence...' King checked his watch. 'Backup should be here by now.' Drummed his fingers on the dashboard. 'What if we've got this wrong?'

'Then we look like a pair of idiots and the press sink their fangs in our backsides.' Which was probably going to happen anyway. 'Besides, where else would Haiden and Mhari be?'

'Hmmm... How about that painting on Gaelic Gary's wall? The stone circle. Haiden's ex said the whole family were obsessed with stone circles.'

Dear Lord, that was stupid.

'So, what: they're keeping their victims in abandoned fridge freezers in the middle of a stone circle?'

'Yeah, now you say it out loud.' He checked his watch again. 'Where the hell are our Thugs?'

And, as if by magic, Steel's MX-5 appeared in the rear-view mirror. Closely followed by a pair of patrol cars – blue-and-whites flickering off as they climbed the hill. No sirens.

'Ha!' King faced front again. 'OK, the cavalry has arrived. Can we go do this now?'

'With pleasure.' Logan put the Audi in gear and hared down the track, slithering to a halt on the parched grass in front of the rusty Mini. Scrambled out of the car with King close behind.

He tried the front door: locked.

King stuck his hand out. 'Keys.'

'Why would I have keys for their house? Are you—'

'*Car* keys! Wheel brace in the boot, remember?'

'Right.' He tossed them over and King sprinted back to the Audi, popping the boot as Logan braced himself and slammed his foot into the front door, right beside the lock. The whole thing bounced and shuddered, letting loose an echoing BOOM. But it didn't fly open.

He had another go.

Answer the phone. Answer the phone. Answer the *bloody* phone...

Haiden sags against the dirty linoleum. Lying on his side in a slowly expanding puddle of red.

Please, answer the phone...

Please...

Every breath is a short, spiky thing, getting colder with each gurgling lungful.

And then her voice comes from the phone's speaker. *'Who is this?'* Cindy.

He tries to tell her, but the only sound that comes out is the crackle of popping blood bubbles.

'Oh very, funny. A dirty phone call with heavy breathing. Well you can take your pitiful *little cock and shove it right up your—'*

'Cindy.' Forcing the word out. 'Cindy it's ... it's me.'

'Haiden.' She says his name with all the warmth of a frozen turd. *'What have I told you about calling me?'*

A muffled boom comes from somewhere round the front of the house, but it's too late to worry about that now. Far too late. For everything.

'Is ... is Marty ... there?'

'You threw away your visiting rights when you started seeing that Mhari bitch. You threw them away when you got arrested again!'

Tears fill his eyes, making the kitchen blur. 'Cindy ... Cindy, please.'

'Have you been drinking?' A sniff. *'You know what? I don't care. You can cry and beg and whine all you want: you're not going to infect my son with your lies and failure and garbage.'*

Another boom.

The phone slithers out of his hand, clunks onto the blood-slicked linoleum beside his head. Can't pick it up again – his hands don't work any more. Nothing does.

'Please ... please, Cindy...'

Her voice is faint, but still there, sneering out of the phone's speaker *'You're weak. You've always been weak. You're pathetic. Enjoy France, you useless bastard.'*

'Tell Marty ... tell Marty ... I love...'

The screen flashes 'CALL ENDED' at him. She's hung up.

Hot tears roll down Haiden's cheek, the word barely a whisper: 'Him.'

Another boom from the front of the house, this one ringed with splintering woody noises.

Maybe it's time? Yeah. Maybe it's...

*　　*　　*

The frame finally gave way and the door bounced off its hinges, tumbling down into the hallway.

Logan stepped aside and King rushed the entrance, wheel brace held up, over his shoulder, as if it was an extendable baton. Ready to crack someone.

He followed, pushing through a tiny porch into a hallway-cum-living-room with tired green wallpaper and an exhausted brown couch. A saltire flag pinned up above the fireplace, a rampant lion on the wall opposite. No TV. A bookcase full of *Oor Wullie* and *The Broons* annuals. And a thick line of dark red along the carpet by the wall, emerging from the open bedroom door and disappearing into the open kitchen one.

That was a *lot* of blood.

King did a quick three-sixty, checking the living room. 'Clear!'

Logan checked the bedroom – old-fashioned and dear God that was a *huge* puddle of blood by the window. He ducked down and checked under the bed. No one there. 'Clear!'

'*Logan!*' King's voice. '*Logan it's Haiden Lochhead! He's been stabbed. Jesus...*'

Out into the living room again.

King's feet were visible through the open kitchen door, the soles shiny with blood. 'Haiden? Can you hear me?'

OK, King had the kitchen; that left two more rooms. Logan threw open the door to a small bathroom – chipped enamel tub, stained avocado toilet, a threadbare towel. 'Clear!'

The last door opened in another bedroom, this one with wooden bunkbeds, the mattresses naked and stained tobacco-brown with sweat. 'Clear!'

He joined King in the kitchen. Wood panelling lined the walls, painted a revolting shade of spearmint green, and playing host to about a dozen framed photos of chickens and pigs – the colours faded to muddy orange. A rickety table with the Audi's wheel brace sitting on top of it. An old white fridge and ancient electric cooker. A door lying open, showing the fiery yellow broom and crystal blue sky. Haiden lay on his side in front of it, completely naked, one leg curled up, the other stretched out, face pale and shiny where it wasn't stained dark red.

His back was clarted in gore, a black slit, about two inches wide, below his right shoulder blade. More blood around his mouth and down his chin. And then bubbles popped between Haiden's lips... He was still *alive*.

'Haiden?' King stared up at Logan – his suit scarlet-soaked all down the sleeves – then down at the bleeding body. Grabbing his waxy shoulder and shaking it. 'Haiden, stay with me, buddy, OK?'

Logan pulled out his phone and dialled Control. 'I need an ambulance, and I need it now!'

'Haiden? Can you hear me?'

'Roger that, Inspector, where do you need it?'

'Haiden? You're going to be all right.' King was getting louder. 'We're getting help, OK, Haiden?'

Logan stuck a finger in his ear and retreated to the living room. 'Ceanntràigh Cottage, Cruden Bay. We've got an I-C-One male, stab wound, *heavy* blood loss.'

'One second... Right we—'

Whatever came next was drowned out by King, shouting now: 'WHERE ARE THEY, HAIDEN? WHERE DID YOU HIDE PROFESSOR WILSON AND THE OTHERS?'

Logan made for the far side of the room, where three small windows looked out over the curl of parched grass and the North Sea beyond. 'Say again?'

'They've dispatched the air ambulance, it'll be with you soon as they can.'

He glanced at the kitchen: King was bent over Haiden, ear pressed close to the burbling scarlet froth coming out of Haiden's mouth, as if he was taking a final confession.

'Tell them to hurry.'

The hole where the front door used to be rattled as Steel and Tufty burst into the room, stabproofs on, truncheons and pepper spray at the ready.

Steel slithered to a halt, teeth bared. 'Where is the daft wee shite?'

Tufty swept the room. 'Clear!'

As if Logan and King hadn't already done that.

Four uniformed officers battered in after them, kitted out in full riot-police body armour, complete with gauntlets, shin and elbow guards, helmets with face shields, batons drawn. They pretty much filled every available inch of the living room. Stubby and her Thugs.

Stubby flipped up her face shield and peered into the bloody kitchen. Then furrowed her dark hairy eyebrows at Logan. 'Is the property secure?'

'Mhari Powell's missing.'

Tufty stuck his head into the bathroom. 'Clear!'

Logan pointed out through the little windows. 'Search the clifftops, she can't have gone far. And watch out: she's armed!'

A nod from Stubby. 'Greeny: you and Ted, out front. Glen: you're with me.' And with that they thundered off again.

Tufty tried the spare bedroom. 'Clea— Ow!'

Steel hit him again. 'Cut it out, you prawn-flavoured arse-magnet.'

'Only doing my job.' Rubbing his arm. 'And that *hurt*, thank you very much.'

She stood in the kitchen doorway, looking down at King and Haiden. 'What a cocking mess.'

Now there was an understatement.

Then King sat back on his haunches, shook his head, and stood. 'He's dead.'

Logan closed his eyes, massaging the ache growing in his forehead. 'Sodding hell.' So close. If they'd kicked the door in five minutes earlier, they might have saved Haiden. Instead, they were all royally screwed.

When Logan opened his eyes again, King was wiping his bloody hands on his shirt.

He stood there, staring down at Haiden's body, then huffed out a shuddering breath, picked up the wheel brace, face a sickly green-grey colour as he turned and stumbled out through the door, into the sunshine.

Couldn't blame him: someone dying in your arms like that? Wasn't easy. Didn't matter how much of a scumbag they'd been...

Steel sighed. 'Aye, Kingy'll be off spewing his ring again.' She leaned against the kitchen door frame, half-hanging into the room, frowning at Haiden's naked corpse. 'It true they were brother and sister?'

'Mhari can't have gone far – Haiden would've been...'

Wait a minute, was that an engine revving? It was – coming from the front of the cottage.

Logan marched for the battered-open front door, just in time to see the Audi's four wheels spinning on the grass, then grabbing hold. The car shot forward with King in the driving seat. 'Hey!' He ran outside, waving both arms above his head. 'COME BACK HERE!'

But the Audi didn't come back here, it roared away up the track, leaving nothing but a trail of dust behind.

'Damn it!' Logan hurried inside.

Steel was thumbing away at something on her phone while Tufty had his head buried in an *Oor Wullie* annual. The pair of them standing about like the useless sods they were.

'King's nicked my car!' He jabbed a hand at Steel. 'Give me your keys.'

She didn't even look up. 'Aye, that'll be shining.'

'Oh for... He's *up* to something! He was asking Haiden where the bodies were, then he rushed out of here and stole – my – bloody – car!'

'Pffff...' She stuck her phone in her pocket. Then pointed at Tufty. 'You: Oor Wanky, secure the locus. Pretend you're a crime-scene manager, or something. No one in or out, access log, blah, blah, blah.'

A grin. 'Cool.'

Steel cricked her head from side to side, flexing her shoulders as she sauntered for the door. Cracked her knuckles like a concert pianist. Nodded at Logan. 'Well, come on then. It's hot pursuit time.'

Keys out, she slid behind the wheel of her MX-5, Logan scrambling into the passenger seat as the engine started with a throaty growl.

'Right.' Steel flicked open the car's roof catch. 'Before we do this, can you confirm to me that you're commandeering this vehicle for the benefit of Professional Standards in the pursuance of an ongoing investigation?'

Seriously?

'Will you put your foot down?'

She pressed a button on the dashboard, and the folding roof whirred down. 'And that any damage sustained by my vehicle will be covered and remediated by Police Scotland at their expense?'

'Yes, fine. Whatever. Now go!'

A grin. 'Hold tight.' The Mx-5's engine bellowed, the rear end slithering from side to side, wheels spinning, like a terrier winding up, then the tyres gripped and the wee car shot forward, hammered between the parked patrol cars, and out onto the dirt track. 'YEEEEEEEEEEEEEEEEEEEEEEEEE-HAW!'

Fields flashed past the car windows, *much* faster than they seemed to when Logan was driving. The dust King had kicked up in the Audi was thinning, caught by the offshore breeze, which at least meant they could see where they were going. But, given the way Steel was driving, maybe wasn't such a great idea.

Logan gritted his teeth, holding onto the seatbelt with one hand and the seat with the other as she threw the car into a warren of tight bends at ludicrous speed. He closed his eyes. Maybe the inevitable crash would hurt less that way?

She shouted at him, over the roar of the engine. 'Don't be such a Jessie!'

OK. OK...

He forced his eyes open, dragged out his phone, brought up his contacts list, and called King.

It rang twice, then: *'What?'*

'What the hell are you playing at? You stole my bloody car!'

'I'm doing my best, OK? You heard Hardie – I'm treading water with sharks here. I can't afford to screw this up!'

'Then don't be stupid! We'll—'

'This is my last chance, Logan. I need this.'

'You can't charge off without...' Logan pulled the phone from his ear and frowned at the screen: 'CALL ENDED'. Oh no you sodding don't. He poked the icon to redial.

The MX-5 slithered around a hard right, shoving Logan against the door as the phone rang.

'Dear God, what now?'

'What did Haiden tell you? Where are Matt Lansdale and—'

What sounded like a horn blared out from King's end. *'Jesus!'*

'Where are—'

A screeching noise.

'Do you want me to crash your car? Is that what you want?'

'No!'

'Then stop calling while I'm driving!'

The MX-5 fishtailed as Steel wrenched them into a sharp left, leaving the tarmac for a moment as they flew over a bump.

Logan jammed his legs against the walls of the footwell, holding himself in place. 'Don't be a...' Complete silence from the other end. When he checked the screen, there it was again: 'CALL ENDED'. He scowled across the car at Steel. 'Bloody King keeps hanging up on me.'

She hurled the car around the next bend. The road stretched ahead of them, long and straight. No sign of Logan's Audi. 'Ah...'

'Please don't tell me you've lost him!'

'I've no' *lost*-lost him, I just ... don't know where he is. A wee bit.' Steel hammered it along the straight, worrying at her bottom lip, her frown growing deeper with every small side road they passed. Whin and broom crowded in on either side of the MX-5, blocking out the world.

'We're slowing down.' Logan turned in his seat. '*Why* are we slowing down?'

'Could've turned off anywhere.'

'Oh for God's sake!'

She raised herself in her seat, peering over the top of the windscreen. 'Can you see him? I can't see him.'

'AAAAAAARRRGH!' Logan stabbed a finger down on the redial button.

It rang as the MX-5 drifted to a halt. Then, *'You've reached*

Detective Inspector King. I can't answer the phone right now, so please leave a message.' Followed by a hard electronic *bleeeeeep*.

'WHERE THE BLOODY HELL ARE YOU?' He hung up and sat there, seething at the gorse-flamed drystane dyke sitting next to the passenger door.

Steel poked him in the shoulder. 'Do we feel better now, after our little outburst?'

'No.' Difficult to imagine what *would* make him feel better at this point, though forcibly inserting his size nine boot up DI King's rectum was probably a good start.

'Out.' She pulled on the handbrake. 'Go stand on a wall and see if you can see him.'

Maybe *both* boots.

Logan climbed out of her car.

The roadside verge was a narrow strip of dry yellow grass, followed by a deep ditch, then the drystane dyke with its crown of Day-Glo-yellow flowers and spiky thorns. About ten foot down the road was a patch of bare stone and he scrambled up onto it.

Fields stretched away on either side of the road, irregular shapes and sizes that followed the features and contours of the land, instead of some ordered grid. On the right, the land fell away to the sea; a thin line of woods to the left; the little granite houses of Cruden Bay, straight ahead. Could see for miles from up here... But there was still no sign of Sodding King and Logan's Sodding Audi.

Lots of whin and broom, though, the thieving git could be parked up almost anywhere, hidden behind a clump of it. They'd have to search every single road and track to be sure.

Deep breath. 'AAAAAAAAAARRRRRRGH!'

All emptied out, Logan slumped. He clambered his way over to the car and crumpled into the passenger seat.

Steel patted him on the leg. 'Look on the bright side, Laz: maybe Kingy's wrapped your car around the arse-end of some teuchter's tractor and right now he's little more than a big blubbering sack of bloody mince in a fancy-pants suit.'

He glowered at her. 'You're not funny.'

'No' *my* fault the man's a dick.' She drummed her fingers on the steering wheel, frowning. 'Honestly: sodding off like the Lone Ranger. Supposed to be a team, here.' As if that had ever stopped *her* from doing all the crap she'd got up to over the years. A sigh, then she released the handbrake and set off down the long straight road again at a less hell-for-leather pace. 'Come on, we'll have a wee search for him. He's got to be *somewhere*.' Steel shook her head. 'But between you and me: see operation King-Logan? It's a sodding disaster.'

Yeah, he was well aware of that.

Logan got his phone out again and called Control.

'*Air Ambulance ETA is five minutes.*'

'You can cancel that – victim's dead. Better get the Pathologist, Procurator Fiscal, and duty undertakers out instead.'

'*Oooh, OK. Will do.*'

'And while you're at it, ping the GPS on DI King's Airwave handset. I need to know where he is, and I need to know *now*.'

Steel slowed at the next side road, peering off down the track, then speeding up again.

'*OK, system says DI King is at Divisional Headquarters. Do you want me to patch you through?*'

Logan covered his eyes. 'Oh for God's sake.' The silly sod had left it behind, at the station.

'*If you need DI King, we can probably still find him through GPS. Which pool car does he have?*'

Gah...

'He's not *in* a pool car, he's in *my* car.'

Bloody Detective Bloody Inspector Frank Bloody King.

'*Sorry. If he calls in, I'll tell him to give you a shout.*'

It wasn't easy forcing the words out between gritted teeth, but Logan did it anyway. 'Thank you.' Then he hung up and put his phone in his pocket. Straightened the seam in his police-issue itchy trousers. Took a nice deep breath. And bellowed a scream into the passenger footwell.

Steel sniffed. 'Yeah ... Kingy has that effect on me too.'

40

Frank parked halfway down a narrow lane. Brambles loomed on both sides, hemming the car in. He opened the door and clambered out.

Yeah… Logan wasn't going to be very happy when he saw what had happened to his beloved Audi. A deep gouge wormed its way along the driver's-side wing, through the door, and off to the rear wheel arch and panels, ringed with bright scrapes of raw metal where large chunks of the paintwork had come off. Dents in the wheel arches. A big one in the bonnet. And, let's be honest, the exhaust sounded like a smoker's lung and the engine wasn't much better.

He reached in, turned it off, and plucked the wheel brace from the passenger seat. Creaked the door shut and limped down the lane – every step making his right knee and ribs hiss – keeping low to avoid being seen.

At the end of the lane he hunkered down behind a low wall and peered around the corner.

The two-storey house was nearly buried by the weight of ivy growing up the dirty granite walls – green tendrils reaching up beneath the eaves and into the roof. Poking out through holes in the tiles. Probably looked impressive at one point, with its bay windows and portico, but not now it'd decayed to a crumbling wreck.

A rusty grey Transit van sat next to it, its bodywork slowly succumbing to green and black mould. Marooned in a sea of brambles. Didn't look as if it'd moved in years.

Right. He tightened his grip on the wheel brace and limp-jogged across the tussocked grass to the front door. Flattened himself against the wall. So far so good. If he could—

His phone launched into its generic ringtone.

Sodding hell…

He fumbled it from his pocket, fast as possible before it started ramping up the volume. The words, 'INSP. MCRAE' filled the screen. Of all the *stupid* times to call.

He hit 'IGNORE'.

And just to be safe, switched it off as well. Stuffed it deep in his pocket.

Trying to get him killed.

Honestly.

Frank stood on his tiptoes and peeked in through the nearest window.

A bedroom – collapsed metal bedframe and the decayed remains of what used to be a mattress. Holes in the walls and ceiling. No sign of a knife-wielding maniac.

The window on the other side of the door was too buried in bramble-barbed-wire to look inside. Which left only one option: the door.

He crept up the stairs.

Huffed out a breath.

This was *definitely* the right place – no one installed six shiny Yale locks on an abandoned building unless there was something inside they wanted to hide. The wood was wasp-eaten and bloated. Probably wouldn't take much to boot it in. But then Mhari Powell would know he was there and going by what she'd done to her brother, that wasn't a great idea.

A brass plaque sat above the letterbox, the metal pitted and stained: the words 'RENFIELD HOUSE' half consumed and obscured by verdigris. Someone had a sense of humour, naming their house after Dracula's bug-eating minion, when Slains Castle was just over the hill there. Oh yes, Whitby might *claim* Bram Stoker wrote and set the whole thing down there, but that was the English for you, wasn't it? Always stealing what was right-fully Scotland's.

He reached for the door handle. After all, you never knew your...

The door swung open as he touched it.

Six Yales and not one of them locked.

About time his luck changed.

Frank slipped inside.

Gloomy in here, even with the evening sun beating down outside. Cool too. The air tasted grey with dust and mould, the sharp mucky scent of rodents. A hole in the plasterwork showed off the room he couldn't look into from outside – a fusty kitchen with sagging units and a broken table. Straight ahead: a bathroom with black-and-white tiles littered with jagged chunks of collapsed plaster. A staircase off to one side, reaching up to the first floor, the wood rotten and treacherous, untouched beneath a thick film of pristine dust.

Which left the cupboard under the stairs and—

He froze.

Was that *singing*?

It was – a woman's voice with no accompaniment:

'And so we came to Branxton Hill, and raised our pikes on
   higher ground,
The guns they roared the archers shot, but dirty weather
   spoiled the lot,'

It was coming from down the corridor, on the right.
He inched his way over, sticking to the wall.

'The wind and rain fought harder still, but King James'
   courage, well renowned,
He led the charge at Surrey's flank, panic spread through
   English ranks,'

There was a door at the far end, its paintwork blistered and peeling. The singing was coming from the other side.

'Vengeance ours, this day, would be, for Henry's bloody
   treachery,
Vengeance ours, praise God we'd see, another Scottish victory.'

He stuck his ear against the door.

'We bathed in blood, the fields ran red, the English foe we
   routed,
A slash of blade, and on we rushed, Surrey's men would soon
   be crushed,'

OK, she definitely hadn't heard him coming – wouldn't be
singing away to herself otherwise. He raised the wheel brace,
took hold of the door handle, and burst through into what
was probably once a living room, looking out over the cliffs
towards the sea. Should have been bright in here, with the
sun blaring down outside, but somehow it made the room
gloomier. The view through the broken windows like a vision
from a past life.

'The cowards ran, the battle fled, as we our war cries shouted!
And brave King James he spurred us on, the English ranks
   their courage gone.'

What?

There was no one here, just five chest freezers, three of which
were smeared with dried blood, one of which was switched on,
all of which had words spray-painted on them in bright-red
gloss. The stomach-clenching scent of rotting meat. The droning
buzz of great big shiny bluebottles. And the singing, of course.

It was coming from a mobile phone, perched on top of the
chest freezer with 'WALLACE' on it.

'Vengeance ours, this day, would be, for Henry's bloody
   treachery,
Vengeance ours, praise God we'd see, another Scottish victory.'

He picked the phone up, slid his thumb across the screen to open it. Wasn't locked.

'But the Devil's luck, upon us come, with—'

Frank hit pause. Why would Mhari record...
Oh.
Something cold and sharp pressed against his throat.
The room hadn't been empty after all – she'd been hiding behind the door. And now she was right behind him, holding a massive hunting knife.
Her breath was warm against his ear. 'Drop the weapon.'
He did and the wheel brace clattered against the filthy floor. Returned the phone to the chest freezer's lid. Kept his voice level and *in charge*. 'OK, let's not do anything we'll regret.'
'Why would I regret anything? I'm not the one about to get my throat slit.'
Don't think about that. Don't think about it. You're in charge. She's not going to kill you. You're going to live through this.
She killed her own *brother*.
King swallowed. 'It's not too late to—'
'How did you find me? This place? How?'
'I... Haiden told me. Before he died. Look, this isn't—'
'I should've slit *his* throat too. Still, I won't make that mistake again.'
The knife pressed harder into Frank's neck.
Yeah, she was definitely *dangerously* unhinged, but that didn't mean he couldn't salvage this. Calm breaths. Sound like you're still in charge, damn it. 'Come on, Mhari, I'm not your enemy here. You've seen the papers, right? I was in the PASL when your dad was in charge. We were friends.'
The only sound was the hum of the working freezer and the drone of the flies.
Then, 'Yeah, I saw the papers. You betrayed us, didn't you?' Spitting the words out. 'You abandoned the cause, went to work for the enemy!'
She twisted the knife and cold pain snapped across his throat. Followed by a warm trickle.

Oh Jesus, she was going to kill him.

'Wait! Wait...' All pretence at being in charge gone, voice rank with the stench of panic. 'Robert Drysdale!'

'What about him?'

Many, Many Years Ago

The bothy lurks in darkness, all its windows panned in, the door warped and buckled. It sits in the middle of nowhere – surrounded by rough fields and ditches, the snow-capped peak of Beinn a' Bhùird lurking in the background. The kind of place where ghosts stalk the moonlit mountainside.

Only the bothy's about to get itself another ghost...

Frank shifts in the passenger seat, trying not to look at the silhouettes in the broken window. At the dancing torchlight as they go about their business. Belting out some old Corries song about battering the English foe.

'Oh Jesus...' He raises the bottle of Grouse and takes a swig, shuddering as it goes down hard and hot. Has another drag on his trembling cigarette.

He's only sixteen, for God's sake. Sixteen.

Should *never* have come here. Should *never* have agreed to help. Should *never* have had anything to do with "Gaelic Gary" Lochhead and his gang of mad bastards. But it's too late now.

One more slug of whisky goes down like burning petrol, souring his stomach.

Maybe, he could do a runner? Climb out of the Land Rover and bugger off into the night. Scarper back to civilisation and never, *ever*—

A monstrous face appears at the passenger window, teeth bared, eyes wide. Hideous and terrifying. A wee scream bursts its way out of Frank's throat.

Gaelic Gary grins at him, torch held under his chin to make him look like even more Hammer House of Horror than he already does. 'Come on, wee man, you're missing all the fun!'

Frank's words don't come out right, bumping into each other in their rush to escape. 'I … I don't think… It, it, it's not… I can't—'

'No!' Gary yanks the passenger door open and grabs a handful of Frank's jumper, pulling him closer, voice a hard dark snarl. 'You get your arse out this car and in there, or you'll be next.' He tightens his grip and hauls Frank and his whisky bottle out into the night. Their breath mists in the torchlight as he shoves Frank towards the bothy.

Then Gary wraps his arm around his shoulder, voice all warm again. Like they're best of friends. 'See, there's no *passengers* in a civil war, wee man. You're either driving, or you're being knocked down. You don't wanna be roadkill, do you?'

'Course not!'

'Good.' A squeeze of that massive, powerful arm. 'Come on, this'll be the stuff of legends!' Gary propels him through the bothy door into a manky wee hallway. A bunch of the floorboards are missing and drifts of bird crap lie beneath the house martin nests dotted around the walls, up by the sagging ceiling.

There's a door straight ahead and Gary boots it open. Pushes Frank over the threshold and into hell.

Oh Jesus. Jesus. Jesus…

Hell is a grubby room, devoid of furniture, with scrawled graffiti on the peeling wallpaper. A broken Belfast sink and rusting old range cooker. Most of the ceiling's caved in, leaving the roof beams exposed, all the way up to the roof above. But that's not what makes it hell. Nor is it the pair of singing bastards – both of them heavyset and powerful. Both of them in kilts, hiking boots, and Scotland rugby tops. Both of them singing and laughing. Both of them reeking of whisky. Both of them swinging their torches around like it's a disco.

No, what makes it Hell is *the man*.

The man hanging from the rope that's been looped over a beam in the middle of the room. Face darkening as his legs kick and his body sways. Turning slow as a lump of doner meat in a kebab shop window.

One of the kilts takes a swig from a bottle of Bell's and roars in the man's face. Spits in it. Grins. 'No' so bloody clever *now*, are we, Robert?'

Gary gives Frank a push, sending him stumbling against the hanging man. 'BOYS! LOOK WHO I FOUND!'

A ragged cheer goes up from the kilts.

The spitter turns his grin towards Frank, eyes big and dark like a shark about to bite. 'Go-an yerself, wee man! 'Bout time!'

His mate shakes a can of spray paint and graffitis a big red capital 'J' on the wall – the letter thick, paint dribbling down like fresh blood. Then a 'U'.

Gary reaches into his coat and pulls out a hammer. Dips his other hand in and produces a plastic bag that jingles and rattles as he bounces it in his palm.

A 'D' joins the two spray-painted letters.

'Hoy, Frank...' Gary tosses the bag at him.

It bounces off his chest and Frank has to scrabble to grab it before it hits the floor. The contents are jagged and rough. Sharp against his skin. He looks down at the bag.

Oh Jesus.

It's full of nails. Each of them about as long as his little finger, with a big round flat head.

A wink from Gary. 'One at a time, eh?'

Oh. Jesus.

The whisky boils in his stomach, threatening to rush up his throat and spatter everywhere.

He can't do this. He *can't*.

But if he doesn't, Gaelic Gary will kill him. *You don't wanna be roadkill, do you?*

He's only sixteen.

He doesn't have a choice...

So Frank swallows it down. Forces it to stay there with another swig of Grouse. Shudders. Hauls in a deep shaking breath. Then nods. Opens the packet.

An 'A' gets sprayed on the wall as Frank fumbles one of the nails from the bag and holds it out. Tries his best to keep his hand steady.

The final letter, 'S', makes the word complete.

'Good boy.' Gary takes the nail from him then turns to the man struggling at the end of the rope. The man who, up until ten o'clock this morning, had been a trusted member of the People's Army for Scottish Liberation. The man whose last half hour on earth was going to involve a lot of screaming.

Now

Frank licked his lips and pulled his chin up an inch, but the blade in Mhari's hand stayed right where it was. 'I was there! I was … I *helped*, OK? I passed your dad the nails. Please don't do this!'

'How do I know you're telling the truth?'

'I'm on your side!' Voice going up an octave, the words stumbling over each other just like they'd done all those years ago. 'I am. I promise! I came here on my own, didn't I? I didn't tell anyone where you were. I'm on your side!'

'Hmm…' She took the knife from Frank's throat.

He was still alive.

Oh thank you Jesus, thank you Jesus, thank you Jesus.

Frank collapsed to his knees, both hands clutching his bleeding neck. Blinking tears and sweat from his eyes. 'I can help you. We can help each other…'

She stood over him, the knife glittering in the dim light. 'Start talking.'

41

'No, but what I *would* call it is a complete and utter balls-up.'
Logan paced towards the cottage again, phone against his ear,
sweat prickling between his shoulder blades.

The Scene Examiners' Transit was parked next to the one
remaining patrol car, Steel's dust-covered MX-5, and the duty
undertaker's discreet grey van – its rear doors lying wide open.
Waiting.

All they needed now was the Procurator Fiscal, Pathologist,
and six tons of hostile media coverage to make today complete.

Superintendent Bevan's New Zealand accent was perfect for
sounding incredulous. *'And there's no sign of him* anywhere?'

'I've got a lookout request on King and the car, the entire
team's going door-to-door in Cruden Bay, patrol cars out
searching the roads...' He made it as far as the living room
window – where the SE team were clearly visible photographing
and fingerprinting and sampling everything – turned around
and paced towards the cliffs again. 'I don't know what else we
can do.'

'Logan, it's DCI Hardie.'

Oh great, Bevan had him on speakerphone.

Logan made a silent wanking gesture. 'Yes, Chief Inspector?'
You miserable useless git.

*'Are we saying this is connected to the revelations in today's
paper?'*

'No. Maybe. I doubt it.' He stopped at the edge of the cliffs, where a line of blue-and-white tape cordoned off a path down through the gorse and broom to the beach below. Not that they'd get a lot of joy from the beach – the tide was nearly all the way in, stealing any footprints and trace evidence Mhari Powell would have left behind. Sunlight sparkling gold off the deep blue water. 'Actually, you know what? *Yes, it is.* He's out there taking risks because someone threatened his job this morning. Thin ice, treading water, sharks. Remember that?'

Hardie cleared his throat. '*Yes. … Well… I'm sure there were faults on all sides.*' The defensive tone got replaced by something altogether more belligerent. '*But if he's got nothing to hide, why hasn't he called in?*'

Moron.

'How are we getting on with a warrant for his mobile phone's location?'

'*Logan? It's me again.*' Bevan. '*They're rushing it through now. But if he's got his phone switched off…*'

Which, given that every time Logan called the thing it went straight through to voicemail, he probably had. Idiot. 'I'm worried he's caught up with Mhari Powell and she's done the same thing to him that she did to her brother.'

Hardie made a strange growling sound. '*Well, if no one else is going to say the obvious conclusion, I will: what if he's joined her?*'

Oh, that deserved another wanking gesture. 'With all due respect—'

'*He was in a nationalist terrorist cell when he was younger, what's to stop him being in an Alt-Nat one now?*'

'But—'

'*Are you saying it's impossible?*'

Oh for God's sake.

Logan sagged. Ran a hand over his face. 'No. But why would he pick—'

A new voice joined the call, clipped, tight, and far too loud. '*We've got a press conference in fifteen minutes, what exactly am I supposed to tell them?*'

Logan held the phone away from his head, so she wouldn't

hear him groan. Then forced a smile into his voice: 'Jane. Didn't know you were there.'

'The media are already ripping our backside wide open with this one, can you imagine what they're going to shove up it when we tell them that A: we still have no clue who Mhari Powell actually is. B: she's killed her brother, Haiden Lochhead, who, by the way, we told everyone was the criminal mastermind here.' Jane got even louder, till she was almost shouting. *'And C: DI King, who's all over the papers as a former bloody terrorist, might have run away to join forces with MHARI SODDING POWELL!'* A small scream of rage belted down the phone. *'Did I miss anything out, in this cavalcade of cocking disasters?'*

'Yes.' Logan pulled his shoulders back. 'That I'm an inspector with *Professional Standards* and I don't take kindly to people yelling at me!'

Bevan stepped in again. *'All right, all right. Things are a bit heated right now, but let's take a deep breath and remember we're on the same team here. All right?'*

No one said anything.

'All right.'

He turned away from the cliffs and started towards the cottage again. 'You *can't* tell them King's joined forces with Mhari Powell. Superintendent Bevan?'

'Logan's right.' She could've put a bit more conviction in her voice, but at least she was on his side. *'There's no proof the Detective Inspector's done anything of the sort.'*

Jane groaned. *'It's a lovely thought, Superintendent, but trust me: that's not how the media works. This isn't about* proof, *it's about* perception. *If we try to spin this like he's a hero and it turns out he's run off to join his terrorist mates, the media will crucify us.'*

'So don't tell them anything.'

'Then, when it comes out, they'll crucify us for trying to cover it up!'

Well, there was no point arguing with Jane – Media Liaison Officers were like bulldogs, only less flexible – maybe Superintendent Bevan could be the voice of reason? Worth a go, anyway.

'Boss? You're the senior officer here.'

'We can't lie to the press, Logan. And we can't lie by omission either.' A sigh. 'Besides, if you're swamping Cruden Bay with officers flashing DI King's photo, someone's going to connect the dots.'

'Probably all over social media as we… Yup. Here, look at this.' Scrunching noises came from Jane's end. 'Look at it!'

Then a grunt from Hardie. 'Oh sodding hell. That's all we need.'

'Now we have to make a statement.' Jane's voice got louder, as if she was looming over the speakerphone. 'You listen to me, Inspector McRae: you – need – to – find – him. OK? You need to find him now, before this utter cluster-wanking disaster gets any worse!'

'I'm doing my best.' He hung up, stuffed his phone away. Shook his head.

Oh, it was easy shouting the odds and making demands from the safety of Divisional Headquarters, wasn't it? Didn't see any of *them* out here trying to actually make a bloody difference.

The duty undertakers emerged from the cottage, carrying a silver-grey plastic coffin. Looked heavy.

What the hell did everyone expect him to do: magic a result out of thin air? 'Izzy Wizzy, Let's Get Busy!' wasn't going to cut it this time.

Sodding DI Sodding Frank Sodding King. Why did he have to go make everything *worse*?

The duty undertakers levered the coffin into their van and clunked the doors shut. Goodbye Haiden Lochhead.

Come on, Logan. Finger out. Let's go find DI King.

And kick his backside for him.

Hard.

Steel leaned back and draped her elbows over the metal hand-rail, face turned to the setting sun. Basking in all her wrinkly glory. E-cigarette poking out the side of her mouth, making thin plumes of fruity fog. Pineapple, going by the smell.

Logan scowled down at the river below, where it disappeared under the bridge, its summer-drought level augmented by the high tide. 'They still there?'

'Hud oan, I'll check.' She tutted a couple of times. 'So far we've got about two dozen journos, five camera crews, and five outside broadcast vans too.' Another puff of pineapple vapour. 'I stand corrected – *six*, outside broadcast vans. That's Sky News turned up.'

'Great.' Logan banged his hand on the railing, setting it ringing like a miserable bell. 'How could he just disappear?'

Steel shifted, turning so she was next to him, facing the coast. 'Longest day of the year, today.'

'Bloody feels like it.'

'Oh, no, wait, that was *yesterday*. It's Friday today?'

Logan straightened up. Risked a glance across the river at the Kilmarnock Arms Hotel, with its besieging horde of the nation's press. 'If he's lying dead in a ditch somewhere...'

A pineapple-scented sigh. 'Look, there's bugger-all we can do the now, right? Till we find Kingy, or your car, we might as well go grab a bite to eat. I'm starving, are you starving? I'm starving.' She pushed away from the railings and wandered off, in the opposite direction to the cameras. 'Starving, starving, starving.'

How could she even *think* about food right now?

What if they couldn't find King? What if Mhari had him? What if—

'HOY, LAZ: FINGER OUT, EH?'

Logan scrunched up his face. Nodded. Then followed her.

The sky deepened overhead, fading to a heady purple at the horizon. Stars twinkling away out to sea. No sign of the sun, from here – it was hidden behind the old-fashioned Scottish houses that lined the easternmost edge of Boddam – but its light still painted that side of the heavens with pale blue and gold.

'Come on, Laz, eat up.' Steel stuffed a chunk of battered haddock in her gob and worried at it. 'Had to pull strings to get you that. Chippy was meant to be shut.'

She'd parked her MX-5 next to a sandstone shed thing that had a slate roof, a Scottish Water Authority sign, and a view out over the wee bridge to a cheery red-and-white salt-shaker of a lighthouse, gilded and glowing in the setting sun.

Logan picked at a pale-yellow chip. 'Not really hungry.'

'Fish supper, pickled onions, tin of Irn-Bru, and a Mars Bar for dessert – all of which I'm claiming on expenses, by the way.' She popped a chip of her own, chewing with her mouth open. 'Besides, it's a beautiful evening. What's no' to love?'

'How about the fact that our *colleague* might be dead?'

A sigh. 'You've got to compartmentalise, Laz. If you're full-on, weight-of-the-world, bleeding-heart, troubled-cop-tastic the whole time, all you're gonna get is ulcers, depression, and an early slot at the crematorium. There's nothing we can do right now.' Another chunk of fish disappeared. 'Might as well keep your strength up.'

'Not the point.' He scowled down at his congealing fish. 'And you can't claim this on expenses – I paid for it.'

'Kingy will be *fine*. Stop wetting yourself: he's a big boy. He was in the People's Army for Scottish Liberation, wasn't he?'

'Yeah, but—'

'There you go, then. Mhari Powell's no' going to hurt one of her own, is she?'

Logan stared at Steel as she gnawed lumps out of a pickled onion. 'Mhari Powell *literally* stabbed her brother in the back.'

Steel frowned. 'Ah. There is that.' A shrug. 'Now shut up. You're putting me off my chips.'

Steel stamped on the brakes and hauled her MX-5 off the main road and into a potholed car park. It wasn't huge: only a dozen spaces, each one marked out by logs. A lone patrol car sat sideways across the far corner, blocking the track that led away across the landscape to Slains Castle.

The ruins were visible in the distance, lurking at the end of the world, where the land fell into the North Sea. Broken walls sticking up like jagged teeth. Other than that, the countryside was a lumpy plain. Fields of wheat and grass. A flock of sheep nibbling away in one littered with big round straw bales.

The sun had finally given up on the day, leaving it to the pale-blue glow of twilight as night took hold. Quarter past ten, so they'd have about an hour to search for DI Vanishing Bastard King before they'd have to break out the torches.

Steel killed the engine and scrambled out, Logan following close behind.

A uniformed officer appeared from the patrol car, pulling his peaked cap on. One of Stubby's Thugs – Greeny, wasn't it? Mid-twenties, with a hint of quarter-past-ten-o'clock shadow, his hair all floppy on top and buzz-cut at the sides. He nodded at Logan. 'Inspector.' Then led the way, down the track, towards the castle. 'A wee wifie called it in. White Audi, abandoned on a side road about midway between here and Dracula's house.'

Steel grimaced. 'That's *at least* half a mile. I'm no' walking all the way over there!'

'Nah, only about a quarter. Be there in no time.'

Logan caught up with him. 'When was this?'

'About fifteen minutes ago? Glen's gone down the castle to check it out. I stayed here to block stuff: vehicles and that, you know?'

'Can we no' drive down instead?'

'Need the patrol car for a roadblock.' Greeny pointed over his shoulder. 'Sergeant Stubbs is on her way. Think we should cordon off all the access points before she gets here?'

Logan nodded. 'Couldn't hurt.'

'Oh aye, because *that* won't tip the press off, will it? You're a pair of morons.'

'She's got a point, Guv.'

'Course I do.' Steel pulled out her e-cigarette and puffed up a cloud. 'Let's see what we've got first, eh? Might be nothing. Just cos it's an Audi, doesn't mean it's Laz's, right? Could be anyone's.'

They tromped down the track, then up a small hill.

From here, Slains Castle looked more like a ruined country house. A *massive* tumbledown one, but the big windows and thin walls didn't have that air of solid, dingy … castliness that Dunottar, Fyvie, and Crathes had.

Logan kept going… Then stopped.

A small lane snaked away off the track to the right, partially hidden by a frozen explosion of brambles. And there, abandoned a hundred yards along it, was Logan's Audi.

He scuffed his feet down the lane, staring at what was left of his poor car.

All those years wanting a nice car of his own. A proper one. A new one. One where bits of it weren't held on with duct tape and prayer. And *now* look at it.

'Noooo…'

Scratches, dents, gouges. The rear bumper buckled and hanging off. The exhaust battered and dragging on the ground.

'My car…'

More dents and a huge scrape down the driver's side.

'Bloody King!'

Logan grabbed the driver's door and hauled it open, but there was no one inside.

'I'll sodding *kill* him!' He poked the boot release and it clunked open. But when he checked, there was nothing in there either. Well, except for the pair of high-viz vests King had turned his nose up at.

Logan slammed the boot shut and leaned on it, scowling down at the damage. The chipped paint. The huge dents. 'AAAAAAAAAAAAAAAAAAAAAARGH!'

Steel stuck her hands in her pockets. 'You need a moment? Maybe have yourself a wee weep?'

He marched around to the front of the car and tested the bonnet. 'It's cold.'

'Aha!' A nod from PC Greeny. 'Been here a while, then.'

Steel hit him. 'Aye, thank you, Constable Obvious.'

The lane twisted away to the left, the brambles blocking out whatever it led to. Logan took a couple of steps in that direction, then stopped and turned to Greeny. 'Where's your mate … Greg?'

'Glen. He went up the castle.' Greeny took hold of the Airwave handset fixed to his stabproof vest, pressed the button and talked into his own shoulder. 'PC Low, safe to talk?'

A tinny voice, amplified by the handset's speaker: *'Aye, aye, Greeny.'*

'Any sign of DI King?'

'Give us a chance, min. Any idea how big Slains Castle is? Gar-sodding-gantuan, that's how big.'

Logan pointed off down the lane. 'Where does this go?'

A sniff from Steel. 'Somewhere sharny, is my bet.'

Probably.

He waved for Greeny's attention. 'Go, back your mate up. But if you find something, you don't take any risks, OK? Mhari Powell's armed and *extremely* dangerous.'

The constable nodded, then loped off, down the road towards the castle, talking into his shoulder again. 'Hold fire, Greg, I'm coming to give you a hand...'

Right. Let's try this way then.

Logan followed the lane, between the towering waves of spiny brambles.

There was a big pantomime sigh, then Steel shuffled after him. 'I could be home eating pickled onion Monster Munch and drinking ice-cold Chardonnay...'

'Well, you're not. Now earn your fish supper and call Control. I want a dog unit, firearms team, and anything else they can give us, ASAFP.'

She rolled her eyes at him, then dug out her phone. 'Aye, Shuggie? ... Steel. ... Listen up, I'm after Dogs, Thugs, Guns, and anything else you can get me. Top priority.'

They kept going, past the remains of an agricultural building that had succumbed to time and gravity.

'Well I don't know, do I? ... Get your finger out and do it, you wee turd! ... *Thank* you.' She hung up. 'Shuggie's on it.'

'He give you an ETA?'

'If they floor it out here with lights and music? Half an hour? Maybe forty minutes?'

'Great. That's ... marvellous.' The sky was darkening, the shadows on either side of the lane growing deeper and bluer with every minute that passed.

'So, you want to wait for them in the car?'

'Yes.' Logan pulled in a deep breath and sighed it out. 'But if King's in trouble—'

'Aye, which he *better* be, after all this.'

'If he's in trouble, half an hour could be too late. Could be bleeding to death right now, like Haiden did.'

The lane curled around a stand of trees, the canopy thick and dark above their heads.

'Yeah, that's what I thought too.' Steel pulled the corners of her mouth out and down, like an angry toad. 'But see if he's *no* dying when we find him? Bags I get first go kicking him in the nadgers till they pop out his lugs.'

'After what he did to my Audi? Join the queue.'

They emerged from the trees and stopped. A rundown house lurked straight ahead: two storeys of crumbling dirt-streaked granite in the process of being digested by ivy and brambles. House martins wheeled and curled out from the eaves, chasing the evening's bugs in simulated dogfights. Elegant feathered arrows, out hunting in the dusk. No cars. No sign of life.

The house's dead windows stared out at them from its grey and green face.

Steel grabbed Logan's arm and pulled him to a stop. '*Promise* me you'll no get stabbed this time.'

'Promise.' He pulled out a pair of blue nitrile gloves and snapped them on, dropping his voice to a whisper as they started towards the house again. 'Just checking: you've got your pepper spray on you?'

'Course I have. And no: you can't.' She snapped on gloves of her own. 'Should've come prepared, shouldn't you?'

'Fine.'

He picked up a fallen branch from the edge of the trees. About the size of a baseball-bat, only less elegant and more lumpy. Heavy enough to cave someone's head in.

Hopefully...

42

Logan hunched over and scurried across the rutted lumpy grass, battering-branch clutched in both gloved hands.

Steel hurried along beside him, keeping her voice down. 'You want front or back?'

Probably both as bad as the other, but at least *this* side was closer. 'Front.'

'King better appreciate this...' She crouch-jogged away, around the side of the house and out of sight.

OK.

He slunk up the steps to the front door. Had to be half a dozen Yale locks there, the brass fronts all new and shiny... But the door wasn't even shut – it hung open an inch, letting out the grimy scent of mildew and rotting wood.

He nudged the door with his stick. It swung open, creaking and moaning on ancient hinges.

The scent of decay got thicker as he stepped over the threshold.

Dark in here. Shockingly enough, what with it being after sunset.

Should've brought a torch, you idiot.

Yeah, well it was too late for that. He'd have to improvise.

Logan dug his phone out and opened the torch app. Swept its pale grey glow around the grubby hallway. Not great, but it would have to do.

He crept forward.

A floorboard creaked under his feet.

God, it was manky in here: the whole place filthy and crumbling. Holes in the floorboards, the foul black Tic-Tac shapes of rat droppings scattered along the skirting. Drifts of leaves had blown in through the broken windows, gathering in the corners like trolls. What was left of the wallpaper peeled off in sagging curls. Dry and brittle after the hottest June on record.

He peered through a hole in the wall to what must have been the kitchen – collapsing units and curling linoleum. No King.

OK, try the open doorway on the right.

It led into a bedroom. Childish drawings scrawled their way across the walls in ancient crayon, a sagging metal-framed double bed rusting against the wall, its mattress little more than decaying skin and spring bones. No King.

Logan turned back towards the hall and a thundering clatter erupted in his face. Forcing him backwards. Stumbling. Battering down against the ancient floorboards, hands raised in self-defence, heart thudding like a blowout on the motorway, phone skittering away.

The house martin squeaked, wings crackling as it did a circuit of the gloomy room, then swooped out through the broken window.

Oh God...

He shuddered, forcing his breathing to slow down. 'Bloody hell.'

It was only a bird. Not Mhari Powell with her dirty big knife. Still alive.

He pushed himself up to his knees. Then his feet. Pulse pounding at the base of his throat as he bent to pick up his phone. Cracks spidered out from one corner, reaching across the screen. 'Wonderful.' Because the car getting ruined wasn't bad enough. Things *had* to get worse.

He crept into the hall again. Opened the door to the kitchen, just in case. Still no King.

A filthy bathroom at the far end.

Stairs – the treads rotten and blistered as they reached up

into the darkness. Sod that. Besides, there was no way King had climbed them. Anything heavier than a small terrier would probably go straight through the wood and crash down into the basement. Plus: no footprints in the dust.

Which left the door at the end of the hall. Only this one was closed.

Logan stuffed his cracked phone in his pocket, raised his battering-branch, and reached for the handle. Took another deep breath.

In three, two, one...

He threw the door open and charged inside.

A cloud of bluebottles growled into the air as he staggered to a halt in the middle of what must have been the living room. Maybe 'living' was the wrong word for it. A collection of five chest freezers lurked in the dark, little green lights down by the base of the units showing that they were on, accompanied by a low gurgling *hummmmmmmmm*.

Logan dug out his phone again and played its wheezy glow across the chest freezers. They all had one of Mhari's horrible messages spray-painted on them. The only one *not* switched on was 'WALLACE'.

The room's windows looked out over the cliffs to the North Sea, everything reduced to shadows and silhouettes as the night grew. The air warm, and ... sickly, smelling of hot metal and rancid meat.

No King.

One by one, the flies settled onto the blood-smeared lid of the freezer marked 'JUDAS'. It wasn't the only freezer with stains on it, but the blood on 'THREE MONKEYS', 'THE DEVIL MAKES WORK', and 'SPITE' had dried to dark muddy brown. 'JUDAS' shone a fresh bright red.

Logan stepped towards it and his foot skidded forward.

Aaaaaaa...

He braced himself, arms out, swinging them to keep upright.

Lurched to a stop. Then stared down at whatever it was he'd stood in. It glittered in a wide puddle that stretched from here to the base of 'JUDAS'. Yeah, that was definitely blood.

'Jesus.'

Every fridge freezer except for 'WALLACE' was padlocked, but for some reason 'THE DEVIL MAKES WORK' and 'SPITE' had chains wrapped around them too – an extra brass padlock securing each in place. As if there was something in them that Mhari *really* didn't want getting out.

Logan inched his way closer.

Closer.

Bluebottles staggered through the fetid air, buzzing around his head, glittering in the phone's glow.

Closer.

He licked his lips.

Closer.

Reached for the chain and—

A pale face appeared in the broken window behind the freezer, ghostly and horrible and it screamed at him and he screamed back and they both flinched away. Then Steel clicked on a wee torch and shone it through the window. 'You trying to give us a heart attack?'

'Don't *do* that!'

'Nearly crapped myself, there...' She puffed out a breath and lowered her torch. 'Kingy's no' out here.'

Logan looked around the room again: the chest freezers with their spray-painted words. 'Think I might have found Professor Wilson, Councillor Lansdale, and Scott Meyrick.' He leaned on 'THE DEVIL MAKES WORK' and frowned at her through the window. 'We're going to need a whole heap of SE techs to—'

A something thumped into the lid beneath his hands and he flinched away.

Steel let out another wee shriek. Then, 'What?'

Holy buggering hell. Logan backed away from the chest freezer; there was someone *in* there. Someone—

His left foot hit something and he staggered again, nearly crashing down into the puddle of blood. Whatever he'd stepped on, it clanged and rattled against the floorboards.

Another thump from 'THE DEVIL MAKES WORK'. Then

another. And another – the whole thing rocking and shaking. Muffled screams coming from inside.

Logan grabbed the padlock holding the lid shut and twisted. Yanked at it. But it was solid. Break it. Break it off. He raised the battering-branch, swinging it overhead and down on the padlock, setting it rattling. 'CAN YOU HEAR ME? THIS IS THE POLICE!'

The thumping got louder. So did the screaming.

Logan hammered at the lock again. Twice. Three times... The branch snapped in his hand, its top half spiralling away to thunk against something in the darkness.

Sodding...

He swept the phone's half-arsed glow across the floor.

There – the thing he almost fell over – the wheel brace from his Audi.

Logan grabbed it and smashed it down onto the padlock. Didn't do anything to the padlock, but the bit of fridge freezer it was attached to snapped clean off.

The lid banged up as far as the chain would allow and a sliver of cold-white blared into the room as the internal light came on. A pair of eyes stared through the gap, breath seeping out in a cloud of pale grey. 'HELP ME! PLEASE! HELP ME!'

Professor Wilson – it had to be. No mistaking that plummy voice, even under all the panic.

Wilson shoved the lid up again and again, rattling the chains, making the internal light pulse off and on. Causing the room to strobe. *'HELP ME!'*

The living room door banged open again and Steel marched in. 'What the bloody—'

Logan pointed the wheel brace at her. 'Switch them off! Switch them all off.'

'GET ME OUT OF HERE!'

He stared at the chain, then at the next chest freezer in line: 'SPITE'. It was padlocked too.

Steel dropped to her knees, torch clasped between her teeth as she fumbled about behind 'THE DEVIL MAKES WORK'.

Logan marched over to 'SPITE', tightened his grip on the wheel brace.

'*NO! DON'T LEAVE ME!*' Wilson's voice cracked on the last word. '*Get me out!*'

He battered the lock twice, denting and deforming it. But the third go snapped the padlock off. Logan yanked the lid up as far as the chain would let him and the internal light bloomed its hard white glow. Difficult to see what was inside, because of the angle, but the interior was smeared with more dried blood. 'Hello?'

Professor Wilson broke into sobs. Getting quieter and quieter, as if he'd used up the last of whatever he had left. '*Please! Please ... get me ... get me out ... of here.*'

Was that groaning coming from inside 'SPITE'? Difficult to tell with Wilson making all that racket, but it definitely sounded like groaning.

Logan grabbed the fallen padlock and wedged it into the gap – propping the chest freezer's lid open.

Then turned to 'JUDAS'.

No chain on this one, just the padlock. He battered it off and threw the lid open.

The internal light burst out into the gloom. Logan shielded his eyes, peering inside. Swore.

Detective Inspector King lay naked in the bottom of the chest freezer, curled up on his side, *covered* in blood.

Oh God...

She'd killed him.

Mhari Powell had killed Detective Inspector Frank King. Dozens and dozens of flat round nailheads glittered in the light, each one sticking out of King's flesh on a short metal stalk. And they were everywhere: hammered into his arms, legs, chest, head. One poking out of his closed left eye.

'*Get me out, get me out, get me out.*'

A faint curl of white fog oozed out from King's bloody lips. He was breathing.

He was *alive*.

Logan turned to Steel. 'He's still alive!'

'*Please, please, please, please, please...*'

Steel must have finally found the plug, because the light

inside 'THE DEVIL MAKES WORK' died, leaving its occupant in darkness.

'You have to let me out!'

She picked her way past the pool of blood on the floor and peered into 'JUDAS'. Blinked. Shook her head. 'Holy mother of...'

'Please!'

Logan looked across the room to 'THE DEVIL MAKES WORK', down at the wheel brace in his hands, then marched over there and rammed the metal rod between the chain and the freezer, turning it like a ship's wheel, tightening the chain. It pulled the lid shut, sealing in Professor Wilson's sobs.

Come on...

He leaned into it, pushing, twisting, teeth gritting, the muscles in his arms screaming at him, the scar tissue across his stomach joining in. Getting louder. Another heave, putting all his weight into it. Still nothing.

He glanced at Steel. 'Little ... help?'

She grabbed one end and he took the other, the pair of them straining and straining and straining until between them they'd managed to bend the wheel brace.

'Buggering flaps of sharny shite!' Steel staggered off a couple of paces, panting.

More thumping from inside the chest freezer as Professor Wilson started screaming again – but the lid remained securely closed, held there by the tightened chain.

She wiped a hand across her forehead and pointed at 'THREE MONKEYS'. 'We not going to open that one?'

Three Monkeys: that had to be Councillor Lansdale. Missing for the longest. And Mhari hadn't bothered to put a chain on his chest freezer. Yeah, no prizes for guessing what they'd find in there.

Logan huffed out a breath. 'Suppose we'd better.'

He unwound the wheel brace from the chain around 'THE DEVIL MAKES WORK'.

Professor Wilson must've found a last reserve of panicked energy, because the lid bounced up again. 'GET ME OUT OF

HERE! I DEMAND YOU GET ME OUT OF HERE!' Screaming and crying. 'PLEASE!'

Steel grimaced at Logan. 'He never shuts up, does he?'

Logan raised the bent wheel brace and hammered the padlock off the last chest freezer. Raised the lid. Cold white light spilled out of 'THREE MONKEYS'.

She stepped up beside him and stared down at the twisted, bloody shape at the bottom of the chest freezer. Lansdale: skin a pale candle-wax yellow, where it wasn't bright red, all of it covered in a thin sheen of jagged frost, partially wrapped in the remains of a shower curtain.

Logan closed the lid.

43

The world exploded with light and noise as the Air Ambulance howled from the field behind the building. Its search beams swept across Renfield House as it turned, then they were gone, fading with the bellowing roar of the helicopter's engines.

Logan watched it disappear.

Then shook his head and started back towards the front door.

The SE Transit was parked right outside, a line of white-suited figures making their way in and out of the building. Carrying things in blue plastic evidence crates. A diesel generator grumbled in the background, work lights blazing away behind the house's broken windows.

PC Greeny's patrol car was parked there too, its blue-and-whites casting flickering shadows in the brambles and ivy.

Steel scuffed her way through the front door and down the steps. Stuck her e-cigarette in her gob and her hands in her pockets as she lumped across the grass to Logan. Vaping up a storm. 'Any news?'

'They're not hopeful.'

'Aye...' She nodded. Looked away. 'And before you say anything: don't. You never think it's going to happen, do you? Not to people you know.'

'Not even if those people are "dicks"?'

'Oh, you can *hope* it happens, but see when it does?' A

shudder rippled its way through her. Then she jerked her head towards the house. 'Still, could be worse, I suppose.'

A uniformed officer led a shuffling figure down the steps and over to the patrol car. Scott Meyrick, wrapped in a crinkly golden space blanket. Crying, head down, one hand covering his face as he was helped inside.

Steel puffed out a thick bank of strawberry fog. 'Meyrick's in shock, but he'll keep till the regular ambulance gets here, long as Greeny remembers to crank up the car's heater.' She cleared her throat. 'Shirley says Lansdale's frozen to the bottom of the chest freezer. All that blood. They'll have to cart the whole thing off to Aberdeen, if they can get a spare van with enough room.'

'Meyrick say anything?'

'Pfff... They attacked him in his house, battered him over the head. Next thing he knows, he's waking up in a chest freezer – it's chained shut, but they've left him enough slack to let air in. Then, about two, three hours ago he hears screaming. After that, Mhari padlocks the freezers and turns them on. Leaves him to die.'

'Jesus.'

'Yup.' She pointed in a vague southward direction, where the helicopter had gone. 'What about Wilson?'

'Tough as old boots. He'll live.' Logan scrubbed a hand across his face. 'You know who Hardie and the rest are going to blame, don't you?'

'Hardie? He's one of them dicks we were talking about.' She pulled the e-cigarette from her mouth and spat into the long grass. 'You thinking what I'm thinking?'

Probably.

'The fifth chest freezer, the empty one – "Wallace"?'

'Aye: Mhari Powell's no' finished yet.'

A low throbbing hum infused Aberdeen Royal Infirmary's High-Dependency Unit. The lights were dimmed, blanketing the ward in a sticky warm gloom that marked the boundary between the living and the not dead yet. The clinging on and fighting.

Hopefully.

Logan leaned against the corridor wall, looking in through the window to one of the darkened rooms.

They'd given King the hospital bed nearest the wall, not that he knew it. He lay there, still as a corpse, as a team of three nurses hooked him up to machines and bags. Wires and pipes and tubes everywhere. Most of the nails had been removed – replaced by blood-spotted gauze patches and the occasional section of fibreglass cast – but the ones in his head still glittered in the bedside light. Whatever antiseptic they'd swabbed him down with had left mottled orange-brown blotches on his pale skin, like a botched fake tan.

Logan checked his watch: five past three.

Four hours in surgery didn't seem a lot, considering. Yet there King was. Still breathing.

'Inspector McRae?'

Logan turned.

A woman stood in the middle of the corridor, in blood-smeared scrubs and hospital clogs, hairnet on her head, bags beneath her drooping eyes. Facemask dangling under her chin. A name badge with 'MR KATE HILLS' on it. 'I've seen some things in my time, but this?' She shook her head. 'He's lost a *lot* of blood. We're pushing fluids. Will it make a difference?' A shrug.

'Is he going to…?'

She took off her hairnet and sagged even further. 'The irony is, if it wasn't for the chest freezer he'd probably be dead already. Yes, you've got an air-tight seal, but the cold lowers your metabolic rate so you don't consume so much oxygen, and you don't bleed out so fast. Which means more time for clotting to occur. But still.' She reached into her pocket and pulled out a plastic box – about the size of a takeaway container. When she held it up to the light, the galvanised clout nails inside glimmered a dull red. 'Seventy-five millimetres long, that's about three inches in old money. You can cause a lot of internal damage with thirty of them.' She handed it to him. 'You'll need to sign for that.'

'Thanks.'

'I don't even want to *touch* the ones in his skull till he's stronger. Assuming he survives the night.'

Logan raised his eyebrows at her and she shrugged again.

'Thirty / seventy. At best.'

The same chance they had of finding Mhari and Haiden at Ceanntràigh Cottage.

She gave Logan a pained smile. 'To be honest, he's lucky he made it this far.'

Scott Meyrick's hospital room wasn't as cluttered as King's – no cortege of nurses fussing around, no bank of machinery to bleep and ping and flash warning lights. He was on his own, sitting up in his bed, with an IV in his arm. Eyes screwed shut, tears spilling down his cheeks, shoulders heaving as he sobbed.

A large gauze pad sat in the middle of his face, held there by a cordon of surgical tape. Red and yellow dots stained the pad's centre, where his nose should have been.

Poor sod.

Logan settled on the edge of the bed. 'How are you?'

Meyrick turned his face away, one hand coming up to hide the padding. His voice was strange – hollow, flat and thin. Jagged with crying. 'They … turned … me into … a *monster*. … I'm a monster!'

Logan put a hand on his leg through the covers. 'The reconstructive surgeons are very good here. Some of the best in the country.'

'I was going … to be on … *Strictly*.'

'Did they say anything to you, Scott? When they grabbed you, or when you were in the … in the freezer? Anything at all?'

He dropped his hand and stared at Logan. 'Look at me.'

'Doesn't matter how small a thing it was, anything you can tell us might help us catch her.'

'LOOK AT ME!' He grabbed at the gauze pad and ripped it down, exposing two narrow slits. Raw and bloody. All that was left of his nose. Mhari had carved it away, right down to the bone. 'Look at me…'

Logan picked the gauze pad up from the scratchy NHS sheets and placed it over those two bloody slits again, smoothing the sticking strips down. Doing his best to sound as if he knew what he was talking about: 'It'll be OK. I know this all seems horrific and overwhelming, and that's because it is. It *will* get better, though. You have to give it time.'

'I was ... I was ... going to be ... someone!'

Oh God.

He wrapped his arms around Scott Meyrick and held him as he sobbed.

What was it about the paintings lining the hospital corridors? You'd think, after all this time, they'd have lost their ability to dredge up the past, but every time he saw them it was the same. The boredom of limping up and down for months. The vague nausea that accompanied every gelatinous overcooked glob of beige cauliflower cheese. The tugging, nagging pain of stitches. And yet another vow *never* to get stabbed again.

He turned the corner into the Monitoring Ward – the paintings swapped for corkboards covered in memos, notices, and the odd thank you card.

A uniformed PC sat on a plastic chair, parked outside one of the private rooms. Small and dark-haired, the sleeves of her Police Scotland T-shirt stretched tight by huge biceps. She looked up from her celebrity gossip magazine as Logan approached, and smiled. 'Guv, I heard you were back. How's the stomach?'

'Slightly less stabby.' He pointed at the observation window behind her. 'What about our friend, Professor Wilson?'

She grimaced. 'DS Steel's in with him now.' Then lowered her magazine. 'If I'd known I was going to be stuck here all shift I'd have brought a book.'

'Has he said anything?'

'Oh he's said *lots* of things, mostly about how incompetent Police Scotland are and how he's going to sue us for not rescuing him earlier.'

Of course he was. Because no one said thank you any more,

did they? No, it was all lawsuits this and formal complaints that.

Logan looked in through the window – all the lights were on in the room, showing Steel, sitting in one of the visitors' chairs with her feet up on the bed. Professor Wilson was slumped against the pillows, the stumps of his wrists covered in fresh bandages. Two IV lines hooked up to one arm.

Odd.

'I thought there would be more ... shouting.'

The constable nodded. 'Oh, there was to start with, but she's calmed him down somehow.'

'Probably doubled the morphine going into his drip.' The smile faded on Logan's face. 'You don't think she'd *do* that, would she?'

'With Steel, who can tell?'

He knocked on the glass and the Wrinkly Horror looked up. Nodded at him.

Two minutes later, the door opened and Steel slouched out, cracking a huge yawn. Then a shudder. And a sigh. 'Pffff...'

Logan stepped in front of her. 'Have you fiddled with Professor Wilson's morphine?'

'Course no'.' Scuffing past. 'But you'll be happy to know he's no' threatening to sue us any more.'

Really?

She wandered off down the corridor.

He turned and looked through the window again. Professor Wilson sat there, with his stumps in his lap, face pinched, shoulders trembling as he cried. OK...

Logan hurried after her. 'How did you manage that?'

'You really don't want to know. How's Kingy?'

'Not good.'

Another yawn. 'Told you this whole thing was an utter disaster.'

The car park opposite the hospital's main entrance was lit up like a very ugly Christmas present that had been wrapped by an undertaker.

According to Logan's watch it wasn't even twenty to four

yet, but faint blue was already creeping into the dark violet sky. Marking the coming dawn.

A wee auld mannie sat hunched in his wheelchair, beneath the portico lights, sooking away on a roll-up, holding the smoke down as if it was more vital to his health than the oxygen tank he was hooked up to.

Steel stepped out into the night air, pulled out her e-cigarette and vaped up a cumulonimbus of watermelon steam. 'You can't blame yourself, you know that, don't you?'

Logan leaned against one of the bollards. 'Yes. But I still do.'

A sigh. 'Yeah, me too.' She had a good industrial-strength sniff. 'Who do you think this "Wallace" is?'

'Been wondering that myself.' As if they didn't have enough imponderables on this sodding case. 'I'll get Nightshift to go through the HOLMES data, see if anyone called Wallace has cropped up anywhere.'

'Mind you, there wasn't an actual "Judas", was there? Maybe...' She stopped, turned, and stared at the little old man. 'What the hell you think you're looking at, Grandad?'

The grey wrinkly chin came up. 'Havin' a fag.'

'Aye, well sod off and do it somewhere else, this is police business.'

He scowled at her. 'That's no'—'

'Go on, hop it. Before I do you for loitering with intent.'

He stubbed his cigarette out and grumbled away on his wheelchair. Muttering about fascists and living in a police state.

Logan raised an eyebrow. 'Was that really necessary?'

'He's on an oxygen tank. Silly sod shouldn't be smoking anyway.' Steel took an extra hard drag on her e-cigarette as if to emphasise the point. Then blew it all out at Logan. 'As I was saying, before I was so *rudely* interrupted, maybe "Wallace" represents an idea instead?'

Maybe.

'Like "Three Monkeys"?'

'Aye: ears, eyes, tongue; "Devil Makes Work" is hands; "Spite" is nose; "Judas" is thirty pieces of silver. Well, thirty galvanised seventy-five-mill clout nails, but it's the thought that counts.'

'So what the hell is "Wallace"?'

She frowned out at the pre-dawn light for a bit, puffing away at her personal storm cloud. Then shook her head. 'Buggered if I know.' Another huge yawn shuddered through her. 'Lovely Roberta needs her bed. And maybe a nightcap.' She jiggled one leg. 'And I wouldn't mind a wee, either.'

So much for that.

Logan patted her on the shoulder. 'Go home, I'll see you in the morning.'

'What about you? You look like something Mr Rumpole sicked up.'

Felt like it too.

'Nah, I want to check in with the team first.' He pointed away towards the car park. 'Go on, away with you. I'll get someone to run me back to HQ.'

'Fair enoughski.' She sauntered across the road, leaving a steam-train cloud of vapour in her wake.

Logan waited till she'd climbed the stairs and disappeared inside, then sighed. Turned around and went in search of a lift.

Their MIT office … well, *Logan's* MIT office now – at least until the top brass came in at seven and assigned someone to replace DI King – was virtually empty. A couple of saggy-faced support staff hammered away at the HOLMES suite, adding in details from Ceanntràigh Cottage and Renfield House to the database.

The rest of Divisional Headquarters was like a mausoleum, though, not even the distant dubstep *whub-whub-whub* of a floor polisher to break the sepulchral silence.

Logan perched on the edge of a vacated desk and frowned up at the whiteboard nearest the door. The one he'd printed the word 'WALLACE?' on in big green letters.

Who, or *what* was 'Wallace'?

One of the support staff got up from behind her desk, stretched, and slouched over to the laser printer as it *burrrred* and chugged. Picked a sheet of paper from the output tray. Handed it to Logan.

She didn't do a very good job of stifling her yawn. 'There's no one called Wallace come up in the investigation – searched for first *and* last names, aliases, and addresses. Did every variant spelling and potential typo I could think of too. Sorry.'

Bugger it.

Logan nodded. 'Thanks.'

She shrugged and went back to her computer, leaving him with the piece of paper that said exactly what she'd just told him, only in fewer words: 'No Match For "Wallace" In System.'

He dumped it in the wastepaper basket and frowned up at the whiteboard again.

Wallace.

It wasn't a random word, it couldn't be. It *meant* something to Mhari Powell.

But what?

Maybe she meant *William* Wallace?

But he was a national Scottish hero. Three Monkeys, The Devil Makes Work, Spite, Judas – they were all pejoratives. Betrayals and punishments. No way she'd lump William Wallace in with that lot.

So 'Wallace' had to mean something else.

Wallace. Wallace. Wallace...

'Who *are* you?'

44

The Transit van rattles and pings as Mhari pulls into the car park and switches off the headlights. This time of night, the only other vehicles belong to the overnight staff – going by the manky Citroën Picasso and the tricked-out Renault Clio, that would be Stupid Steven and Grandma Mags – abandoned near the main doors for a quick getaway when their shifts end.

Mhari takes the ancient Transit and parks it in the corner nearest the residents' wing. Where Grandma Mags won't be able to see it from reception.

She pulls on her black leather gloves and slips out into the warm night. Dressing like a ninja probably isn't necessary, but it's traditional, isn't it?

Not as if Mags pays any attention though. Could drive a herd of buffalo through here and she wouldn't notice.

Look at her, sitting behind the desk with her head buried in a breeze-block sized Stephen King, all lit up by the reception lights, because she doesn't see why *she* should have to sit there in the dark. Not that it's all that dark. Four in the morning, but the sky's already slipping from navy to eggshell blue. Be sunup soon.

Better get a shift on.

Mhari jogs along the side of the building, past the dark windows of the residents' lounge and around the corner. Pauses at the staff break room. The window's open a crack, letting a faux-Scottish accent ooze out. One with more than a hint of the down-under about it. Banging on about freedom and battering the English army.

She peers in through the window and there's Stupid Steve – big and burly, with a spade-shaped forehead, slouched in an armchair in front of the telly, one hand tucked into the waist-band of his trousers, mouth moving silently as he recites the words in time with the film. Hollywood karaoke, for the permanent wanker.

Mhari keeps going, around the rear of the building, till she finds the fire exit she wants. The one that's just down the corridor from where she needs to be. The one that's never alarmed.

She jimmies it open with a wee wrecking bar in about thirty seconds and slips inside.

Course the other benefit to using *this* particular fire exit is that the nearest security camera faces the other way. And it's not like they splurged on a fancy one that moves, either.

A wheelchair sits in a small recess opposite, blocking the door marked 'Linen Closet'. She wheels it down the corridor to her dad's room: 'saor alba' even thought it *should* be 'alba shaor'. Still, that's men for you.

She lets herself in.

The reading light is on above the bed, bathing its occupant in warm golden light.

He's asleep, flat on his back, with an oxygen mask on his face. Much paler than last time. Skin like paper stretched over a thin bone frame, tinged blue and purple and yellow. As if his whole body's one big bruise, fading out of life. Even his tartan pyjamas look ready to die.

Mhari reaches out and takes hold of his foot. Gives it a soft shoogle. Keeping her voice down. 'Dad? You ready to go?'

'Mnnnghnn...' He shifts a bit, then settles into the pillows again.

She gives him another shoogle. 'It's time, Dad.'

He blinks, fumbles his way to consciousness. Face pinched, looking around like he's never seen the room before. 'Gnnn...? I'm... What?'

Poor old soul.

'I understand, Dad. Come on, we'll get you sorted.'

She pulls the horrible blue blankets off of him and piles them up on one of the visitors' chairs, positions the wheelchair by the bed, sticks the brakes on, then scoops her arms around his chest – under his arms. Up close he smells sour and sickly sweet, all at the same time.

In his heyday, "Gaelic Gary" Lochhead was a huge man, powerful, terrifying. But there's so little of him left, it's like he's made of balsa wood. She lifts him into the wheelchair and covers him up with the blankets again. Clips the oxygen tank onto the support struts. Does the same with the morphine drip.

'Haiden? Haiden, are we going home?'

'No, Dad.' She kisses him on his papery forehead. 'We're going somewhere much, much better, remember?'

He nods, eyelids drooping as she makes him comfortable. And soon his breathing is shallow, but regular. She wheels him out through the door.

Down the corridor.

Turn at the emergency exit and...

Damn it.

Stupid Steve is right outside the door, standing there, facing away from the building, smoking a joint and fiddling with his phone. Paying no attention to anything but himself.

Mhari sets the brakes on Dad's wheelchair again and slips her hunting knife from its sheath. Sharp and glittering. Then creeps across to the other side of the emergency exit and flattens herself against the wall.

Waiting.

Waiting.

Stupid Steve finishes his joint, pinching out the tiny roach and sticking it in a wee metal tin – the kind you get breath mints in. He puts his phone away, spits out into the dawn, turns and steps inside again.

Stops dead and frowns down at the wheelchair and its occupant. 'How did *you* get out here?' A sigh. A shake of the head.

'Bloody crips. Crips and old farts, far as the eye can see. Pfff... Come on then, you old git, let's get you—'

She steps up behind him and puts the knife to his throat. Twists it a little, so he knows what it is.

Gets a wee squeak in return.

Probably working his way up to wetting himself.

Mhari leans in close to Stupid Steve's ear. 'That "old git" is more of a man than you'll ever be, Steven. He's a *hero*. What are you again?'

'M... Mary?' His voice trembles. 'Have you lost your—'

She gives the knife another twist and he lets out a tiny strangled scream. There's the sound of water hitting the lino and the scent of warm fresh piss.

'There are civilian casualties in every war. Do you want to be one of them?'

'No!'

'Then turn around. *Slowly.*'

Stupid Steve puts his hands up. 'Please don't kill me! Please don't—'

'Turn around, or I *will* kill you.'

And he does: cheeks wet with tears, blood trickling down his neck and into the collar of his nurse's whites, bottom lip trembling. Aw, shame. Poor wee thing.

She smashes the hilt of her knife into his forehead, hard. His knees wobble, eyes rolling back, then he collapses like a bag of wet laundry into the puddle of his own making. Should rub his nose in it. But instead she hooks her hands under his armpits and drags him over to the door marked 'Linen Closet'. Unlocks it with the keys hanging from his belt. Bundles him inside.

Hmm...

Stupid Steve's a bit too big to fit in the narrow space – what with all the shelves full of towels and bedding and the like. Never mind, she can make it work. Mhari shoves and kicks until everything but one arm is stuffed in there. Bad luck, Steve: she stomps on it till the bones snap and his arm bends enough to get the door shut.

Mhari turns the key, then breaks it off in the lock.

Well, wasn't as if he didn't *deserve* it.

'Come on, Dad.' She clicks off the wheelchair's brake and pushes him out through the emergency exit and into the dawn.

Only been a few minutes, but it's already brighter out here. Birds warming up for the dawn chorus. Some lights flickering on in the airport way beyond the chain-link fence.

'It's OK, Dad. The plan's changed, but everything's going to be fine.' She wheels him down the side of the building, towards her ancient Transit van, a smile pulling her face wide. 'Trust me.'

45

The canteen vending machines buzzed and gurgled in the gloom. Yes, *officially* the sun had risen, but it hadn't climbed high enough to clear the grey granite walls of King Street yet, so gloom it was. Especially as Logan hadn't bothered to switch on the lights.

After all, when you were trying to force down a plastic cup of 'Instant Brown Horrible' from the machine, not being able to see it was probably a bonus. How did they manage to get coffee to taste like that? As if someone had set fire to a used nappy and then boiled the blackened remains for three and a half—

The overhead lights *bing*-ed and flickered, warming up to a soulless white glow.

Tufty let the door swing shut behind him as he squeaked across the canteen. Yawning. Bags under his eyes. But dressed in his full Police Scotland black. He gave Logan a wee wave: 'Sarge.'

'What are you doing in at ...' Logan checked his watch. 'half four in the morning?'

Tufty grimaced and plonked himself down on the chair opposite. 'I've got alerts set up so if someone posts certain "somethings" it pops up on my phone.' He dug his mobile out, poked at the screen, and slid the thing across the tabletop. 'Woke up to this.'

Pale pink filled the screen, then a galvanised nail appeared

– long and dark, with a round flat head, clutched between a couple of fingers. A hammer slid in from the other side.

Logan flinched away from Tufty's phone. 'Please tell me that isn't...'

The point of the nail rested against the pink and the hammer battered down on the head, driving straight in. Blood welled up around the nail shaft as the hammer swung in again and screaming bellowed out from the speakers. The footage shaky, going in and out of focus as the hammer battered into shot again and again and again.

The instant coffee turned to battery acid in Logan's stomach.

'Jesus...' He pushed the phone away. 'Get it taken down. Get it taken down, now!'

Tufty paused the video. 'I'm trying. But soon as it went up it got spread across the Alt-Nat message boards like Marmite.' A long deep sigh. 'Not sure if it's bots, or people in the US, or *what* spreading it, but you'd think all our home-grown nutters would be asleep right now.' He curled his top lip and turned the phone screen-side down on the tabletop. 'Some people are sick.'

Logan groaned.

They were screwed. Completely and utterly screwed.

'It'll be all over the morning news, won't it?'

Just when things *couldn't* get any worse: they did.

'Sorry, Sarge. Don't know if this means we missed the Scotty Meyrick video, or if Mhari didn't bother posting it, because this one was better.'

He thunked his head on the table, making his plastic coffee jiggle. 'Steel was right: I should've gone home to bed!'

'Yeah... Erm, Sarge? I bumped into Bouncer on my way in. From Scene Examination? Wanted me to give you this.' Tufty held out an Audi key fob. 'Said they've finished doing the swabbing and taping and photographing and you can have your car back now.'

Logan closed his eyes and groaned again.

'They've parked what's left of it in the Rear Podium car park.' A pause. 'He says sorry about all the fingerprint powder, but they didn't have time to clear it up, what with everything going on out at Renfield House.'

Even better.

Logan sagged in his seat. 'I *hate* this job.'

Tufty tried for a smile. 'Anyway...' He picked up his phone and poked at the screen again. 'I'm still not having any joy finding out who the fake Mhari Powell really is. Her social media profile twists like an eel in a tumble dryer, and it's got all these *weird* layers to it too. Loads of different aliases and usernames, but they're all definitely her.' More poking. 'Some of her accounts are screamingly Alt-Nat, some of them are rabid Alt-Brit-Nat. Sometimes she starts flame wars with herself, then goes quiet and lurks as everyone else piles in. Poking the bear every now and then.' Tufty frowned as he scrolled. 'It's weird.'

'You've got nothing at all?'

'Only that she's been using "Mhari Powell" as an alias for about two years.' He scooted forward in his seat. 'But you'll like this: I does has a hypothesis! The *real* Mhari Powell works in a psychiatric facility, so maybe that's where the *fake* Mhari Powell met her? Maybe we should try sending the fake Mhari's photo to the real Mhari and see if she rings any alarm bells?'

What?

Logan tried to keep his voice level. 'Are you telling me no one's actually done that yet?'

'Nope.'

Oh for God's sake, he was working with MORONS.

He covered his face with his hands and strangled a small scream.

How could King not get that organised? How could he be so sodding...

Lying, unconscious, in a hospital bed, with nails sticking out of his head.

Gah...

Logan stared up at the ceiling tiles.

Steel was right: the whole thing was a complete and utter *cocking* disaster.

'Erm, Sarge? Does that mean you want me to try?'

403

He forced the word out between gritted teeth. 'Please.'

'Okeydoke.' More fiddling with his phone. 'Done. Emailed it off to that bloke at Northumbria Police with the warty nose.'

Though, knowing their luck, it would be a complete dead end. As per.

Logan sagged even further. 'What does "Wallace" mean to you?'

'And Gromit?' A pause – and swear to God, you could actually see the hamster wheel inside Tufty's head spinning until he finally got it. 'Oh, from the *chest freezer*. Right. Yeah. Probably not "and Gromit" then. So...' He wrapped one arm around himself, the other hand tapping at his forehead. Then his eyes widened. 'Ooh, ooh, I know: *William* Wallace!'

Well, asking Tufty had always been a long shot. It wasn't as if he was renowned for his Sherlock-Holmes-style steel-trap intellect, was it? He wasn't *completely* thick – the boy was great on sci-fi trivia, so if *Star Trek*, *Buffy the Vampire Slayer*, or *Battlestar Galactica* came up at a pub quiz, he was your man – but actual police work? Might as well ask a drunken hedgehog to fill out your tax return.

'Nope: already thought of that. Wallace is a hero to her, the other chest freezers are named after punishments. Betrayals. It doesn't fit.'

Tufty rolled his eyes. 'No, listen, Sarge: they captured him at the battle of thingummy and took him down to London, didn't they? Hanged, drawn, and quartered him.' Wrinkles appeared on that hollow forehead. 'Though *technically* it should be drawn, hanged, and quartered. A lot of people think drawing was taking out your inside bits, but it was really them dragging you through the streets to your place of execution. And if we're being pedantically technical, it should be drawn, hanged, castrated, disembowelled, and *dismembered*. Cos they hack you into more than four bits and they're not of equal size, so—'

'OK! I get it: Wallace is a hero *and* a punishment.' Logan held up a hand. 'You can stop talking now.'

'Oh, and after they cut off your gentleman's relish they burn it in a fire, right in front of you. Then do the same with your intestines: the world's most horrible barbecue.' A nod. 'You should ask Rennie about it. He's the history buff. I only know this stuff cos it was in a game of Dungeons and Dragons.' Tufty smiled, eyebrows up. Eager. 'Have you played?'

'No, *genuinely*: stop talking.'

'Honestly, it's not just for kids, you should try it!'

Logan covered his face with his hands again. 'Kill me now.'

'I'm playing a dwarf called Tuftin Oakenbeard and she's got this enchanted axe that—'

The canteen door banged open and a uniformed PC bustled in, red-faced and breathless. Lanky, with a prominent nose, like a human ice axe. She had a quick scan of the empty room then hurried over. 'Inspector McRae!'

'Oh, thank God.' Saved.

'Been trying to get you on your Airwave. And I was up and down them stairs a million times looking for you! I'm absolutely—'

'Can we skip straight to the message, please?'

'Oh, right.' PC Godsend pouted a little, as if she'd been rehearsing her moan and now didn't have anyone to perform it for. 'OK, well, there's been a break-in at that Ravendale Sheltered Living Facility. Someone's abducted "Gaelic Gary" Lochhead.'

Logan stared at her, then at Tufty.

Tufty's eyebrows climbed up his forehead.

Then they were both on their feet, running for the door.

Bang: out into the stairwell.

Tufty screeched to a halt on the grey terrazzo flooring, arms pinwheeling to keep himself upright. 'Wait, wait: stabproof!' He turned and scurried off down the stairs, voice echoing against the concrete. 'I'll catch up; don't go without me!'

A couple of security lights broke through the grey shadows that swamped the Rear Podium, reflected in the windscreens of half a dozen parked patrol cars. And what was left of Logan's Audi.

Overhead, the sky was already heading towards a bright cheery blue, but down here it was definitely bloody horrible.

His poor car…

Sitting there, exposed in the security light's merciless glow, it actually looked *worse* than it had when he'd found it abandoned near Renfield House. More battered and scraped. More falling to bits.

He was still staring at it, mourning, when Tufty lurched up, struggling under the weight of two stabproof vests and a pair of utility belts.

'Argh… Heavy, heavy, heavy!'

Logan popped the boot and Tufty dumped the lot inside with a grunt.

Then staggered away a couple of paces, wiping at his shiny face. 'I nicked one off the rack for you too, and a full Belt-O'-Many-Things as well. Don't tell anyone, but I might have forgot to sign for it, OK?'

'Promise.' Logan clunked the boot shut and climbed in behind the wheel.

The inside was dusty with fingerprint powder – making it look even more grey in the dim light – and turning the key set the engine rattling and groaning like a tractor. His lovely Audi was *not* a well car.

Tufty got in the passenger side, mouth stretched wide and down, eyebrows pinched up in the middle. 'Oh dear.'

It backfired twice as Logan reversed it out of the space, and again on the way down the ramp onto Queen Street. He frowned: there was something buzzing and squeaking that didn't buzz or squeak before.

'Erm, no offence, Sarge, but maybe we should take a pool car instead?'

Logan glowered at him. 'Oh … shut up.'

A patrol car sat outside Ravendale's main door, sideways, taking up four parking spaces. Logan pulled up next to it in his groaning growling squeal-and-rattle Audi. Switching off the engine was a bit like a mercy killing.

Soon as he hauled on the handbrake, Tufty was out, scurrying around to the boot, phone clamped to his ear. 'I know, but according to the Many-Worlds theory, you were already awake in a parallel universe, so it's not that bad is it?'

He held the phone away from his ear, grimacing as Logan walked around to the boot and popped the lid. Tufty helped himself to one of the stabproof vests – *scrrretching* a Velcro side panel open. 'No, Sarge. ... Yes, Sarge. ... Sorry, Sarge. But Inspector McRae says—' His eyes widened and pink rushed up his cheeks as he wriggled into his vest. 'I'm not telling him *that*, Sarge!'

Tufty grabbed a utility belt and Logan thunked the boot shut again – headed for reception.

'No, Sarge...' Phone pinned between his ear and his epaulettes as he followed, hooking himself into the belt. 'Yes. ... OK. ... It's not my fault! I'm only—'

Logan grabbed Tufty's mobile, talking into it as he pushed through the main doors. 'Listen up: I want a nationwide manhunt organised. Alert every station in the country, ports, airports, bus stations, motorway service stations, and everything in between. Now get your hairy backside out of bed and into DHQ, you useless sack of cat jobbies!' He handed the phone back. 'Don't let Rennie bully you.'

All the colour vanished from Tufty's cheeks. 'Yeah... That's not Sergeant Rennie on the phone, it's DS Steel.'

Oh sod.

Still, too late now. 'Tell her to get her arse in gear, then.'

It wasn't the usual bland grey-and-beige man behind the reception desk – he'd been replaced by an older lady in a brown cardigan and oversized spectacles, fussing over a big lump of a man in a nurse's uniform. Holding an ice pack to his forehead as he squirmed.

His right arm was in a sling, the fingers poking out the end like mouldy sausages, all purple and swollen. He was working on a pretty stunning pair of black eyes too.

No sign of whoever turned up in the badly parked patrol car.

Logan marched over to the desk and nodded at Nurse Black Eyes. 'Are you the one who called it in?'

Black Eyes had barely got his mouth open before Granny

Cardigan jumped in. 'Naw, that was me. Heard crying and banging coming from the linen cupboard and thought one of our residents had got a bit lost.'

'I *wasn't* crying, I was calling for—'

'Key was snapped off in the lock. Had to kick the door in.' She didn't look capable of kicking the skin off a bowl of custard, so God alone knew how she'd managed that. 'And there he was.'

'I wasn't crying!'

Logan took out his notebook. 'Did you see who took Gary Lochhead?'

The black eyes narrowed. 'Oh I saw her all right. She—'

'It was that Mary Sievewright. Can you believe it?'

The nurse turned a squinty glower at her. 'Can I tell—'

'She was such a *nice* wee thing when she worked here. Never said boo to a duck.'

Wait a minute: 'Mary Sievewright? Who's Mary—'

'She hit me!' Black Eyes slapped Granny Cardigan's hand away and she lowered the ice pack, revealing a round circle of red, about the size of a golf ball, bruised into the skin between his bloodshot eyes. 'Could've fractured my skull!'

Tufty wandered over, stuffing his phone into his pocket. 'DS Steel's on her way, Sarge. So's Sergeant Rennie.'

Logan nodded at him. 'Have you heard of a Mary Sievewright?'

'Sievewright?' Tufty pulled his phone out again and poked at it. 'Sievewright, Sievewright... Yup. Mary Sievewright's one of her social media aliases.' He handed it to Logan.

A Facebook page filled the screen. The username might have been 'MARY SIEVEWRIGHT' but the profile pic was definitely Mhari Powell, only blonde and wearing glasses.

Tufty pointed at his phone. 'Alt-Brit-Nat account. *Very* sweary.'

'Sweary?' Granny Cardigan pulled her chin in. 'Oh, that doesn't sound like our Mary at all. She made a lovely sticky toffee pudding.'

A harrumph from Nurse Black Eyes. 'Bet I've got concussion now.'

Logan showed him the profile pic. 'This her?'

'*Bitch*. She snuck up on me! Otherwise...' He mimed strangling someone.

Yeah, he looked the type.

Logan turned the phone's screen so Granny Cardigan could see it. 'I need her employment records.'

46

PC Guthrie leaned against the wall of Gary Lochhead's room, hands tucked into the armholes of his stabproof vest. Smiling like a cheerful potato, with a number two haircut and a big sex-offender moustache in various shades of grey. 'She got in through the fire door down the corridor.'

'Hmm...' Logan flipped through Mary Sievewright's file again. No disciplinary notes, always on time for work, excellent rating for her six-month appraisal.

'The duty nurse keeps the alarm turned off so he can sneak out for a,' Guthrie gave Logan a knowing wink, '"cigarette" whenever he fancies. She nicks a wheelchair and bashes Mr Nursey on the forehead with the heel of her knife.'

Top marks on the internal training courses. Commendation for saving a resident's life by administering CPR.

Guthrie sniffed. 'He's lucky she didn't use the stabby end.'

Logan stared at him and he shrugged.

'No offence, Guv.'

'Mhari's face has been on every news broadcast and front page for days. How come Nurse Black Eyes didn't recognise her?'

'Nurse...? Ah, OK, you mean the dick with the broken arm. There's a very good reason for that: he works nights and is a bit thick.'

Tufty appeared in the doorway and gave Guthrie a wee wave.

'Hey, Al.' Then slouched over. 'I did a search for "Mary Sievewright": no criminal record and the address she gave the care home is a rental bedsit in Stoneywood.' He pulled a face. 'The current tenant was *not* chuffed with me phoning at ten past five in the morning.'

'Current tenant?'

'Been there two months.'

Logan closed the file. 'So about the same time Mhari stopped working here.'

'Yup. It's like she adopts a new persona every time she needs something, then ditches it and moves on to the next. Well, except online. She collects those.'

Hmmm...

On the other side of Gary Lochhead's window, through the chain-link fence, Aberdeen Airport was winding up for its first flight of the day. Wee trucks bumbling about, people in high-viz doing their best to look busy. Logan watched a couple of them manoeuvre what had to be a fuel tanker alongside a 747. 'Why would Mhari abduct her own father?'

Guthrie held up a finger. 'Ah, but maybe she doesn't *know* he's her dad.'

'Bit of a coincidence if she doesn't.'

'Ooh!' Tufty's turn. 'Maybe it's an escape attempt?'

Behind them, someone cleared their throat. Everyone turned to face the door.

Nurse Black Eyes stood there, with his ice pack, sling, and scowl. 'Janice wants to know if you want tea or coffee. Like I'm a sodding tea boy.' He tucked the ice pack under his arm and fingered the lump growing between his eyes. 'And it *can't* have been an escape, cos there's nothing to escape from. Gary Lochhead's free to go at any point – he's not being detained here, it's palliative care. At the taxpayer's expense, by the way.'

Interesting. 'How palliative is palliative?'

'If he's not snuggled down in his coffin by next week, it'll be the week after. I've seen enough OAPs kick the bin to know "end-stage" when I see it.'

411

Heartless little sod.

Logan gave him a cold smile. 'In that case, we'll have two teas and a coffee. Milk in all three, two sugars in the coffee. And see if you can rustle up a packet of biscuits, eh? Constable Guthrie is partial to Jaffa Cakes.'

The scowl deepened, then Black Eyes turned and stomped off. 'Like I'm a sodding tea boy; I'm badly injured here...'

Tufty puffed out his cheeks. 'Nice to see compassion is alive and well in the private healthcare sector.'

A nod from Guthrie. 'Told you the man's a dick.'

Logan waved a finger around the room. 'You searched all this yet?'

'Not so much as a porn mag under the mattress, Guv. That's the problem with the internet, it's killed the joy of discovering unexpected boobs, willies, and exciting combinations thereof.'

Damn.

Logan did a slow three-sixty: door, en suite shower room, bedside locker, hospital bed, visitors' chairs, wheelie-table thing, window, and last, but not least, Gary Lochhead's painting of that recumbent stone circle. 'What about this? Did you search it?'

'Funny you should say that, Guv,' all innocent, 'but I was *just* about to when you came in.'

'I'll bet you were.' He reached up and unhooked the painting from the wall.

Nothing hidden behind it. So he turned it the other way around. Nothing tucked into the frame either. 'LOUDON WOOD STONE CIRCLE' was printed on the bare canvas in black Sharpie, above Gary Lochhead's signature, a Saint Andrew's cross, the word 'BARLINNIE', and '4TH MAY 2016' – presumably the date it was painted. So no sodding use at all.

Worth a try.

Logan hung it on the wall again.

Guthrie raised an eyebrow. 'No porn?'

'If you're Mhari Powell, and you've abducted your terminally ill father, where do you take him?'

'Ah, *now* you're asking.' A big happy potato smile. 'I've always fancied going back to Padova.' Sigh. 'There's this wee restaurant, Corte dei Leoni, does a *gnocchi in salsa di formaggio* that's—'

Tufty hit him. 'Meanwhile, in the *real* world: Gary Lochhead's dying, right? Maybe he wants to do it somewhere special? Maybe that's why Mhari got him out of here? I mean, most people want to die at home, right? Only he can't, because he doesn't have one any more, but maybe...'

There was something about the painting. Not just the colours, or the light. Something special.

'Sarge?'

Otherwise why would Gary Lochhead keep it there all these years?

Tufty tugged on his arm. 'If you like it, don't think anyone would mind if we took it in as evidence.'

A nod from Guthrie. 'It's pretty good, really. Not *Gustav Klimt* good, but as paintings go?'

'Ooh, it'd look great in the incident room! DHQ could do with a bit of brightening up.'

All these months, lying there looking up at a painting he'd done years ago in a Glasgow prison.

'Sarge? Earth to Planet Sarge? Come in, Planet Sarge.'

Logan turned and grabbed Tufty by the shoulders. 'You, my geeky little friend, are a genius!'

Tufty stuck his arms in the air. 'Yay!' Then lowered them as Logan barged out through the door. 'Wait, what did I do this time?'

Logan's Audi roared and spluttered its way across Dyce, the siren sounding as if it was trapped underwater. Only one of the blues worked, flickering off and on like a demented Christmas tree as they made for the nearest on-ramp to join the ring road.

Tufty fiddled with his phone, tongue poking out the side of his mouth as he clicked and scrolled. At least it kept him quiet, which was more than you could say about Steel.

Her voice groaned through the hands-free kit. *'Are you kidding me?'*

'I know it's a stretch, but—'

'I only got into the sodding office two minutes ago – after about an hour's sleep, by the way, thank you very much – and you want me to go out again? I'm organising a major buggering womanhunt here!'

He threw the Audi around the roundabout. Accelerating out of it in the gravelly growl of a broken exhaust pipe. 'It's not—'

'And Rennie's getting me a coffee. Can I at least drink my coffee?'

'Mhari's been building up to something and she needs a big finale. Her "Wallace".'

The dual carriageway lay empty in front of them as the speedometer crept up to seventy, the engine sounding like a slow-motion explosion in a tuba factory. The steering wheel juddering in Logan's hands.

'Aye, and what about backup? You remember what happened last time? Assuming this isn't all some huge spud-funting waste of time.'

She'd walked right into that one.

'Well, since you're volunteering: sort out a firearms team, dog unit, OSU, and everything else you can get out to Loudon Wood Stone Circle. And do it quick: we're on our way there now.'

'Oh, in the name of God's sharny—'

He poked the 'END CALL' button before she could get going.

'Err, Sarge?' Tufty waved at him from the passenger seat. 'Shouldn't we get King's team involved too? They've kinda got a vested interest.'

True.

'Go on then.'

Tufty took out his phone and dialled. 'Sergeant Gallacher? It's Tufty.' A pause as he smiled and nodded. 'Yes, I *do* know what time it is, thanks.'

The needle nudged eighty and the noise got worse. With any luck the car would make it as far as Loudon Wood before the engine managed to eat itself...

The sky shone a brilliant blue as they hammered up the A90.

'Sarge?' Tufty poked away at his phone, face all scrunched up. 'I has a worry that this stone circle is going to be an absolute bumhole to find. All the websites say it's buried away in the woods.'

'If Mhari can find it, *we* can find it.'

Traffic was getting heavier, as the morning commute from Ellon to Aberdeen kicked off. All those lucky sods who didn't have to be at work till six, when Logan was still there from seven o'clock the previous sodding morning.

'Yeah, but what if we get lost in the woods, Hansel and Gretel style?'

'You've got GPS on your phone, you idiot.'

'I *know* that. But it's the woods. And it's dark. And in the middle of nowhere. And there's probably Druids lurking with sickles waiting to sacrifice nubile young police officers to the ancient bloodthirsty gods.'

Logan overtook a bread van. 'Thought you said it was two minutes outside Mintlaw?'

'That just means the Druids have a shorter commute.'

Mind you, the proximity to Mintlaw wasn't a bad thing. Not a bad thing at all. 'Traffic Unit's based there – give them a call and see if they'll lend us some officers. They've got to have *someone* on nightshift.'

'Okeydoke.' He pressed the button on his Airwave. 'Control? Can you put me through to whoever's in charge of the Divisional Road Policing Unit nightshift?'

A bored voice crackled out of the handset's speaker. *'Connecting you now.'*

It was replaced by a wailing siren overlaid on the sound of a racing engine and a woman shouting over their combined racket. *'THAT YOU, TUFTY?'*

'Sergeant North? Dude! Well, Lady-Dude. Er ... I mean: safe to talk?'

'NOT HUGELY, CHASING A BMW ON THE A947 NORTH OF FYVIE. MAN'S DOING NINETY!'

'Have you got anyone we could borrow? We need to chase down a murder suspect in the woods outside Mintlaw.'

'GOT ONE CAR IN PETERHEAD, AND THE OTHER'S IN PORTSOY. WHICH WOODS?'

'Loudon.'

The racing engine noises got louder. *'LEAVE IT WITH ME. GOTTA GO!'*

'Thanks, Sarge.'

But she'd already hung up.

Tufty let go of his Airwave and grimaced at Logan. 'No way they're going to get to us in time. Not from Peterhead, Portsoy, and Fyvie.'

Logan tightened his grip on the shuddering wheel. 'Then it's you and me, isn't it?'

'In the woods. With the Druids.'

47

The Audi made a gurgling, grinding noise as Logan wrestled it along the twisting road, west out of Mintlaw. Sheep and barley – caught in the early morning sunshine – no longer streaked past the car windows, because no matter how hard he tried, the damn thing wouldn't go faster than forty any more.

Tufty hunched over his phone, staring at the map. 'Soon...'

Great chunks of Forestry Commission pines marched across the landscape, curling over the hilltops or standing in gloomy regiments – breaking up the patchwork blanket of fields.

Heather's voice fizzed and crackled out of the car's speakers. *'About a mile south of Ellon, blues-and-twos all the way.'*

'Thanks, H.'

Tufty pointed through the windscreen at a road sign not-so-rapidly approaching on the left-hand side of the road. 'Skillymarno', 'Strichen', 'White Cow Wood Forest Walks', 'White Cow Wood Cairn', and most importantly: 'Louden Wood Stone Circle 2 ½'.

The wee lad bounced in the passenger seat. 'There! Take a right.'

Logan stamped on the brakes and threw the Audi around the turn. Tyres squealing. Something clanging ominously under the bonnet as if it was in the process of falling off.

'Guv? DI King, is he...?'

Good question. 'They're doing everything they can.'

'OK. Well, then, it's up to us, isn't it?' One of the chunks of forestry pines loomed up on the right. '*Guv? If you see her – don't let her get away this time. Run her over if you have to. But she spends the rest of her life in jail.*' There was a pause. '*And take a care, OK?*'

'We'll do our best.' He ended the call.

Tufty looked up from his phone. 'Not far now.'

The road twisted and turned, skirting the edge of the woods.

'OK, Sarge, should be a right coming up ... there!'

Logan slammed on the brakes again and the Audi slithered past the entrance to a dirt-and-gravel track down the side of a converted bungalow. He stuck it in reverse, getting a horrible grinding noise for his trouble before the gears finally meshed. Front nose dipping as he wheeched backwards. Then into first again to ease around onto the track. Killing the gurgling siren and what was left of the lights.

The trees closed in on either side of the car.

Tufty grimaced at the canopy above them and shuddered. 'Not meaning to put the jinx on it or anything, but last time you and I went for a drive in the woods, things didn't end so well.'

'Yes, *thank you*, Officer Quirrel, for bringing that up.'

'What I mean is we should be extra-super careful this time.'

'You keep this up and it won't be Mhari Powell or rabid Druids you have to worry about. It'll be me.'

The car lurched and rolled along the uneven track, suspension making ominous thunking noises with every pothole. Heading deeper into the dark-green forest depths.

Even with the morning sun blaring down, it was dark in here – the light blocked by thick layers of leaves overhead. On either side of the track, the earth was a blanket of pale grey needles, spread between the trunks. Blaeberry bushes lurking in the shadows.

The car's speakers crackled and burred for a bit, announcing an incoming call as the word 'CONTROL' appeared on the display. Logan hit the button. 'What's happening with my Thugs, Dogs, and Guns?'

'*Inspector McRae, safe to talk?*'

'Are they on their way?'

'*OK, so I spoke to the Duty Superintendent and she wants to know why you haven't done a risk assessment, resource allocation request, and filed a—*'

'Because it's an evolving situation! Because I'm trying to catch a killer.' Getting louder. 'And because Mhari Powell isn't going to sit on her backside waiting for me to fill out four tons of bloody paperwork!'

There was a pause, then, '*I see. And you'd like me to pass that on to the Superintendent, would you?*'

'Yes. And feel free to add some expletives!' He stabbed the 'END CALL' button. 'AAAAAAARGH!'

Tufty grimaced. 'So they're *not* on their way?'

A fork in the track up ahead.

'Left or right?'

Tufty consulted his phone. 'Left.' He fidgeted in his seat. 'You know, maybe we *should* wait for backup?'

'Be irresponsible not to.'

'Only I don't want Mhari Powell capturing me, cutting bits off, and posting them to the BBC. I need my bits. All my bits. They're very nice bits. Kate's quite fond of some of them.'

'No one's cutting bits off anyone.' A sigh. 'But if we sit on our thumbs, waiting for backup, and she kills Gary Lochhead...?'

'I know. "Blundering on regardless" it is.'

The woods opened up on the right, turning into a patchy scrub of felled stumps and bushes. A fox hopped out from them, onto the track, and froze, staring at the approaching wreck of Logan's Audi, before padding across and away into the wood on the other side.

Logan put on a reassuring voice. 'Besides: Steel's right. We're probably wasting our time. There'll be nothing here.'

'Ooh, and *that* means we can go for great big breakfast butties at...' His face did a distressed-frog impersonation. 'Oh dear.'

A filthy Transit van sat at the side of the track, two wheels up on the needle-strewn verge. Rusty, streaked with mould. The kind of van you found dismembered body parts in.

Tufty licked his lips. 'Is it me, or does that look hella ominous? I think it looks ominous. It looks ominous, right?'

Logan parked behind the ominous van and killed the Audi's engine. Well, put it out of its misery anyway. 'Might not be hers.'

'Yeah, right, right. Maybe it's just Druids? They like stone circles, don't they? Like in *Asterix and Obelix*? Nice, *friendly* Druids.'

'Thought you said Druids were going to sacrifice us to the elder gods?' Logan climbed out into the morning heat. Barely gone six and it had to be at least eighteen degrees – the warm air thrumming with the sound of insects and birds.

Tufty emerged from the car, talking into his Airwave handset. 'I need a PNC check on a white Transit…'

Logan left him to it and picked his way over to the van instead. The side door lay open, but the only things inside were two empty cardboard boxes – one for a camera tripod, the other for a phone-mount, going by the packaging.

He turned.

A path led away into the woods, right in front of the van's open door, narrowing as it went. Swallowed by the gloom.

Logan checked the van's cab: nothing but an empty Twix wrapper and a crumpled tin of Irn-Bru. When he stepped down onto the track, Tufty was waiting for him.

'Van belongs to one Jeffrey Moncrief – same guy who owns Ceanntràigh Cottage. No valid tax, insurance, or MOT.' Tufty kicked the front wheel. 'Tyres are bald too.'

He took a step towards the path, then stopped. 'Tufty? No risks, OK? If it all goes wrong, you don't play the hero, you get the hell out of there and wait for backup.'

'OK. But *only* if you put on that stabproof vest and Belt-O'-Many-Things I got you.' He held up a hand before Logan could say anything. 'No point me stealing it, otherwise, is there?' A small cough. 'Well, not *stealing*, stealing: borrowing. You know, what with you being Professional Standards and all. Borrowing. Definitely not stealing.'

'Deal.'

*   *   *

The path into the woods barely deserved the name, it was so overgrown and lumpy. Outside, in the real world, the sun was blazing down, but in here gloom ruled. The scent of pine sap, sticky and thick in the dusty air.

Four feet from the 'path', the forest floor was shrouded in a darkness that swallowed everything. And they'd only been in here a minute.

But at least they knew they were going the right way: a pair of parallel indentations scoured the tracks through the fallen needles beneath their feet – thin and about a metre apart. The kind of marks you'd make with a wheelchair.

Tufty sniffed. 'Course it might *not* be.'

Logan kept going, slow and careful. 'Shut up.'

'Might be a couple of kids out on their bikes.'

Something moved in the shadows off to the right and they froze. Maybe it was that fox again? Or a homicidal maniac with a dirty big knife... The sound faded. Tufty puffed out a long, slow breath.

Onward.

A clump of blueberry bushes beside of the path, the fruit a hard, unripened green. A wheelchair lay on its side, abandoned next to it.

'Kids on bikes?' Logan pulled the wheelchair upright. Across the back, in big white letters, were the words, 'PROPERTY OF RAVENDALE ~ DO NOT REMOVE FROM SITE'. Bit late for that.

Drag marks led from the chair away into the woods proper.

Tufty shuffled his feet. 'Should I check on our backup, Sarge?'

'We did that ninety seconds ago, you muppet.'

'Ah. Right.' He eased his extendable baton from its holster, sniffing the air. Dropped his voice to a whisper. 'Can you smell that?'

Logan took a deep breath... A warm, crackling smell familiar from years of bonfire parties. 'Wood smoke.'

'The world's most horrible barbecue...'

Oh sodding hell.

Logan snapped out his baton. 'We're too late!' Charging into the woods, shoving branches out of the way, stumbling over the uneven ground, breathing hard.

They burst out from the trees into a wide clearing full of knee-high grass and weeds. Clumps of reeds. Scrambling coils of brambles reared like frozen explosions, punctured by the vivid-green curl of ferns. And, at the centre of the clearing: a ring of stones, their grey surfaces speckled with lichen and moss. Most of them had fallen over, but a few still stood as tall as they had five thousand years ago. Ancient and feral.

The recumbent stone lay on its side at the opposite end of the circle, like an altar, flanked by a vertical on the right and a fallen stone on the left. A fire crackled beside it, coiling out pale grey wood smoke. But it was what loomed *behind* the altar that really caught the eye: a rough wooden tripod, fashioned from fallen trees – about twelve foot high and tapering to a point. The individual trunks weren't that big around, barely more than you could encircle with one hand, but together they were clearly sturdy enough to support Gary Lochhead's weight.

He dangled from the apex, dressed in a pair of tartan jammies, a noose around his neck, the rope looped over where the trunks were lashed together.

He wasn't dead yet, though. His legs twitched, bare feet swinging, shoulders shaking, both hands behind his back, face scarlet but heading rapidly towards purple. Eyes bulging as Mhari sliced his dusty pyjama bottoms off with a huge shiny hunting knife.

Or at least, it was *probably* Mhari – difficult to tell with the black hood over her head, but who else could it be?

Logan broke into a run. 'YOU THERE! STOP! POLICE!'

'YOU HEARD HIM!' Tufty charged through the tussocks and undergrowth, waving his baton over his head. 'DROP THE WEAPON!'

Mhari turned, her knife glinting in the sunlight. She'd cut two eyeholes in the hood, but up close it looked more like a pillowcase. Baggy and square-cornered. 'You're too late.'

Closer.

'DROP IT! DROP THE KNIFE NOW!' Tufty peeled off, heading for the right-hand side of the recumbent stone.

Logan took the left. 'It doesn't have to end this way, Mhari.'

A genuine laugh. 'Yes it does. Of *course* it does.'

Gary Lochhead's struggles were getting weaker as his face darkened. Naked from the waist down.

Tufty made it behind the stone, slowing, his free hand up, palm out. 'Come on, Mhari, he's your dad. You can't do this.'

She looked at the knife in her hand, then up at Gary's body. He wasn't struggling any more. A nod, then Mhari pulled at a slipknot and her father's body crashed to the ground.

Oh, thank God for that.

Logan inched nearer. 'That's better. Now, put the knife down.'

'I dragged him here. I hanged him till he was barely conscious.' She tilted her black-hooded head to one side. 'Why would I put the knife down? This is where the *important* bit starts.'

Tufty edged closer. 'He's your *dad*, Mhari!'

'WHY DO YOU THINK I'M DOING IT?' She wiped at her eyes through the hood. 'Lung cancer.' Jabbing the knife towards Gary's half-naked body. 'He's a hero! All his life he's been fighting for Scotland and you think he's going to die in some crummy care home?'

Couldn't be more than six foot between her and Logan now. He stepped around the recumbent stone – past a bright-blue duffel bag and an abandoned shovel – closing the gap. 'Put the knife down and you can tell us all about it.'

'Our generation needs a William Wallace moment of its own. Something relevant to the slack-jawed masses sleepwalking their way through life. Something to wake them up!'

'Inspector McRae's right, Mhari: butchering your dad isn't going to do that. Come on, let us help him, yeah? Before it's too late?'

'Oh I'm not butchering him, "Mary Sievewright" is.' Mhari pointed at another tripod – a smaller one this time. A smartphone was mounted on top of it, a little red light winking on the screen. 'Mary's doing it as revenge for Professor Wilson, Councillor Lansdale, and Scott Meyrick. Filming it and posting it to every Unionist website she can find. "LOOK WHAT I'VE DONE!" she'll cry. "LOOK WHAT THESE SCOTTISH *BASTARDS* DESERVE!"' Mhari whipped off her hood and beamed at them, eyes wide. 'And *our* side will turn that into a rallying cry. The people who were asleep will answer and join us. Together, we'll drive the English from our country like the scum they are!' Finishing with her arms out as if expecting a round of applause.

Unbelievable.

Logan shook his head. 'It's too late, Mhari. They'll know it was you who killed him.'

'They won't *care*.' She lowered her arms and stepped towards Logan. 'Welcome to the post-truth world, Inspector. Welcome to alternative facts and conspiracy theories, echo chambers and filter bubbles. People don't care what's true any more, they care about what reinforces their beliefs.'

Tufty had made it as far as Gary Lochhead. 'Sarge? I don't think he's breathing.'

'It's over, Mhari. Put the knife down.'

'His death can *mean* something. We can cast the English out of Scotland! Rise up and be the nation again!' Hauling in a deep breath to bellow it out: 'FREEDOM!'

Yeah…

Maybe not today.

Logan unclipped the pepper spray from his utility belt and emptied half the canister right into her face.

She spluttered, staggered away a couple of paces, eyes screwed shut, free hand coming up to wipe the liquid from her skin… Then screaming rang out across the clearing as she dropped the knife and clawed at her cheeks. Fell to her knees. *Wailing*.

Tufty lunged for Gary Lochhead, kneeling beside him and wrestling with the noose. Hauling it free and feeling for a pulse. 'He's *definitely* not breathing!'

'CPR. Mouth-to-mouth. Don't let him die!' Logan shoved Mhari onto her front and pulled out his cuffs. 'Mhari Powell: I am arresting you under Section One of the Criminal Justice, Scotland, Act 2016, for the murders of Councillor Matthew Lansdale and Haiden Lochhead…'

48

The fire had gone from a crackling blaze to a hot red glow, perfect for cooking. But, thankfully, Gary Lochhead's innards were no longer on the menu. A couple of paramedics knelt beside him: one working away at chest compressions and humming 'Another One Bites the Dust' to herself, while her partner fiddled about with a defibrillator.

'Clear!'

Paramedic Number One stuck her hands in the air and Gary Lochhead spasmed. Then she felt for a pulse. 'Come on, come on, come on...'

On the other side of the stone circle, Steel scuffed her feet through the long grass, vaping away and talking to someone on her mobile phone. Rennie was on his phone too, pacing around one of the upright stones, face creased. Both of them too far away to make out what they were talking about.

Not that it mattered.

Not now they had 'Mhari Powell' in custody.

She sat with her back against a fallen stone, her face a study in beetroot and scarlet. Cheeks glistening with tears, top lip and chin glistening with snot. The delightful aftermath of a face full of pepper spray. She glowered up at Logan through bloodshot, swollen eyes. 'This changes *nothing*.'

'Oh, I think it does.'

She sniffed and spat. 'So you lock me up, so what? I won't

be the first political prisoner to lead a revolution from inside a jail cell.'

'Political prisoner? You abducted and mutilated *four people* including a police officer. You murdered two people – maybe three if the paramedics can't save your father. I don't think anyone's going to have a hard time telling you and Nelson Mandela apart.'

'Nelson Mandela led the armed resistance, you moron: he was a founding member of *Umkhonto weSizwe*. So *yes*, like *him* I'll be a martyr for my country.'

Tufty joined them at the fallen stone. 'A *nutjob* for your country, more like.' He hooked a thumb over his shoulder, to where the paramedics were wrestling Gary Lochhead onto a stretcher. 'They've got his heart going again, but can't say if it'll stay that way, so they're wheeching him out of here, ASAP. Air ambulance is on its way.'

Mhari kept her puffy eyes fixed on Logan. 'And your "police officer" had it coming.' Her smile looked obscene on that swollen scarlet face. 'I *was* going to cast Edward Barwell in the role of Judas, dirty little two-faced journalist dickbag. You know he used to be pro-independence? But soon as his paymasters changed, so did his opinion pieces.'

'And then DI King caught up with you.'

'He offered to "help me disappear" for a share of the gold. Can you believe that? He betrayed the PASL and he betrayed *you* as well.' Her snot-slicked chin came up. 'You should be thanking me.'

Over on the other side of the stone circle, Steel pulled the e-cigarette from her mouth and made a loudhailer with her other hand. 'HOY! SOMEONE'S DUG A BIG HOLE HERE!'

Tufty stuck his chest out. 'Was that where you were going to bury Gary Lochhead's body?'

'*Bury* him?' She laughed, the sound thick and sticky with mucus. 'I was going to quarter him and send the bits to the four corners of Scotland. Post his head to Holyrood and his heart to the First Minister. This is your early morning alarm call: rise and bloody shine, and *do* something instead of talking about it!' She snorted. 'Bury him.'

Then what was the hole for?

Logan stared at Mhari, then over at the recumbent stone. Pointed at Tufty. 'Keep an eye on her.' He picked his way across the rutted grass.

That bright-blue duffel bag was still there, along with the spade. He snapped on a pair of nitrile gloves and undid the zip.

Inside was another bag, only this one was ancient – the leather rotting and caked with earth. Trying to open it made a chunk of bag come away in his hand, creating a gap the size of his fist.

Something inside *gleamed*.

Was that really...? It was.

He reached in and pulled out a gold ingot. Much, much heavier than it looked. Solid. Expensive. Wow. There was another one in there, every bit as shiny and impressive.

Steel stepped up beside him and gave a low whistle. 'Think anyone would notice if we nicked one of them and split the proceeds?'

'Yes.' He slid the ingot into the crumbling bag again where it made a very satisfying *clink*. Then stood and marched back over to Mhari, grinning.

'You sure we can't nab *one* of them?' Steel followed him, glancing over her shoulder at the bag. 'Just a teeny weenie one?'

'*No.*' Logan stopped in front of Mhari. 'Well, well, well. Looks like we've—'

'Doesn't matter.' Her angry-pink chin came up. 'There's plenty more where that came from. Hidden in secret caches *all* over Scotland. Waiting to fund the revolution. Guns, and bombs, and explosives aren't cheap, but they're worth every stolen penny.'

Steel squatted down in front of her. 'See me? I'm all for independence. But I want a Scotland of the Enlightenment; a nation of fairness and equality; a nation that cares about the smallest, weakest person living here every bit as much as the biggest, richest one. A nation that welcomes *everyone*: aye, even the English.' She patted Mhari on the leg. 'What I *don't* want

427

is some sort of apartheid shithole full of racist, moronic, ethnic-cleansing wankspasms like you.'

Rennie slumped over, face turned down at the edges, phone still clutched in his hand. 'Guv? That was Control. The hospital say DI King passed away half an hour ago.'

Mhari looked up at Logan again. 'Told you: you should be thanking me.' She bared her teeth at Steel. 'Now, if you don't mind, I think I'll save my voice for my lawyer.'

Logan pulled into the kerb, the Audi coughing and spluttering like a sixty-a-day man. Half the dashboard was dark, and the bitter smell of roasting plastic oozed out through the blowers. When he turned the key, the engine kept going for a couple of seconds, before finally grinding to a halt.

He sat there, both hands on the wheel.

The road was one long line of granite tenements, broken up by modern flats. Some sort of builder's merchant on the other side, its yard full of bricks and racks of timber.

Black wires were draped across the front of King's building, like an unconvincing combover, trying to hide the dirt-streaked stone and failing.

King's flat was up there – second floor right – the windows ablaze with sunlight.

Deep breath.

Sitting in the passenger seat, Steel sighed and put a hand on his knee. 'You want me to go in and tell her?'

Yes.

'No. I should do it.' He tried for a smile. 'You stay here and look after the loon.' Hooking a thumb over his shoulder.

'Hmmm?' Tufty didn't look up from this phone, completely absorbed in whatever he was fiddling with.

Logan reached for his peaked cap, turning it in his hands. 'It all went so horribly wrong.'

'Aye. But look on the bright side: we caught Mhari Powell, or whoever the hell she really is, we saved—'

'Ooh! Ooh!' Tufty bounced in his seat. 'I does has a result!'

Steel glowered over her shoulder. 'Shut yer yap, Spongebob

Crappants, the grown-ups are talking.' She frowned at Logan. 'Where was I? Oh, aye: we saved—'

'No look, look!' He poked his phone between the front seats, screen angled so they could see it. 'Sergeant Wartynose, from Northumbria Police, has been to see the real Mhari Powell. He showed her *fake* Mhari's photo and she recognised her!'

Steel snatched the phone from his hand and squinted at the screen. 'Why have you got the font so small, how's anyone supposed to read this?'

Tufty rolled his eyes in the rear-view mirror. 'Turns out *our* Mhari shared a flat with the real one years ago, when they were both training to be psychiatric nurses. Called herself "Margaret Lochleat" in those days. Apparently she was kinda obsessive and, I quote, "a bit of a weirdo". Which is putting it mildly, given what we caught her doing.' A grin. 'See? I said that, didn't I? I said she'd probably been—'

'Blah, blah, blah.' Steel tossed the phone over her shoulder – Tufty scrambling to catch it before it landed.

'Hey!'

She turned to Logan again. 'As I was saying, before I was so *moronically* interrupted: we caught her, we saved Gary Lochhead, and we recovered about...' She pursed her lips. 'About four hundred grand's worth of stolen gold bullion? And you didn't get stabbed this time. So I'm going to call it a win.'

Logan stared up at King's flat again. 'Then why does it feel like I've let everyone down?'

She gave his leg another squeeze. 'Come on, we'll get this done then head down The Questionable Gentleman for a huge fry-up and all the Stella you can drink.'

'Can't. The paperwork alone is—'

'The paperwork can wait. You've been on since seven yesterday morning, Laz. Twenty-six and a bit hours. You did your best. Don't make me be nice to you.'

He nodded and climbed into the morning sun.

Its heat wrapped itself around him, squeezing the air out of his lungs, pushing down on his shoulders like a heavy weight. Someone had propped the tenement's door open with a bicycle, so he didn't have to buzz. Instead he stepped inside and trudged up the stairs to the second floor. Stopped on the landing and straightened his uniform. Tucked his peaked cap under his arm. Shoulders back, chest out, like a police officer. Raised a hand to knock on the door, then stopped...

Voices inside. Too muffled to make out what they were saying, but one of them definitely sounded familiar. A man. His tone cheerful, even happy.

Well that was about to change. Delivering a death message tended to spoil the mood.

Logan knocked.

Took another deep breath. Rehearsing it: *I'm very sorry, Mrs King, but I'm afraid I have some bad news. Can I come in?*

Didn't matter how often he did it, it always felt like ripping someone's heart out.

Mrs King? My name's Logan McRae, I work with your husband. I'm afraid I have some bad—

The door swung open and there was Detective Chief Inspector Hardie. A bit pink in the cheeks. Smile fading on his face as he stared at Logan. He cleared his throat. 'Inspector McRae.'

Logan blinked. 'I ... came to deliver the death message.'

'Yes, well, I've already done that, so you can—'

'*Stephen?*' An English accent from somewhere inside the flat. '*Who is it?*'

'It's all right, Gwen, I'm dealing with it.' Hardie pulled his chin up, looking down his nose at Logan. 'I think you'd better go now.'

A woman appeared behind him, drying her hands on a tea towel. Short and petite, with long black hair and full red lips. Strange – would've thought she'd be crying her eyes out in grief for her murdered husband, but hers weren't even blood-shot. As if it didn't matter. As if it might even have come as a bit of a relief. As if Frank King's death wasn't important enough to get upset about.

Logan looked from her to Hardie. The Detective Chief Inspector's blush deepened.

430

She's sleeping with someone at work. And not someone at her *work,* someone at mine.

So that's how it was.

He nodded at Mrs King. 'I'm sorry for your loss.' Then turned on his heel and marched away downstairs again.

The bloody pair of them deserved each other.

— one year later —

49

A massive metal manta ray broke through the clouds, topped with ringed exhaust ports – glinting in the setting sun. Huge, imposing, and opulent. Its attending school of biplanes circled it like cleaner fish, the sky around them laced with vivid pinks and darkening blues. A caption faded up on the screen: 'THE ARGONAUT ~ MÒR-CLASS PASSENGER LINER ~ ESTIMATED VALUE 4,000,000,000 CREDITS'. Stirring music swelled.

Logan helped himself to another Malteser, sooking the chocolate off before crunching the malty interior.

The screening room was probably big enough for forty people, but it wasn't even half full. Zander, his FX guru Hoshiko, and a handful of her team, took up most of the back row. Steel and Susan had commandeered the middle seats in the middle row, with Rennie sitting on one side of them, and Logan on the other. And, in the front row, all on his own, with a huge tub of popcorn: Tufty.

The wee lad pretty much fizzed with excitement.

The screen took up the entire wall in front of them, glowing with colour as the *Argonaut* passed, then darkening as the scene switched to the inside of another ship. Its wheelhouse was a strange mix of new-fangled electronics and Heath Robinson levers, cogs, and dials. Moving bits turning other bits. More bits going in and out. The *Argonaut* clearly visible through the windscreen – below and unsuspecting.

An older woman stalked into the middle of the shot. Handsome and imposing, with a cascade of curling flame-red hair and a clockwork corset. She took off her top hat and tossed it to a stitched-together part-man-part-dinosaur creature, who caught it with a mechanical arm.

A half-naked Conan type lumbered on, complete with loincloth and furry boots. Only instead of Arnold Schwarzenegger's head at the top, a cat sat inside the stump of Conan's neck – wearing goggles and a silk scarf – operating levers to make him move.

'Excuse me.' Tara appeared at the end of the row, one hand on her swollen belly as she squeezed past Rennie. 'Sorry. Coming through. Thanks.' Smiling as Susan, Steel, and Logan stood to let her past. She thumped down into the empty seat next to him and groaned.

Logan took her hand and squeezed it.

She leaned closer, voice dropped to a whisper. 'Did I miss anything?'

Tufty bounced up and down in his seat. 'Any minute now!'

The handsome woman in the corset snapped her fingers. *'Poltron, Scartbreak, release the grappling spears!'*

Frankenstein's Tyrannosaur nodded. *'Yes, Baroness.'*

A jump cut and the picture switched to outside again, sweeping down from the wheelhouse windows, past the ship's mascot and 'THE BURNING FOX', looking up past the ship's hull to the elliptical balloon it hung from, its propellers a blurred whurrrrrrr.

Hatches popped open all along the ship's length and harpoons with grappling heads levered out, before roaring away like guided missiles, trailing ropes and chains behind them.

The screen filled with the *Argonaut* again as the grappling spears thunked into her hull. One cracked into a biplane on the way in, pinning it to the ship like a lepidopterist's butterfly.

Tara shifted in her seat. 'My bladder's got the attention span of a sodding goldfish these days.'

Tufty turned and scowled, one finger up to his lips. 'Shhh!' He gazed up at the screen again. 'Here it comes!'

The baroness snapped her fingers again. *'Arachnox!'*

Apparently, Arachnox was a human head in a jar full of blue liquid, mounted on a mechanical body that looked like the unholy love child of a silverback gorilla and a tarantula as it unfolded itself from the ceiling and clicked down onto the wheelhouse floor.

The head in the jar looked an *awful* lot like Tufty's.

Arachnox's voice was a grating electronic rasp. Wet and sibilant. *'Yesssss, Baronessssss?'*

'It's time for your children to come out and play.'

'Of courssssssse.'

Doors and levers sprung open all over the solid parts of Arachnox's body and sharp red eyes glowed in the darkness. *'Ssssssssscurry, my little onessssss. Ssssssscurry and feassssssst!'*

A whole heap of mechanical spider-rat-things fell from his body – twisting to land on their metal feet – and scampered out through small holes in the bridge's skirting boards.

The camera followed the biggest spider-rat as it scuttled through the gloom and out onto one of the chains stretched between *The Burning Fox* and the *Argonaut*. Following its brothers and sisters as they swarmed across to the bigger ship, drill-head teeth spinning.

Tufty let out a little squeal of delight, bouncing up and down in his seat.

Yes, he was an idiot and a pain in the hoop, but you had to admit he made a pretty good mechanical-gorilla-spider-sidekick for an evil genius.

Logan turned and smiled at Tara. Leaned in, closed his eyes and kissed her. Her lips tasted of warm cherries and vanilla ice cream.

The kind of taste you'd never get tired of.

The kind of taste you could spend the rest of your life with.

On the screen, people started screaming.